PRAISE FOR S

Wanting Mr. Cane

"A smoldering love story that will melt the screen right off your phone! Five forbidden stars!"

—Sierra Simone, *USA Today* bestselling author

"A scrumptious morsel of forbidden love dusted in sugary, sexy urgency. This story had me hungry for more, long after I turned the last page."

—Dylan Allen, *USA Today* bestselling author

The Perfect Ruin

"A shocking, sensual thriller."

—Tarryn Fisher, *New York Times* bestselling author

"Twisty and impossible to put down! 10/10, would recommend."

—Claire Contreras, *New York Times* bestselling author

"I was hooked from the very first twist."

—Alessandra Torre, *New York Times* bestselling author of *Every Last Secret*

"With diabolical turns and surprises at every corner, it's an ideal summer read."

—*Booklist* (starred review)

"Williams is an award-winning author of romance and suspense novels; her tale of revenge will find an easy spot in fiction collections. Tailored for book clubs and for those who like to read about the sleazy side of rich elites."

—Library Journal

The Other Mistress

"Fans of *The Wife Between Us*, by Greer Hendricks and Sarah Pekkanen, won't be able to put this one down."

—Booklist

"A fast-paced psychological trip with a climax that will shock the most voracious readers. Recommended for fans of Alyssa Cole, Liv Constantine, and Megan Goldin."

—Library Journal

BEAUTIFUL BROKEN LOVE

OTHER TITLES BY SHANORA WILLIAMS

Ward Duet

The Man I Can't Have

The Man I Need

Cane Series

Wanting Mr. Cane

Breaking Mr. Cane

Loving Mr. Cane

Being Mrs. Cane

Nora Heat Collection

Dirty Little Secret

Caress

Crave

My Professor

Stand-Alones

Bad for Me

Coach Me

Temporary Boyfriend

My Fiancé's Brother

Doomsday Love

Until the Last Breath

Series

Mr. Black Duet

FireNine Series

Ace Crow Duet

Venom Trilogy

Thrillers

The Perfect Ruin

The Wife Before

The Other Mistress

The Bitter Truth

BEAUTIFUL BROKEN LOVE

SHANORA WILLIAMS

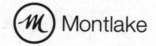 Montlake

Text copyright © 2024 by Shanora Williams
All rights reserved.

Published by Montlake, Seattle

www.apub.com

Amazon, the Amazon logo, and Montlake are trademarks of Amazon.com, Inc., or its affiliates.

ISBN-13: 9781662518881 (paperback)
ISBN-13: 9781662518874 (digital)

Cover design by Hang Le
Cover image: © Federica Giacomazzi / Stocksy; © s8, © Kirill I,
© Michael Kraus / Shutterstock

Printed in the United States of America

To my beautiful niece Dez

AUTHOR'S NOTE

Dear reader,

Though *Beautiful Broken Love* is an angsty, emotional sports romance, I realize some people may go into reading it expecting lots of fluff, and while there is some in there, I want to mention that this story goes much deeper than that. It's about finding yourself after loss, dealing with grief, trusting your heart, and healing along the way.

With that said, I do want to mention a few trigger warnings involved, like death of a loved one, childhood abuse, graphic descriptions of suicide, childhood trauma and neglect, the mention of anxiety medication, and detailed depictions of panic attacks.

Protecting your mental health should *always* come first, and there are aspects to this story that may be too heavy for some to bear. I didn't want to put this book out without giving a heads-up first!

No matter what you decide, I'm happy you're here, and if you continue forward, I hope you enjoy Deke and Davina's story!

ONE

DAVINA

"You can't say he isn't fine, Vina." Tish turned the screen of her phone my way to show me a picture of Declan Bishop.

Leaning forward, I studied the photo and cracked a smile to indulge her. "He *is* really cute, but I feel like you say that about every man."

She shrugged, setting her phone down on my desk to pick up her nail file. "Well, I mean it about this one. I'd have all his babies."

I laughed right along with her.

Tish and I arrived at work early so she could fill me in about our eleven o'clock meeting with the famous Declan Bishop, an NBA player *many* people obsessed over and one of the most popular athletes on the East Coast. The ladies loved him, and based on all the pictures Tish presented, I understood why.

He was one of the biggest faces in sports at the moment, and that's what made it so shocking that *he* agreed to meet with us. A fuzzy feeling stirred in the pit of my stomach from the reminder that I'd be speaking one on one with him soon.

"Think I have time to stretch my legs and take a walk before he gets here?" I rose from my chair, pressing my palms into my back and pushing my hips forward. It felt good but did absolutely nothing to calm my nerves.

"You can stretch all you want, but I don't suggest leaving the building." Tish glanced at me as she blew dust from her filed nails. "I know how you get when you start walking outside and reach Confetti's. We can't afford you being late because you can't decide on which donut flavor you wanna try."

"Hey." I threw both hands in the air in a guiltless gesture. "It's not my fault their donuts are good."

"The meeting is"—she flipped her wrist—"forty-five-ish minutes from now. Promise you won't drift too far."

"I won't," I assured her, already making my way to the door. "I'll be right back, I promise. Want anything from the break room?"

She looked at me from beneath her brows. "Only if there's wine."

I huffed a laugh, waving a hand at her.

Most of our days started like this, but on this particular morning we were trying our hardest not to be frazzled. Though Tisha Cole was my secretary and best friend of thirteen years and we'd conquered a lot of achievements together, we had no idea what to expect from this meeting with the NBA star.

Still, we'd prepped as much as possible, and if Tish hadn't been by my side, I wouldn't have felt confident enough to go through with it. In fact, I wouldn't have had *half* the success that I did if it weren't for her.

She was part of the reason I became CEO of a skin care company— one that went viral on social media, thanks to an actress named Atish Monoi.

Atish tried our products on a whim, and she loved them so much she gave them a shout-out. Since then, Golden Oil Co. had skyrocketed.

Our company now had over fifteen employees, who all seemed to love their jobs and were paid well. Our goal was to keep the GOC ship steady for them.

Tish had reached out to Declan's manager several weeks ago, when a video of him putting lotion on in the middle of one of his games went viral. Afterward, one of the reporters asked him why he was applying the lotion, and he told them he forgot to moisturize before the game and didn't want his ashy elbows caught on camera.

Gotta admit, that was funny to me.

Tish was watching the game with her boyfriend when she saw the interview, and she immediately claimed Declan's response as an opportunity for us.

To our surprise (and after *many* emails with his manager), Declan had agreed to test our products. He liked them so much, he agreed to meet us to discuss an endorsement.

After making a cup of tea in the break room and snagging a muffin, I took the route back to my office. My heels clicked on the marble floor as I walked past a wall of mirrors.

I shot a glance at my reflection, and my outfit was on point—a chic ivory blouse tucked into peach-colored high-waisted suit pants. However, one of the curls on my head was astray.

I smacked my teeth when I saw it was the curl closest to my right temple. No matter what style I rocked with my hair, whether it was a twist-out, Bantu knot-out, or braid-out, that curl always pointed the opposite way.

I smoothed it down with my free hand as best I could before pushing my office door open. Tish had disappeared, but a partial view of the Charlotte skyline was there to greet me instead.

The sky was nearly aqua, not a cloud in sight. I soaked in my workspace—gold and black decor, black vegan-leather furniture, and floor-to-ceiling windows.

I placed my tea and muffin down, then picked up the manila folder Tish left behind. The name **DEKE** was written in bold permanent marker on top of it. I opened it and studied the details, printed interviews, and even his career stats.

Declan Bishop was thirty-three years old, was shooting guard for the Atlanta Ravens, and had a Doberman named Zeke that he loved showing off on his Instagram. His favorite color was orange. He'd formerly played for two other teams, but his jersey number remained the same. Seventeen.

There was a sheet of paper attached about rumors of him dating a model named Giselle Grace. A lot of people said they were in a committed relationship, while other people thought they had an open relationship. Neither had been confirmed or denied by them.

I wasn't sure why that mattered, but Tish highlighted it as if it were an important detail. Knowing her, she was just trying to be funny.

Sunlight filtered into my office and bounced off the glass surfaces as I nestled into the chair behind my desk. My eyes wandered from the steaming cup of tea to the picture frame next to my computer.

A black-and-white photo of a familiar couple smiled at me. The woman wore an ivory A-line dress, her hair braided into a halo, while the man wore an all-black tux, even down to the tie. My chest tightened, while my throat thickened with emotion.

Me and my husband Lewis. We'd eloped in Hawaii. I found the courage to smile back at the photo, which was progress, seeing as it'd been seven months since he died.

I reached for my chest, digging beneath my collar until I felt the dragonfly pendant attached to my necklace. The metal and colored gems were warm, the wings pressing into the pads of my fingers.

Lew had given it to me on our second anniversary. He had said dragonflies brought love and promising changes. I thought how he had it all wrong, because our change wasn't promising. It was *damaging*.

Sniffling, I tucked the pendant back into place, blinked my tears away, then picked up my tea to take a much-needed sip.

This meeting with Declan was important, and I couldn't let my emotions screw it up.

TWO

DAVINA

I hardly ever got nervous before meetings, and normally I knocked them out of the park.

Signing a deal to be featured as a Target Black-owned brand? No problem.

Signing a contract to be on display at a women's expo? Not a single worry.

Having a launch party with Ulta? No biggie.

But for some odd reason, meeting with a professional athlete felt different. Declan was the first famous Black man to give our products a chance. If I screwed this up, it would set back many of my plans—and therein lay the problem.

I was a planner who lived life by routine, which meant this meeting *had* to go well. I had to keep Declan in my back pocket and make sure he was happy that day, because if I didn't, I would feel like a complete failure.

Hmm. Maybe that was my ego talking.

I waited at my desk, chewing on a thumbnail while going over my notes. It took only a few minutes for Tish to send me a text with the words HE'S HERE!

My heart skipped a beat, but I played it cool by taking a sip of tea and then walking around my desk to wait.

Less than a minute later, there was a knock at my door.

With the door halfway open, that knock was more of a courtesy from my best friend. Tish walked in first, dressed to impress in a black pantsuit, with her hair brushed into a sleek puff. She wore gold jewelry with her outfit because "gold is for queens" (her words, not mine), and her gold eye shadow made her umber skin pop.

She grinned at me like she was going to burst into a fit of giggles. I had to look away from her before I started laughing. That was one of the silly problems about us being friends. We laughed at the dumbest shit and always at the worst times.

I cleared my throat as a short, bald man with warm ivory skin entered my office, and trailing behind him was a man the polar opposite of him.

Tall, with satiny brown skin, prominent cheekbones, and a sharp jawline, it was none other than Declan Bishop. His coarse black hair was short and lined up, the natural waves like ocean currents in the night. A light trace of stubble was peppered along his jaw and chin like he'd shaved a day or two ago.

He wore a crisp linen shirt with the sleeves rolled up to his elbows and three buttons at the collar undone. A gold chain hung around his neck, a crucifix pendant dangling from it, and square diamond earrings pierced both ears.

The NBA player swept his downturned eyes around my office, and as if he were impressed with his surroundings, he smirked and provided a slight nod.

There he was. In the flesh. Star shooting guard for the Atlanta Ravens and a man worth *a lot* of money. The pictures online did not do him justice.

His brown eyes landed on mine and locked with intention. I couldn't help noticing they were a deep, rich brown, but the sunlight pouring through the windows revealed the slightest hint of cognac within his irises.

He gave me a look I couldn't read. I couldn't tell if he was trying to find my flaws or drinking me in.

"You must be Davina," the short man said, offering me a hand. I accepted it, giving it a generous shake.

"I am. And you must be Arnold Glass."

"That's me." Arnold smiled, revealing a rather cute gap between his two front teeth. It suited him, made him appear friendlier. Arnold fixed his blue tie, cleared his throat, and said, "And I'm sure you already know Deke Bishop."

My eyes slid up to Declan's again, and he leaned forward, offering a hand to me. I took it and gave it a firm shake. His hand was twice the size of mine and surprisingly soft.

"I'm well aware of who Mr. Bishop is," I said with a warm smile.

"Mr. Bishop?" Declan raised a brow with a crooked smile. As he did, a set of dimples adorned his cheeks. *Good Lord.* I forgot the man had dimples. "You can spare the formalities. Just call me Deke."

"Okay, *Deke.*" I released his hand as he assessed me with his eyes. "It's very nice to meet you in person."

Both corners of his mouth turned up. "Likewise."

I gestured to the love seat near the windows. "Please, have a seat. Can I get you some coffee or anything to drink before we get started?"

"Water for me," Arnold said.

"Got any Gatorade?" Deke requested.

I glanced at Tish, who shook her head. "We don't," I answered. "But I can have Tisha run out to grab you one. There's a market right up the street."

"Nah, it's all good." Deke relaxed in his seat, spreading his long legs and placing an arm on the arm rest. The other hand rested in his lap, very close to his groin. I focused on his face, trying not to let the placement of that hand distract me. "Make it water for me too."

Tish nodded, trotting away and leaving the office to get their drinks.

I stood in front of my desk, allowing myself a minute to collect a breath while my heart steadied to a calmer rhythm. When I faced them again, I went for it.

"Well, firstly, Deke, I'm so glad you loved our products," I said, and he nodded, looking into my eyes. I don't know what it was about the way he looked at me, but it was like he was staring into my soul.

Most people put their attention elsewhere or plucked lint off their clothes, because they hated eye contact. It made me feel out of sorts that he wasn't doing *any* of that, so I shifted on my heels, ignoring the thought and his powerful presence.

"I'm really honored that you agreed to meet us," I continued. "I know it's the offseason and you'd much rather be hanging out with family and friends than coming to boring work endeavors, so thank you."

Another nod from Deke. "It's my pleasure."

Tish returned with two cold water bottles and placed them on the table in front of the men. Then she smiled at me, giving me big side-eyes that screamed *GIRLLLLL!*

I wanted to shoo her out of the office before my professional facade cracked.

"I see you like to do a lot of small talk." Deke grabbed his water bottle and opened it.

"Oh. Is my small talk bothering you?" I asked.

He shrugged a shoulder after taking a sip of water. After a wet gasp, he said, "A little."

"Okay." I kept the corners of my lips turned up. "Well, then let me cut to the chase." *Jerk.* "We were hoping you'd sponsor our products for five months. In exchange, we're willing to give you four hundred thousand dollars."

Deke smirked. Nothing more, nothing less. He then glanced at Arnold, who raised a bushy brow and bobbed his bald head.

"Okay," Deke said. "Seems like a fair deal, coming from a small company."

"Really?" I sat up taller, my eyes stretching with surprise. We were lowballing him—I knew this—and I expected him to immediately counter it, which I was prepared for, but still.

"You want the truth?" Deke asked, and my smile slipped a bit as he leaned forward and placed his water bottle on the table again.

"Um . . . the truth?" I gave pause. "Sure, give me the truth."

"Well, the truth is four hundred grand or so ain't nothing to me. I can make that in a day."

I avoided a frown, which I nearly failed to do, because his arrogance was stinking up the room. I kept a neutral face, though, as he continued.

"But I'm willing to agree to this deal as long as I get to negotiate something else."

I blinked, confused. "Like what?"

Deke shifted his attention to Arnold. "Arnold, think you can give me a moment with Ms. Klein?"

As if Arnold was used to this, he hopped up and said, "You got it." He collected a mint from the candy bowl, picked up his water bottle, and left the office as quickly as he'd entered.

I glanced over my shoulder as Arnold shut the door behind him, and from the corner of my eye, I noticed Deke shift on the love seat. I faced him again.

The last thing I had time for was games. I didn't care if he was some famous basketball player that everyone loved.

"What is this about, Mr. Bishop?" I asked, keeping my voice level. This was a practiced calm—one I'd used many, *many* times before. Trust me, he wasn't the first person with lots of money to ever waste my time.

"Deke," he corrected, which I found funny because he kept addressing me as Ms. Klein.

"Okay, *Deke*." I folded my arms. "What is this about?"

He looked me up and down, tilting his head a bit. "Am I getting under your skin?"

I sighed. "You want the truth, Deke?"

He leaned back on the sofa, spreading his legs farther apart. "Sure. Give me the truth."

I avoided a smile. He was using my words against me, just as I'd done to him. "The truth is you *are* getting under my skin."

"Honesty." He gave me a lopsided grin. "I like it."

"Look, you showed up here for a reason. There are many places you can be right now, but you're here. You clearly love our products and you don't mind sponsoring them, so what is this really about?"

"It's about *you*," he stated simply.

I hesitated. "*What* about me?"

He rose to a stand. This man was a giant—six feet and four inches, according to his Wikipedia, but I think sometimes players lie about their height by adding an inch or two. And Deke was tall, but more like three over six to me. Lewis was six one, and Deke couldn't have been *that* much taller.

Still, he took up a lot of space and towered over me like a giant.

"As I said, four hundred grand is easy to come by. And for five months of my time, I normally request more to sponsor stuff like this."

"We can go up in price," I assured him. His cologne tickled my nose. Damn, he smelled good, like cocoa butter and mahogany. "That's no problem. What are you thinking?"

Truth is, it *was* a problem. We couldn't go past $500,000. Anything more, and it would really put us in a financial bind. Offering so much was already a risk, but it was one I was willing to take because I knew it'd pay off.

"That won't be necessary," Deke said, and relief washed over me, but that didn't stop the frown from taking over my face, because I wanted him to know I was confused and, frankly, getting frustrated.

If it wasn't necessary, why was he dragging this out?

"Dinner." Deke's eyes traveled down the length of me like I was some kind of snack he was ready to eat.

I shifted on my feet and tucked my hands deeper beneath my armpits. "Dinner?"

"Yes. I'm in Charlotte for the next two days. I want you to have dinner with me so I can personally get to know the mind behind this company and make sure it's truly worth backing."

A laugh snuck out of me before I could stop it, and I clamped my mouth shut for the lack of professionalism.

"Oh wow. Um, I'm sorry." I cleared my throat, pressing a hand to the center of my chest. "Are you being *serious* right now?"

He lifted a brow. "I'm dead serious."

"So *this* is how you get the women." I nodded at the aha moment.

As if to entertain me, he asked, "How's that?"

"You do a little bickering, ask them to dinner, make your move, do your whole bachelor-famous-athlete thing, then you drag them to a hotel or something, right?"

Deke let out a hefty chuckle. "I usually don't have to ask."

"Right. Because women just show up to dinner because you tell them to."

He shrugged. "It's that easy for me."

Man. Tish didn't mention how cocky he was.

"Well, that's nice." I flipped my wrist and checked the time, feigning disinterest. "I suppose I can move some things around on my schedule to meet you for dinner." I narrowed my eyes at him. "But it will *only* be for dinner and to discuss the deal. Purely business. Yeah?"

"Are you always this uptight?"

My eyebrows shot up. *"Excuse me?"*

Deke's head tilted as he looked me over, and as if he hadn't heard me, he continued with "When's the last time you've been wined and dined?"

"I'm not sure why that matters right now."

"Matters a lot, actually." He scanned my face like he was searching for the answer. Those eyes of his were electrifying. I found it hard as hell to look away from them. From *him*. "What's your favorite restaurant?"

I blinked up at him before finally snatching my eyes away. "I don't have one."

"Of course you do. You're a woman who clearly knows what she wants. The confidence radiates off of you, and I gotta admit, it's damn hard to ignore. So tell me, *Davina*. What's your favorite restaurant?"

I huffed a laugh, which was an attempt to ignore the delicious twist in my stomach. The way he said my name was deep and husky enough to make a woman's toes curl. I knew the game he was playing, but I was *not* about to be the woman moaning his name that night.

I just wanted to close this deal. I didn't have time to drag this out or bother entertaining this man longer than necessary. But the sooner we had dinner, the quicker I could lock it in.

And I supposed basketball players needed their own entertainment too. If I played along, I could hook him.

"Silver Wolf in South End. We can meet at seven, but I have to be out of there by eight." I wasn't about to tell him my actual favorite was Valentine's, a little steak house in the heart of uptown that was a regular for my date nights with Lew. That place was too sacred.

"Silver Wolf at seven," he said, his gaze falling to my lips. I swallowed, once again fighting that spiral of heat in my lower belly. "See you there, *Davina*."

He walked to the door, and I don't know why I expected him to look back, but when he didn't, a breath of relief escaped me. It was a good thing he didn't look back. It meant he was just flirting and hoping to get lucky. But he wouldn't.

We could have dinner, a couple of drinks, and I'd lure him into signing the deal. His ego would be fed, and my business would continue thriving.

All I had to do was hook, line, and sink him.

THREE

DEKE

"You're meeting her *outside* the office?" Camille cut her eyes at the phone and stopped the rapid tapping on her keyboard.

It was Thursday, the day of the week when my sisters and I reserved at least thirty minutes of our time for a FaceTime call. Between her and my other sister, Whitney, they made me want to bash my head into a wall.

As much as they made me want to do that, though, I always looked forward to talking to them. It was better seeing their faces virtually than going months without.

When we were kids, it was easy to check in with each other and keep in touch, but as adults who were successful in their careers, we'd found that spare time was rare.

My sisters had pulled me out of some of the darkest seasons of my life, so though they could get under my skin like no one else, I made sure I carved out time in my schedule to catch up with them.

"That boy never listens," Whitney said around a mouthful of puffy Cheetos.

"We're just gonna have a couple of drinks while we discuss business. Why y'all tripping about it?" I adjusted the collar of my shirt, focusing on my reflection in the mirror.

Camille sighed and clacked away on her keyboard again. "You only take women out when you're interested in them, Deke. We know you."

"That's a false accusation."

"Please. If she was a man, would you have asked her to join you for *drinks and business*?" Whitney countered.

"I might've." I couldn't help smirking at that.

No, I wouldn't have, but unless I was hanging out with my boys Javier and EJ, there was no point in hanging around dudes outside of work. I was a man, but even I knew hanging with other men got boring as hell after a while.

"No! See, look at you! Grinning! Camille, talk some sense into this boy, please!"

Camille removed her glasses with a long-winded sigh.

"Uh-oh. Not the glasses coming off." I slid my watch onto my wrist as Camille pursed her lips.

Camille was the oldest of us all, and she got tired of me and Whitney's shenanigans real quick. Not that she *wasn't* patient, she was just hella mature—way more than we were. Camille didn't sugarcoat a damn thing she said, and she definitely didn't play any games. It was why she was so good as a family law attorney.

"Yes, the glasses are coming off, because I need you to look me in the eye and promise you won't do something stupid tonight. Just sign the deal, help the lady out, and be on your way. Her products are really good. I put on some of the shea lip balm at the office earlier, and it lasted me hours, and if you mess up that endless supply of lip balm for me, I *will* fight you."

"And I'll be jumping in to tag team your ass," Whitney added with a breathy laugh. "I used the honey shea lotion after a couple of my showers, and it had my skin feeling like a newborn baby's booty. Do not mess this up, Deke."

"Look, it's just drinks, all right? I'll sign the contract as soon as we meet."

"Should've done that at her office," Camille muttered, settling her glasses on the bridge of her nose again. "You've made a terrible habit of roping people in just to let them down, Declan. Don't go ruining people's lives because of your inflated ego."

"First of all, you know I hate when you call me by my real name. Secondly, I'm not going to ruin anyone's life, all right? This Davina chick has a good vibe. I just want to know more about her business to make sure this is the right fit. And like y'all said, you love her products and want more, so why not build on that?"

"Sounds like a load of bullshit."

"Whitney, seriously? Eli is in the room," Camille said, sighing.

"Oh, sorry, Eli! Love you, baby! It's not like he's listening anyway. He's always on his iPad."

"*Anyway*," Camille replied curtly. "Sign the contract, Deke, and move along. What is it about her that makes you want to build the business relationship, anyway? That sounds really weird coming from you. Any other time and you let bigmouth Arnold do all the talking 'cause you hate the business part."

Camille's question caught me off guard. She was right. I *did* hate talking business.

Don't get me wrong, I loved money, but talking about it along with sales figures and percentages irked the fuck out of me. I stared at my reflection and pressed my lips as I searched for the answer.

"I don't know," I said. "I guess I just respect her grind. She's humble, and she has a good thing going with this skin care thing. Y'all know how hard it is for Black women to succeed out here. Gotta work twice as hard. Plus, she reminded me of y'all with the hustle and the confidence."

I wasn't going to tell them her sex appeal was a hell of a bonus. One look was all it took for me to lock in and memorize her heart-shaped face and her upturned brown eyes, which were like whiskey in the light.

She was so effortlessly put together, with a head full of tight natural curls, curvy hips, thick thighs, and a smile that could make any man stop dead in his tracks.

All the qualities I was looking for in my dream woman: Davina Klein had them.

"Aww," Whitney cooed.

"Okay, that's fine and dandy, but if I see any news leaks about you sliding your *you-know-what* in this woman, I'm not backing you up—especially if she decides to sue you down the line. Because you know that can happen, right? You're inviting her to dinner, buttering her up, and throwing hella mixed signals. She could say you initiated the manner of your relationship, if her business declines."

"Now you just sound like an attorney," I said, gripping the edge of the counter and focusing on Camille. "Out of respect for her and her company, I wouldn't let that happen."

"All right," Camille murmured. "Well, I know I can't tell you what to do, so just be careful. Okay, playboy?"

I flashed her a smile. "I'm always careful."

"And put some of her good lotion on your ashy-ass face," Whitney said as she opened another bag of chips.

I couldn't help laughing at that. "I'll hit y'all later."

"Bye, Deke," Whitney sang.

"Behave, brother," Camille added with an inclined brow.

When the screen went black, I studied my reflection again. All I could think was maybe my sisters were right. My ego *was* making me do some dumb shit.

But the night was already set, and though I could've had Arnold contact Davina and cancel, something told me I would regret not seeing her again.

And if there was one thing about me, I was going to follow that inner voice.

I didn't know what it was about that woman. I admit, it had been the curve of her ass in those bright-peach pants and the full breasts beneath her shirt that had caught my eye first.

But then I looked at her—*really* looked at her—and felt like I'd been struck by a tiny bolt of lightning. Something buzzed between us—something I couldn't quite explain.

All I knew was that I had to know more about her.

Who was this woman, and where had she been for the past thirty-three years of my life?

Davina was a magnet. From the moment I'd entered that office, she'd had an intense pull on me, and oddly enough, I wanted to feel that pull again.

FOUR

DAVINA

I was right. Deke *definitely* wanted his ego stroked.

Standing at the back of the restaurant, Deke grinned with two women in short, shimmery dresses while holding one of their phones in the air.

"Give me a smile, ladies," he said, his voice as smooth as satin, and the women giggled behind bright smiles, hands on hips and elbows popped out as they peered up at the phone for a selfie. "There you go."

He handed the phone back to one of them, and they thanked him graciously before wandering to their seats. That didn't stop them from giggling and gawking at him, though.

When Deke caught sight of me, his mouth turned up, and those dimples of his made yet another appearance. With his eyes all soft and relaxed, he looked innocent, boyish even.

"Did I interrupt your little threesome?" I asked.

Deke's smile slipped, and his eyes widened. "My *what?*"

I felt a prickle on my forehead. Yeah, I was about to break a sweat from the stress of this moment. Why would I ask that? *Just be normal, Davina!*

To my good fortune, Deke busted out laughing, and my shoulders relaxed.

"I'm sorry. That was so unprofessional of me." I laughed nervously and waved a hand, hoping to dismiss the awkwardness.

"Trust me, I've heard worse. Don't sweat it," he said.

A man in all black waltzed up to the table, with a tray in hand and two cocktails on top of it.

Deke took both drinks off the tray and offered one to me. "They say this drink is the best in the house."

"Oh, I, um . . ." I glanced down at the drink. It looked yummy enough, topped with flowers, sugar crystals, and a purply liquid. It was very aesthetic . . . but I couldn't drink it.

"Shit. Let me guess." Deke set the spare drink down on the table. "You don't drink?"

"I . . . don't as much anymore. Just a personal choice. I'm so sorry." I forced a smile at him, adjusting the strap of my purse on my shoulder. I was butchering this night.

"Ah, see. That's my fault for assuming things."

"If that poses any issues, I apologize," I added as he signaled for the waiter to come back.

"An issue? Over *alcohol*? Nah. If anything, you've gained more of my respect. Do you know how hard it is *not* to drink in America?"

I couldn't help laughing at that. He had a point.

"Hey, man. You think you can take these back and bring us some waters, please?" he asked the waiter. "Lemon in mine would be good." Deke's head swung so that his eyes met mine. "Lemon?"

"Uh, sure. Yeah."

"Lemon in both," Deke told him. "And don't let those drinks go to waste. Send them to the girls over there." He pointed at the two he'd taken a selfie with.

The waiter nodded, collected the pretty drinks, and scurried away. I watched as he placed them down on the girls' table and said something. The girls immediately looked at Deke and squealed "Oh my God! Thank you!" in unison.

He gave them a swift nod before returning his focus to me. Pulling out one of the chairs at our table, he gestured to it and said, "For you."

I sat and gave him a grateful smile. "Thank you so much."

He walked to the opposite side of the table and sat down, resting his back against the chair and spreading his legs. "So, you don't drink. Not to be all up in your business, but why choose a place with a bar if you don't bother with alcohol?"

"You want the truth?" I asked with a nervous smile.

His mouth twitched. "Yeah. Give me the truth."

"Well, the truth is I've never been here before. Tish told me about it, and it was the first thing to come to mind when you asked about a favorite restaurant."

Deke chuckled, nodding. "I see."

"To be fair, I would've been fine going to Outback or even Olive Garden, but I didn't think that would impress you as much." We both laughed. "And just so you don't think I'm recovering from a drinking addiction or anything, I *do* have a drink from time to time. It's just not as often as it used to be a year ago." He nodded like he wholeheartedly understood, which made me want to further explain. "I toned it down last spring when I decided it was time to develop a new lifestyle. Now that I'm thirty-two and busier than ever, I'm sure my liver thanks me for it." I laughed, and he smiled. "But if I'm celebrating or if there's a major event happening, I'll have a drink or two. There just hasn't been much to celebrate lately, so . . ."

"This night isn't cause for celebration?" He gestured to the space around us with a hand.

"Not unless we're closing this deal right now." I pursed my lips and looked into his eyes, challenging him. Deke fought a grin, embracing the challenge. Then he leaned forward in his chair to dig his phone out of his back pocket.

"It's an e-signature, right?"

"Yes," I said as more of a question than a statement.

He was quiet for a moment, tapping and scrolling away at the screen of his phone. Then he placed the phone flat on the table and used his index finger to sign in a box.

"There," he said, tapping the Submit button. "Signed. All you have to do is complete it with your signature, and this partnership is official."

"Wow." I blinked rapidly. "You didn't even read it."

"Didn't need to. Arnold took care of that for me. He said it was legit, and I trust him."

I swallowed. "Um . . . okay. I guess you gave those drinks away for nothing." I bubbled out a laugh as I glanced at the girls in shimmery dresses, now taking pictures of each other posing with the drinks. They were definitely enjoying the free cocktails.

"Nah." Deke glanced over his shoulder to where the waiter was preparing our H_2O at the bar. "We can stick with the basics tonight. I don't wanna throw off the lifestyle thing you have going on. And, like you said, this is business. But next time we'll be celebrating with proper drinks. You feel me?"

"Oh, there's a next time, is there?"

He lowered his eyes to my chest, then brought them back up again. "Absolutely."

I crossed my legs, feeling a tingle between them that I hadn't felt in a long time. Thankfully, the waiter appeared with our waters and took our orders.

I wasn't sure what we were going to do or talk about now that he'd signed the contract. I'd had some things in my mind that I'd wanted to mention, like sales figures and what we used in our products. Fortunately, I didn't have to lead many of the conversations, because Deke took the floor.

Before he started, though, I noticed him glance at my wedding ring as I collected my water. His face had warped a bit, and when he noticed *me* noticing *him*, he cleared his throat and forced a smile.

I could tell he had questions—or that maybe he was regretting his wine and dine initiative with a woman he didn't realize was (or had been) married—but if he felt any sort of way about it, he didn't show it. He still acted himself . . . and still stared at me like I was naked.

I should've told him about Lew—about why I still wore the rings—but I wasn't sure I'd be able to hold back the tears. It was better to let it be and let it go. After all, I doubted Deke and I would be having any more one-on-one "business" dinners after this.

"What made you get into skin care, anyway?" Deke asked after chatting about how packed his summer schedule was going to be.

"Well, believe it or not, I used to make my own body scrubs and creams when I was younger. All in my mom's kitchen. I went to a community college and got my bachelor's in business and figured I'd put that degree to use doing something else I loved."

"And that's how GOC was born," he said.

"Yep. Exactly."

"Seems to be doing well for you. Don't know what you need me for." His eyes lit up as he waited for my response.

"I mean, sure, it's done well, but it can always do better. And by the way, I'm really glad you're doing this with us, Deke. Seriously. Having you as the face of our products is going to change a lot of things for us."

"You don't have to thank me. You did the work, and it paid off. But let's make a sober toast to it," he said, picking up his glass of water and raising it in the air.

I snorted a laugh, picking mine up too. "Okay."

"Here's to Golden Oil." His eyes twinkled beneath the warm lighting as he studied every detail of my face. "May it continue to prosper for you."

"To Golden Oil," I said, tapping his glass.

As we locked eyes and sipped, I tried very hard to ignore that warm, fuzzy feeling inside me.

FIVE

DAVINA

While we ate, I found it surprising that Deke was such a great conversationalist. Most athletes loved talking about themselves, but not him.

"Were you born in Charlotte?" he asked me.

"No, born and raised in Maple Cove, but Charlotte is my second home."

"Oh." His eyebrows dipped a bit. "Where's Maple Cove? I don't think I've heard of it."

"It's about a two-hour drive from here, just outside of Asheville. It gets lumped in with Asheville, because it's such a small town."

"Oh. That's cool. I'll have to check it out. So what about siblings?"

"A sister, two years younger, and a brother, sixteen years younger."

"*Sixteen years?*" His eyes stretched as he gaped. "Mama got busy!"

"Yeah." I laughed. "She did."

"That makes you the oldest, then."

"Sure does."

"That must've been a burden growing up."

I shifted in my seat. "What makes you say that?"

"My oldest sister grew up as the caretaker. She was like a second mom, when I think about it. She was always taking care of me. Then again, I'm the youngest, so . . ." He shrugged like it was no big deal, but that small statement seemed loaded.

"Hmm. Well, there are downfalls and perks to being the eldest."

"Really?" He sat up taller in his chair, placing both elbows on the table. "Care to share any?"

"One of the downfalls is that your parents are harder on you, but only because they're afraid of what the world will do to you. You're basically this guinea pig, and they're trying to figure you out and how to get you to navigate the world properly. But as you age, they begin to trust you, so much so that they want you to watch over their *other* kids. But with that comes the annoyance of babysitting on weekends, when what you really want is to go out and have fun with your friends—and you can't, because your 'parent' has to work, or they end up having things planned for themselves."

I fiddled with my fork, hoping it'd distract me from the brewing frustrations. I didn't want to think about my childhood, and I was glad Deke didn't notice how worked up I was getting. I sipped my water to calm down.

"Okay. I hear that. What are the perks?" he asked.

"The perks . . ." I chewed on my bottom lip. "Well, one of them is the independence that comes with being the oldest. We learn how to do a lot on our own. Sure, there can be burdens, but being older means getting out first, exploring the world first, becoming the most responsible—well, sometimes. In my case, it paid off. Being the oldest made me work harder for the things I wanted so I wouldn't have to share with my siblings forever. Believe it or not, I had to wear my sister's hand-me-downs. She grew up bigger than me."

Deke gave me a warm smile. "That's usually how it goes, isn't it?"

"Yep." I sighed, then looked him over, grinning. "So, you're the baby."

"I am."

"I bet you're so spoiled."

He belted out a laugh. "Spoiled? Nah, I wouldn't say all that. I may be the baby of the family, but I grew up to be a respectful gentleman."

"And a charmer, apparently." I took a sip of my water like it was hot gossip tea.

"What gives you that impression?"

"You're trying to charm me right now."

"You think so?" A smooth smile tugged at his lips. "How am I doing?"

"It's sweet. Unfortunately, it won't work on me."

His eyes dropped to my ring finger, and this time he made it very clear that he was aware of it. He tapped the cushion-cut diamond while holding my gaze.

"I assume it's because of this?"

I glanced at the ring, trying hard not to react to the heat of his finger. Instead, I gingerly pulled my hand away from his to pick up a slice of bruschetta. "That's part of the reason."

I tried not to think how ridiculous it was to still be wearing my wedding rings so many months after my husband died. Just like the dragonfly necklace, they felt sacred—like something I couldn't take off, not even in the shower.

Deke's lips pushed together before he said, "I respect that."

"I'm glad you do. That makes you a *true* gentleman."

"Can I ask you something, though?" he asked.

I eyed him. "Sure."

"Are you happy with the man who put that ring on your finger?"

My back straightened like a board as I fought a frown. I hesitated before asking, "Why do you ask that?"

"Because you don't seem happy. Overall, I mean."

"How do you mean?"

"I don't know." Deke's cognac eyes penetrated mine, then he dropped his gaze to my rings again. "I think it's your eyes. There's a sadness or a longing in them, but they still hold a lot of passion. And it's like you want to pour all that passion out and place it somewhere, but he won't let you . . ." He paused, twisting his lips. "Or maybe you can't. Long distance. Marital issues. Lack of trust, possibly. I'm no relationship expert, though."

I pulled my gaze away, and my guard went up like a steel wall. What was he, a shrink now? "It's none of those."

I was getting uncomfortable with where this conversation was heading. My eyes prickled with heat, and I blinked to cool the burn as I checked my phone for the time. It was nearing nine, and the contract was signed. There was no need to entertain him any longer. I had to get out of here before I started bawling at the table.

I darkened the screen of my phone before putting my focus on him.

"So, listen, dinner was great, Declan."

"Deke," he corrected.

"Sorry. *Deke.*" I collected my purse and pushed out of my chair. Deke stood too. "Tish was right. This place is incredible. Thank you for the invitation to dinner, the endless cups of water, and for agreeing to endorse us. I'll leave some cash so you can pay."

I was about to undo the clasp of my purse, but Deke stopped my hand with his. My breath hitched as I focused on the brown hand that felt like it was searing into my skin.

When my eyes dragged up to his, I didn't expect to find him so close to me. His cologne was intoxicating, and those damn eyes, bordered with impossibly long lashes, were hooking me good.

Why did he have to look at me like that? Like he owned every part of me, down to my blood cells. This man oozed sex appeal, and he *knew* it.

Deke had a way of making a woman feel special, like he only had eyes for her and like she was the only woman in the room. I understood it now—what drove the fans crazy (and probably the women he encountered on a daily basis).

I was positive I wasn't the first person he made feel this way, and I damn sure wouldn't be the last. Not that it concerned me. This fluttery, nervous feeling I got with him wasn't going to matter when the night was over.

"Don't worry about paying," he said, taking his hand away.

"Huh?"

"The bill. I've got it," he said, the corner of his mouth quirking up. "Come on. I'll walk you out."

"Right. Yeah."

My heart sped up a notch as he followed me out of the restaurant. *So much for that steel wall going up.* When we made it to my car, he stopped only a few steps away from me while I unlocked it and opened the door halfway.

"Thanks again," I said, unsure what else to say.

"Don't sweat it."

"And for signing the deal. This is going to be great for you! You'll see. We'll make it worth your while. Tish will email you and Arnold about the photo shoot and all the other details within a week or so."

"Sounds good." Deke continued smiling, but I don't think he really cared about the deal or the emails that would follow from Tish. He kept watching me, his eyes shimmering beneath the streetlights.

He revealed those dimples again, and that's when I had to look away. He really *was* sexy. I needed to get away from this man. He was making me feel things I shouldn't have felt.

I fumbled with my keys as I slid into the car. Taking a step back, Deke threw his hand up and tossed me a wave as I started the engine.

I waved back before pulling out of my parking space, but as I drove away and looked in the rearview mirror, his head was bowed and a big, adorable grin was on his face.

He was smiling like a schoolboy with a crush.

SIX

DEKE

The bass of the music pulsed through my shoes as I sat on a leather sofa, a drink in one hand and my phone in the other. I was at one of EJ's many offseason parties in the private house he owned in Atlanta.

I didn't want to be there, but EJ was my teammate *and* one of my closest friends, and he'd sent me an invite. Plus, I had nowhere else important to be. If I weren't at the party, I'd have been at my condo, curled up in bed with all the lights out.

I couldn't do this party alone, though. I hit up my boy Javier Valdez and told him to join me. He wasn't fond of parties, and I knew he'd have rather been home with his three-year-old daughter, Aleesa, but it was a Saturday night, and his nanny of the month often kept an eye on her every other weekend. This was one of her on-duty weekends, so he had no excuse to bail.

I looked at Javier, who was frowning, with his arms folded loosely across his chest.

"You can at least pretend you wanna be here," I said, nudging him with my elbow.

"That is the point. I do not want to be." His accent was thick as he glared at me with dark eyes.

Javier Valdez was an Argentinean six-foot-five recruit for the team. He'd been popular in his home country, and the NBA had noticed him. The Ravens had signed him four years prior, and he was one of the best centers in the game.

Ever since I'd met him, he'd been a generally serious person who hardly joked around, but we got along pretty well. When his wife died, though, the word *serious* may as well have become his last name.

He hadn't been the same since Eloise passed. I could count on one hand how many times I'd seen him smile the past year, and all those smiles had been given to his daughter.

"I would rather be at a bar or something, catching a *fútbol* game," Javier went on. "EJ is always inviting weird people to these parties."

I took a look around as the lights flashed neon colors through EJ's dumbass fog machine. I didn't know half these people. The women were half-naked, and the men were desperate for their attention.

A cloud of weed smoke passed my nose, and I smashed my lips together. There were a few other teammates here and some B-list celebrities, who had people with cameras following them around for the perfect photo op.

"We'll give it ten more minutes, then we're out. I'll hit up EJ, let him know we're about to bounce."

Javier nodded, satisfied with my response. I unlocked my phone again and shot a text to EJ with our ten-minute countdown, then swiped to the Instagram app.

A photo appeared on my feed of me and Davina standing in front of her work building. At the sight of it, my heartbeat quickened.

I sat up taller and swallowed as I brought the screen closer to my face. In the picture, I was shaking her hand—a sign that we'd closed a new deal. I'd met Davina the morning after our little dinner, just before my flight, and I remembered her hand being soft and delicate in mine and the way her eyelashes fluttered as she peered up at me.

I didn't know what the hell it was about that woman, but she made my body do weird shit. I mean, she was so simple, and perhaps that's what it was that I was attracted to. The simplicity.

She had a nice smile, wasn't too heavy on the makeup, and she was herself. In a world full of bullshit and plastic, it was a nice reprieve to be around a female who was her authentic self. If she didn't have those rings on her finger, she would've already been mine.

I couldn't believe I'd missed the rings when I first saw her in the office. Or maybe I was just being willfully ignorant. Seeing them at Silver Wolf was a wake-up call that filled me with disappointment. I never would've asked her to dinner if I'd known she was married. I could get down with a lot of things, but fooling around with a married woman wasn't one of them.

I tapped the photo, and her username popped up: *thatvinachick*. I gave it a tap and a follow, then did something I never did with any other female. I started a message.

You look good in that pic of us. Glad we're working together.

I hovered over the Send button before giving it a swift tap. I don't know why I bothered sending it. I guess it felt necessary—like something I *needed* to do to prove to her how important this opportunity was to me too. She was passionate about her company, and I was glad to help . . . or maybe I was just looking for another reason to talk to her again.

Willfully ignorant.

Despite knowing she was taken, I couldn't stop thinking about her. It was frustrating as hell. To her, that dinner was probably nothing more than a business transaction, but I'd felt a connection there. I wasn't tripping. I'd been sure she could feel it, too . . . but she had a man, so that was that.

"Damn, who is that?!" someone yelled over my shoulder. EJ, our top point guard, hopped over the couch and wedged his six-foot frame between me and Javier. "Nah, for real. Who is that?" EJ asked while panting like a dog.

I side-eyed him. "Why the hell are you breathing so hard, man?"

"Oh, when you sent me that text, I was fucking Lula on the balcony. You know how it is, bruh." EJ supplied a shit-eating grin. "Who you looking at?"

"Nobody." I turned my phone away from him. "Just a girl I work with."

"You fucking her?" he asked. This dude. So damn nonchalant.

"No, dumbass."

"So why you all in her pics, then?"

"It's not like that," I muttered, then stood and slipped my phone into my back pocket. "We're heading out."

Javier followed my lead, giving EJ a nudge on the side of the head with his fingertips. "Choose better people to surround yourself with, EJ. This is ridiculous. I saw a woman in the bathroom with her fucking face in the toilet."

EJ followed us to the door, going on about how *lit* his parties were, but of course we didn't make it out without getting stopped over a dozen times to take pictures or to talk to a few of those B-list celebs.

When we were clear, I found my Ferrari and told Javier I'd meet him at our favorite bar, Rossi's. I went through more of Davina's pictures at the stoplights. I couldn't help myself.

She didn't post much, and she didn't have many images of herself either. Most were of her products or scenery images from places she'd traveled to. There were a few off guards of her peppered throughout the feed, one of her showing off a dragonfly necklace she was clearly proud of, and then a picture posted four years ago.

She was in an ivory linen dress on the beach wearing a straw hat, and a man was holding her from behind, his hands low on her belly and his chin resting on her shoulder.

She seemed to be midlaughter as he gazed into the camera. He had tan skin, like he might've been biracial, curly dark hair, and bright eyes.

Ah.

So he was the lucky man.

I shut the screen of my phone off and gripped the steering wheel tighter. When the light turned green, I peeled off, ready for a strong drink to wash away my desire for a married woman.

SEVEN

DAVINA

"Today is fucked," I grumbled. I blew out a gut-deep sigh and faced Tish, who was already standing beside me.

"No, it's not, Vina. It'll be fine," she insisted. "We still have Kenji, and we're on schedule." Kenji was our backup photographer.

It was Deke's photo shoot day, but our original photographer had ended up getting into a car accident on the way to the studio we booked. That was the last thing we'd expected.

"You're right. You're right." I wrung my fingers around my phone while biting into my bottom lip.

"Stop that before you make yourself bleed," Tish scolded, before dropping her eyes to her clipboard again.

"Sorry—I'm just . . . I really need things to go smoothly for the rest of the day." That was a fact. I hadn't been able to sleep the night before, too busy thinking about Lew.

I'd been thinking about him a lot more since that dinner with Deke. A part of me felt guilty for enjoying my time with another man. Acting like I hadn't been clinging to my husband's dead body just months ago.

"Everything will be okay. Relax." Tish's voice snapped me back in place. "Deke is getting dressed now, and Kenji is setting up. It'll be great."

Tish was right. Other than the terrible news from our photographer, the shoot went well. Deke was skilled, and watching him in action was a sight to behold. He didn't complain and didn't mind being instructed on what to do or how to pose with the products.

It was fun watching him be so calm and relaxed, shifting from pose to pose as if he did this for a living—well, let me retract. He *did* do this kind of stuff for a living, but never with body oils and lotions. It was always for sportsy stuff—Gatorade or Nike.

Deke was photogenic, to say the least. It was no wonder the media loved him.

When Kenji instructed him to take his shirt off, a few people whistled, and he couldn't contain his smile. I found it hard to look away after that, drinking in the sleeves of ink on his arms, the sculpted abs glistening from one of *my* body oils. I was almost jealous of the assistant who'd helped spread the oil all over him.

Dear Heavenly Father, he was just too much. I had to grab a water and chug some of it down to calm myself.

When the shoot was wrapped up, relief washed over me, because it meant there could be no more hiccups. Kenji showed me a sneak peek of the raw images, and hope blossomed inside me. They looked *so, so* good. After editing, the images of Deke were definitely going to change the game.

During cleanup, Tish gave Kenji a bottle of water, then passed one to Deke, who thanked her with a wink. He carried his eyes across the room and linked them with mine as a smile materialized.

I tried ignoring the fact that he was still shirtless. He shot me a thumbs-up while mouthing the words *Was I good?*

I threw him a thumbs-up in return and mouthed, *You did great.* He sent me a wink and graced me with a dimple. I refused to acknowledge what that wink did to me internally.

When Tish came back my way, she said, "I'm going with Clarise to pick up the lunch for everyone. When I get back, we can finish up with Kenji and Declan."

"Sounds good."

I watched her leave the studio, before turning to look at Deke again. He was already looking at me . . . or maybe he'd never looked away. I ignored the rapid beating of my heart and turned for the snack table to grab a pastry.

I glanced over my shoulder, nibbling on a glazed donut, and was fortunate to see one of the stylists had approached him with a sheet of paper and a Sharpie. Deke smiled, graciously taking the items to provide an autograph.

While I was in the clear, I weaseled my way to the seating area and sat to check notifications on my phone.

I'd purposely kept my distance from Deke all morning, and sure, it was a bit immature, but I had to. The Davina from two weeks ago would've bounced on over to speak to Deke like an adult, but a week and a half ago I'd received an Instagram message from him.

I had no idea why he bothered messaging me, let alone *followed* me. Seeing his name in my inbox was a surprise, to say the least. I actually had to check his profile to make sure it was him. The page was verified, so it was.

I went to the app to read his message again:

You look good in that pic of us. Glad we're working together.

He was referring to the picture of me and him shaking hands in front of the company building. The photo was posted on our company's official Instagram page and website, and I assumed he found me because my personal account was tagged.

His message seemed like a double-edged sword. At first, I was going to respond to only the *glad we're working together* part, but I changed my mind just as quickly when I looked up and saw a picture of Lewis staring back at me.

While I was on the app, I clicked his username, *bishopdeke*, to view his profile. I tapped the first photo on the page, an image of him on the court last season, dressed in his black-and-red uniform, the bold number seventeen in the center, sweat glistening on his sculpted upper arms.

Finishing my donut, I scrolled down until I came across an image of him with some supermodel. She was slender yet curvy in all the right places. Her hair was dark and curly, her skin a shade lighter than caramel. They were at an event, her arms draped over Deke's neck, him hugging her by the waist. She had to be Giselle Grace, the woman he was rumored to be dating.

"You left me on read," a deep voice said next to me.

I gasped and flipped my phone on its face as Deke stepped into view.

He looked from the phone on my lap to my face again with a funny look. "Did I interrupt something?"

"No, no—I was just . . . checking some things. Um, what do you mean I left you on read?" I asked, swiftly changing the subject.

"Sent you a message on Instagram a couple weeks ago."

"Oh, yeah. I'm so sorry about that." I tugged on my shirt to smooth it out. "When I saw it, I got caught up and completely forgot to respond."

"You're busy. I get it." He shifted on his feet, clutching the bottled water in his hand and taking a thorough look around the studio. I drew in a breath and slid over, tapping the available cushion next to me.

"You should sit," I offered. "Are you hungry? Tish went to grab lunches for everyone, but in the meantime, there are donuts and cookies at the refreshments table. I doubt an athlete wants to eat that junk, though."

He chuckled, lowering to the sofa. "It's the offseason. This is the time when I eat whatever I want, D."

"*D?*" I repeated with a confused laugh.

"Yeah, D. I can call you that, right?"

"Uh . . . sure. If you'd like."

I wriggled in my seat, twisting my wedding band. I didn't want to tell him it was normally family who called me by that nickname. It was either D or Vina. Most times it was Vina. My dad was the one who called me D the most, so it was a little strange hearing it from Deke after not hearing it for so long.

Deke sat back, twisted the cap off his water again, and took a few chugs.

"If it makes you feel any better about your message, I appreciate the compliment, and you looked great despite those unnecessary gold chains around your neck."

Humor filled his eyes. "Oh, you think the chains were unnecessary?"

"I mean . . . I guess I don't get the point." I laughed. "Why do ball players wear that heavy-ass jewelry, anyway?"

"Nah, see, you got it all wrong. People love seeing the bling."

"Well, I think it's just a way for people who used to be *nobodies* to show off the fact that they're *somebodies* now." It was a mindless statement, but when Deke turned to look at me, I instantly regretted those words.

The smile melted from his face, and his thick brows puckered. "Damn, Davina. Way to chop me at my knees."

"Oh—no. I'm sorry! I didn't mean *you*!" I barked out an embarrassed laugh. "It's just . . . I know men like that. Using all that glitz and glam to prove to people they're important. But you don't need all that, Deke. Your personality speaks for you. People love your energy."

He fought another smile. "I appreciate that, but the chains are here to stay."

I laughed.

After a silent second, he added, "You have good energy too."

Our eyes connected, but neither of us pulled away. My pulse crawled to my ears, and I swallowed.

"I bet I do," I said, pressing an exaggerated hand to my chest. I wanted to change tempo. I *needed* to. "I'm, like, the best person you'll ever meet. I'm like those tulips on the refreshments table. I can brighten up any room if I want to."

"Oh, really? You like tulips?"

"I do. They're gorgeous."

"Well," he said, glancing at the flowers briefly before locking on me again. "That's good to know. And about you brightening up a room, I believe that's true. There's a light in you. Shines bright. I like it." He winked, and my heart fluttered.

I fought a blush as I dropped my eyes to my lap.

When Arnold called his name and Deke turned away, I was mildly relieved. Arnold meandered his way through the studio, stopping a step or two short of Deke. "Hey, Deke, uh . . . G. G. called. Said it's urgent." Arnold's voice was low, like he didn't want anyone else to hear, but I heard the words clearly.

Deke's forehead crinkled as he looked Arnold in the eyes; then he glanced at me. "Give me a second, D."

He followed Arnold to the dressing rooms, and I watched as he shut the door behind him, before picking up my phone again and checking his Instagram.

I tapped the picture that appeared, and the username *gisellegrace* popped up. Her page was full of half-naked images, duck-lipped selfies, and designer outfits.

Some images of her and Deke stood out, where they held hands while cameras flashed around them or she kissed his cheek while glaring into the camera.

In all the images with Deke, it was like she wanted it to be abundantly clear he was hers and no one else's. I wasn't sure what it was, but their relationship didn't look real. It seemed forced, *fake*. Deke hardly smiled with her.

I didn't get it. If he was with her, why the hell was he trying to flirt with me? Because that's what this was—all the back-and-forth banter. *Flirting*. Then again, that was a dumb question. Famous and rich men alike did this sort of thing.

Flirted.

Lied.

Cheated.

Made it a game of cat and mouse. It shouldn't have come as a surprise to me.

Deke's dressing room door swung open again, and I noticed that he'd changed into his regular clothes—a white T-shirt that hugged his body, jeans, and a pair of colorful high-top Nike Dunks. I was almost positive those shoes were custom made.

His eyes snapped to me instantly, and this time I darkened the screen of my phone to prepare for his presence.

"I have to go, but thank you, Davina," he said as I rose to my feet. "I hope the pictures work for you. If not, we can set something up later and do it again."

With a smile, I offered a hand to him, and he looked at it in a funny way before taking it and shaking. I bet he was expecting a hug, but I had to keep this man at a distance. I had a feeling if I hugged him, I'd melt in his damn arms.

"Thank you for everything, Deke."

"Sure." He started to walk away but caught himself and cut his eyes to me again. "I heard some of the proceeds for the rebranding are going toward a spinal-cancer charity or something like that."

"Oh, yeah. Solid Spines." I nodded, hoping my throat wouldn't close up on me from the mere thought of it. I cleared the blockage in my throat and said, "Ten percent of each sale will go to them to help people in need and to fund research for the cancer."

"That's a specific choice for a charity." Deke gazed deep into my eyes. I didn't like the way he was looking at me. It was like he was reading me, trying to figure me out. "What made you choose it?"

One of my shoulders lifted up and dropped down in response. I wasn't about to get into a whole spiel about it. The last thing I wanted was Deke's pity. Plus, I didn't like talking about Lew's terminal illness with anyone other than my family and Tish.

"Let's just say it's a cause that's close to me," I told him.

Deke scanned my face. "Cool. Well, I'll be in town for a couple days. I'll be hanging with the Charlotte Wasps to school some kids on basketball. If you wanna catch a few waters at a bar, hit me up."

I couldn't help the laugh that bubbled out of me. "I'll consider the offer. Have fun with the kids."

With a smirk, Deke sauntered away with Arnold, and when he exited the studio, I realized my heart had been racing during our entire conversation. I'd been professional with a lot of men during my career, but with Deke . . . I don't know. Being around him made me feel so . . . *different*.

The jokes.

The banter.

The natural flow of our conversations.

But a workplace setting and a bar were two *very* different atmospheres. One had boundaries, and the other didn't. If I wanted to continue this deal and keep him the face of our brand, I had to maintain a safe distance.

He was my colleague. Not my friend. Not my buddy. *A business colleague.*

Regardless, planning to keep a distance from him was much easier said than done.

EIGHT

DEKE

I was a man born and bred in sunny Orlando, Florida, so you'd think I could call it home. The truth is, there was no better place for me to be than in Atlanta.

I'd signed on as a rookie to play for New York, but that only lasted me a year before I got traded to Memphis. It was hard for me to get along with the coaches at Memphis, so my agent found a home for me in Atlanta.

It'd been two years since signing with Atlanta, and after all the bouncing around prior, I felt I had to prove myself. Atlanta needed a shooting guard, and I was that guy. I took my training much more seriously and focused heavily on the fundamentals, while adding my own *razzle-dazzle* to it.

As soon as I signed, I knew Atlanta was the place to be. The team welcomed me with open arms, and I was cool with the majority of my teammates.

To put it simply, this city was my home. I had friends, a place to call mine, and passionate fans who loved me. Apart from my mama and my sisters, I'd never truly felt love in Orlando.

I dropped my keys off with the valet before heading toward my condo building. Justin, the doorman, put on a big grin when he spotted me. He was in his fifties, dark skin, salt-and-pepper beard. A man for-ever young in spirit.

"Deke Bishop is in the house!" he yelled, throwing both hands in the air.

I laughed as we clapped hands and bumped shoulders. "What's going on, Justin? Your grandbaby still keeping you awake, man?"

"Every night. Swear my wife is about to strangle *me* because *she* can't sleep. She's the one who let our daughter move back in! She signed up for that, not me." Justin laughed.

"You know what works? Flowers, man. Women love getting them for no reason." According to Camille, anyway.

"I'll have to bring some home for her. Oh, and just a heads-up. You've got company." Justin gave me a look that said *Sorry, man*, and I sighed, throwing my head back and closing my eyes for a second.

When I lowered my chin, I released a slow sigh, thanked Justin, and made my way into the building.

I took the elevator up to my penthouse, but I didn't have to unlock the door. It was already unlocked, which annoyed the hell out of me because she always left it unlocked.

The first thing I smelled when I walked inside was an overly sweet candy-scented perfume. I was growing to despise it. I dropped my bag by the door as Giselle walked around the corner in spiky heels and a ruby-red dress that hugged her body.

Giselle Grace, the woman everyone assumed was my girlfriend. That was a stretch by this point. Her red lips split apart as she smiled and placed a hand on her cocked hip. Zeke, my two-year-old Doberman pinscher, rushed around her, his paws tapping on the floors as he charged toward me.

"What's up, man?" I bent over, scratching behind his ears, and as usual, Zeke flipped onto his back to show me his belly. "Damn, Zeke," I laughed, giving him a rub. "Justin might be feeding you too much. Look at that belly."

"Um, hello?" Giselle called.

I cut a glance at her before returning my attention to Zeke. "What's up?"

"*What's up?*" she scoffed, her Caribbean accent thick. "Is that it?"

"Wasn't expecting you to be here."

"Well, I'm here, and I'm glad you made it back. I booked reservations for us at this new restaurant. Everyone says it's really nice and it's so aesthetic. You'll love it."

I stopped rubbing Zeke's belly to stand up straight. "Giselle, I'm not in the mood to go anywhere. I just got back and wanna chill, to be honest with you. Plus, I'm working out with Javier tomorrow."

"Well, it's been a full week since I last saw you, Deke. Plus I ran out of pictures of us." She put on a faux smile, and I blew a breath, peering out the wall of windows across the room.

I admit, when I first met Giselle, I found her sexy as hell. Every man in the world wanted her, and when she showed up at one of my games dressed in leather pants and a crop top to show off her tits, batting her long eyelashes at me, I could tell she wanted me. I wanted her, too . . . but that was *before* I realized there was a catch with her.

This woman only wanted me for the attention it would bring her. Think of it as a gold digger, but for the media's sake. She was so desperate for the public's attention, always insisting that I kiss her during our outings or hug her a certain way when cameras were around.

She started showing up at some of my games wearing the most *ridiculous* outfits, to sponsor whatever designer was paying her. Suffice to say, I was over it real fucking quick.

She wasn't an entirely bad person, which was why I had given her a key to my apartment early on. She would swing by between my home games so we could fool around, and then she'd leave.

Despite how superficial she was, it was nice spending time with *someone* rather than being alone and drowning in my thoughts. There was only so long I could be around her, though, and she could sense I was pulling away. I could see it in her eyes. Sadly, I didn't care.

"Fine," I mumbled. "Let me take a shower first."

"'Kay. Hurry up, though. The reservation is in an hour."

After showering, getting dressed, and posing in front of this snazzy new restaurant Giselle was so eager to go to, we were seated in a booth.

Pictures were taken by the other diners, and Giselle was aware. She had her back straight and was trying her hardest to be sexy for the "random" shots that'd float around on the internet.

In between her poses, Giselle talked about her schedule and how she had to fly to Paris for a fashion show. She was going to be there for two weeks. Good. I already needed the break, and we weren't even an hour into dinner yet.

As she talked my head off about some makeup collection she wanted to launch, my phone buzzed in my pocket. I pulled it out, surprised to see a notification from Davina on Instagram.

I hurried to open the app.

Sorry for missing out on bar waters. Maybe another time?

Btw, I got a few pics of yours back from the shoot and they look really good.

Below her message were three photos of me posing with her products in my hand or on a stand next to me. There was one I particularly liked, where it looked like I was tossing a container of face cream in the air like it was a mini basketball aiming for a goal.

For the sake of skin care, they'd asked for a few shirtless shots, and this was one of them. The photo shoot was creative as hell and would make a splash. Gotta say, I never knew I could make skin care look so damn good.

"What are you smiling about?" Giselle's high-pitched voice caused my smile to slip away.

I lifted my gaze and watched as she stabbed a fork into her seared chicken, her eyes on me.

"Nothing." I shut the phone screen off, and as I dug into my chicken, too, I made a mental note to message Davina back as soon as this dinner was over.

NINE

DAVINA

Past

Three weeks before Lewis died, I noticed his depression had worsened.

I wasn't sure how to help him or what more I could do as his partner. He was slowly withering away. I still held out hope that things could turn around, but deep in my gut, I knew they wouldn't.

Wilmer, his personal caregiver and a man who'd become a very close friend of ours, suggested that we all plan a trip to the beach.

Lew perked up at the idea, and though I was nervous to travel anywhere with him while he was so frail, I figured why not. He needed the experience after so many hard months, so during the last three weeks of his life, we planned and prepared.

We made a short drive to the Outer Banks so the ride wouldn't wear him out, but there was one night of the trip that stuck with me most. One that would haunt my dreams so badly they would keep me awake at night.

We sat by the pool as the sun set and the ocean waves roared in the distance. I didn't want to go inside yet, but Lew was tired and ready to lie down. I helped him with a shower, assisted with the pajamas, then got him into bed.

Afterward, I brushed his buzz-cut hair. There wasn't much of it left, but he loved the feel of the soft bristles on his scalp. He used to have gorgeous curls, which I'd apply moisturizer and water to so I could comb them and make them bouncier. I had done it all the time before he got sick, and he'd loved it, said he'd never had his hair played with before.

Lewis caught my eye as I placed the brush down and smiled up at me.

"What is it?" I asked, smiling back.

"You're just so beautiful, Davina."

His words caught me completely off guard, along with the wide, proud smile taking over his face, and the shine in his eyes. He had a cute smile. One of his front teeth was slightly chipped at the tip—hardly noticeable unless you were up close and personal with him. He told me it chipped while he was playing a free game of football with his friends.

"Come here." Lewis reached for me, and I climbed onto the bed to lie next to him. He was quiet for a moment. While he was, I listened to the dishes clinking in the kitchen as Wilmer cleaned up.

"I can't stop thinking about when we first met," Lew said with a soft laugh. "How upset you got when I bumped into you and spilled your popcorn all over the floor."

I laughed at the reminder. "I think I had a right to be upset. Movie popcorn ain't cheap, and I was already broke."

"You're right. It's not cheap. But I bought you another one—a jumbo size, remember? With a Diet Coke?"

"I remember." I stroked the tiny bits of fuzz on his chin and jaw as my brows dipped. "What are you getting at, Lew?"

His hazel eyes glistened as he looked into mine. I sat up straighter as his lips parted, and it was like he had so much to say but couldn't articulate the words.

"Babe, what is it?" I asked. "What's wrong?"

"You were the prettiest woman I'd ever seen, Davina," he said after a sharp exhale. "I remember thinking that I wanted to marry you right on the spot. I know it sounds crazy, but it's like all these moments flashed before me when I looked into your eyes that day. I could see you walking down the aisle to marry me, us buying a house together and me kissing you at the threshold while I held you in my arms. Making love . . . having kids . . .”

At the last statement, his eyes dropped, and his throat bobbed when he swallowed. A tear ran down his cheek and landed on the top of my hand. My throat closed in on itself as I placed my fingers to his chin and tipped his head back up.

I wanted to cry. *Badly.* But I also wanted to keep my emotions level. Lew hardly ever talked like this.

“Why are you saying all of this?” I asked in a quiet voice.

“Because I want you to know that even though we vowed to spend the rest of our lives together, you should be happy. Whether I’m here or not.”

“Lew.” I shook my head, swallowing to soothe the burn in my throat. “Stop.”

He took one of my hands in his and squeezed it tight. “I mean it, Vina. I want you to be happy. No matter what happens to me, I want you to live on, baby. I know the last year has been brutal, and you’re wanting things I can’t give you.”

“Lew. I mean it.”

“You can talk to other people,” he went on, ignoring me. “You can be with someone else and let them make you happy, just like I did. You can fall in love again, so long as you’re living your best life.”

“Stop talking like that. Please,” I pleaded, but the words came out hoarse and thick.

Oh, God. My chest was hurting so badly. The dam was going to break if he kept going.

Lew smiled at me as he used his free hand to swipe one of my tears away. “I love you, Vina Boo. But I know you, and I don’t want you shutting the world out when I’m gone.”

“You’re not going anywhere,” I countered, fighting a sob. “You’re here to stay, Lewis. You’re here, and you’re mine, and we did *not* fall in love just for it to be cut short. We didn’t. You can still beat this.”

Without another word, Lew cupped the back of my head and brought my forehead to his chest. That's when I broke down completely. His body was my home, and I loved being there. No one wanted their home to crumble—to deteriorate and vanish. It was unfair.

No one else could comfort me like he could.

No one else could embrace and accept me through every single one of my flaws like my husband could.

There was no way he was leaving me. No way at all. He was alive and breathing. How could such a beautiful life be stripped away from him?

I swear, it's always the best people who are dealt the worst situations.

"I love you," he whispered into my hair. He said it again while stroking my arm, but I noticed how hard that was for him to do. I could hear the strained noises in his chest, feel the rigidness of his movements. Even while sick, he wanted to comfort me.

"I love you, too, Lew Boo," I finally whispered.

I'm not sure when we fell asleep that night, but when I woke up, a stretch of sunlight was spread across the bed, and its warmth lingered on my face. My eyes were still tight and raw from crying, and my heart ached at the sheer reminder of our conversation.

I turned to Lewis, who was still sleeping, and snuggled closer to him. I kissed his upper arm, then shifted upward to kiss his cheek. I remained nestled against his body . . . but it only took me several seconds to realize he wasn't breathing.

"Lew?" I sat up, giving his shoulder a shake.

I pressed an ear to his chest, waiting for that heartbeat I loved hearing every night.

Nothing.

I listened harder, but his chest was hollow, empty. Not a single thump.

"Lew!" I tapped his face rapidly, and when that didn't make him budge, I shook him by the shoulder again. "Lew, no. Please, get up.

Lew. Get up! Oh, God! Wilmer! Get in here! *Please!*" I didn't stop shaking my husband. "Open your eyes, baby, please. Lewis, *please!*"

The bedroom door burst open, and Wilmer rushed in. "Davina? What is it? What happened?"

I tried answering him—I did—but my chest felt like it was caving in, and my heart was in my throat. The ache inside me was raw and deep, and it sliced me in two because I knew exactly what was happening. I knew it but couldn't fathom speaking the truth.

All that talk from him about moving on, about me being happy . . .

No. Why did I fall asleep? Why didn't I stay awake with him? All I could think was that I could've prevented this if I'd just been awake—if I'd gotten up to check on him.

"Please do something, Wilmer!"

Wilmer checked for Lew's pulse by the wrist and then switched to his neck. When he lowered to a squat and studied Lew's body with misty eyes, he gave his head a deliberate shake and said, "I'm sorry, Davina."

It couldn't be real. It couldn't be true. I looked from Wilmer to Lewis. He looked like he was sleeping. He had to be sleeping . . . *right?*

"Lewis, please." A sob rocked my entire body. "Please, baby. Don't do this. I need you. Please don't leave me."

The sound that ripped out of my throat was one I'd never heard before. Never in my life had I felt so much pain, so much *hurt*. I'd lost my daddy, yes, but I was so young and clueless then. I didn't fully understand what I'd lost until I was older.

But Lewis was my partner and my better half. Can you imagine half your heart being ripped out of your chest? The other half keeps beating, but it's damaged beyond repair, and not a damn thing can mend it.

You're hopeless this way. You fold into yourself and are left with no choice but to feel every wave of emotion, every clench of the belly, every halted breath as you slowly wish for the oxygen to leave your lungs, because what's the point of breathing anymore? It feels like you'll never survive such agony—like you'll never recover . . . like *you're* dying too.

I dropped my head onto my husband's chest. I don't know when I stopped crying that day.

My safety.

My rock.

My best friend.

My *everything*.

He was gone, and I was completely shattered.

TEN

DAVINA

I gasped, springing up in bed as I scanned my bedroom.

It was dark. My heart was pounding. My throat felt like sandpaper.

I was searching for someone. Searching for *Lew*.

I reached for the water on my nightstand and guzzled some of it down. With a wet gasp, I pressed my back to the headboard and dug the heels of my palms into my eye sockets, fighting the memories and controlling my breaths.

Breathe, Vina. Just breathe. You're home. You're safe. Just breathe.

I settled into bed again, sniffling as I swallowed my emotions.

There are no words to truly define grief, but if I had to imagine them, I'd say grief is a beast who likes to stomp, claw, and bite until you're stripped of everything. Then, when you finally gain some balance, it returns for another round, and the cycle continues, until you're nothing but a hollow shell waving a white flag.

That's grief, I'm afraid. And it's so damn cruel.

~

I woke up groggy when my alarm went off.

It was a Saturday, and I didn't have to work, so it was completely unnecessary for me to be awake at seven in the morning. I'd found that if I stayed in bed too long, though, I'd never leave.

Perched on an elbow, I peered around my room as strips of sunlight lingered on the walls and highlighted my wedding photos as well as the old hoodies and baseball caps hanging on the wall rack. It was better to get up and keep the routine.

I got ready for the day and made a list in the kitchen of groceries I would need. Later, as I shopped, my phone rang in my purse, and I dug it out. When I saw who was calling, I beamed.

"Octavia!" I answered with a squeal.

"Vina!" she sang.

"You finally had time to call me back, huh?"

"Nah-uh. Don't be like that, okay?" my sister said, laughing. "I'm a busy woman. And besides, not everyone has their life together like you do."

"Girl, bye. I wish I had my life together." I pushed the shopping cart forward.

"I was thinking about heading to Charlotte to see you next weekend. Roger's parents are going out of town, and they're taking him with them, so I'll be free."

"Who is Roger, again?"

She sucked her teeth. "The kid I nanny now. He's such a spoiled fucking brat, Vina. You know he got gum stuck in one of my locs."

I gasped as I grabbed a tub of vanilla ice cream from one of the freezers. "No, he did not!"

"Yes! I went to my loctician, and she had to cut the loc off. I wanted to cry. He's lucky it was on the back of my head. Can't really see where it was cut. But still. My hair is my joy, and he tried to rob me of it. Little asshole."

I huffed a laugh. "Isn't he, like, three?"

"Yeah, but I'm telling you, Vina. Three-year-olds are emotional terrorists."

I couldn't help laughing at that. I didn't have any kids, but I knew many people who did, and all of them had shared a gripe or two about toddlerhood.

"Well, if you come next weekend, I'll have the guest room ready." I paused as I scanned the shelf for cinnamon.

"Have you talked to Mama?" Octavia asked, and I stopped my eyes from shooting to the ceiling.

"Not much lately," I answered dryly.

Octavia sighed so hard I may as well have felt her breath in my ear. "You need to stop remembering the old version of her. She's trying, Vina."

"Yeah, and it only took her sixteen years to do so." I tossed the cinnamon into the cart with more force than intended.

"If I can forgive her, you can too. You know I couldn't stand how she used to be—and look at Abe. He's doing good. Going to school. Going to his cute little spectrum basketball camps. Getting fed hella grilled cheese sandwiches 'cause that's all he'll eat. Plus, she was there for you when Lew died. She dropped everything and came running, so that proves she cares and that she's changed."

My chest tightened as I headed to the checkout, remembering how Mama cooked every morning and night, left little DOVE chocolates on my pillows after my showers in the morning. She was there for a whole week.

I was so consumed by grief that I hardly acknowledged it, but now that I remembered, I felt guilty.

"Just call her, all right? She said she's been trying to reach you. She misses you, Vina."

I cleared my throat. "Yeah, well, just like you, I've been busy, sis."

"Sure. Whatever. Where are you anyway? What's all the beeping?"

"I'm at the store. I'm making an apple-crumble cake later."

"Oh, Lord. Please don't burn your house down."

"Bite me, bitch. I can bake too." Not as well as my sister could, though.

"I'll call you when I'm on the way to your house."

"Okay." I dug into my purse for my wallet. "Love you, Poop-Butt."

"Love you, too, Stinky V!"

I chuckled, slipping the phone back into my purse. After collecting my bag of groceries, I walked past a magazine stand to get to the exit but ended up doing a quick double take when I spotted Deke Bishop on the cover of a sports magazine.

His hands were pressed on top of a basketball, and he wore a black T-shirt with the number seventeen on it. As usual, gold chains hung from his neck. The thick veins in his hands ran all the way up to his inked forearms, and his lips were quirked up on one side just enough to reveal his amusement.

And though those veins were a sight to behold, nothing caught me more than his eyes. They stared right back at me with a confident glint.

I drew in a breath and left the store.

I swear, even when he wasn't around, he was flirting with me.

ELEVEN

DEKE

"Well, I think that went pretty well." Arnold pushed the side door of the building open and stepped outside with a triumphant sigh. The sun was beaming, even with the shadows of the buildings hovering above.

I stepped out, and the humidity was enough to make me sweat in a matter of seconds. My black Armani button-down was sticking to me like glue.

It was the start of summer in New York City, so the heat was expected, but I didn't think it'd be *this* damn hot. We'd just had a meeting with a team from Nike to discuss a massive lifetime endorsement deal. I'd been endorsed by them before, but not for a lifetime.

When I was a kid, getting endorsements was one of my goals. The first was to get good enough at basketball and make it to the NBA. The next was to make sure I was a top player on my team. Then I'd go for the endorsements just to prove I was worth it to the world.

It all sounded pretty sweet . . . but all I could think now was how exhausting it was. When I was a rookie, getting endorsed was hella cool, but that was years ago. The sweetness of it all became bitter pretty damn fast. Still, I was fortunate. Not many people could say they were endorsed by Nike.

"You're hot right now, Deke," Arnold went on with a chuckle. "Everyone wants your face with their brand. Keep playing like you did last season, and you'll be seeing more of it."

I looked toward the oncoming traffic, where a sea of yellow cabs mixed with other vehicles whizzed by. The thing I liked about New York was that everyone minded their own business.

People walked right past me with their faces buried in their phones or hustled to get to their destination. A few would look back as the familiarity registered, but they never stopped.

"I'm sure that'll be the last deal I take for a while," I said. "These busy summers are wearing me out."

Arnold wiped sweat from his forehead. "Yeah, I feel you, big guy." I hated when he called me that. "But hey. Let's not make any promises to ourselves right now. Someone might approach with an even bigger check—you know what I mean?" He let out an obnoxious laugh, and I tried not to roll my eyes as he whipped his phone out.

Don't get me wrong, Arnold was a dope manager—I wouldn't have gotten half the endorsements I had without him—but the dude could be annoying as fuck.

"I'll let the driver know we're ready. Oh—by the way, if you're stressed about your schedule or anything, you've got a lucky break next weekend. Golden Oil reached out, said they're rescheduling their rebranding party. Oh—car is right over here."

"Wait, why are they rescheduling?" I asked, automatically thinking of Davina.

"The CEO—that Davina chick—decided to take a week off for mental health reasons. Apparently, her dead husband's birthday is around the same date as the party was, and she changed her mind. Talk about a mood killer." He chuckled. "I told them it was no big deal and that we could discuss a date that worked for you later."

Arnold continued his trek to the car, but I stopped in my tracks, digesting all the words that came out of his mouth for once.

Davina's husband was *dead*? How the hell didn't I know this? I mean, with that ring of hers, I figured . . .

Wait. At the dinner, when I tapped her ring and she tensed up, she wanted nothing to do with me after that. It was like she couldn't get out of the restaurant fast enough. And that look in her eyes . . . damn.

I was right. She *wasn't* happy, not because her husband was a piece of shit or they had a long-distance thing going but because he was *dead*.

Suddenly it all made sense—the spinal-cancer charity she was donating to, the way she kept her distance at the photo shoot. The slight standoffishness.

"Hey, Deke!" Arnold called. I peered up, and he was frowning at me from the open door of the SUV. "You comin' or what?"

I shuffled forward, but something about that news wasn't sitting right with me. I don't know why I cared, but it was bugging me now, knowing she was grieving a loss.

Grief is a whole other pain, one I'm *very* familiar with, yet there she was, smiling and going to dinner with me like her life hadn't been forever altered.

I climbed into the SUV, and when the chauffeur closed the back door behind me, I asked my manager, "Do you have her email address?"

"Who?" Arnold asked absentmindedly as he scrolled through his phone.

"Davina, man. I want to send my condolences."

Arnold finally looked up and tilted his sweaty bald head. "Oh, you don't have to worry about that, Deke. I did it for you. Sent an email on your behalf. Plus, he died sometime last year. Wouldn't make sense to bring it up again."

Normally I would've been fine with Arnold taking that initiative, but this time was different. Davina *needed* to hear from me personally.

"Nah. I need to reach out to her myself."

Arnold hesitated as the chauffeur slid into his designated seat behind the steering wheel. "Uh, yeah. All right. I'll text her email address to you right now."

"Appreciate it, *big guy.*"

TWELVE

DAVINA

My husband is dead.

Some mornings I forgot . . . until the reality sank in.

I squeezed my eyes shut to cool the burn and soothe the hangover. My head was throbbing, and I could do with some water and aspirin, but judging by the dishes clinking from afar and the missing wineglass that had been on my nightstand the night before, my sister was still around.

If I left this room, she'd make me leave my house to *shake things up*. Though we'd had a few drinks last night to celebrate Lew's birthday early, I wasn't up for much that morning.

There was a knock on the door, and I buried myself deeper beneath the comforter. "Go away," I groaned.

I heard Octavia's footsteps as she rounded the bed, then felt the mattress dip as she sat at the bottom of it. The weight of her hand pressed down on my leg, and silence lingered for a few seconds before she said, "You know it's almost one o'clock."

"Yeah. So?"

"So, what can I do to get you out of bed, sis?"

Nothing. There was nothing she could do to get me out of this bed right now. If I could have, I would've molded to it.

When I didn't answer, she yanked the cover down, and I tried yanking it back up, but she had a better grip and threw the whole thing onto the floor.

"Davina, come on. I need you to get out of bed. I love you too much to let you rot in here."

"I'm grieving," I grumbled, pressing a hand to my forehead.

"Oh, *now* you want to grieve?"

I frowned. "What is that supposed to mean?"

"All you do is work, and if you're not working, you're pretending to be busy with other things. The only reason that rebranding party isn't happening is because Tish didn't think it should be so close to Lew's birthday. You agreed with her for a reason. I've hardly seen you cry since the week he died."

I burrowed my face into the pillow. I hated that she was right. Other than that day I'd realized he was dead, I hadn't cried much— not because I hadn't wanted to, but because I'd known that if I did, I wouldn't stop.

There had been a few tears here and there, but I'd never really sat and let it hit me. I'd never let the emotions take over until I was a blubbering mess who could hardly breathe.

"I bought your favorite Native soap—that coconut-and-vanilla one you like. I went to Target while you were sleeping and got some of that, a new body scrub, *and* some DOVE chocolates. I know you love those." I cracked one eye open, and she was smiling as she slid closer. "Yeah, I got you with the chocolates, didn't I? All you have to do is walk to the kitchen and get them."

"I don't feel like getting up, Tavia."

"Please get up, Vina. If not for me, do it for Lew."

At the second mention of his name, both of my eyes peeled open, and that quick action made my head throb. I stared at my little sister in all her natural glory—her golden brown skin and big round eyes. The tiny mole above her upper lip, which girls from our school used to think she penciled in. Her full lips, which always made her look like she was doing a cute pout.

The tips of her straw-size locs were long enough to touch her collarbones, but today she had them pulled up into a pineapple. She was one of those people who didn't need makeup to stand out. She was effortlessly beautiful and had been since she was born.

"Lew wouldn't want you stuck in bed like this so close to his birthday, and you know it." Octavia's eyes glistened, and I don't know what it was about her eyes that day, but they caused a wrenching in my chest. My sister wasn't much of a crier, either, but I think seeing me like this was doing something to her.

Oh, God. I couldn't be *that* person—the type to ruin someone's mood through bitterness and selfish acts. She needed me just as much as I needed her right now.

"You're right." I pushed up on one elbow and gazed down at my ratty shorts and the UNCC hoodie that Lew gave me when we first started dating. Well, he didn't give it to me. It was more that I kept it because it was comfortable and never gave it back.

"Yeah?" Octavia's sad brown eyes lit up as she grinned. She hopped off the bed and said, "Cool. I'll get you some Advil."

She hurried out of the room, and I hoisted myself up to rest my back against the headboard. I cradled my head in one of my hands, sighing.

When Octavia returned and passed me the ibuprofen and a bottle of water, the doorbell rang.

"Who is that?" I asked.

Octavia went to the window to peer out. "Not sure. There's a white van with flowers on it." She glanced at me before leaving the room again.

I heard some distant chatting after she answered the door, a laugh from Octavia, and then the door closing again.

When she returned, she said, "It was a flower delivery. Are you dating somebody and didn't tell me?"

"What? No! What are you talking about? They're probably from someone at work. The whole company knows I rescheduled the party so I could have time to myself."

"Oh." Octavia's eyes bounced around. "Well, come on. Go shower, and I'll make you a really late breakfast, lazy ass. Something greasy should get you back on your feet."

I huffed a laugh, then palmed my head again. "Oh my gosh, Tavia. Don't make me laugh right now, please."

Octavia planted a hand on her hip. "No one told you to drink a whole bottle of wine last night. That was your grown-woman choice, and now you're paying for it."

Oh yeah. It was a full bottle, wasn't it? I hadn't drunk in months, but I went to the market last night and collected a bottle of my favorite red wine. I downed the whole thing like it was water. I wanted to avoid the emotion—to fight the ache. It didn't help much.

I groaned on my way to the bathroom. When I shut the door behind me, I faced the mirror. I looked horrible. Absolutely *horrible*. My hair was sticking up all over the place and appeared matted in some areas. My skin was chalky and dry from so many tears, and my lips were chapped.

I dragged my hands down the length of my face before planting them on the countertop. I lowered my head, letting my eyes close for a second before drawing in a breath, exhaling, and opening them again.

My gaze flickered over the counter to Lew's favorite hair pomade that I *still* didn't have the balls to move or throw away. Some mornings, I liked to open it and smell it.

We used to spend so many mornings in this bathroom getting ready together. He'd be doing his weekly shave, and I'd be popping an earring in or applying makeup. We'd always been in each other's way without fully being in the way, and I'd loved it. I would've given *anything* to have those days back.

I stood up straight and swiped at my eyes, turning for the shower to start it. But the shower was just another reminder of what we had. All the laughter, the making out, the *sex*.

I washed up and tossed a cotton robe on. I tied it at the waist, moisturized as much of my body as I could stand before my head started spinning, then left the bathroom.

Octavia was in the kitchen, scrambling eggs while bacon sizzled in a skillet. She peered over her shoulder when she heard me coming and said, "There she is! Don't you feel better?"

"Don't even." I noticed a burst of color in my peripheral and turned my attention to the dining table. There was a large bouquet of pink, white, and yellow tulips with white carnations hugging them from the outside.

Tulips weren't a common flower I'd received. Most people sent white roses and lilies—even gardenias. But *tulips*? That was different.

"I didn't check, but who do you think those are from?" Octavia asked over her shoulder.

"I'm not sure," I murmured, unable to take my eyes off the flowers. I spotted a white card on a pick in the center of the bouquet and plucked it off.

My first name was printed on the thick cream envelope. I flipped it open, took out the card, and read it.

> Davina,
>
> I am so sorry that I'm just now finding out about your loss. I know we just met, and I'm several months late, but I hope these flowers make up for my lack of awareness and can bring some light to your day. Here if you need me.
>
> Deke

"Oh. *Wow*."

Deke's name was the last one I expected. He must've heard about Lew through Arnold. Tish did tell me she was going to reach out to him first about rescheduling the party to make sure Deke's schedule aligned.

"What?" Octavia set a plate down on the glass table. "Who is it from?"

"Um . . ." I read Deke's name again, waiting to see if it'd transform to someone else's, but nope. It was his. "Just a colleague." I sat as Octavia went back to the kitchen, murmuring the words *orange juice*.

I couldn't stop staring at the flowers. They were gorgeous, and on this gloomy day, they truly had brought a little light. But it wasn't the beauty of the flowers that had me so surprised to see them. It was the significance.

I'd mentioned tulips being my favorite flower at the photo shoot a few weeks prior. I couldn't believe he remembered such a small detail about me—something so minuscule during a mindless conversation.

I picked up my fork and smiled.

THIRTEEN

DAVINA

After my sister had forced me to get dressed and grocery shop with her, we decided to sit on the deck, with the string lights glowing.

It'd rained earlier, and the weather had dropped to a cool seventy degrees, which was a nice reprieve from the blazing-hot start of summer.

I cozied up on one of the upholstered outdoor seats with a glass of wine as I inhaled the fresh, damp air. We'd had dinner, and I helped myself to two glasses. Hell, I'd already guzzled down a whole bottle the night before. I didn't see the point in stopping now. *So much for that lifestyle change.*

I mean, technically, we were celebrating Lewis's birthday. We even bought cupcakes again, so that made it an occasion.

The reason I changed my drinking habits was because everything had changed after Lewis's diagnosis. I'd been so strong for him when he cried, lost his hair, and lived in pain. But behind every strong person is an even stronger vice. Mine was wine.

I wouldn't have considered myself an alcoholic, but whenever I'd needed to loosen up and kill the noise, I'd grabbed a bottle. I'd have a glass or two every night after work, but when life got harder, I'd tack on another glass.

There had been one night in particular, when I created my vow to slow down on drinking. Lew was feeling ill, so I helped him get into bed early. I thought he was asleep, so while I worked, I drank about two or three glasses of wine. Eventually, the work was put aside, and I fell asleep on the couch.

What I didn't realize then was that Lew woke up in the middle of the night and vomited several times. Meanwhile, my sorry ass was passed out a room away and oblivious to it.

When he told me about it the next morning, I wanted to cry. I felt so guilty for not being there for him. He kept assuring me it was fine, that he was okay, but none of it was okay. I'd drunk myself into a damn coma while my husband had been suffering all night.

It was that day I had promised him and myself I'd cut back on drinking. I'd needed to change anyway . . . but I suppose none of that really mattered anymore.

Octavia took the chair next to mine and spread a blanket over her legs.

"Hey," I called as she held her glass in the air to adjust herself without spillage. When she looked up, I smiled. "Thank you for being here for me these last couple of days, Octavia—hell, the last couple of *months*. It means a lot."

"Oh, girl. Stop. That's what I'm here for." She waved a dismissive hand at me, but I didn't miss the proud grin on her face.

"No, I mean it. I wouldn't even be functioning right now if it weren't for you."

"Well, you know Mama and Abe were here too. Did you call her?"

"Here we go. Just take the gratitude, Tavia." I swirled my wine in the glass.

Yes, my mom and little brother had come down once they'd heard about Lew, and they'd been there for the funeral. But that's what mothers were *supposed* to do, right? Be there for their daughters? Make sure they were okay?

I wasn't sure why this feeling had come over me the last few years, but I'd developed a bitterness toward my mother that I couldn't shake. It was stupid, because all I had to do was let it go and pretend nothing was wrong, like I had all those years ago, but that was hard to do when I realized how short life was.

The decisions she'd made when I was younger affected me even now. I bet my life could've been so much better had she stepped up to the plate, but she hadn't until I was almost out of high school.

"I'm just saying!" My sister threw an innocent hand in the air. "If Abe didn't have camp, she'd be here right now."

I pursed my lips. I wanted to ignore Octavia, but when I met her eyes, I softened.

"I know." I sighed, glancing at my little sister again. She gave me a *you know what to do* look. "I'll call her tomorrow."

"See? So easy, girl."

My mouth twitched just as my doorbell rang.

"Who is that?" Octavia asked, eyeing me.

That was a good question, considering it was nearly eight o'clock at night.

I checked the security camera app on my phone, but when I saw who it was, I grimaced. "You've got to be fucking kidding me."

I climbed out of my chair and went inside to open the front door. A woman stood on the other side, her snow-white skin flushed and her hair in a neat chestnut bun atop her head.

Her brows were so thin they may as well have been penciled in, and her eyes . . . well, I couldn't hate them, because they were just like Lew's. Hazel and surrounded by thick lashes. It was my former mother-in-law, Gloria Roberts.

I leaned against the frame of the door and folded my arms. "Have you ever heard of a phone call, Gloria?"

Gloria turned her nose up at me. "It's the first birthday of Lewis's since he passed," she stated.

"I'm well aware of that."

"I was on this side of town and thought I'd visit his grave. That's when I remembered the photo album with all his baby pictures in them. He asked to borrow it so he could show them to *you*."

She looked me up and down in my sweats and hoodie, like she was searching for whatever it was about me that appealed to her son.

"Do you want your photo album back?" I asked, ready for her to get out of my face already.

"I do," she replied curtly.

I stepped back to let her into the house, and she closed the door behind her. I retrieved the baby-blue photo album from the cabinet of the TV stand and carried it to her.

"None of the pictures have been removed, have they?"

"No, Gloria. I can assure you all the pictures are there."

She narrowed her eyes at me, then pointed her attention over my shoulder. Octavia was walking inside, her lips pressed and her arms crossed as she looked my mother-in-law from head to toe.

"Is that all?" I asked, and Gloria put her focus on me.

"Yes, that's all."

"Good, because we were in the middle of enjoying wine and cupcakes to celebrate Lew's birthday."

Gloria's eyes watered as she averted her attention to the box of cupcakes on the counter. Her throat bobbed, and she hugged the photo album to her chest. I felt sorry for her, and that was a rare thing to feel for a woman like her.

"Would you like to join us?"

She swallowed and swiftly shook her head. "No. I have a busy night. Goodbye, Davina."

I watched her walk out the door and shook my head. Why couldn't she be a normal person? Always with her dramatic entrances and judgment.

I hate saying it, but Gloria Roberts was a stuck-up bitch, and though I hated the stigma of daughters disliking their mothers-in-law, I truly did *not* like mine. She'd made it that way, though, and it'd only gotten worse after Lewis died. She kept telling me I should've tried harder for him—that I should've been awake when he died, as if I wasn't carrying enough guilt about it.

When it came to Lew's wake, Gloria had been the *worst*. It was common knowledge that she liked to be the center of attention, but that day she made *everything* about her.

She didn't like the food, so she ordered a meal from DoorDash she could eat. She didn't want to see images of me and Lew together inside my house, so she stayed outside the majority of the time, smoking her cigarettes and shit-talking.

She didn't even say goodbye when she left, but she kept popping by for little things afterward, like Lew's football jersey from college, or the fedora his dad had passed down to him. It was vintage, and she felt it was important to hold on to.

I had never minded giving her those things. The only thing that bugged me was that she never provided a heads-up. She just showed up at my doorstep like I was *meant* to be at her service. She'd blamed me for everything that went wrong in Lew's life, even his cancer.

"You're the one who's killing him. You're the reason he's so sick!" I could still remember her shouting that in my face when Lew told her about the diagnosis.

"Why is that heffa always popping up?" Octavia grumbled when we were back in our seats on the deck.

"I don't know, but I swear I might end up going off on her one day. She's really been testing my patience."

Octavia laughed as my phone vibrated. It was a notification for a new email, but I had to read who it was from twice, because I thought my mind was playing tricks on me.

Davina,

I hope you don't mind me reaching out to you like this. I told Arnold to give me your email address.

Just checking in with you. Hope you're good. I know you've probably heard this a million times and are sick of it, but I'm truly sorry for your loss. If I'd known, I never would've brought your husband up at Silver Wolf.

Keep your head up.
Deke

I tugged on the string of my hoodie while reading the email again. First the flowers to my house and now this?

I probably shouldn't have emailed him back so quickly—he *was* my colleague, after all—but he'd sent the tulips, which were pretty and thoughtful, and the man had carved time out of his schedule to type up a personal condolence letter.

I pressed Reply.

Hey Deke,

Thank you for reaching out and for checking on me. You didn't have to do that. Seriously. But thank you. The flowers are gorgeous. I'm surprised you remembered tulips are my favorite. I am curious how you got my home address, though. Don't tell me you're stalking me now.

Also, very sorry the rebranding party got rescheduled but I hope you can make the new date!

P.S. Why an email this time instead of a DM?

Thanks again for checking in.

Talk soon,
Davina

I read the last question in my reply again, debating whether to keep or delete it. Deke wasn't a man with a lot of time on his hands, and any other person would've just given condolences the next time they saw me or not brought it up at all.

Not Deke, though, and I wanted to know why.

I pressed Send and sipped red wine as I waited for his response.

"Who are you texting?" The blue light of Octavia's phone highlighted her face.

"It's the basketball player we signed to endorse Golden Oil. Deke Bishop. He *emailed* me."

At that, Octavia lowered her phone and gave me her full attention. "How in the world did you manage that?"

"I didn't *manage* anything." I laughed. "He's the one who sent the tulips. I guess he was making sure I got them."

"He sent you flowers *and* a follow-up email? That's dedication."

"Dedication for what?"

She sucked her teeth. "To get in those panties, girl! Don't act like you don't know what I'm talking about!"

"Octavia! No!" I waved a dismissive hand at her, fighting a laugh. "First of all, it's too soon for any of that. Second of all, it's not even like that with him. He's pretty cool for a famous athlete."

"Yeah. Okay." She delivered a playful scoff and lifted her phone. "If that's what you wanna tell yourself."

As she scrolled, I couldn't deny that Deke trying to get in my panties wasn't a thought in the back of my mind. He'd made it perfectly clear at Silver Wolf that he was into me, that he wanted to get to know me, and that the only things stopping him from making a serious move were the rings on my finger.

But back then, he thought I was still married, and fortunately, he respected that. I didn't know how to explain it, but after receiving the flowers and the email, I didn't feel like it was an agenda or a scheme from him. Or maybe I was just being naive about it, and he really *was* doing this to catch me at my lowest and make his move.

That would've been *extremely* shallow of him, though, and a title like that didn't suit a man like him.

Still, I had to be careful. I wasn't looking to be serious with anyone right now.

I guzzled down the rest of my wine, climbed out of my chair, and said over my shoulder, "I'm getting a cupcake!"

FOURTEEN

From: Deke Bishop
To: Davina Klein-Roberts
1:22 a.m.

I'm back. My bad. Just touched down in ATL. Had to shoot a commercial in Cali. About knowing your home address, I reached out to your girl Tisha. She gave it to me, but not willingly. She told me I'd owe her . . . should I be scared? lol

And why the email vs a DM? Well to be real with you, DMs are impersonable. I don't post on IG like that unless I want to or I'm contractually bound to. Plus sending my condolences on an app would've been lame AF, D. Come on. I'm better than that. And why wouldn't I remember what your favorite flower is? You were all starry eyed over them.

But real talk, I'm glad to hear from you.
Deke

From: Davina Klein-Roberts
To: Deke Bishop
1:28 a.m.

Well, your reasoning about the email vs DM thing seems solid. I'll allow it. As for Tish—yeah, I think you should be a little afraid. She's going to make you repay that debt somehow.

Glad you had a safe flight.
Davina

From: Deke Bishop
To: Davina Klein-Roberts
1:38 a.m.

Oh, so I was on trial, huh? Damn. Glad I wasn't found guilty lmao. What are you doing up so late? Thought you'd be sleeping . . .

From: Davina Klein-Roberts
To: Deke Bishop
1:46 a.m.

I can't sleep much anymore. I doze off for a bit, but always wake up around 3 or 4 am. My sleep schedule is shit, I know. I was prescribed something from my doctor to help months ago but it makes me feel like I've been hit by a truck when I wake up so I don't take it.

And yes, you were on trial. Too many people in this world pretending to be something they're not.

From: Deke Bishop
To: Davina Klein-Roberts
1:53 a.m.

Well that's the good thing about knowing you. I don't have to pretend to be anything but myself when we talk. Glad I'll be able to make it to your rebranding party. It'll be nice seeing you again and making sure you're OK.

From: Davina Klein-Roberts
To: Deke Bishop
2:00 a.m.

Ah, yes. The rebranding party. Everyone will be excited to see you. Going to try and sleep now. Goodnight, Bishop.

FIFTEEN

DEKE

I shut the screen of my phone off and placed it on the nightstand. The neon clock on the wall read 2:03 a.m., but I wasn't sleepy. All I could think about was Davina.

After that last email she sent, though, it was pretty clear she wanted to be left alone. I thought we were having a moment, but I went and fucked it up, just like I always did.

I mean, she brought her assistant into it with no laughs, no smiley faces—nothing. Then again, Davina didn't strike me as an emoji-using "LOL" person. She was straightforward, and I liked that about her in person . . . but she was hard to read by text.

Normally, I'd have turned over and fallen asleep, but a woman showing disinterest in me was rare—and I'm not saying that to be cocky. Okay . . . maybe I am a little. But even married women found a way to sneak a flirt with me.

Not Davina, though, and it intrigued the hell out of me.

I turned over with an exhale, peering out the wall of windows. The lights on the skyscrapers blinked in the night, and the clouds were thick and heavy in the sky. Rain was on the way.

As if he could sense the decline of my mood, Zeke walked around my bed and placed his head on the edge of it. He'd have jumped on if I didn't have a rule about him being all over my expensive bamboo sheets. The last time I let him on my bed, he clawed at them while I was sleeping and ripped them.

"What's up, man?" I scratched behind his ears after he let out a light whimper. "I'm all good. Promise."

Zeke burrowed his head into my palm, and I caved and let him onto the bed. I lightly scratched his head while grabbing my phone with my other hand.

I scrolled through my photos until I found my Favorites folder, then tapped on one of the last pictures taken of me and my brother, Damon. I was fourteen, and he was seventeen. Everyone always said we looked alike. A tightness hit my chest as I stared at it.

All this talk of grief while thinking about Davina and her loss struck something in me. Normally I'd catch a wave of grief, and it would pass. I'd distract myself, hit the court, drop a few buckets, and forget about it. If that didn't work, I'd focus on the good times we shared. But on this particular night, the good times were distant.

People claim grief is a process—like it'll end one day and never be thought of again—but that's far from the truth. Grief is an ongoing cycle and is totally reliant on your mood and vulnerability.

When you feel good, grief can be dealt with. You can go about your day, accept it for what it is, and move along. But when you're down and reminded of your loss—when you're alone at night with no one to talk to and nobody to hold—grief is like a colossal wave. It rises higher and higher, and no matter how sturdy your ship is, it'll smash into it and wreck it, leaving you to drown.

To put it simply, Grief is a bitch, and she likes to hit you where it hurts. I swear she's Karma's two-faced sister.

When the screen of my phone darkened, I slid it off the bed. It landed with a soft clatter on the hardwood floor, and when Zeke went back to his pillow, I turned my back to the window, pulled the sheets over my head, and swallowed my sorrow.

SIXTEEN

DAVINA

"What are you doing here!?" Tish's voice was shrill as she stood within the frame of my office door.

"I like myself better when I'm busy," I told her with a faux grin, and she scoffed. Let's just say she was not pleased to see me sitting in my office bright and early on a Monday morning.

"Davina, this isn't busying yourself. This is *distracting* yourself."

"Well, it's better that than being at home with all the curtains drawn and bottles of wine in rotation," I said, clicking through one of the folders with my computer mouse. I cut my eyes at her. She had her arms folded and a dip in her brow. "Wanna catch me up to speed?"

"I don't like that you're back. I was actually going to come see you tonight and bring Chinese food."

"Well, how about you have the Chinese delivered here later, because it's going to be a long day. We need to get the rebranding party squared away. I know the caterer we hired had a tight schedule, so let's reach out to her about the menu, because we have *a lot* of vegans and she's really good. We'll work through the list for final touches and then get in touch with Kenji to go over the photos that'll be on display for the slideshow."

I purposely avoided my friend's eyes as I clicked away on my keyboard.

After a few seconds of silence, Tish asked, "What is this really about, Davina?"

"It's not about anything." I forced a laugh to prove to her that I was fine, but she wasn't buying it. Her eyes narrowed as she scanned me like paper in a Xerox machine.

"Are you really going to make me say it?"

I stopped typing with a sigh. "Say what?"

"You aren't properly grieving, Vina. You're just burying yourself with work to disassociate with your feelings. You're my girl, and I love you, but I have to be honest. You need to take your ass back home and sit with your feelings. You lost your *husband*, Davina. Your life partner. That's not something you just get over in months."

I folded my arms right along with her. I wanted her to cave, to yield, but Tish was just like Octavia—stubborn as hell and always getting her way.

Or maybe I was just too damn soft.

When I realized I wouldn't win the silent battle, I sucked my teeth and dropped my arms. "Well, since you want to be honest with me, I'm going to be completely honest with you. Everything in that house reminds me of Lew, and spending so much time there is killing me. It makes me want to sleep all day, to drink all day, and I thought I wanted the time off, but it's not healthy for me to be there for hours staring at our pictures or sniffing his hoodies." I paused, looking away. "And sometimes I—I get this feeling that I might—" I clamped my mouth shut, shaking my head.

"Might what?" she asked, her forehead creasing with concern.

"That I might fall into a really ugly depression that I won't be able to pull myself out of. I feel like the walls are closing in, Tish. Like I can't breathe sometimes." She started to say something, but I raised a hand and said, "Yes, I'm still taking my medication. Look, if I stay there all day, no one will ever see me. I'll never leave. I'll turn into a shell of myself, just like I did when my daddy died."

I dragged in a breath. *Oh, God.* Now I was bringing my dad into this. No, I couldn't do that here. Not right now. Talking about Lewis was already hard enough.

Tish stared at me a beat longer before finally dropping her arms and breathing hard through her nose. She then walked into my office and spread her arms wide open. I stood up so I could step into them and hug her.

"Ugh. I love you, Vina," she murmured over my shoulder. "I don't agree that you should be working right now, but I get it." She leaned back and clutched my upper arms. "But you have to promise me you'll take breaks and that you'll leave this office by seven this *whole* week."

"Okay." I laughed. "I will."

"I mean it! Okay? And I'll be checking on you every twenty minutes while you work, just to make sure you're good. Got it?"

"All right, all right." I fought a smile.

Tish gave me a thorough once-over before releasing my arms. She caught me up to speed, and I was grateful she let it go, but just because I promised her I'd leave work at seven, it didn't mean I couldn't take my work home with me.

Around seven o'clock, Tish reminded me that she was coming to my house with dinner after she changed into more comfortable clothes at home. I figured this would give me an hour or so to keep working.

As soon as I got home, I sat at the dining table and opened my laptop. I finished up an email with Kenji and confirmed photos for the slideshow that would be shown at the rebranding party, then responded to my primary investor, Chester Hughes, who was being surprisingly nice to me via email.

I figured that had something to do with Tish announcing my week off—well, more like my three days off. Normally, he was brief and dry, but in our recent emails he'd been very thorough and was signing off with words like *take care* and *be well.*

And just to make it clear, the only time he did that before was right after Lewis died. I guess I'd raked in his pity again. I hated pity, but not as much when it came from a billionaire investor who threw money at every inconvenience.

Once that was done, I decided to go over a few more of the new label designs for our rosewater face mist. As I did, my phone chimed on the table. I gave it a glance, ready to dismiss it—until I saw that familiar name again.

Deke.

Business Davina switched off, and my heart sped up a few notches, which was weird. I tried ignoring the feeling.

As if someone was watching, I played it cool by resting an elbow on top of the table, dropped my chin into my hand, and swiped my phone open to read his email.

> From: Deke Bishop
> To: Davina Klein-Roberts
> 7:34 p.m.
>
> How you holding up?

Oh.

They were simple words, but enough to make me shift in my seat. Was he pitying me too? Was that what all the emails had been about?

I put my phone back down, then closed the lid of my laptop. After I poured myself a glass of water and took a few gulps, the doorbell rang.

"Hey, girl!" Tish sang when I swung the door open. She sauntered past me, and the savory scent of Chinese food drifted past my nose, making my stomach grumble.

I hadn't eaten much that day, just a few nibbles of a sandwich Tish had ordered for lunch earlier. I'd mostly drunk tea to get by, but now I was starving.

"I'm glad you're here." I met her in the kitchen. "I'm hungry as hell."

"Well, lucky for you I got the lo mein and the orange chicken—the owner even tossed in extra fortune cookies."

"I'm positive that man is in love with you, Tish." I grabbed plates and silverware. "Didn't he give you free fried rice one time? And not the plain rice—it had shrimp in it. Name me one restaurant owner who gives away free shrimp."

"Oh, he did do that, didn't he?" She allowed the thought to marinate as I set the plates on the counter. "Well, anyway, a lot of people love me. Take Lorenzo, for example. He wants me to come to Virginia Beach with him. He claims it's for work, but I think there might be something more to it."

"*More* as in?" I glanced at her as I opened one of the food containers. The steam rose from the greasy noodles and danced around my face. My stomach was practically caving in now.

"As in an engagement, girl!" she exclaimed.

"Oh, wait!" I paused, giving her my full attention. "You think so?"

"I do! It's been two years for us now, and I swear I saw him scrolling through wedding rings on his phone a few weeks ago."

"Aww, that'll be nice, Tish. You should go with him to the beach, see if it's actually more than what he says." I plopped some noodles on my plate as Tish opened a new bottle of wine.

"I don't know. We have so much to set up for the rebranding party, and I was supposed to work this Saturday to help out at the warehouse."

I stopped loading my plate to penetrate her with my eyes. "Tisha Cole. I appreciate your devotion, I truly do, but life is too short. Go with Lorenzo. Spend some quality time with him. The warehouse can wait."

I pressed my lips and fought the sudden tug in my chest. Talking about this made me miss Lewis, and to add fuel to the fire, my eyes traveled to one of the photos on the floating shelves.

We were standing hand in hand on the shore of Newport Beach. Lew wanted to learn how to surf but was so bad at it. I was surprisingly good. We were both sandy in the picture, with big white smiles and a grand turquoise ocean behind us.

"Hey." A hand pressed to my back. Tish was standing closer. Her brown eyes searched mine as she asked, "You okay?"

"Yeah. I'm fine." I dropped my eyes to my plate and picked it up. "Just really hungry." I carried the plate with me to the dining table and sat. Tish came my way with two empty wineglasses and the bottle of rosé, pouring both halfway.

After sliding the glass toward me, she said, "You can talk about Lewis at any time, Vina. I promise you I'm here to listen."

"I know. I just feel like I've talked about him with you so much that you're low-key sick of it."

"Girl, shut up! I'm here for you no matter what."

I could hardly see her, because my vision grew blurry. I blinked the tears away. "I know," I murmured. "Thank you, Tish."

"You know it, girl."

As she prepared her food, I shuffled through mine with a fork, my appetite waning. I was relieved when she started talking about diamond cuts and silver or gold bands for her engagement ring. I didn't want to talk about myself or Lew. It'd only depress me further. Plus, I was genuinely happy for Tish. She'd always wanted to get married.

When her phone rang, I was even more relieved, because it was Lorenzo calling, which created more of a distraction for her. She was worried about me, I could tell, but I didn't want her to be. I was fine.

Tish went to the deck, and I took a few bites of food, guzzled down the rest of my wine, then went to the kitchen for my phone. I read Deke's email again, then surfed through our previous emails.

They were bordering on flirtatious. I wasn't sure I liked it. It wasn't that I *didn't* want to talk to Deke . . . I just didn't want to send him the wrong signal.

But I admit it was comforting getting his emails. It felt good to chat with someone so late at night who wasn't insisting that I get some rest. That's all my sister and Tish did.

You need your rest, Davina!

Try to sleep, Vina!

It seemed neither Deke nor I could sleep at night—like we both had a lot on our minds after the clock struck twelve.

I scrolled back down and sent him a response.

> Hey! Definitely hanging in there. Went back to work today actually. Tish thinks I've lost my mind and you probably will too. But I need work, you know? Don't want to spiral too much and keeping busy helps. Thoughtful of you to check in. But why *do* you keep checking on me?

I waited for his response as I poured another glass of wine and carried it with me to the couch. Just like before, my heart sped up a notch when my phone chimed again and another email from him popped up.

> Nothing wrong with working. Everyone copes differently. Can't say I blame you for wanting to busy yourself. And about me checking in. You want the truth?

I couldn't help smiling at his question.

I always want the truth, I returned.

> Well the truth is that unlike 99% of the people I know, I actually *like* talking to you. You're mad cool, D.

Okay. I was smiling again. How was he so good at that?

Are you only saying that because you feel sorry for
me right now?

No. I'm keeping it 💯. Congrats on making it into my
1%.

I bit back a grin, then shook my head as a hopeless sigh escaped me.
I had a feeling he was going to do that—make me feel special, singled
out, *important.*

And though any woman in the world would've been thrilled about
a famous athlete flirting with her by email, I just couldn't be that
woman right now.

Thanks for including me. I'm honored.

I stopped typing, hovering over the Send button.

No. That couldn't be all. I did the dry-and-short thing last time.

Deke was a good guy. I needed to be honest with him now before
it was too late, so I continued my email:

But I feel like I should let you know I'm a mess and
am still grieving my husband. I don't want to lead you
on or anything. I'd love to keep talking to you and we
can keep checking in with each other but can it be
as friends? *Just friends?*

I bit into my bottom lip and pressed Send. Had to rip it off like a
Band-Aid. If I didn't do it now, I never would.

Two hours passed. I cleaned up with Tish before she left, and there
was still no response from Deke. I changed into pajamas and mentally
debated about whether it was the right thing to tell him. That email was
a little rude . . . but it was true, and I didn't know how else to explain it.

Around eleven o'clock that night, there was still no response.

I sulked on the couch, stealing glances at my phone as the TV played an episode of *Martin*. Maybe I was too harsh. Octavia always said I was too direct with text messages. She'd say if she didn't know me personally, she would never be able to tell if I was joking via text.

I picked up my phone and read my email again.

I cringed.

I mean, who italicized the words *just friends*? That took effort and placed way too much emphasis on the matter. I groaned, knowing damn well I wasn't going to hear from him again. I wouldn't blame him.

Toward midnight, I crawled into bed. I sank beneath the comforter, nestled my head into the pillow, and forced my eyes shut.

Sleep wasn't going to happen. This was a known fact. My sleep schedule was so jacked up now, but I was going to try anyway.

As I turned onto my back, my phone buzzed, and I gasped as I scrambled to pick it up. I opened the email with a smile, but that smile slowly slipped away when I read his response.

> You got it, D. *Just friends.*

He'd italicized the words too.

Okay, good.

That's exactly what I'd wanted him to say . . . so why the hell was I so disappointed with that?

SEVENTEEN

DEKE

"I feel like my boobs look way too big in this dress." Whitney huffed a breath as she shifted next to me and adjusted her black halter-top dress.

"They look good to me," EJ said, his eyes sliding from Whitney's chest to her exposed legs and thighs.

"Fuck off, EJ," my sister muttered.

I slapped his chest, and he broke out in a laugh.

"What?" he exclaimed with a stupid grin. "I ain't gonna lie about it. They look good."

We were on our way to Golden Oil Co.'s relaunch party, which had been rescheduled three weeks out from the original date.

I'd called Whitney and Camille and asked if they could join me. Camille had a hearing that morning and couldn't make it, but Whitney was game. When I was on the phone with my sisters, I was working out with EJ and Javier, and of course EJ had invited himself.

Javier probably would've come, too, but he was taking his daughter to Disney World.

"Remind me why you wanted to come again?" I asked as EJ adjusted his red bow tie.

"Because I have skin, too, and if the owner likes me, she might replace your face with mine. I *am* sexier." EJ flashed me a grin, revealing his gold grill.

I huffed a laugh, peering out the window as the limo slowed to a creep. The limo was Whitney's idea. She was all about the uppity stuff. She never settled for anything cheap and loved being pampered. She was just like our mama, but if I told her that, she'd slap the shit out of me.

"Wow," Whitney said. "You have such big dreams, EJ."

"You think that's the only thing I have that's big?"

I gave him a swift smack on the back of the head this time.

Whitney snickered.

EJ winced, rubbing his head. "Bruh, why would you do that?"

"Cause I need you to shut the hell up."

He scowled at me. This dude was like a little brother who knew exactly how to get under your skin. Couldn't take his ass anywhere.

The back door of the limo swung open, and I stepped out in my loafers, adjusting my tie, then dusting off my suit. The venue was in an area of Charlotte called Ballantyne and was taking place in a building that was damn near the size of a castle.

This was supposed to be an intimate occasion, and with Davina's company being on the small business side, there weren't any awaiting photographers or hounding paparazzi near the entrance that I could see.

"Oh my God. There he is! I told you he'd be here!" a woman screamed. "Deke Bishop! Over here!"

I turned my attention to the gazebo a short walk away, and a cluster of women were rushing toward me. *So much for intimate.*

I couldn't help wondering how they knew I'd be around. Something told me EJ had something to do with this. That man posted his entire day on social media.

I gave the women a crooked smile as the two security guards in front of the building stepped toward me.

"It's all good, fellas." I moved past them to greet the fans.

"Oh my God, Deke! Hi!" one of them squealed.

"You're even sexier in person!"

"Can you sign this for me?" One of them shoved a jersey and a Sharpie into my hand.

I glanced over my shoulder as Whitney and EJ walked toward the entrance. Whitney was shaking her head, clearly annoyed by their invasion, while EJ pointed a finger at me and shouted "'Ey! That's my boy, Deke! Best player in the game! Still ain't sexier than me, though!"

I chuckled as I signed the jersey and an area on one of the girls' chests that was close to her left tit (as she so proudly demanded), then thanked them for the love.

Security stepped between us again, and I walked into the building with a smile. I couldn't lie. That was one of the things I loved about being in the league. The recognition, the appreciation, the *love*. Most times, I wanted to be left alone, but when I needed a boost, the fans always showed up.

Sure, most of that love came from women who wanted a selfie or a quick fuck, but it felt good knowing I was *someone* to them. It felt good being recognized solely as Deke Bishop and no one else.

As soon as I was inside, the ambience shifted. Contemporary music played, and dim lighting created a chill vibe. Little string lights on the walls led toward the banquet hall, where most of the people were gathered, and as soon as I entered the room, all eyes turned to me.

There was a rush of whispers and murmurs, then some applauded and others hooted and hollered as I continued ahead.

I smiled and waved, shook hands with a few of the guests, and took pictures with others, and after excusing myself, I scanned the room for Whitney and EJ.

I spotted them by the bar and started their way before another flood of people sought me out. Not that they couldn't find me with ease. I *was* the tallest person in the room.

As I went, my eyes snagged on a woman in a satin indigo dress. Her hair was in bouncy curls that framed her face, her honey-brown skin moisturized and glowing. The mere sight of her made my heart thump faster—a foreign feeling I couldn't wrap my mind around.

Davina.

She was speaking to another woman, and as if she sensed that I was looking, her dark-whiskey eyes gracefully slid my way. Her mouth curved into a smile, and I tossed a hand up with a lopsided grin.

She mouthed the words *excuse me* to the woman in front of her, then wove her way through the cocktail tables.

As she walked toward me, I stopped in my tracks and straightened my back. She looked good as hell in that dress. It was spaghetti strapped, and while my sister may have been complaining about her tits, all I could think was that Davina's were perky and voluptuous as fuck.

I did my best not to focus on her chest as she got closer, and I succeeded there, up until I realized there was a slit at the thigh of her dress so high it made my imagination run wild.

What would I find beneath that slit? Lace panties? Cotton? A thong? How easy would it have been for me to slip a finger beneath the crease and skim her inner thigh?

Fuck. She had to be teasing me right now. Did she not realize the power she held? How the hell could a man like *me* only want to be friends with a woman like *her*? I'm sorry, there was just no damn way. I could try for her sake, but I had *very* little faith in myself that I could commit.

It'd been a little over a month of friendly on-and-off emails. I kept it simple with her, but I wasn't going to lie and say I didn't jack my dick off to the mere thought of her every other night.

She had this one picture on her Instagram where she was wearing a black bikini and sitting on the edge of the pool. It was an off-guard back shot and just enough to make me come.

I'd had some encounters with other women the last few weeks, but ever since meeting Davina, it wasn't the same. It never went past the point of them having my dick in their mouths, and I stopped messing around with Giselle after the last time I saw her.

I didn't want any of them. The woman I wanted was right in front of me, and she wouldn't even let me get a taste of her.

"Deke, hi." Davina's voice was a mixture of sultry and husky, and the sound of it sent a tingle down my spine. She stopped a step away, looking at me from beneath wispy eyelashes.

Fuck. That look. At this point, she was purposely turning me on.

Her perfume slipped past my nose, a sweet warm vanilla. She smelled good too? Yeah. This was gonna be a long night.

"How's it going, D?" I asked, keeping my cool.

"It's going good, yeah," she said with way too much enthusiasm. She fingered the dragonfly pendant dangling from her necklace, the same one I'd seen on her Instagram.

It didn't take a genius to know she was internally stressing. It seemed she was waiting for the other shoe to drop as she scanned the room with wide, bouncing eyes.

"I'm, um . . . I'm glad you made it." She looked from the room full of people to me again.

"Wouldn't have missed it."

Her irises sparkled beneath the chandeliers, highlighting the amber flecks, and her lips were glossed, pouty, and parted just enough for me to see her tongue. She had nice lips. A cute pink tongue.

I cleared my throat and gestured to the bar. "That's my sister Whitney and my teammate EJ over there. I think Arnold told you I was bringing two people with me."

"Oh, yes. He did say so." She nodded while taking a sip of her champagne.

I gestured to her flute glass when she lowered it. "Celebrating tonight?"

"Oh. Yeah. The whole lifestyle thing has been put on hiatus." She wore a tight smile and completely avoided my eyes. I studied her, trying to figure out what else she wanted to say.

"I get it." I bobbed my head toward the bar. "Let me introduce you to Whitney and EJ." I led the way, and of course my sister and teammate were in the middle of yet another heated debate.

These two always got into debates about the most random things, like if Marvel or DC was better. Who would win in a fight, Patrick Mahomes or Russell Wilson? Who's the better artist, Whitney Houston or Aretha Franklin? Tonight, they were debating which song on one of Kendrick Lamar's albums was better.

"I'm telling you, 'Money Trees' is a pure masterpiece. 'Bitch, Don't Kill My Vibe' was more commercial, and you can't say it wasn't, because Jay-Z hopped on the remix, and that man is about nothing but commercial shit," EJ declared. "I don't blame him, though. That's where the money is."

"I still stand by what I said," Whitney said after sipping her drink. Her eyes swiveled to mine as I stepped closer. "Oh, hey, bro!"

"What are y'all arguing about now?"

Whitney handed a flute of champagne to me. "Something EJ is *clearly* wrong about." My sister put her focus on Davina again. "You must be Davina. Hi, I'm Whitney, Deke's big sister." Whitney offered a hand to Davina, and Davina pasted on a big smile as she shook it.

"I am. It's so nice to put a face to one of the names Deke always mentions." She gave me a little wink. I swear on everything, we were having foreplay. "And you're EJ McCoy, right?" Davina asked, eyeing my teammate.

"Look at that? She already knows who I am, Deke!" EJ beamed, showing off the gold grill on the bottom row of his teeth again. "Look, if you ever need a new face for your company, I'm the guy, all right? This skin looks good because it requires a lot to make that happen."

Davina laughed and said, "I'll keep that in mind."

"How do you know who this corny-ass dude is, anyway?" I jerked a thumb at EJ.

"Oh, I looked into the whole team after Tish told me you were coming in to discuss a deal with us," Davina said with a pop of her shoulder. "Thought it'd be nice to familiarize myself with the roster."

"A woman who does her homework." I tossed her a wink. "I feel that."

She brought her glass to her lips, hiding a smile.

"I just have to say, I love your products, Davina!" My sister moved closer to her. "Thank you for all the samples and for the leftover stuff. I told Deke the honey shea body butter is my favorite! My skin is always so soft when I use it."

"Stop. It's my pleasure, Whitney. Really. I'm just glad to hear you love them and that *someone* is putting the products we send your brother to good use." Davina eyed me with a playful smirk.

"Hold on now. You trying to say I don't use your stuff?" I asked, laughing.

"Well, you *did* tell me you only took the deal with me so your sisters could have an unlimited supply of GOC products." Her lips pursed, like that was the end of the conversation.

"He told you that?" Whitney scowled at me.

"No, hold on. Hold on." I dug into my pocket and pulled out a travel-size hand cream. "What's this then, D?"

She dropped her eyes to my palm and saw the hand cream with her company's name on it. When her eyes flickered back up to mine, she murmured, "I stand corrected."

"I'm sorry, what was that? I didn't hear you." I leaned toward her, cupping my ear.

She laughed and loudly said, "I stand corrected!"

"Oh, okay." I smirked. "Good to know."

She looked into my eyes, sinking her teeth into the corner of her bottom lip. I don't think she was doing it to tempt me but more as a nervous habit. Either way, it was turning me on.

"I like the hand cream," I told her. "Keeps my hands soft." I sounded stupid, but I didn't know what else to say. I just wanted to keep hearing her voice. Keep her near me.

"I'm glad it helps." She locked eyes with me for a fleeting second before giving her head a little shake and distracting herself with a sip of her drink.

"Davina?" someone called behind us. I looked back, and it was her friend Tisha. When Davina looked back, Tisha gestured for her to come.

"Well, that's my cue," Davina announced. "Whitney, it was really lovely to meet you. You as well, EJ." She turned to me, placing a hand on the upper arm of my tux. "Deke, thank you so much for coming. I know there are plenty of other places you could be."

I could feel the warmth of her hand through the fabric, her perfume luring me in. I loved a woman who smelled good, and Davina Klein smelled like a snack.

"Like I told you," I murmured. "Wouldn't have missed it."

She blinked up at me, and once again her eyes were on my face, searching it. I wasn't sure what it was she was looking for. Her lips parted, like she was going to say whatever was on her mind.

Instead, she said, "I, uh . . . I hope you enjoy the party." Then she sauntered away to meet her friend.

I sipped my champagne, studying her ass as she walked across the ballroom. For the last couple of weeks, I kept asking myself why I wanted Davina so badly. She was just a woman, and to most men, pussy was pussy.

But . . . I don't know. Davina felt like a different breed of woman. She didn't beg or drop straight to her knees at the sight of me. She didn't tell me things I wanted to hear just to be on my good side. She was honest and naturally beautiful, and her curves, thick thighs, and plump ass were a hell of a bonus.

"I see why you were staring at her IG pics, big dog."

I looked at EJ, who sat in an empty chair close by.

"She's fine as fuck," he said.

"You were *staring* at her pictures, Deke?" Whitney asked, eyes widening.

I wasn't about to answer that. I finished off my champagne and stepped past Whitney to get to the bar again. I needed something stronger than the bubbly.

"Deke. What did me and Camille tell you about her?" my sister hissed.

"What are you talking about?" I flagged the bartender down.

"You need to leave her alone. *Do not* cross that line."

"What line?"

"You know exactly what line I'm talking about. Look, I get it. She's really, really pretty. But didn't you say on our last call that she lost her husband a couple months ago? That's just . . ."

"Just what?" I demanded, dropping my eyes to hers.

Whitney's brows puckered, and she straightened her posture. "That's *messy*, Deke."

"Well, maybe I'm okay with it being messy." The bartender appeared, and I requested a neat whiskey. The irony of my drink of choice wasn't lost on me.

"Okay—you know what? Whatever," Whitney muttered. "Do whatever you want, just like you always do. But, Deke, I'm telling you, if you sleep with that woman, you're gonna fuck her up even more. I saw her eyes. She is *not* okay. She's smiling and looks happy on the outside, but she's *crying* inside. After experiencing that sort of pain firsthand, you of all people should know that tampering with it doesn't help. Don't make matters worse for her."

Whitney took off with those words lingering in the air, and I blew a breath, collecting my drink and leaving the ballroom to find a quieter space.

EIGHTEEN

DAVINA

To my relief, the party ran smoothly.

There wasn't the slightest hiccup, and I was grateful Tish made sure of it. If there was something that went wrong, she didn't bring it to my attention.

It was nearing ten o'clock, and it seemed the party should've been winding down, but instead it was ramping up. The drinks at the bar were unlimited, courtesy of Chester, who was roaming around somewhere, and that was probably why no one was going home.

The guests had everything they needed in this big, beautiful building, which cost a fortune—food, drinks, entertainment—and it was worth staying.

I stood near the stage and watched the slideshow on the screen above it. There was a shuffle of images, some of our employees in action or posing for the camera, others of our products staged nicely on beige-and-white backgrounds.

And of course there were the images of the main man *and* the reason many people had rapidly RSVP'd to the rebranding party, Deke. When an image of him slid across, I peeled my eyes from the screen to find him. He was coming in from the lobby, and as if he were looking for me, too, our eyes connected.

He tossed a hand up with a crooked smile. That was clearly his signature move. It was cute and always caused a flutter in my belly. I gave him a quick wave back, then turned my attention away, gulping some champagne down to cool the simmering in my throat.

"Vina, we're ready for your speech," Tish said from behind me. I turned to find her, and she looked stunning in her black-and-gold gown. Her newly appointed fiancé, Lorenzo, was at the party as well, dressed in matching gold and black and helping himself to as many barbecue meatballs as he wanted.

"Right." I followed my best friend to the stage, ready to get my speech over with.

Tish got everyone's attention and primed the crowd. When it was my turn to take the floor, I thanked the necessary people, then called Deke to the stage.

The crowd went into an uproar when his name was announced. Whistles were in the air, and the spotlight flickered to Deke as he made his way toward the crowd, with a bashful smile, like he was a young boy who didn't know how to receive all that glory.

When he was onstage, I handed him the mic but didn't miss the way his long fingers slipped over mine or how his eyes demanded that I look at them. His cologne wrapped around me, and I cleared my throat as he took center stage.

"Wow. Thank you for the warm welcome. I think that might've been better than it is at my games," he said, and a cacophony of laughter erupted in the room. "I'm not that good at the whole speech thing, so don't expect me to be up here too long. I mean, Davina told me I should prepare one, but I don't have much to say. All I can do is express my gratitude. I appreciate GOC for choosing me to be the face of their brand for the next couple of months and only wish the best for it." Deke extended an arm, gesturing to me. "I admire this woman right here. She's a boss to a lot of you, but she works hard, and I respect that. So thank you, Davina, because none of this would be happening if you didn't have a vision and a plan."

Heat crept to my cheeks, and the silliest smile took me over. I waved and blew a few air-kisses at the applauding crowd, and as Deke finished up his speech, I took a deeper look at all our guests.

Funny. I'd dreamed of this moment—signing a big name for my brand, branching out, and getting wider distribution—but all those dreams included my husband.

There were so many faces in that crowd—a sea of people I knew and some I didn't . . . and *none* of them satisfied me. I stepped back just as Deke handed the mic to Tish. He walked in my direction and gave me a wistful smile, but I couldn't bring myself to return it this time.

Instead, I left the stage as subtly as I could, wove my way through the ballroom while everyone was distracted, and left the building.

NINETEEN

DAVINA

I wasn't sure what it was about that night, but I wanted so badly to talk to my daddy.

Aaron Klein had died from a hit-and-run when I was nine years old. I was fortunate enough to have nine years with him. He'd been the warmest person, with the kindest smile, and his presence was always comforting.

They say no one is perfect, but to nine-year-old Davina, my dad was the definition of perfection. He cooked for me and Octavia every morning before school and ate dinner with us every night.

He made sure we had clothes, shoes, and even the snacks we loved. He'd take us fishing with him or hiking in the fall. He'd brush the kinks out of mine and Octavia's hair and rub shea butter on dry patches of our skin.

He'd even taken care of Mama, though she'd made that difficult for him to do.

I wished Octavia was around for the party, but she had to return to nannying and couldn't make it.

I blew a breath, resting my chin on my knees as I focused on the body of water ahead of me. I was sitting in front of a man-made lake with a fountain sprouting from the center. The fountain cycled through colors, going from green to pink, then red to blue. It was the balm I needed for my emotional wounds.

A rustling noise sounded behind me, and I glanced over my shoulder, expecting Tish to be there, but it wasn't her.

It was Deke walking through the grass.

"You were hard to find," he announced, looking down at me with soft eyes.

Deke had a lot of the same traits my father did. He had the kind of personality that made you want to smile for no damn reason. I resisted, though, and faced the water again.

"Actually, I take that back. You were pretty easy to find," he said. "If it were me, I'd have walked this way too. View is nice."

"Why are you here, Deke?" I mumbled.

"For the party. You invited me, remember?"

I narrowed my eyes at him.

"Not the time for jokes." His lips popped. "Got it."

I looked ahead again, while he took a step closer. I saw him shifting from foot to foot, and when I glanced up at him, he was staring at the ground with mild disgust.

"What's wrong?" I asked.

"I'm debating if I want to sit down with you right now. This is a two-thousand-dollar suit. Armani shouldn't be anywhere near dirty grounds."

I huffed a laugh. Rich men and their materialistic problems. "You don't have to sit. In fact, you don't have to be here at all." I gave him a smug grin.

"And let you drown in the funk you're in? Nah."

A moment of silence passed between us before Deke finally released a sigh and sat on the pavement next to me. "You're lucky I like you," he mumbled.

I fought a grin.

He placed his legs at a bent angle, then put his arms on top of his knees in a relaxed position. I saw all this from the corner of my eye.

I couldn't dare myself to fully look at him while we were this close. I was sure my mascara had run a little and my eyes were red. I probably looked like a hot mess sitting next to this perfect melanin god in his crisp designer suit.

I buried my chin deeper in the gap between my chest and forearms and side-eyed him. He was watching the fountain, seemingly lost in thought. A serenity bloomed around him like he was shining with a new light.

"We can just sit here if you want," he murmured, like he knew I was watching him.

I nodded in appreciation.

When a few quiet seconds ticked by, though, I couldn't stand the silence anymore and looked at him. "I still don't get why you care so much."

"Who says I care? For all you know, I need some fresh air too. Someone in there was starting to smell like a basket of cut onions." He slid his eyes my way, revealing a dimple.

I hugged myself tighter while fighting a smile. "You do that a lot, you know?"

"Do what?"

"Make a joke when I'm being serious. You deflect."

His lips pressed as he contemplated that. "Do I?"

"Yeah. Like saying I'm in the one percent of people you like, the first time I asked why you keep checking on me. I can't imagine how many girls you've said that to."

"I've only ever said that to you." He dropped his arms and leaned closer to me. "One thing you should know about me, D, is that I don't lie. I speak my truth, and I'm a man of my word."

My head went into a slight tilt as I studied the long lashes that framed his brown eyes. "Did you sign with Golden Oil for your sisters, or was it really something you wanted to do?"

He digested the question, turning his gaze slightly to the left. When his eyes settled on mine again, he said, "At first, it didn't matter much to me. I wanted to hear you out because I'd never had a small business like yours approach me. Suppose none of them ever felt they had a chance, seeing as I'm not out here screaming about skin care. But GOC did. And call me crazy, but when I saw you in that office, I wanted to make sure I had a reason to keep seeing you."

I tilted my face to the sky. "Oh, Deke."

"What?"

I dropped my chin, looking into his eyes. "What happened to our *just friends* agreement?"

"We are friends," he confirmed smoothly.

"Well, I don't know what kind of friends you have, but they usually don't say stuff like that."

He released a gut-deep chuckle. "Friends check on each other, make sure the other is okay. I'm here to make sure you're good."

"Well, I'm fine," I said, putting my attention elsewhere.

"Don't do that."

I whipped my head to look at him. "Do what?"

"Don't lie about how you feel. You ran out of the ballroom to sit alone in front of a fountain that has geese shit all around it. You're not fine."

I rested my chin on my arms again. "You probably think I'm an emotional idiot."

"I don't understand why you'd say something like that." His voice was serious—so serious I had to look at him again to make sure he was okay. He was staring at me with his brows drawn together.

"What?" I asked through a breathy laugh. I sat up straight, confused by his sudden change of mood.

"I would never think that about you—or *anyone* who just lost a person they care about."

I swallowed hard and dropped my head, but Deke wasn't having it. His fingers gently grasped my chin, and he lifted my head just enough that I had no choice but to look at him.

His fingers were warm, and I had the faintest urge to sink my cheek into his whole palm just to feel something—*anything*. I hadn't been touched by a man in so long and probably would've done it if he'd attempted. Maybe I was just sad and vulnerable at the moment, but I would've.

There is such a thing as being touch starved. I craved a man's touch, a *possessive* grip—anything that would drive my body wild. I wanted to be comforted and was willing to take it in the form of a mildly cocky, multimillion-dollar athlete . . . so long as there weren't any strings attached to it.

"I think you're smart as hell. And funny. And *real*," Deke said, voice husky. A smile played at the edges of his lips as he held on to my chin. "It's hard finding authentic people in my world, but with you, you're just yourself. So don't sit there and say you're being emotional or that you're an idiot. You're being exactly who you need to be right now, D, and there's nothing wrong with it."

He released my chin, and it was then that I realized my pulse was swimming in my ears. My heart was hammering behind my rib cage, and his words had caused a flutter in my lower belly.

I looked from his eyes to his lips, and he mirrored my action. There was something magnetic humming between us. I hadn't felt this in months, not since Lew, and it both allured and terrified me.

Craving touch was one thing, but feeling a connection *this* powerful was an entirely different beast.

It was then that I looked at Deke—*really* looked at him for who he was. The man behind the suit and the jewelry. The man without the uniform, the round leather ball in his hands, or the cameras in his face.

The fountain transitioned from orange to purple and bathed the profile of his face. There was a light scruff on his jawline and around his mouth. His lips were sculpted, with a cute bow on the upper lip, and with them pressed like that, his dimples made a faint appearance. He smelled good, like expensive mahogany cologne with a hint of cocoa butter.

But it was his eyes that caught me most. Deep with understanding. Soft, but with a sharp awareness of something he recognized. Something he personally understood.

And that's when it hit me.

I wasn't the only person by the fountain who was grieving. He was too. That's why he cared. That's why he came to find me.

Who had he lost?

Who was he grieving?

As if he'd read my mind and didn't like the idea of me finding out his secrets, Deke's throat bobbed, and he pulled his fingers away. "I, uh . . . I'll go get you some water if you want."

"Sure," I whispered. "Actually, wait. I'll come with you. I should clean myself up and get back to the party before other people notice I'm missing."

Deke provided me that warm smile again as I stood and wiped my butt off. I was glad I hadn't sat in goose shit.

We walked side by side, but neither of us was in a hurry. The venue was within sight when we went up a grassy hill, and a few people from the party stood in front of the building, chatting or laughing.

"For what it's worth," I said when Deke dropped his head to look down at me, "I think you're smart, funny, and authentic too. Despite the big gold chains and icy diamond earrings."

At that, he put on a boyish smile. "That's a compliment, coming from you, D."

"Are you blushing?" I asked, grinning up at him.

"Nah. I'm not blushing," he countered quickly.

"Yes, you are! Aww! I made you blush!" I lightly bumped into him from the side.

He bumped me back, and when we reached the doors of the building, he pressed a hand on the area between my shoulder blades and slowly dragged it down to the small of my back. That hand caught me *completely* off guard and seared through my satin gown as he let me walk in ahead of him.

A thought struck me, fleeting and intrusive. I wanted his hand to go lower—to see what it felt like to have that large palm of his grip my ass. It'd been a long time since I was held.

Clutched.

Gripped.

Oh my goodness. No. What is wrong with me?

When Deke pulled his hand away and took that hot touch with him, he lowered his lips to my ear and murmured, "Look who's blushing now."

TWENTY

From: Deke Bishop
To: Davina Klein-Roberts
You up?

From: Davina Klein-Roberts
To: Deke Bishop

I am. Embarrassed myself in front of a famous bball player at my own party and now it's haunting me.

From: Deke Bishop
To: Davina Klein-Roberts

LMAO how is it embarrassing if no one else saw you?

From: Davina Klein-Roberts
To: Deke Bishop

YOU saw me.

From: Deke Bishop
To: Davina Klein-Roberts

Yeah, but I grew up with two sisters and am still close to them. I'm used to seeing women cry.

From: Davina Klein-Roberts
To: Deke Bishop

You're just saying that to make me feel better.

Why are you up? What are you doing?

From: Deke Bishop
To: Davina Klein-Roberts

At my hotel. I'll be heading to FL in a couple days to see family. That's the best part about the off season. Schedule is freer so I get to spend more time with the people I love. I'm up cause I can't sleep. Too busy thinking about you.

From: Davina Klein-Roberts
To: Deke Bishop

Do I need to send you a reminder before every email so you won't say stuff like that to me?! JUST FRIENDS, REMEMBER?

From: Deke Bishop
To: Davina Klein-Roberts

What??? It's true. I am thinking about you . . . but it's not like how you're thinking.

From: Davina Klein-Roberts
To: Deke Bishop

So what's it like then?

From: Deke Bishop
To: Davina Klein-Roberts

Just about how you ran off to be alone. You were hurting. Still are, I'm sure. It sucks when you want to help someone but all their troubles are on the inside.

From: Davina Klein-Roberts
To: Deke Bishop

Oh. Yeah, I get it. It does hurt but I think I'll be okay.

From: Deke Bishop
To: Davina Klein-Roberts

No you won't. No one is ever fine after.

From: Davina Klein-Roberts
To: Deke Bishop

What do you mean?

TWENTY-ONE

DAVINA

I flipped onto my stomach with my phone in my face, waiting for Deke to respond. What did he mean, *No one is fine after*?

While I waited for him to email me back, I searched his name on the internet. Many articles popped up—*way* too many to count.

Most of them were stats. Some were with BOBBLE, a popular source for celebrity gossip. They had pictures of him with that Giselle Grace woman from two months ago.

I ignored the BOBBLE stuff and typed Deke's name in the search bar again but this time with the word *grieving*. With that, not many options popped up. Two appeared but were from four years ago, when a team he used to play for lost a playoff game. There was also a Facebook post with a picture attached to it that the search engine considered a related link.

I gave it a click, and it led me to an image of a boy with russet skin, cornrows, light-brown eyes, and a big smile. He wore a dark-green basketball jersey with the number two on it and had a basketball tucked beneath his arm. The post was made by a woman named Olivia Blake. The caption said:

Damon. Light of my life. Sweet, sweet angel. It's been 3 years too many and our grief has only started healing. Mom, Camille, Whitney, and Deke love and miss you so much. RIH, baby.

"Oh my goodness."

This was his mom's Facebook page. There was a carousel of images along with the photo of Damon—some of him with his sisters and with his mom, but then a picture appeared of him and a teenage Deke.

Deke was smiling from ear to ear with his brother, their faces so close to the camera I almost couldn't distinguish them. But I knew those eyes. I'd become very familiar with them. It was an adorable picture.

Wholesome.

Sweet.

But the sight of it broke my heart.

Deke's brother had died, which meant I was right. He *did* know grief. That glimpse of brokenness I saw during our little intermission at the party was because he no longer had his brother.

I swiped off the internet and sat in the dark for a moment, letting it sink in. Deke still hadn't emailed me back, and with so much time passing, he either had fallen asleep or was purposely not answering because he didn't want to talk about it.

I figured it was the latter, so I went back to our emails and wrote up a new one.

From: Davina Klein-Roberts
To: Deke Bishop

You know . . . I was completely fine during the party and just knew I wouldn't cry about anything. I was distracted, I had my food, I had my drinks, I had my friends . . . but there was something about being on that stage that changed it all.

I looked around the room and saw all those faces. I was searching for something—well some*one*. And it hit me all over again that my husband wasn't there and that he'll never be here again. But his face was all I wanted to see.

I wanted him to be there to cheer for me, to hug me, to congratulate me. Tonight was supposed to be this big success and he was supposed to be a part of it, you know? That's all a partner wants, really.

So . . . that's why I went to be alone. I miss him and my heart was breaking but I didn't want to ruin the night for anyone. I know you probably don't want to hear all that but I guess what I'm trying to say is thank you for coming to find me. Thank you for understanding and caring when you didn't have to, Deke.

I read over my email three times, chewing on my acrylic nail. It was too much information. Too personal. I wanted to delete it—say forget it and force myself to sleep . . . but something in the back of my mind told me Deke *needed* to hear this.

Perhaps if I opened up to him a bit, he'd open up to me too. I wouldn't push it, though. He hadn't pushed me about it when we were by the fountain, and I appreciated that more than he knew.

With a shaky breath, I sent the email, then lay on my back and stared up at the ceiling fan. The blades whirled, and my heartbeat slowed to a steady pace, pulsing in my ears.

I closed my eyes, and just when I felt the regret sneaking its way in, my phone chimed.

From: Deke Bishop
To: Davina Klein-Roberts

Wow. That hit me deep. Sorry you're hurting so much inside right now, D. I get it though. Wanting to put on that brave face even though you're unraveling from every seam. Thank you for being honest with me. Told you you're real.

And I'll always care, Davina. I'm not just saying that. Don't know what it is about you but something keeps nagging me to hit you up and make sure you're good. If it's alright with you I'd like to check in every once in a while to make sure of it. That cool?

I smiled, and this time I didn't hide it or fight it.
That's cool, I replied.

TWENTY-TWO

DEKE

Though I loved the designer clothes, the shoes, and my Ferrari parked in the private garage connected to my condo, when it came to seeing family, I liked to keep it low key.

So what did I do? Rented a Mazda from one of the airport's rental car services so I could pick my nephew up from camp without making a scene.

Camille had called as soon as I touched down in Florida. She was stressing about being late to pick up Eli and how her fiancé would be running late too.

"Sis, I got you," I said, marching through one of the terminals. I noticed a man looking at me as if he was familiar with me, but I pulled my eyes away and kept walking. I was glad I wore a hat. "I'll pick Eli up. Just send me the address for his camp."

"Deke, thank you," she said with so much relief she may as well have melted. "I'll call the camp and let them know you'll be picking him up."

Before I knew it, I was driving with my seven-year-old nephew in the passenger seat, with J. Cole rapping and both of us bobbing our heads to the beat of the songs.

"Uncle Deke! Watch this!" Eli started doing some crazy dance little kids do, shaking his arms and kicking his legs as he rocked to the beat. I snorted a laugh as I pressed a hand to his chest.

"All right, all right, big dog. Slow down. I see you."

Eli grinned from ear to ear as he peered through the windshield. "Are we gonna play basketball today?"

"I don't see why not. You been practicing?"

"Duh! I'm just like you! I make it splash in the net!"

"Oh, word?" This kid was a trip. I loved him to death, though. "We'll see about that when we get to your house. But before we get there, let's get some italian ice. You still like the red kind?"

"No, I like the blue one now. The red one always messes up my shirts."

"That's 'cause you're a messy kid, my dude. Your mom told me you didn't clean your room last week, said she stepped barefoot on a LEGO. You know how much that hurts, right?"

"Yeah, I know," he returned with a hint of sorrow. "But she asked me to do it when I was in the middle of building the *biggest LEGO tower ever*, Uncle Deke!" He was upbeat again. "I still have it up, if you wanna see it!"

"Oh, I definitely wanna see that!"

I loved kids, man. They were the realest people on earth and not tainted by any of the world's bullshit. At least Eli wasn't . . . *yet*.

I'm convinced growing up is a curse. All the emotions hit you harder and the innocence fades when you get a dose of the real world. This earth is supposed to be our playground, and yet every day feels like walking through a war zone.

After we grabbed some italian ice, we headed to Camille's crib. She had a simple one-story home with three bedrooms and a theater room we loved making use of during my longer visits.

I wouldn't be able to stay long this time around. My training with Ken Massey was coming up, and I needed to be prepared. Ken was one of the toughest trainers around, but he yielded impressive results. My main goal was to get better at the game, not worse, so hiring him was a necessity.

I waited at the hood of the car for Eli before heading to the front door of his house. He had a fresh blue stain from the italian ice on his gray shirt, and I huffed a laugh.

When I gave the doorbell a ring, it only took a few seconds for Jack, Camille's fiancé, to answer the door. Jack, an extremely extroverted man with warm beige skin, a big gap-toothed smile, short auburn hair, and shirts tucked into whatever pants he was wearing, would soon be my brother-in-law.

The last man Camille was married to—Elias's father—was a piece of shit, and the complete opposite of Jack, literally down to the skin tone. Her ex talked too much, tried too hard, and wanted everyone to like him, even though he was a narcissistic asshole.

But Jack was a good dude, and he treated my sister well. And to be honest, Jack was only ever himself, and I could appreciate that . . . even if he was a little too handsy and always in someone's face.

"Well, look at that! *The* Deke Bishop is at my doorstep!" Jack announced, raising his arms in the air.

"That'd be me," I said, then cut my eyes to Eli, who was rolling his.

"Hey, Jack," Eli said, squeezing through a gap to get inside.

"Hey, there, Eli! I made some pizza rolls if you want some!"

Jack looked at me again with that same goofy smile and his hands at his hips now. He ran his eyes up and down the length of me in awe.

I raised a curious brow. "You gonna let me in or what, Jack?"

"Oh! Right! Yes, come in, come in!" Jack moved aside, and I stepped over the threshold. It definitely smelled like pizza rolls, and as I entered the kitchen, I spotted Eli standing over the stove, devouring them.

Damn.

Maybe I should've grabbed him a burger instead of shaved ice.

A hand clapped my shoulder, and Jack stood at my side. "The kid's hungry, huh?"

I laughed. "Guess so."

"Hey, listen, Deke. Thank you for picking Eli up. Camille's been so stressed with work and all. I would've gone to scoop him up myself, but I was trying to finish up with one of my patients. Time sort of ran over. Glad I could make it home before you got here, though."

Jack was a physical therapist. Mostly treated sports injuries . . . which was why it was so awkward at times with him, because it was like he was *waiting* for the day I got injured just so he could treat me.

I stepped back, not only to remove Jack's hand from my shoulder but also to face him a step or two away, like most men usually did. "It's all good, Jack. Trust me, I get it."

"Anyway, make yourself at home. Camille should be here within the hour. I've ordered pizza and wings for tonight. Oh—can we take a picture together? My golfing buddies are gonna *freak* when they hear Deke Bishop was in *my* house!"

Oh, man. There was only so much of this I could take.

I took the selfie with him, but not without thinking that my sister needed to get her ass home stat.

TWENTY-THREE

DEKE

"Are y'all going to be out here all night or what?" Camille's voice rang in the air as I passed the basketball to Eli.

I turned to find my sister stepping out the back door of her house and walking through the trail leading to their private basketball court.

"Hi, Mommy!" Eli abandoned the ball to rush to her. He hugged her tight around the waist, and she laughed as she held him back.

"Well, hello to you, too, honey. How was camp?"

"It was good. It was my turn to be the jungle leader today."

"Oh, really? And did you walk in a straight line?"

"Yeah, but some people kept getting out of line."

"Well, as long as you did your part, that's all that matters, baby." She kissed Eli on the forehead, then turned her attention to me. "Declan. Look at you." She sighed, moving closer to me.

I tried not to react to her calling me by my real name. She and my mom were probably the only two people who could get away with it now.

"Wassup, sis?" I hugged her tight as she stepped into my arms.

"I'm glad you're here." She leaned back and gripped my upper arms. "Did you get enough to eat?"

"Oh yeah. Me and Eli killed that pizza."

"Yeah, I see that, and now you and Eli can help with the dishes."

She stepped away and wrapped her arm around Eli's shoulder as he threw his head back and whined, "Aww!"

~

After cleaning up, Eli and Jack put on a movie in the living room, while Camille opened a bottle of red wine. I stood next to the fridge, with my lower back resting against the counter edge and my arms folded.

"You want a drink?" she asked, eyeing me as she placed the wine bottle on the counter.

"Nah, I'm good. I've got training on Monday and drank enough at that party over the weekend." Speaking of the party instantly reminded me of Davina, and as if the universe had read my mind, my phone vibrated in my back pocket.

When I checked it, there was an email from her. It was wild to me that we were still communicating. I mean, technically I fulfilled my end of the contract. I did the photo shoot, she had her party, and it turned out great. All she had to do now was wait for the products to hit the shelves and for people to snatch them up.

But, regardless of all that, I liked talking to her . . . and I wanted her to know it, so I read her email.

> Sorry it's taken me a minute to get back to you. I was at the warehouse today—hectic stuff. Anyway, your training sounds intense. But look at you! You're living your dreams and playing basketball for a living. Not many people in this world can say that.
>
> Don't worry about getting back to me hours later or whatever. You're a busy man so I get it . . . plus I'm sure there are other women you need to entertain first. It's all good!

I couldn't help laughing at her email.

Other women? If only she knew I hadn't slept with a woman since meeting her . . . and by *sleeping with*, I mean actual intercourse. I hadn't felt the urge to *sleep* with a woman unless her first name started with a *D* and her last name with a *K*.

"What are you smiling about?" Camille asked from the other side of the kitchen. She sipped her wine as she looked from my phone to my eyes.

"Nothing." I slid my phone into my back pocket. "Just an email."

"Is it from that Giselle girl?" she asked, her nose scrunching with distaste.

"Hell no. I'm done with her."

"Oh. Well, good, 'cause you know I don't like her ass."

I chuckled. "Trust me, Camille, you have made that abundantly clear."

She smiled behind another sip of wine. "So, if it isn't Giselle, who is it?"

I hesitated.

I wanted to tell Camille about Davina, but I knew my sister, and if Whitney had made a fuss about our situation at the rebranding party, I could only imagine what Camille would say in the privacy of her home.

"It's just a woman I met at a party," I told her, which was partly true. She *was* at the party, and I *did* bump into her at the fountain, only to discover a new side of her.

I'd noticed after my speech that Davina's eyes were a little shinier than usual. Then she took off and left the ballroom altogether.

When she still hadn't returned after ten minutes, I looked for her and found her sitting in front of that fountain.

She hadn't noticed me when I first spotted her. It was clear she was crying, and I felt a twist in my chest and the sudden urge to hold her and comfort her somehow. It would've been inappropriate, though, so I just gave her a moment. When her crying had calmed, I'd shuffled a little louder through the grass so she could prepare for my "random" appearance.

"Oh, yeah. The party. Whitney said it was really nice." Camille's voice pulled me out of the memory. I watched as she refilled her wineglass. "You going to see Mama while you're here?"

"I planned to stop by for a little."

Camille nodded, then pursed her lips as she scanned the kitchen. Several seconds of silence passed, and while she casually sipped, I studied her. She was avoiding looking at me for some reason.

"What?" I finally asked.

Her eyes flickered to mine. "Nothing." She stepped around me to sit at the dining table.

I took one of the chairs closest to hers and could see Eli and Jack in the living room, watching one of the Fast & Furious movies.

"You're thinking about something. You've got that pensive look. What's going on?"

Camille took a big gulp, swallowed it down, then said, "I think Mama has been seeing Dad."

I froze.

Those were *not* the words I expected to hear.

Frowning, I sat back and shifted my attention to one of the windows. Half the sun was beneath the horizon, the sky an orangey pink.

"How do you know this?" I asked. A part of me didn't want to ask. I didn't want to care.

"Last weekend I went to drop off a glass pitcher she'd been asking me to bring for her little margarita night with her book club friends. When I got there, I saw his car in the driveway. I only recognized his car because I saw it the night me and Whitney agreed to have dinner with him at that Italian restaurant, remember? Anyway, I didn't go inside, just left the pitcher on the porch with a note . . . but why else would he have been there?"

I inhaled deeply, letting the frustrated breath collect in my chest before releasing it. "She promised she wouldn't go back to him," I muttered.

"She's lonely, Deke. I mean, she has me, Eli, and Jack most weekends, but I can't say I'm surprised if something is going on. And, you know, it seems Dad has turned a new leaf. When we saw him at the dinner, he said he'd been going to AA and he's a coach for a youth basketball team at his church—"

I sniffed and pushed back in my chair so hard the legs scraped the floor. Jack and Eli twisted their necks to find the commotion.

"Declan," Camille murmured evenly, her eyes hardening.

"I'm gonna head to my hotel," I said when Jack and Eli looked away. I couldn't sit here anymore. If I did, I'd blow the fuck up, and the last thing I wanted my nephew to see was his uncle getting angry.

I walked out the back door and took the trail to the court, which had a path near it that wrapped around the house and led to the driveway. My keys were in my pocket. I could leave right now.

"Deke, come on." Camille rushed after me. "He's trying to change."

"No, see, that's the fucking problem, Camille!" I whirled around to face her, and she stopped dead in her tracks. "I don't believe that shit. Not for a second. So, what, he goes to a fucking alcoholic group, joins a church, and that makes him a saint? *Fuck that!* He hasn't changed, and you know it!"

"What happened between you, him, and Mama was so long ago, and we were all in a dark place, okay? I get it, trust me. I understand why you're angry, but people *can* change, Declan."

"Stop calling me that shit," I snapped, giving her my back. I fished my keys out of my jeans pockets and marched toward the path. "Tell Eli and Jack I'll see them tomorrow before my flight."

"Deke!" Camille called, but I kept walking until I reached the Mazda.

I slammed the door behind me, huffing rapidly as I started the car and backed out of the driveway.

I was too fucking mad to drive, though.

Every car was in my way.

Every person crossing the street was a hindrance.

I pulled to the side of the road, bleary eyed and full of rage, and without thinking, I yelled and punched the steering wheel so many times my knuckles split.

TWENTY-FOUR

DAVINA

It was right after leaving the nail salon when I spotted an email from Deke that I knew would cause a rift in our friendship.

Can we text instead?

He'd included his number in the email too.

I blew a breath, dropping my phone into the cup holder and driving home. I wasn't sure why his simple question made my heart stutter. I tried not to think too much about it. Tish would be coming over again, and this time she was bringing sushi. I figured I'd discuss the Deke matter with her later.

I decided to drive the long way home—the one that took me past the graveyard where Lewis was buried.

It'd been almost three months since my last visit. Each time I went back made me feel lonelier and made the reality harder to bear. A part of me didn't think he was there. His soul was with God now, and that body in the grave was just a deteriorating vessel. Still, it was nice knowing his physical presence was *somewhere* I could find.

Tish was already parked in my driveway when I pulled up, and it was no surprise that she was in the house when I walked in. She and Octavia were the only two people with keys to my place.

Tish had already prepared a tray of various types of sushi along with a mini saucer of soy sauce and a glass bowl of edamame. She carried the tray to the coffee table in the living room as I placed my purse and keys down.

"You're just in time for some good ole sushi!"

On this night, the premiere of some reality show involving a bunch of rich, dramatic housewives was streaming, and Tish loved that kind of stuff. Whatever it was, I wasn't very tuned in. I was too busy reading the email from Deke again as I popped edamame beans into my mouth.

Why did he want to text *now*? Texting him would have been taking a step up . . . and it was a step I didn't want to risk. And not only that, but he didn't respond to my last email, like I thought he would.

I mean, sure, the whole *entertaining other girls* bit was a little over the top, but I thought it'd be funny or that he'd get a kick out of it. And, okay, maybe a part of me wanted to know if he *was* entertaining other women and, if he was, why he was wasting time emailing me. Not that it mattered much, but still. Emails were just that: emails. I could get back to them whenever I had time, but texting was more prompt. More intimate. Texting required a sort of personal dedication.

". . . and then she had the nerve to let the door close in my face. Uh, hello?" Tish snapped her fingers in my face, and I blinked up at her. "Where is your head at?" she asked with a soft laugh.

"Sorry. Yeah, it's here. What happened again?"

"What are you thinking about?" she asked, biting into a piece of tempura sushi.

I watched as she chewed, then followed it with a gulp of strawberry Fanta. I rested my upper back against the nearest sofa and set my phone down.

"It's just Deke."

Tish's eyes expanded as she took another bite. *"Deke?"* she garbled around a mouthful.

"Yeah. We've been emailing each other here and there. And I told you about the other night at the party, remember? How I needed some air and a little time to myself because I was thinking about Lewis?"

"Yeah?"

"Well, what I *didn't* tell you was that Deke found me."

She tilted her head, swallowing the bite of sushi. "He *found* you? What do you mean?"

"I was sitting by myself near the fountain. I guess he noticed I was upset and he came looking for me."

This time her mouth twitched, and she tried bottling her amusement. *"Ohh,"* she sang.

I fought a smile. "Tish, no. It's not like that."

"A famous athlete who could've been using his free time to do literally *anything* else decides to go after a crying woman and check on her? Yeah, okay." She scoffed. "Tell me how it's *not* like that?"

"Okay—maybe you're right. But when it came to the party, I think he was genuinely concerned, so he checked in. I told you he lost his brother, right? And he knows about Lew. Maybe he just wanted to be nice."

Tish pursed her lips and rolled her eyes.

"What?" I asked. "What are you not saying?"

"How long have you two been talking to each other?"

"He reached out around the time you sent the email about me taking a week off. He sent his condolences, but it's like ever since then, we haven't really stopped staying in touch with each other. It's been a few weeks now. And it was okay at first, you know? Just harmless. But he just sent me his number today. Look."

I unlocked my phone and showed her the email. Tish read it, then took the phone from me to scroll through all the others.

"Tish!" I laughed.

She lowered the phone and looked into my eyes. "He likes you, Vina."

"No," I moaned. "Don't say that." I pressed the heel of my palm to my forehead.

"Oh my goodness, Vina, this is just like a rom-com movie where two people coincidentally meet each other and they start getting to know each other through love notes or text messages. I *love* shit like this!"

I leaned forward to snatch my phone out of her hand. "I think it's nice that he cares and that he checks in to make sure I'm okay, but I've already told him we can only be friends. I'm not looking for anything more than that right now. I just feel bad because I don't want to text him."

"Why? Because you know it'll lead to something you can't resist?"

I opened my mouth but clamped it shut again.

Tish smirked. "Listen, he's a *man*, Davina. You think he gives a fuck about that *just friends* thing? In your last email you said something along the lines of him entertaining other women, but if you take a step back and look at the bigger picture, a man like Deke Bishop can't entertain more than one woman at a time. At least not with emails and texting. He's a busy person who is constantly on the move. I doubt he has time to sit around emailing a bunch of women all day and night, but he makes the time in his schedule for *you*. Do you see what I'm getting at here?"

"Nope, sure don't," I said as she stood up with her empty plastic cup.

"All I know is for a man who is *famous*, with a schedule as hectic as his, that means something. People make time for the things they want, Davina. If he's finding time to send your favorite flowers, to email you for weeks just to stay in touch, *and* to find you near fountains during parties, that's more than friendly territory, even if you don't want to admit it. Just give him your damn number already, girl. It won't kill you." Tish walked around the ottoman to reach the kitchen, and while she refilled her cup with red soda, my heart sank to my stomach.

She was right, but I still couldn't bring myself to text him.

Instead, I darkened the screen of my phone and figured I'd take a step back from whatever this thing was Deke and I had going on.

TWENTY-FIVE

From: Deke Bishop
To: Davina Klein-Roberts
July 15

Been three days since I heard from you. Everything good?

From: Deke Bishop
To: Davina Klein-Roberts
July 17

If I've offended you somehow, I apologize. Just wanna hear from you, D. Make sure you're okay.

From: Davina Klein-Roberts
To: Deke Bishop
July 18

I'm good, Deke. Not offended. Hope you're well too.

From: Deke Bishop
To: Davina Klein-Roberts
July 18

Tell me what I did wrong.

From: Davina Klein-Roberts
To: Deke Bishop
July 18

You didn't do anything wrong. I've just been really busy. I'm sure you understand what that's like.

From: Deke Bishop
To: Davina Klein-Roberts
July 18

We're all busy. And sure, I can say I understand but do you wanna know the truth?

From: Davina Klein-Roberts
To: Deke Bishop
July 18

I always want the truth.

From: Deke Bishop
To: Davina Klein-Roberts
July 18

Truth is I think you're bullshitting me and for someone who always wants honesty and truths, I find it
ironic that you can't return the favor. So tell me what
I did wrong, D.

TWENTY-SIX

DEKE

It'd been a whole day since my last email to Davina, and it was taking everything in me not to send another one.

She'd stressed the *just friends* thing every time we talked, and I accepted it for what it was, because I liked talking to her any way I could.

I couldn't explain it, but emailing felt limited—like there was a barrier between us. Clearly I'd overstepped by asking to break through that barrier.

I only gave her my number so I could hear her voice before I broke something. After hearing about Mama and my piece-of-shit dad, it seemed like talking to her would calm me down. That was my bad for relying on a woman so wounded, though.

Because I was pissed, I ended up launching a water glass from my hotel room at the wall and breaking it to deal with the frustrations. I paid for it when I checked out.

"Bishop!" Javier chucked the basketball my way with furrowed brows. I caught it before it could hit me in the face, and the leather slammed into my palms. "Come on, man! Ken gave us the drill. What are you doing?"

Right. I was supposed to be training.

We were practicing in Element Recreation Center, the members-only gym I co-owned with Javier. We often left it open to members after we did our workouts and training, which was usually four times a week from six to eleven in the morning.

Some of the money made from memberships went into the gym for our employees or for repairs, but nearly all of it was used as donations for our nonprofit charity, Kids in Element. Sometimes we brought the kids in and would shoot hoops with them.

During Christmas, we made sure the kids had gifts they could unwrap, and if a utility or medical bill was brought to our attention, we took care of it for the parents. I was damn proud of our charity and wouldn't have co-owned it with anyone else but Javier.

It was easy to get lost in time at Element, surrounded by basketball goals and the scent of sweet orange leather. This was the perfect place for me to sweat out all the stress. That was what I wanted to do that day—work out all my frustrations and focus on getting better for the next season—but it just wasn't happening for me.

I chucked the ball back at Javier. He caught my equally hard throw, tucking the ball under his arm and resting it on his waist. "What the hell is going on with you, eh? You have been off all morning. It is like your head is not in the game."

"Yeah, well, maybe it's not," I muttered.

Javier blew an irritated breath as I turned away to grab my water bottle. "You asked *me* to come and train with *you*, Deke. You made me put up money for this time with Ken. If you are not in the mood to train, then why the hell am I here?"

"I asked you to join me two weeks ago," I said over my shoulder. "A lot of shit changes in two weeks."

"Even so, you never let whatever is bothering you interfere with training."

I glanced over my shoulder, and Javier's forehead was wrinkled with concern. Some of his black hair was glued to his forehead, and sweat stained the upper half of his shirt. I turned completely as Ken made his way back to us in his tracksuit. He'd run off to call his wife.

I sat on one of the chairs on the sidelines and guzzled down more water. Javier walked my way, lifting the bottom half of his shirt to wipe the sweat off his face. I never understood why he did that. We had clean towels in literally every corner of the basketball gym and even in the strength training and conditioning rooms.

With a sigh, Javier sat next to me and lifted his water bottle, giving it a squeeze as he held it above his mouth. After guzzling a few sips down, he said, "I know you, Deke." His gaze was ahead, focused on Ken, who was setting cones up for another drill. "You are in your head." Through my peripheral vision, I saw his head turn to look at me. "What is *really* going on with you?"

I stared at the white lines on the glazed wooden floors. "You're gonna think it's stupid."

"I don't think anything you say can be more stupid than whatever comes out of EJ's mouth."

I huffed a laugh. "Yeah, you're right. It's not *that* stupid."

Javier leaned forward, resting his elbows on top of his thighs. When he crossed his fingers, he said, "Tell me what's up."

I flicked my gaze to his, and he looked at me closely, waiting for me to speak. I wanted to tell him about my parents and what my sister told me, but I'd never spoken to anyone about that situation. It was too personal—too fucked up—and though that was a major reason why my head wasn't in the training, it mostly had to do with someone else.

"It's this girl," I said, sitting up straight again.

"Ah." Javier fought a smile. "I had a feeling."

"I know what you're thinking, but this isn't about Giselle."

That caused his smile to slip. "No?"

"No. It's this woman I've been working with. Her skin care company endorsed me, and when I met her, there was just something about her that I liked. I couldn't pinpoint it, but it was *something*, you know? I mean, yeah, she's sexy as hell—more than a ten, in my opinion—but that's not what kept me wanting to know her. When we talked, we had this automatic connection. It was like our dynamic wasn't forced. Conversation was easy with her. You get it, I'm sure. About forcing conversations for the sake of it?"

"Oh, trust me. I do get it," he said. "So you like this woman?"

"I do like her . . . but she's a little complicated and hard to read sometimes, especially through text. We've been emailing back and forth for a good month and a half, but I sent her my number a few days ago so we could text or call, even, and ever since then, I feel like our dynamic has changed."

"Well, why wouldn't she want to call you after all those emails?"

"Because we're only supposed to be friends. I can tell she doesn't want more than that."

Javier scoffed. "Why the hell not?"

"I told you her situation is complicated, man." I paused, prepping myself to tell him the worst part. "Look, she lost her husband sometime last year. He died from spinal cancer."

Javier's dark-brown eyes stretched while all his other features collapsed. "Oh." Then his eyebrows dipped as he said, "*Shit*, Deke." I had a feeling this was striking a chord with him by the way he hunched forward.

"Yeah. I know. I've been checking in with her, and I know she's not ready to move on from him. I mean, he was her husband, right? She needs that time to process, so I get it, I really do, but at this point I'm thinking I need to back off, because I can't be just a friend to her. I'm greedy, Valdez. I want more."

"Yes, well, I agree about backing off. She needs time to heal herself," he said.

"I know."

"Because I can tell you, after I lost Eloise, I did not know who I was or what the point of living was. I still feel that way sometimes, but Aleesa keeps me going. Perhaps that is what this woman is feeling too. You cannot make a person move faster with something like this."

"But I'm not," I countered. "I *want* her to process it. I *want* her to acknowledge it. I don't even mind being there while she does. Don't ask me why, but I care about this girl and her well-being. I can relate to her in so many ways, and yes, I do want to know more about her, but I can't do that if she doesn't let me in."

"Okay, okay. I get it." Javier raised his hands in the air, a gesture for me to slow it down. "But you need to listen to me, Deke. You say you do not want to be just friends with her, but what if that is what she needs right now? A *friend*. And perhaps all those emails you shared made her feel like you were a friend she could talk to. It proved that you did care. Sending her your number probably made her realize you are seeking more from her, and she does not want to hurt you, so she's keeping quiet. Her emotions are all over the place. She probably doesn't even feel like herself. I think you should just keep being that friend to her. If there is true chemistry, it will be one day. And when she is ready, she will call."

I nodded and sighed, dropping my head again.

"Bishop! Valdez! Get off your asses and start these drills!" Ken shouted across the court. "It's not my money you're wasting!"

Javier capped my shoulder before rising to his feet, and I followed suit. As we walked across the polished floors, he asked, "Have you ever been friend zoned before?"

"Hell no, Javier! Are you serious? Look at me." I gestured from my face to the rest of my body. "Not a single woman I've met has *ever* attempted to put me in the friend zone!"

"Ah, that is right. Because you are Deke Bishop," he said, chuckling.

"Damn right." I smirked.

"So this woman bruised your ego. Are you sure that is not why you want her? So you can prove to yourself that you can get her? That you have still *got it*, as you Americans like to say?" Javier asked as Ken tossed a basketball to him.

"First of all, that is *not* how we say that shit."

Javier's laugh filled the gym.

"Secondly, it's just like I told you. I care about her. She's rare, and I think she deserves the best."

"Interesting you say that," he said.

"How's that?" I asked, scooping up a ball from the rack. I moved to the spot Ken was pointing at.

"Because if she deserves the best, will you be capable of giving that to her?"

I stared at Javier as his words sank to my stomach.

Damn. That was a good question.

I wasn't the best guy, and I'd made my mistakes. I had a cloudy reputation as some bachelor athlete, and I couldn't say some of the rumors about me weren't true. I'd had my fun, but those days were behind me.

Now I could see why Davina was hesitant. She probably didn't think I was serious—or maybe she thought I was chasing her for one thing.

I realized that day what went wrong. She didn't trust me worth a damn. And the worst part about the realization was that I had no clue how to fix it.

TWENTY-SEVEN

DEKE

After I hopped out of the shower and threw on a pair of basketball shorts, I went to the kitchen to warm up the lunch my personal chef had delivered earlier.

It wasn't until I'd popped a slice of asparagus into my mouth that my phone rang on the counter.

MA

I sighed, setting my fork down with a soft clatter.

"What's up, Ma?" I answered, tapping the Speakerphone button.

"Deke, honey, how are you?" My mother's voice was loud and vibrant. "I haven't heard from you in a while. Everything okay?"

I shoveled some brown rice into my mouth and garbled out, "Everything's fine."

"You sure? It isn't like you to *not* call me at least once a week. I mean, I would call you, but I know you've been busy."

"Yeah, it's fine, Ma. I have been busy. It's why I haven't been able to call."

"Hmm." It was a noise of disapproval, which meant she had more to say and I needed to coax it out of her.

I stood up from the barstool and walked toward the window with a sigh. "What's up, Mama?"

"Well, it's just that Camille told me you were at her house, and I recalled you saying you were going to stop by, but you never did. It would've been nice to see my son while he was in town."

"I had to get back for training."

"Declan. Do not lie to me," she countered, her voice stern.

I sighed and walked to the couch to sit. Zeke sat up on his pillow and cocked his head at me. "Camille told me she saw your ex-husband at your house."

"Oh, good Lord," she muttered.

"That's why I didn't go. Because if I would've swung by and he was there, I'm positive I would've lost my cool. And the reason I haven't called you is because I'm not good at faking how I feel about him, like my sisters can, and I didn't want to ruin your mood."

"Deke, baby. That situation is not what you think it is."

"No? So why was he there, Ma?"

"Look, I ran into him at the grocery store a few days before that and invited him to come over. He'd asked me to join him for lunch one day, but I turned it down. I felt guilty seeing him at the store, all run down and tired looking, so I invited him over. He comes around every couple of days or so to make little repairs around the house and to catch up. That's all."

"Oh, is that all? You sure?"

"Declan, I know you don't want to believe it, but he *is* changing, okay? Holding on to a grudge like this will only make you bitter."

"Ma, you know I don't like when you call me by my real name."

"I don't care! That's the name I gave you and the name on your birth certificate. You have to get over what happened, *Declan*! You have to let it go! He can't do those things to you anymore!"

I shot off the couch. "Get over what happened? Ma, he was literally beating your ass and mine every day until he got arrested!"

"Don't you curse at me," she scolded. If she were with me in person, she'd probably have slapped me upside the head.

I closed my eyes for a moment, breathing in through my nostrils and then exhaling. "Listen, I'm sorry. Okay? I'm sorry. You may have forgiven him, Mama, but I can't. So if you decide to get closer to him or to let him back in, I won't act like I'm okay with it and I won't come by the house."

"You pay for this house, Deke. You're allowed to come whenever you want."

I ignored her. "Just promise me you won't let him move back in."

She was quiet a moment, but I could hear her sighing. "You know I wouldn't allow that, but he's changed, son. He's not the same man he was all those years ago."

"People don't change, Ma. They just fake it until the people around them believe they have. *He* taught me that."

"Declan, I love you, okay? And I'm not getting back with your father, but you have to remember that regardless of what he's done, he *is* the father of *all* of my children. I was married to him for *twenty-one* years, and all those years weren't bad. All that time doesn't just go away, you know? All we're doing is catching up. Being human. That's it. It's okay to show a little grace sometimes."

"Yeah, well, you do you, Ma. I gotta go. I love you." Then I tapped the phone to hang up before she could call my name to stop me.

TWENTY-EIGHT

DAVINA

"Make sure your core is nice and firm, Davina."

I glanced up at my Pilates instructor, Betsy, a passive-aggressive blond woman with a nose so small and surgically chipped away she may as well not have had one. She forced a smile at me, then sauntered away to criticize the next victim.

Okay. So, I'd gotten a little out of shape the last couple of months. Sue me. The last thing that'd been on my mind was working out. I remembered now why I'd stopped coming to this Pilates class with Tish before Lew passed away. Betsy was a *B-I-T-C-H*.

A loud thump sounded behind me, and then a sharp gasp pierced the air. I looked at Octavia, who had collapsed from her kneeling side kicks.

"You must keep your core *engaged*, Octavia!" Betsy shrilled from across the room.

Octavia grimaced at me, and I snorted a laugh.

When class concluded and we left the building, Octavia said, "Remind me to never do another class like that with you ever again."

"Oh, I won't be returning. Trust me," I laughed, rubbing the back of my neck. "I forgot how hard it was."

Inside the car, Octavia took big gulps of water before stabbing me with a glare. "Betsy out here thinking we all have cores built like Roman soldiers. Like, girl—we are not all made like you! Some of us love cake!"

I broke out in a laugh as I started the engine. Octavia was going to be with me for a few weeks, since she was no longer nannying that spoiled kid she always talked about. His parents had let her go, said they didn't like what she was teaching him. I knew exactly what my sister was teaching that kid: *manners.*

We drove to our favorite smoothie spot, and as we waited at the drive-through, Octavia gasped and said, "Oh snap! Did you see this?"

"See what?"

"Look." She gave me her phone, and the first thing I saw was an image of Deke in his basketball uniform midair as he released the ball. Then there was an image of a familiar beautiful bronze-looking woman with slightly oversize lips and long, glossy black hair.

Giselle Grace. The picture was split in half to showcase both of them. It was an article.

"Tavia, I don't wanna read this." I handed the phone back to her. Truthfully, I *did* want to read it, but I already felt bad enough about Deke's last email. The last thing I wanted was to be reminded of him.

"Didn't you say you keep in touch with him?" my sister asked, eyeing me.

"Here and there, yeah." I grabbed the smoothies from the employee at the drive-through window. "But I don't need to know about his love life."

I thanked the worker and drove away, glad Octavia had her smoothie and could keep her mouth busy with that.

But of course, when we got home, she blurted out, "Why don't you just fuck him already?"

"Octavia!" I frowned as I dropped my keys and purse on the kitchen countertop.

"What? I'm just asking. If I had direct contact with an NBA player, I'd be getting my fix. You know they're my kryptonite. I usually hate men, but an NBA or NFL player could get it—but only because I know they won't cling to me, you know? They've got other stuff to worry about. Plus, they're consumed with their careers."

"Well, it's not like that with Deke, so I wish you and Tish would stop trying to make nothing into something."

"Okay, look. I get it. You lost Lew, and that was hard. It still *is* hard! I can't imagine what you feel walking into this house every single day and seeing pictures of him at every corner."

I swallowed, trying not to search the walls and shelves for said photos.

"Lew was like a brother to me, and I loved him, but you can't possibly think you'll never be serious with another man again, Vina. Come on. You're thirty-two, not eighty-two."

"I *don't* want to be serious with anyone else, Octavia." I grabbed my strawberry-banana smoothie and finished it off.

"So you don't plan on dating or getting married ever again?" she asked, hand on her hip.

I cocked a brow. "Do you?"

She pointed a stern finger at me. "You don't get to do that! You know I hate dating." She visibly shuddered. "Such a waste of time."

I smirked.

"You can't say you haven't at least thought about it," my sister went on. "At least a quick fuck or a fuck-buddy type of thing."

I tossed my empty smoothie cup into the trash bin. "You know, before he died, Lewis told me I could move on and find love again. He said I deserved to be happy." I looked into my sister's eyes, giving my head a light shake. "But I just don't see how that's possible when he's the one who made me feel that way."

"Aw. Sis." Octavia set her cup down and walked to me. When she wrapped her arms around me, I rested my cheek on her shoulder. "But how will you ever know what else makes you happy if you don't give it a chance?"

"It's too soon."

"Well, why not go back to what I said and just fuck the basketball player? Nothing else has to happen."

I huffed a laugh. "I can tell Deke wants something more than that from me. There's this look in his eye . . . a longing. I don't think I can give him what he's looking for."

"Let me ask you this. Have you fucked anyone since Lew died?"

"Oh my—*what*?" I pulled away from her, flabbergasted. "Why is that your business?"

"I'm just asking!"

I turned away and busied myself with turning on the faucet and washing some of the dirty dishes. There was no way I was about to answer that. The answer was embarrassing, to say the least.

No, I hadn't slept with anyone. The last time Lewis and I did anything was months before he passed, right before his cancer became worse. I hate saying it, but I could hardly remember what that last time with him was like. His head was somewhere else, and he was already losing his confidence.

I had to be honest with myself, though. I *did* miss sex. When Lew was sick, my vibrator was my best friend, but vibrators can only do so much for a woman.

What I really craved was intimacy. I wanted to be owned, pleased, to submit to a man . . . and the thought had crossed my mind that Deke could be the person to dominate me. But having sex with Deke Bishop wouldn't have been right unless that was all it was for him too. Just sex.

Octavia got a FaceTime call from our little brother, Abe, and dropped the conversation, much to my relief. After chatting with Abe, taking a shower, and checking a few work emails, I ventured back to the string of emails I shared with Deke.

His last one really got to me. Every fiber inside me wanted to respond just to let him know he was doing absolutely nothing wrong. He literally was doing everything *right*, but I didn't deserve that. All that time and energy he was investing in me would be for naught, and he needed more than that.

I figured if I stopped emailing and being so personal, then he'd get the point and move on. It'd been three days now, and he hadn't sent any more, so perhaps the message was received.

~

That night, I lay in bed and stared up at the ceiling. I had my vibrator fully charged and grasped in hand, my eyes closed, and memories of my husband on my mind.

I thought about all the good times we shared, all the amazing sex we had before he was diagnosed, his beautiful face and soulful eyes. How deeply connected we felt when he was inside me.

I closed my eyes and moaned as I started the vibrator and placed it between my thighs, clinging to that feeling, but the closer I got to coming, the more his face changed.

His skin became darker, his jawline sharper, and his eyes lowered to calm, downward slits. The hazel shifted to deep brown, and the hairless face was covered in scruff.

I sucked in a breath, scrambling for that image of Lewis again, searching for it behind my eyelids, but it was gone. It'd been replaced by the man I was trying desperately hard to avoid.

I. Was. Imagining. *Deke. Bishop.*

I wanted to stop—to bring this fantasy to an end—but the vibrator felt *too* good, and I was close. *So close.*

I remembered his hand on the small of my back at the party and how badly I'd wanted him to lower that hand to cup my ass. How his warm breath brushed my ear as he lowered himself to my height to murmur the words *Look who's blushing now.*

Oh, yeah. I was done for.

I detonated on the bed, bringing a pillow to my face and crying out my orgasm as I let the vibrator finish me off.

When the climax settled, I moved the pillow away, clicked the vibrator off, and muttered the word *fuck*.

It was clear to me now. Deke was in my head, and having sex with him was *exactly* what my body needed.

TWENTY-NINE

DAVINA

It was a Thursday, and I couldn't concentrate for the life of me.

Not only because of how I let my imagination/fantasy run wild the night prior but also because the picture on my desk, which revealed me and Lewis, was drowning me in guilt.

"Don't look at me like that," I muttered, turning the frame to the left. *Ugh.* I was being so petty and ridiculous about this.

So what? I fantasized about Deke. I was sure many women in the world fantasized about him. And it wasn't like he or anyone else would ever find out. I wasn't going to see him again for several months, and that would be to renew our endorsement contract (if he even wanted to do it). I figured by then, he'd have completely forgotten about our emails and found himself a new lady to flirt with.

There was a knock at the door, and then it rapidly swung open, before I could say anything. "What's up, sis!" Octavia barged in with a black jumpsuit on and a peach-colored bag hanging from her shoulder. "Why are you sulking in here?" she asked, dropping the bag on the coffee table.

"I'm not. I'm fine." I placed my pen down and straightened in my chair. "What are you doing here?"

"Oh, right." She opened the peach bag and dug out a glass container, giving it a little shake. "I made that chopped salad you really like—you know, the one with the cranberries and walnuts."

I gasped. "You didn't!"

"I did, and I made you some double chocolate chip cookies."

"Stop! You know I love your cookies, Tavia!" I really did. Octavia learned to bake when she was twelve. She was really good at it then, but a master at it now. I often teased her about going on one of those Food Network baking competitions. "Remind me again why we did that Pilates class?"

She snorted, handing me a container of salad. I took this moment to sit on the sofa and take a break from work. Maybe after a good meal, I could get my head back into business and stop with all this Deke nonsense.

But of course there were hardly ever any free moments in my life. This one ended when Tish stuck her head through the gap of the door and said, "Chester is on the line."

"You've gotta be kidding me. Tell him I'm having lunch, Tish."

Tish sauntered into the office and grabbed the container of cookies. "I would, but he says it's urgent, and you know how he gets."

Octavia stood and snatched the cookies away from Tish. "I know you aren't thinking about eating these without asking me."

"Octavia, give me a cookie before I fight you in this office," Tish hissed at her, trying to reach for the container. Octavia was reeling her elbow back, so Tish missed every time.

"I will—but only if you agree with me that Brent Faiyaz is better than Frank Ocean." Octavia cocked a brow and smirked.

"Are you still on that?" Tish shifted her eyes toward the ceiling before dropping them to Octavia again. "Okay, fine. Brent is better. Now give me a damn cookie." Tish snatched the container away, and Octavia cackled with glee as she sat back down with her salad.

I thought my relationship with my sister was a hot mess, but Tish and Octavia took the cake. They may as well have been sisters too.

I'd met Tish in community college, both of us weaving through the aisles of the campus bookstore, trying to find the same book. There was only one copy left, and she grabbed it first. That day, we laughed about it and agreed to split the cost of the book. Then we swapped numbers so we could text each other when we needed it. Eventually, our texting led to study sessions and general hanging out. I never looked back after that. She'd become my best friend, and my family had adored her as soon as they'd met her.

"Send the call through, Tish," I said, returning to my desk. I forked through my salad as my best friend walked out. A few seconds later, my desk phone rang.

"Chester! Hi!" I answered with way too much enthusiasm.

"Davina, how's it going? Listen, there's something important I need to ask you."

I refrained from sucking my teeth. It was just like Chester to jump straight into business. The *how's it going* bid was merely to assure himself that he was a nice person who cared about others' well-being. News flash: he didn't care much at all.

Chester Hughes was your typical mega-rich male born from the pipeline of generational wealth. Egotistical, with bucketloads of money and very slim patience. He was nearing sixty, was bald, and had heavy wrinkles around his mouth from all the frowning of disapproval he'd done throughout his life.

"Okay. I'm all ears."

"How do you feel about baby products?" he asked with a hint of rare excitement.

I couldn't avoid the slight dip in my brows. "Baby products?" I glanced at Octavia with a *what the fuck?* look.

"I might have a great opportunity for you that could expand Golden Oil exponentially."

The dip in my brows transformed to a slow incline. Now he was talking. "Go on."

"I'm meeting with Kyla Cox tomorrow. She's the co-owner of Bubbles and Swaddles. They're an up-and-coming Black-owned brand that sells baby products—mostly shampoos and bath soaps. Anyway, her brand is looking to include body creams, lotions, and oils in their line, and they're looking for a larger Black-owned brand to collaborate and distribute with. I was thinking this could be a great opportunity to not only bring the GOC brand more awareness with the quality of your products but to also tap into the market of moms and babies. I'm not sure you're aware of this, but baby and maternity products are an infinite market, Davina. There are new mothers and babies born every second of the day. A collaboration like this is the ticket you need to be making *millions* more."

I worked to swallow as I glanced at Octavia again. She mouthed, *What's he saying?* but I turned away in my chair to let Chester's words sink in.

He was right. Baby and maternity products had an infinite market. Moms—especially first-time moms—spent loads of money on their babies. They wanted to give their offspring the world, so the price tag didn't matter. So long as it made their baby happy, they'd purchase it.

"Davina, you there?"

"Uh, yes." I cleared my throat. "Still here."

"Great. What do you think?" he asked. "You interested?"

"Uh, sure. Yeah. Absolutely. When would I get to meet Kyla?"

"That depends. How soon can you hop on a flight to Miami?"

"That also depends."

"How about tomorrow?"

I gaped. *"Tomorrow?"*

"Yes. This is big, Davina. Kyla's company has received a lot of recognition, and there are many eyes on her. An opportunity like this won't present itself again."

I turned in my chair again, not even realizing Tish had walked back into the office and she and Octavia were staring at me while nibbling on cookies.

"Sure, Chester. I'll be in Miami tomorrow. Just send me the details."

"I knew you'd make the right decision. I'll have Logan send you everything. This is going to be huge. I can feel it."

I placed the phone on the receiver and swung my head to the girls.

"What did he say?" Tish asked.

"He wants me to go to Miami to meet with a company that sells baby soaps. Apparently, they're wanting to branch out and add lotions and creams. He wants us to meet with the co-owner tomorrow to see if we can work out a collaboration deal."

"Damn. Well, that sounds like it might be worth it," my best friend offered.

"Wait . . . so you're going to Miami *tomorrow*?" Octavia asked.

"Looks like it," I said, blowing out a breath. "Tish, do you think you can look at flights for me?"

"Absolutely, babe. I got you."

"Uh, make that a flight for two," Octavia added, throwing up two fingers. "I'm going with her."

Tish glanced at me as she stopped at the door.

"No, Tavia. This is business, not leisure. We won't have time to do whatever it is you're thinking about doing."

"Come on, Vina! I'll behave, I promise!" she pleaded, walking closer to me, with her hands clasped together in prayer mode. "Please! I'm your baby sister. You love me. Take me with you!"

I looked her up and down, and when she realized I wasn't going to buy it, this girl dropped to her knees to milk it. "Pleaseeee."

"Oh my goodness! Okay! Fine," I laughed.

"Yes!"

"Y'all are a trip." Tish chortled on her way out the door.

"You have my word I'll walk a straight line. But once the business part is over with, that's a whole other discussion."

"Tavia," I warned.

She broke out in a laugh as she flopped down on the couch. "I'm just playing, girl!"

THIRTY

DEKE

When Javier had told me he was flying to Miami for a meeting, a part of me had yearned to go, because there were three things I knew I'd encounter that always turned my bad mood around: liquor, nightclubs, and of course, the women.

Yeah, I know I said I didn't want to fool around with another woman unless she was Davina, but that was over with now, so to me, it was free game.

Javier probably wasn't going to do any clubbing, but I had a few dudes who played ball for Miami who I was cool with and could meet with them.

I needed to let loose and forget about Davina. Javier said to be her friend, but she hadn't emailed me back in days. It was clear now. She didn't want to deal with me, so it was whatever. I'd give her space and stop sweating the situation if that's what she wanted.

I watched Javier walk down the steps of the private jet, with Aleesa in his arms. I was surprised he'd brought her with us, but his nanny was newly pregnant, and her morning sickness was kicking her ass. He'd have to look for a new one soon, but in the meantime, his mom would be flying in to help out.

I walked across the tarmac to get to the black SUV waiting for us. The sunlight bathed the back of my head and neck, and it felt good after being on that cold jet.

When I climbed into the SUV, my phone vibrated with a text.

Whitney: I saw that article about you and Giselle. Glad you're done with her. She was mad superficial.

I darkened the screen of my phone again. I wasn't in the mood to even *think* about that fucking article and definitely not about Giselle's snobby ass.

She was the reason it was even floating around. She was telling everyone we weren't seeing each other anymore because I wasn't a good person and that I wasn't romantic. It was a whole bunch of bullshit.

"Deke. Candy?" a little voice said next to me. It sounded more like "Dee. Canny?"

I looked at Aleesa, who was locked into her car seat, with a smile pasted on her face. She had big green eyes and sandy-colored curls. That beautiful three-year-old looked just like her mom. I was sure it pained Javier every day to see the spitting image of his deceased wife in his baby girl.

I cut my eyes to her dad, who was sitting in the passenger seat and giving the driver the designated address; then I dug into the pocket of my jean jacket and took out a pack of jelly beans. I'd brought three packs just for Aleesa.

Our candy affair had started when she was one and I'd had to swindle her with a STARBURST. She literally wouldn't even look at me when I came around, and for a while there, I could've sworn she hated me. I shared that tiny strawberry fruit chew with her, and her entire mood flipped. Suddenly, I was her best friend.

It'd gotten to the point where she started reaching for me whenever I entered a room she was in. Yes, I bribed her with sugar. No, I don't regret it. She was my little road dog now, and believe it or not, I helped Javier out from time to time by babysitting her if I was free.

Aleesa did a little squeal, and I pressed a finger to my lips. She cupped her mouth with one hand as I opened the packet of jelly beans and dropped some into her tiny palm. She couldn't help giggling.

While she did, Javier peered over his shoulder.

"Dee canny, Daddy," she said, already chewing.

Javier turned the soft gaze he had for his daughter to me, transforming it into a full grimace. "Seriously, man?"

I threw my hands in the air. "That's the last pack, I swear."

"You know I do not like her to have candy, Deke. She turns into a little gremlin, running throughout the whole house and jumping off of the walls."

I laughed as Javier faced forward again, then pointed my gaze at Aleesa, who was chewing and smiling at the same time.

"You're gonna make your dad beat my ass," I murmured to her.

"Deke!" Javier shouted.

"What, man?"

"I told you about using bad words around her!"

"Oh, shit. Sorry, Valdez."

"You did it again!" he yelled, and Aleesa giggled louder, getting a real kick out of our exchange.

~

After dropping our bags off at the rental house Javier booked, we went to a high-end water-view restaurant called Wave 47.

The walls were painted black and accented with white vertical and horizontal zigzags. Green plants were threaded throughout the place, wrapping around the columns and clinging to the walls, and the round pendant lights were dim.

The hostess led us straight to the back, where she slid a curtain aside to reveal a private dining area with windows overlooking an endless ocean.

A woman with sable skin, black bangs, and a white pantsuit was already seated at the table. I assumed she was Kyla, the owner of the baby products company Javier had mentioned.

"Javier Valdez!" Kyla stood and rushed to him, her hand already stuck out for him to shake. "I'm so glad you could make it. This means so much to me to have you here."

"Well, I am just happy to be here," Javier said with hardly any enthusiasm.

I kept telling him he needed to work on his people skills. With that tone, he sounded like he'd have rather been anywhere else than at the restaurant. I knew that wasn't the case, though. For a few weeks now, he'd been talking about this meeting and how good Kyla's products were for Aleesa's skin and hair.

"And is this little Aleesa?" Kyla cooed, her eyes melting into puddles as she focused on the little girl in Javier's arms. Aleesa rested her head on his shoulder with a shy smile. "Oh, she's so beautiful, Mr. Valdez."

"Yes, she is," he said, nodding in agreement. "And please, call me Javier."

"Javier it is." Kyla turned my way, pointing a knowing finger at me. "And you are the one and only Deke Bishop. How great it is to be in your presence."

I took the hand she offered and shook it. "Nice to meet you, Kyla. Hope you don't mind my presence. I'm just here to help out."

"Well, that's wonderful and kind of you," she said. "Please, let's have a seat. Javier, I mentioned to you that we have a few more people that will be joining us for lunch. I spoke to a potential collaborator on the phone last night and have really high hopes about this."

"Yes. That is okay."

Not long after settling into our seats, a familiar pasty man in a tailored suit walked in, and Kyla sprung right up to greet him like she had with us.

"Chester! Hi!" she sang. "It's so great to see you again!"

Chester gave her a closed-lip smile. "Pleasure's mine, Kyla."

The name Chester sounded familiar. There weren't any Chesters in my world, but I was almost positive that name was mentioned somewhere recently.

Just as the thought occurred, a curvy silhouette near the sliding curtain appeared in the corner of my eye. My heart dropped a notch when I saw who it was.

The drop wasn't in a bad way. No, this was one I could recover from, like being on a roller coaster and reaching that adrenaline peak, only to hit a rapid descent and be brought back to level ground. It throttled me but also made me feel alive.

There she was. The woman I couldn't get out of my damn mind. The woman who'd been ignoring my emails. The woman who looked sexy as fuck in a powder-blue dress, her hair in a curly afro and her almond skin bright and flawless, with full, glossed lips I wanted to do so many things to.

Davina.

I picked up my water and took a much-needed swallow.

When Davina caught me in the room, she stopped dead in her tracks, and her eyes widened like saucers. She'd been calm and collected when she first entered, but at the mere sight of me, she was flushed, her throat bobbing and her lips parting as she searched for words.

After lowering my glass, I smirked and said, "You're blushing, D."

THIRTY-ONE

DAVINA

This could *not* be happening.

Out of all the places in the world, Deke was right here in the heart of Miami and in the same restaurant I was in. I should've known. *I should've known!*

Chester said Javier Valdez would be joining us for lunch, and I'd read up on Deke enough to know Javier was one of his closest friends and teammates. I didn't think they'd be together, though! Out of all the places he could've been, he was *here*. I swear God was trying to punish me for something. Didn't Deke have some event to go to, or an offseason game to play?

I ignored Deke, who remained seated while I shook hands with Kyla Cox. After greeting Chester, I drew in a breath and sat next to Octavia, who was sitting across from Deke. That left me to sit diagonally across from him. I'd have traded spots with Javier, but his daughter, Aleesa, was at the head of the table.

Everyone knew that adorable three-year-old. She was the sweet little girl who giddily cheered for her dad from the sidelines. Other than on the court, you'd never catch Javier Valdez without his daughter.

I cleared my throat, then picked up the full cup of cool water in front of me to take a few gulps.

Octavia bumped me with her elbow. "What is wrong with you? Just say hi."

I peered around the table, after Kyla took the seat directly across from Javier. Chester sat across from me, and Deke was to his right. I inhaled, setting my glass back down and finally giving Deke my full attention.

That was a mistake.

He was already looking at me as he leaned casually against the back of his seat, with his arms folded over his chest. His hooded eyes traveled from my mouth to my bosom, then slowly dragged up to my eyes again.

His freshly cut hair was lined up neatly, the dark waves glistening beneath the pendant lights. His gold chain may as well have blinded me with how thick and shiny it was. He wore a blue jean jacket, with the sleeves rolled up, over a solid black T-shirt and black pants. A gold watch was on one wrist and a bracelet to match on the other. I studied the sleeves of dark ink on his forearms, all of various designs, and those bulging veins that were like arm porn.

Good Lord, he looked good. *Too* damn good.

"Uh." I cleared my throat. "How have you been, Deke?"

"Wouldn't you want to know that via email, Davina?" He raised a brow, mouth twitching. The waitress appeared and took his order first, and I was glad for the distraction, but as soon as she left, his eyes were locked on me again.

"Davina's company makes some of the best body butters. All the ingredients are organic. Right, Davina?" Chester asked.

I whipped my head to look at my investor and nodded. "That's right."

"I just love that," Kyla said. "And Javier, I want you to know that I always source the best ingredients possible. Little Aleesa here already loves our bubble bath, right?"

Javier nodded. "She does."

"So, imagine a whole collection created for a bath-and-bedtime routine, with your name featured on it. I know you don't want her advertised too much, and I completely respect that, so I talked to my publicist about your concerns, and she had some really great ideas. One of them was to take pictures or footage of you and Aleesa but with her back to the camera the entire time. We could hide her face, which we think would draw more interest to the consumers."

"Well, the whole world has seen her face, so I don't think that really matters," Javier said, huffing a laugh. He shifted in his chair, glancing at Aleesa, who was watching something on an iPad in a purple case.

"Oh—um, yes. That is true." Kyla put on a smile, but there was unease swirling in her eyes. It was clear she was thinking of something else to say.

Kyla was new to this world, and though she seemed to be confident right now, I could tell when I shook her hand that her nerves were fried. I remembered being just like her when I first started, thinking I was a fraud, thinking I wasn't worthy as a Black woman in a world as daring as this one. I couldn't let her drown.

"Javier, I think what Kyla is trying to say is Aleesa would be safe. You two will be our top priority throughout whatever the process is. It can be daunting to have your child advertised on screen and especially online. I get it. You don't want the publicity to go sideways or for it to become overwhelming for either of you. It's one thing for people to see her and be in awe on the courtside, but it's a completely different thing when her image would be put directly in people's faces. But you love Bubbles and Swaddles products, right? And you love Kyla's cause?"

"I do," Javier agreed.

"I say start small." I gestured to Kyla. "Right, Kyla?"

"Yes, absolutely," she said, bobbing her head rapidly.

"I, for one, am very excited to be collaborating with Kyla, and if you ask Deke, here, I think he would agree we had a great time working together on our collaboration too." Though I didn't want to, I shifted my gaze to the other basketball player at the table, who snorted a laugh into his drink.

"Wait . . . you two have worked together?" Javier asked, looking between us with narrowed eyes.

"Oh, yeah, man," Deke answered before I could. "She's the woman who endorsed me for her skin care company. It's been great working with her and being *just friends* and all."

Okay. *Seriously?*

"Oop." Octavia pulled her lips in and looked anywhere but at me, while I glared a hole into the side of her head. As my sister, she was *not* supposed to instigate this.

"I see," Javier said, shifting his eyes between us as if he was connecting a few dots.

"Anyway, I think this'll be great, Javier," I went on, returning my attention to the Argentinean player. "And I do agree with Kyla about the pictures and footage. Perhaps we can start with Aleesa's facial profile or show images of just her eyebrows and up when it comes to the shampoo. You'd be more of the highlight, and I'm sure you're aware of this already, but women *love* when they see a father caring for his kids in ads. The women are already celebrating you for being such a great father and putting her first. This could further that image, if it's something you'd like to pursue. All I know is that regardless of what you decide, there will be no loss for you and your baby girl."

"So, you're officially on board then, Davina?" Chester asked. He may as well have had dollar signs in place of his eyeballs.

I smiled at him, then looked at Kyla. "I am."

Chester clasped his hands together.

Kyla let out a sigh of relief. "That is so great to hear, Davina. Thank you. And Javier, I'm willing to do *whatever* it takes to champion you and Aleesa. I'm all about loyalty, trust me."

Javier tipped his head with a bit more positivity.

"I'm glad *someone* around here is," Deke muttered.

I frowned at him, and of course, Octavia was trying her hardest not to snigger. Our waitress appeared with the appetizers, and while everyone was focused on their food, I drew in a breath to compose myself.

This was only the start for Deke. He was *not* happy with me, and he was going to use every single minute of this lunch to make sure I was completely aware of it.

THIRTY-TWO

DEKE

Not much could shock me in today's world, but the fact that Davina could sit diagonally across from me at the table and hardly look at me was one hell of a surprise.

She held a good poker face, I could give her that, and when it came to business, she didn't let feelings interfere with it. I respected that. But as a man who wanted only a slice of her attention, I found that this bugged the hell out of me.

I wasn't going to ruin her day any further, though, and to be honest, I was starting to feel bad for being a dick to her. Making it awkward wasn't helping a damn thing, and this was a big moment for not only Davina but Javier and Aleesa too.

Apparently Davina was going to make a new baby cream and lotion exclusively for Javier and Aleesa's collaboration. The last thing I wanted to do was ruin this deal for my best friend, so I discontinued my jabs at Davina.

Plus, Javier shot me a text and told me to *shut the fuck up and be cool.*

When lunch was wrapped up and the waitress handed Chester the bill, he dug into his pocket and said, "I'll be having a little get-together at my condo tonight around eight. I'll have a few friends over just to catch up and have a few drinks. You should all come."

"I'd love to," Kyla said much too eagerly.

"I wish that I could," Javier said, "but that is after Aleesa's bedtime."

"Oh, I understand."

"I'll come," I offered.

Chester turned his eyes to me with a look of surprise. "Will you really?"

"Sure." I raised a shoulder. "Why not?"

"Hey, I'd love to have you. I have to warn you, though, my friends might crowd you a bit," Chester responded with a snicker.

"I'm used to it." I turned my gaze to Davina. "You should come, too, Davina."

Davina lowered her phone to glare at me. "I can't, actually."

"Why not?" I fought a smile as I tipped my head sideways.

"I have a lot of work to catch up on, and I have an early flight tomorrow."

"Oh, come on, Davina!" Chester boomed with a pompous laugh. "You can swing by for a few minutes, chat with some friends of mine. A few of them also invest, so it'd be a great way to network."

She pulled her lips in and pressed them together, looking from Chester to me again. This time, I allowed the smile to take over me as she narrowed her eyes briefly before focusing on Chester again.

"Uh, sure. I'll swing by for a bit." She forced a smile at him, and Chester nodded, proud of himself.

Meanwhile, I tried my hardest not to laugh.

~

When we left the restaurant, I spotted Davina standing with her sister near the curb.

Javier was already at the SUV, buckling Aleesa into her car seat. I strolled over to Davina, who noticed me coming and gave me her back.

"Glad you'll make it to Chester's," I said.

"How far away is the Lyft, Tavia?" she asked her sister, ignoring me.

"Four minutes," Octavia announced.

"'Ey, Deke!" Javier called as he shut the back door. He gestured for me to come on. I held up a finger before putting my attention on Davina again.

Her sister grinned as she looked between us. Then she said, "You know what? I'm gonna introduce myself to Javier again. I'm a nanny . . . maybe he'll be interested."

"Octavia, no. Why would you—" Davina clamped her mouth shut as her sister sauntered across the parking lot to meet with my teammate. Davina inhaled deeply before exhaling, with her eyes shut.

"So you're not going to talk to me?" I asked, taking a step closer.

"I did talk to you," she countered.

"I'd say you talked *at* me, not *to* me."

She dropped her arms to finally face me. "Deke, you shouldn't take the email thing personally, okay?"

"Why shouldn't I? The emails *were* personal. I thought we were cool, D."

"We are cool."

I heard giggling and looked to find it. Aleesa's window was rolled down, and Octavia was talking to her while lightly squeezing her chin. Javier stood close by, looking between them with his arms crossed.

"Look . . . just come to Chester's, all right? We can talk it out there, and we'll be honest. Okay? No bullshit."

Davina swung her head my way. Her shoulders lost a bit of the edge as she sighed. Then she took a step back and faced forward again. "Fine."

"Cool." I stepped off the curb and headed for the SUV. "See you at the party."

As I walked, I tried my hardest not to look back at her. I didn't want her thinking I was desperate or anything. I was surprised I stuck it out as I rounded the truck.

When I climbed inside, I heard Javier ask Octavia, "And how many years of experience do you actually have?"

"I've been a caretaker for many years. My brother has special needs, so I take care of him a lot, but I got into nannying and babysitting five years ago."

"Hmm. Well, I will have to look into it. Email your information to me anyway. Where is your phone?"

She dug it out of her back pocket, and once it was unlocked, Javier took it and typed something on it. When he handed it back, he gave her an agitated once-over before turning away and climbing into the SUV.

Octavia made a face like she was slightly annoyed with Javier's demands and bluntness. She'd learn Javier was a very direct person and that the angry faces were nothing to take personally.

The SUV rolled away with us inside, and through Aleesa's open window, I gave in to my urge and fixed my gaze on Davina.

She looked at me, eyes soft and sparkling, before tearing them away just as quickly.

THIRTY-THREE

DAVINA

The last place I wanted to be was at Chester's.

It was enough having to deal with him for work and lunch during meetings with people like Kyla—not that I had a problem with Kyla. I liked her so far—but to put it simply, Chester was the kind of person you only spent time around for money's sake. Not for fun.

I'd planned on spending the rest of the night reading for a little bit or watching TV while I sifted through emails, but that'd been pushed to the side, thanks to Deke. He knew exactly what he was doing, and I was not pleased that it worked.

Of course, my sister was excited to go. She looked up the address for Chester's condo, and it was the definition of luxury, with its water views, its glass balconies, and a whole restaurant and bar on the main floor.

"I'm about to add every single moment of this night to my stories," she said as we pulled up to the towering building in an Uber. "It's so nice having a rich sister."

I scoffed. "I am not rich."

When the car came to a complete stop, we climbed out, and I braced myself for the night ahead. Once we were checked in with the doorman, we took the glass elevator up. Octavia held her phone up in the air to record a video of herself in the transparent box.

"You weren't joking about adding every single moment, were you?"

"Uh, no. All my followers are about to know I'm *that* girl," she said, tapping away at her screen. I laughed.

The elevator opened with a soft chime and welcomed us to the penthouse floor. I could hear music playing from a distance and spotted Chester's room number at the end of the hallway.

"We aren't gonna be here all night, okay?" I fixed my dress, a black bodycon with thick spaghetti straps. The dress was Octavia's, and it was riding up my damn legs. I forgot Octavia liked her clothes a little risqué.

Other than the dress I'd worn to lunch, I had no other cute outfits to go out in, and something told me showing up to a party at Chester's required a fresher fit. All that was left in my suitcase was a set of pajamas and a comfy jumpsuit that I was saving for my flight back to Charlotte.

"Okay, but if this is an open bar type of situation, let's at least stay for an hour and take advantage of it." Octavia finger-combed her locs as she peered at her phone screen, with the front camera open.

"We'll see." I gave the door a knock, and it was answered in a matter of seconds. A woman appeared, older, with pale skin. Her hair was mousy brown and stringy, and she had fine lines around her mouth.

"Hi! Davina, right?" she asked.

I threw my hand up. "That's me."

"Come in, come in!" the woman insisted, gesturing for us to hurry inside.

We walked into a spacious, dimly lit condo. Jazz music poured from hidden speakers, and there were at least twenty or so people here, with drinks in hand, mingling or laughing. "Chester has told me all about you! I'm his wife, Caroline."

"Nice to meet you, Caroline." I gave her hand a shake while trying to remember a time Chester mentioned having a wife. He didn't wear a wedding band . . . then again, when I looked at her hands, I noticed she wasn't wearing one either.

"Follow me. I'll show you to him." Caroline was already walking across the room, and I trailed behind her in my heels.

She stepped through two french doors that revealed a glass balcony with a skyline view of buildings peppered in gold lighting. Chester was outside, chatting with a tan man with bright-green eyes. I started to smile when I saw my investor, but as I stepped farther out, that's when I caught Deke on the other side of him.

Shit. I was really hoping he wouldn't show. He had better places to be. Why would a man as lively as him voluntarily come to a party full of old bores?

"Chester, honey! Davina's here!" Caroline sang, and when she did, Deke's head swung to find me.

I forced a smile, avoiding Deke's searing gaze while giving Chester a quick hug.

"Glad you're here, Davina. Please, help yourself to the hors d'oeuvres and drinks. We have two bars set up, and drinks are on the house."

"This is why I love rich people," Octavia murmured. "Be right back." She left the balcony to find the nearest bar.

Chester introduced me to the tan man next to him, but once that was over, they returned to their conversation from before.

I tried not to look but couldn't help myself when my eyes connected with Deke's.

"You look good," he said, stepping closer. A drink with ice in a short glass tumbler was in his hand. His silky gray shirt was paired with dark-wash jeans and a pair of designer loafers. Two chains hung from his neck, one thick and one slim, and his diamond earrings glinted beneath the dim lights. He smelled just like he did the first time we met.

"You look good too," I said, doing my best to keep my heart from racing. Impossible. My heart always sped up around him. He made me so damn nervous, which was crazy, because I had no reason to be.

Deke finally took his eyes off me to gesture inside. "Want a drink?"

I nodded. "Was just about to grab one."

I entered the condo, with Deke close behind me—so close I could feel the heat of his body on my backside. I made a beeline for the bar where Octavia had ordered herself a cocktail. It was a signature drink for the night, called the Hey, Miami. I found it on the short menu and ordered one for myself.

Octavia moved away from the bar but only to stand next to Deke. He turned a fraction to face her, a slow smile materializing.

"Octavia, right?" he asked.

She provided a little curtsy. "That's me."

I collected my drink, when it was ready, and stood next to her.

"What's up with your friend Javier? Is he always an asshole?" she probed.

"When it comes to looking out for his daughter, yeah," Deke answered with a chuckle. "Why? What'd he say?"

"I was giving Aleesa a little tickle, and he was all 'Oh, do not tickle her right now. She is very tired and needs a nap.'" Octavia frowned while taking a sip of her drink. "He's a helicopter parent. Those are the worst."

"Are they?" a voice asked behind us. Octavia whirled around, only to find Javier standing a few steps away with Aleesa in his arms.

"Oh—Javier! Hey!" Octavia chimed, but he wasn't having it. He looked my sister up and down in her beige jumper and heels with a deep frown.

"Aleesa could not sleep. Probably because she had way too much *candy* today." He shot a pointed look at Deke, who twisted his lips like he was innocent. "So I figured I would bring her to the party tonight to burn some energy and so she can get to know you a little more. Chester said it was okay to bring her, so I figured it could not hurt. But since I am the worst and too much of a helicopter, as you put it, maybe this was the wrong decision."

"Oop," I quipped, then hid a smile behind my drink.

Octavia hit me with her elbow and caused some of my drink to spill. "I didn't mean it like that, Javier. I just meant—I mean, I get why you're so protective of her." Octavia looked from me to Deke, searching for an out.

Deke provided one by capping Javier's shoulder and saying, "She didn't mean it like that. But you gotta admit, you *are* an asshole sometimes, man."

Javier didn't smile, but his shoulders did drop a notch. He returned his attention to Octavia, then lifted a mini pink backpack, offering it to her. "Let's see if you can do better."

Octavia's eyes widened, and she immediately set down her drink and took the backpack, sliding it onto her shoulder.

Javier placed Aleesa on her feet, and Octavia smiled as she lowered to one knee. "You wanna go see the city lights?" my sister asked.

"Lice! Yes!" Aleesa clapped her hands.

"Yeah? Come on." Octavia scooped Aleesa up and headed for the balcony. Javier followed right after.

"You might want to tell your sister that working for Javier will be the worst decision of her life." Deke laughed, standing next to me.

"Meh." I shrugged. "I think she can handle him."

"Good luck to her, then." Deke's body moved a bit, and he stood so close to me I could feel the heat of it again. "Will you walk with me? I wanna show you something."

THIRTY-FOUR

DAVINA

I followed Deke out of Chester's condo, and he led the way to the elevators.

"Where are you going?" I asked, glancing back at the door before looking at him.

"You'll see." The elevator chimed, the doors parted, and Deke disappeared inside.

After shooting off a quick text to my sister to let her know I would be back, I rounded the corner to get into the elevator with him. Deke pressed the button to go up, and when the doors pulled together, I drew in a breath, realizing we were alone. *Again.*

He shifted closer to me, and the back of his hand brushed mine. It was the faintest feeling, yet it sent goose bumps up my arms. I cleared my throat, relieved that the elevator had stopped to let us off.

Deke stepped out first, pushed a door open, and led the way outside. My heels clicked on the cement as I followed his lead, and suddenly he was bathed in blue light.

We were on the rooftop, where a turquoise pool radiated its light on every surface. White lounge chairs were lined neatly around it, with buttoned gray-and-white umbrellas between them. Three canopied cabanas were on the opposite side of the pool, along with a vacant bar only steps away.

Deke drained his drink and set the glass down on a nearby table before walking toward the canopies. I brought my drink close to my chest, taking careful steps after him.

I watched as he pushed one of the curtains of the canopy away to reveal a cushioned bed inside. When he pinned the curtain back, he asked, "Wanna sit?"

I fought a smile, finished my drink, set the glass down, then kicked out of my heels. I sat on the edge of the canopy bed, letting my feet rest on the step below. Deke followed suit and kicked out of his shoes before sitting next to me.

He tipped his chin, looking toward the gold-lit skyscrapers and the dark, endless ocean ahead. Chester's condo was in the heart of the city. I heard cars driving on the street below and the ocean roaring in the distance. Paired with the drink I had, the sounds were a soothing combination.

"This is nice," I sighed.

"Yeah?" He glanced at me. "Figured you'd like it."

"I do. But I'm still mad at you for setting me up to come here in the first place," I told him, fighting a grin.

He released a belly-deep laugh, then ran his tongue over his bottom lip. "How else was I going to see you again?"

I faltered when his eyes fell to my lips before slowly dragging back up to connect with mine. "You'd have seen me again one day," I managed to say. "We work together, remember?"

"Yeah, well, tonight feels better. One day could've been months from now." He faced forward again, the skin around his eyes softening. "So be real with me, D. Why did sending my number make you wanna stop talking to me?"

I swallowed and lowered my line of vision to the ground. "I told you. I got really busy with work." The lie slipped straight through my teeth.

As if he sensed that lie, he said, "I don't believe you."

"Why not? You aren't the only person with a crazy schedule, Deke." I dared myself to look up at him, and his face was serious. The rippling waters reflected off his warm eyes like jewels, and my breath caught a bit. His jawline was defined beneath the scruff, his lips supple and freshly damp from his tongue.

"No bullshit, remember?" His voice was lower, breathier.

I dropped my head again, staring at my hands now. I rubbed the wedding band and the cushion-cut ring that still occupied my finger.

"Okay. You're right. No bullshit."

He sat up taller, waiting for me to speak again.

"It's just . . . I was talking to Tish, and she mentioned a few things about how you treat me and the attention you've shown me recently, and I tried to think nothing of it, because I was okay with us being friends and staying in touch. But then you sent your number, and to me, that felt like a step above friends, if that makes sense. Because we would've been talking even more, and texts would've transitioned to calls, and I don't want you having the wrong idea, Deke. I mean, I *really* like talking to you. You're a great human with a great heart, and any woman would *kill* to have that, but I don't want you pouring all your attention into a woman who is in fucking shambles. It'd be a waste of your time, and you deserve better than to be someone else's leftovers." I paused. "Plus, I'm not looking to be with anyone else right now . . . in a serious way. I just don't think it would be a smart move for me."

He looked me up and down. "You call wearing this little black dress and the one you had on at lunch being in shambles?" he asked, completely disregarding my last statement.

I bubbled out a laugh and playfully slapped his arm. "Stop doing that."

He threw his hands in the air. "Doing what?"

"Deflecting and being so damn charming."

"Ah. So you think I'm charming? That's gotta count for something, right?"

I fought a smile as I took a sweep of the rooftop again. "How did you even know this pool was up here?"

"Every rich White man like Chester has a rooftop pool in a seaside condo they own. Plus, I looked up the address before we got here. Saw it on the website."

I threw my head back to laugh at that. "You sound like my sister. She was so excited to come here just to capture everything on her Insta stories."

"Shit, can't say I blame her? It's a nice place. Not really my style, though."

"What *is* your style?"

"Something more low key and chill. I have a penthouse in Atlanta. I'm hardly ever bothered there. You should see it sometime. My room-mate would love you."

"You have a roommate?" I asked, avoiding a frown. This was news to me. Was he talking about Giselle? I mean, not that it mattered . . . but I was curious.

"Yeah. His name's Zeke, and he looks serious as hell at first glance, but he's goofy and playful. He also has four paws and is a Doberman."

"Oh my goodness, Deke! You are *so* corny!" I laughed, and he chuckled.

When silence fell between us again, it was welcoming. Comforting.

He was sitting close to me, his hand resting on the edge of the canopy where mine was. One lift of my pinkie, and I would be touching him.

What was it about him that made me want to touch him? I couldn't figure it out, but it wasn't good to want so much from someone I didn't want to get serious with.

I ignored the thought just as Deke sighed. His head was down, and he was staring at the ground.

"What's wrong?" I asked.

His head tilted enough for his eyes to connect with mine. "You want the truth?"

A smile tugged at my lips. "Always."

He turned toward me so that his knee was touching mine. I glanced down at where we were touching before dragging my eyes up to his.

"Well, truth is being just friends with you is killing me slowly." His eyes fell to my lips, and I froze a little.

"Why?" I dared myself to ask. I shouldn't have asked. This was testing the limits and going against all the things I told him I *didn't* want.

"Because from the moment I met you, I wanted you, D. And wanting someone has never felt so complicated."

"I told you I'm in shambles," I whispered as his mouth moved closer to mine. "I'm so broken, Deke. You don't need that."

"You think you're the only one here who's broken?" he rasped, and I instantly thought of his brother, the post I found on Facebook by his mom. "You say you're in shambles, but that can be fixed."

He was closer now, his lips only a hair's breadth away. My heart pounded when he slid a warm hand over my thigh. The frozen parts of me unthawed. My heart pumped faster. His hand was smooth, and he carried it up my hip. My breath hitched as the tip of his nose touched mine.

"But my shambles are like glass," I whispered.

"That so?" His mouth was right there, the heat of his breath spilling down my chest. His large hand—the same one that palmed basketballs for a living and shot perfect three-pointers—went beneath the hem of my dress and cupped my hip.

"Yes," I breathed.

"Well, for you, I don't mind getting cut a few times."

He inched his face closer. At this point, I could feel those lips— that, or I imagined I was feeling them.

"Can I kiss you now?" he murmured on my mouth.

I nodded way too quickly for my own good, and he gripped my hip tighter. As soon as his lips came down on mine, my whole body charged to life. My heart pounded faster, and a moan filled my throat as he laid me back on the canopy bed to shove my dress higher up my thigh.

He was between my legs in a millisecond, claiming my lips and kissing me so deeply I spiraled. I got lost beneath the solid weight of his body, the scent of his skin and cologne, and when he coaxed my mouth open with his tongue, I felt a clench between my thighs. He tasted like whiskey and citrus. He tasted *good*.

A deep groan rattled in Deke's throat as his tongue played with mine. Then he hissed through his teeth after breaking the kiss and looked me in the eyes.

"You good?" he breathed. I was nodding before he'd even asked the whole question. It'd been too long since I was kissed or touched like this. Too long since I'd been *dominated* by a man who exuded nothing but masculine energy.

Deke came back down for more, slipping his tongue between my lips and eliciting another moan from me. He pushed the hem of my dress farther up to reveal my panties, then glanced down at them. They were black with a white lace trim.

"Fuck," he rumbled as he pressed himself deeper into me. He was rock hard already, thrusting himself against me. Every shift of his hips caused the friction to build and made me ache.

I circled my arms around the back of his neck and let him lay kisses on the hollow of my throat. He sucked on the soft flesh at the bend of my neck, then said, "I wanna fuck you so bad right now, Davina," as he pressed the ridge of his dick harder on me. He ground his hips up and down, groaning as he carried his mouth back up to mine and claimed my lips.

This moment was overwhelming in the best way possible. I could feel Deke *everywhere*—the heat of his breath caressing my cheek when our lips parted, the softness of his full lips as they covered mine. His hips kept grinding so the bulge of his dick could rub against my clit, and I swear I was about to come from the friction alone.

I hated that his jeans and my panties were in the way but was also glad, because if they weren't, we'd have been fucking like horny teenagers on this canopy.

Just when I felt I was about to roll into an orgasm, Deke snatched his lips away and murmured, "Stay just like that."

He climbed down my body until his face was between my legs, then he tucked a finger beneath my panties to tug at one side of them.

It was that action alone that made me freeze. But when he said, "I need to taste you," I sat up.

"Wait," I breathed, pushing his hand away from my panties.

"What?" he said just as breathily. His eyes swiveled up to mine, glossy and confused as he pulled his hand away. "What's up?"

"I, um . . . I haven't done any upkeep down *there* in a while." Three whole weeks to be exact. I used to get a full bikini wax every month, back when Lew was healthy and our sex life was thriving, but lately I'd been resorting to shaving to make ends meet, and I hadn't even done that. I didn't need to, really. Who was I shaving for? No one was going to see what was down there, whether it was bare or a full-blown bush.

But now, someone *was* going to see, and that someone just so happened to be one of the most famous basketball players in the world. That didn't feel right. If I were to ever do *anything* sexual with Deke Bishop, I needed to be ready for it in all ways.

Deke still appeared confused as he looked from my eyes to my panties. "What are you talking about?"

"I haven't shaved or waxed in a while," I finally said. "I've just been so busy with work, and I mean, I've been keeping to myself really, so there was no need to—"

"Wait, wait." Deke huffed a laugh as he briefly closed his eyes to let it all register. When he opened them again, he asked, "Do you *really* think I care about that, D?"

I blinked down at him, unsure what to say.

"Let me put it to you this way," he said, hooking that same finger beneath my panties again. He tugged one side down, and I sank my teeth into my bottom lip as he used that same finger to do the other. "I've wanted to taste you from the moment I walked into your office and saw you in those tight peach pants." He dragged my panties down and removed them with so much ease I was positive he'd performed this action many, many times before. "And I promise you, not a single hair on your body is gonna stop me from eating this pussy."

I shuddered a breath as he spread my legs farther apart and settled his head between them. He peered up at me with hungry, heated eyes, then dragged his tongue over his full lips.

"Now make me a happy man right now, and feed me."

THIRTY-FIVE

DEKE

This moment with Davina was a motherfucking *dream*.

Here she was—this woman I'd been wanting for months, lying right here with her pussy in my face and her hand on top of my head.

She smelled good, vanilla perfume mixing with her natural feminine scent. She was worried about some hair, but that didn't bother me a damn bit.

Who was she kidding? I wanted to bury my tongue in her pussy and *consume* this girl, but I urged myself to do it slowly.

I had to take my time with her and truly satisfy my craving, so I slid my tongue through her other set of lips and pressed in until I found her clit. She pushed out a heavy breath as I gave it a slow, torturous swirl with my tongue. *Fuck.* I knew she'd taste good.

"Oh . . . Deke. Oh my—" She panted as her fingernails dragged over my head. I groaned as I licked, giving her pussy french kisses and then suckling on her sweet spot. All of it riled her up to the point she was breathlessly moaning, and her back arched when I slid my tongue *inside* her. I let my tongue fuck her briefly before gliding it back up to the sweet spot that would eventually make her unravel.

"I see you like having your pussy eaten," I rumbled between licks, and she moaned louder, clutching my head with both her hands.

Oh, I really see now.

She liked being talked to while being eaten. I could roll with that.

"You like how it feels, Davina?" I groaned, kissing her clit. "How I slip my tongue inside your wet pussy?"

"Oh my God," she gasped, trying to shove my face deeper.

"I need you to tell me, baby. Talk to me."

"Yes," she panted. "Yes, I like it."

"Is this what you wanted from me?"

"Yes, Deke. *Yes.*"

"You're so fucking sexy." I flattened my tongue and rolled it over that sweet spot I knew would make her come.

My dick was throbbing at this point, and I was dying to fuck her. As badly as I wanted that, though, I wanted to watch her come apart with my mouth even more.

I kept my tongue on her swollen clit and pushed up just enough to slide my fingers inside her slick entrance. I curled the tips of my fingers, and she breathed faster, bucking her hips on my mouth.

She ground her pussy on my face, pressing her palms to the back of my head to guide me deeper. Damn, she was wild. I loved it.

She was hungry for it and desperate to come, and as I lapped my tongue around her clit, then flicked it rapidly with my tongue, she belted out my name. It sounded so sweet coming out of her mouth, and what made it sweeter was the reason *why* she was saying it.

"Oh my goodness," she whimpered, bucking when I finally pulled my mouth and fingers away. I lay a kiss on her pelvis, then placed one on both sides of her lips. She had a pretty pussy, pink like a rose inside.

I sat up on my knees, and my dick felt heavier than ever. It'd been too long since my last fuck, and that was *only* because the woman I wanted was right in front of me. No other person would do. I was waiting for Davina, and waiting was damn near killing me.

I wanted to unzip my pants, pull my dick out, and thrust inside her until she came again, but based on how she was lying there in a daze, that probably wouldn't have been the right move to make. Plus, if I did it hastily, I would come in a matter of seconds.

If I was going to fuck this girl, it had to be done right, and it had to be someplace better than a canopy on a rooftop.

"You good?" I asked, huffing a laugh.

She sucked in a breath and sat up to eye me. "You're, um . . . you're *really* good at doing that."

I smirked. "I'll take that as a compliment."

Her eyes darted past me, and if I wasn't mistaken, her eyes were glistening like she was on the verge of tears. Her throat bobbed, and she moved past me to climb off the canopy and search for her panties.

"I, um . . . I should go," she said hurriedly, scanning the ground.

I frowned, climbing off too. I found her panties near one of the potted plants nearby and handed them to her. She pressed her lips to smile and took them but still wouldn't look me in the eye.

"You don't have to go, D," I told her.

"Yeah." She slipped into her panties. "I think I do." She tugged on the hem of her dress to adjust herself, then hurried across the roof to snatch up her heels.

"Wait—D!" A humorless laugh escaped me this time as she rushed to the door and gripped the handle. She couldn't be serious. What was happening? What did I do wrong? "If that was too much, I'm sorry. I thought that was what you wanted—"

"Don't apologize," she said, holding a hand up. "I *did* want it."

I shifted on my feet, confused as hell. "So why are you running away?"

Her head shook as she bit into her bottom lip.

I took a step toward her, losing my smile and all the hope that'd bloomed in my chest. I thought she liked what we did. I thought she was opening up to me and embracing this thing between us for once, but the contemplation in her eyes spoke otherwise.

"What are you so afraid of, Davina?"

At that, her eyes snapped to mine. She stared at me for so long it felt like she was looking through me.

Then she swung the door open, dropped her eyes, and said, "*Everything*, Deke. Everything between us scares the shit out of me."

She scurried inside, and when the door slammed behind her, my chest tightened with both longing and frustration. Not frustration with her, but with myself.

"It was too soon," I muttered, slumping down in a chair. "Too fucking soon, Deke."

THIRTY-SIX

DAVINA

The night after I returned from Miami, I chose to burn the midnight oil. I tried distracting myself with work, but all I could think about was what'd happened with Deke on that rooftop.

What the hell was I even thinking? It never should've gotten that far. But he was so close and *so damn sexy*, and having the privacy of that moment made me lose all morals.

The worst part of it all was that I *wanted* more. I wanted so much more. I had no idea he was so good with his tongue, and maybe I'd been long overdue to release an orgasm with a male counterpart, but when I say that I *shattered*, I fucking shattered.

I couldn't remember the last time I'd come so hard and so fast. I mean, sure, Lew was decent at oral, but my late husband didn't even come close to Deke. Lew never talked to me like that. He never spoke to my body with so much carnal *hunger*, and he'd never been able to make me come in a matter of seconds like Deke had.

Groaning, I pressed a hand to my forehead and shut my eyes. *Here I go again, comparing him to Lew.* Deke and Lewis were two completely different men. I had to stop doing that.

I closed my laptop and left my desk to find my phone on the kitchen counter. A part of me was hoping to find a notification waiting, preferably an email. I missed the emails that would appear from Deke when I happened to check my phone. I missed a lot of things when it came to him, and it was an unexpected feeling.

A loud snore filled the room, and my eyes flickered up to Octavia, sprawled out on the couch with her eyes closed and her mouth half-open. Her black satin bonnet had slipped off one side of her head, and a few strands of her locs were hanging out.

I snorted a laugh. At least someone was getting some sleep around here.

After grabbing a blanket and spreading it over her, I tapped the app for my emails and found the thread I shared with Bishop. I hit the Reply button, and because my heart was sick and I felt terrible for leaving him stranded on that rooftop, I searched for a white flag emoji, typed Truce? then added my number below.

I hit Send before I could change my mind or think too hard about it, then carried my phone with me to the bedroom. I fluffed my pillows, put on my satin bonnet, slipped into one of Lewis's hoodies, and curled beneath the comforter.

As I shut off the lamp and settled in, my phone buzzed next to me. When I checked the caller ID, I was sure it was Deke. I felt a flutter deep in my stomach when I tapped the green Answer button.

"Hi, Deke."

"What's up, D?" His voice was deep and gravelly, like he hadn't used it in a few hours. Still, the sound of it caused a delightful twist in my belly.

"What are you doing?"

"Watching *The Great British Baking Show* with Zeke."

I couldn't help the giggle that slipped out. "You're not joking, are you?"

"Hell no. This is my show," he declared proudly. "It's got that cozy vibe to it. You ever look at the desserts they make, hear how the judges describe it, and your mouth starts watering? It makes me want to be a judge."

"You should add that to your bucket list, then."

"Oh, I am."

"I figured you'd be watching one of those sports channels or something," I said.

"Nah. I avoid it. All they do is talk shit between the highlights."

"Hmm." I sat up against the headboard and released a slow sigh. Even when I knew he was upset with me, he still made everything seem okay.

"Listen, Deke . . . I shouldn't have run off on you like that. I'm really sorry. I just . . . well, this whole situation is hard for me, I guess." I paused, trying to think of better words. "It's just that I'm realizing how much I actually like you, and it, um . . . it feels too soon to like someone this much. That's why I said I was scared, because I know that if I get attached to you, there's a possibility I could lose what we have. Maybe not in the way I lost my husband—God forbid—but in some other crazy scenario."

"I understand," Deke murmured. "You don't have to apologize for feeling that way."

My lips smashed together as my eyes bounced around the dark room.

"I shouldn't have made a move on you," he said. "That's my fault. *I'm* sorry."

"No. It's fine. Honestly. Like I told you, I wanted it." It really was fine. What kind of person would I have been to regret being *devoured* by Deke Bishop? I loved every damn second of it. Hell, I couldn't stop thinking about it since leaving the rooftop.

"What are you doing tomorrow?" he asked.

"It's Sunday, so not much. I'll probably clean, get groceries, and do a little laundry."

He huffed a laugh. "You sound like my mama."

"What? Sundays are my reset days." I tugged at one of the drawstrings of my hoodie while biting a smile. "Why do you ask?"

"I wanna take you to brunch."

"Brunch?"

"What? You don't like brunch?" He chuckled.

"Oh, I love brunch. Tish and I go for it at least every other week."

"Well, there's this spot a friend of mine owns in Charlotte. Great food. Bottomless mimosas. It's a pretty big deal. She has private spaces designated for people like me and my guests so we can park and eat in peace. I'll drive to Charlotte early if you'll join me."

"Oh, um . . ." I bit into my bottom lip.

"It's just brunch, D," he reminded me with a smooth laugh. "No rooftop cabanas. I promise."

I laughed at that, then said, "Okay. We can do brunch."

"Yeah?" There was a lilt to his voice. I could tell he was smiling.

"Yeah. I'll be there. Just let me know the time and place."

"All right, cool. I'll text you the info. I love that I can say that now, by the way."

I laughed again. "If you're driving to Charlotte, you better get some sleep, then, Bishop."

"My head is already hitting the pillow, D-Baby."

I busted out laughing at yet another nickname created by him. "Good night, Deke. I'll see you tomorrow."

"Good night, Davina."

THIRTY-SEVEN

DAVINA

Manhattan Rose was a gorgeous restaurant inspired by its first location in Manhattan, New York.

There were only four franchises across the United States thus far, and one just so happened to be located in Charlotte and owned by a culinary chef named Leticia Brent.

After checking in with the valet, I stood in front of the castle-like building, bringing the strap of my purse to my shoulder. The exterior was made of gray cement, and there were three levels, with the upper two having balconies. According to my research, there was also a rooftop with seating and a full bar. Hey, at least there were no cabanas.

When I walked inside, I was greeted with a rush of cool air. Crystal chandeliers hung from a ceiling that seemed endless, and the roof was made of glass. Trees with leafy green tops were spread out like columns, and sofas were inside, occupied by waiting guests. It was like the outdoors had been brought indoors in elegant fashion.

Stairs with black railing led to the upper floors, and when I checked in with the hostess, she guided me to the second level and rounded a corner to a private area, and that's when I saw him.

Dressed in a lavender linen shirt, dark jeans, and a pair of oxford shoes, Deke stood next to an older woman in a black chef's uniform, who was laughing at something he was saying.

Two gold chains hung from his neck, per usual, and there was a small gold hoop earring in one ear and a diamond stud in the other. The lavender shirt was a soft color, but it took nothing away from the masculinity that practically leaked out of his pores. If anything, I found him even *sexier* for wearing it. I knew a lot of men who were afraid of wearing pastels publicly, but not Deke Bishop. Of course he wasn't.

From the information I'd gathered online, I knew the woman laughing and chatting with him was the famous Leticia Brent. She was nearing her fifties but easily could've passed for early forties. Her upturned head swung in my direction when she noticed me, and Deke followed her gaze.

When Deke caught sight of me, he did a double take over his shoulder before turning around to drink me in. Those warm eyes of his traveled down the length of my body, and I was glad he liked what he saw.

I had given this brunch a lot of effort. In the back of my closet I'd found a sienna lantern-sleeved dress with a plunge at the neckline, and I'd plucked out my best push-up bra. And because I couldn't sleep so easily last night, I decided to braid my hair into thick singles and unbraided them this morning for a cute braid-out.

I kept my makeup simple, with some concealer, a few brushes of mascara, blush, and a touch-up of the brows. I also took off my dragonfly necklace, which was bittersweet. I guess I wanted to show up as someone with a positive mindset, not someone attached to their grief.

"Davina." Deke sounded breathless as his eyes kept roaming me, and I bit back a smile as I moved forward and offered a hand to Leticia.

"Hi, Leticia. I'm Davina Klein. I'm so honored to be here right now." I smiled as she took my hand. "Figured I'd introduce myself, since this guy is too speechless to do so." I bobbed my head at him, and he grinned.

"It's lovely meeting you, Davina. I'm glad you could make it. Is this your first time?" Leticia asked.

"It is. I've heard incredible things about your food, so I'm very excited."

Leticia let out a tinkle of a laugh and pressed her hands to her heart. "Aren't you sweet?" She looked between me and Deke, who still hadn't said a word. I could feel him still looking at me, though. "I was happy to hear Deke was coming in for a visit. He's one of my favorites to serve."

"Is he?" I looked up at Deke from beneath my lashes, and he finally snapped out of his silent stupor to point his attention to Leticia.

"Your food is the best, Leticia. You know I had to swing through. I appreciate you for setting me up in a private room."

"Absolutely. Well, I'm going to let you two get to your brunch, but please let me know if there's anything you need. Davina"—she took my hand and shook it again—"so lovely to meet you. Take care of this one." She pointed a thumb at Deke, gave me a wink, then left the room.

Then there were two.

I found Deke's eyes.

"Do, uh . . . do you wanna sit?" he asked.

I laughed. "Please."

He moved around me to pull out one of the chairs beneath the table.

"Thank you." I sat and placed my purse on my lap.

He took the chair across from me, and after he slid in, he cleared his throat and said, "As always, you look divine. Davina the Divine. New nickname?"

"Oh, please no," I snorted. "I'd rather take D-Baby over that one."

His lips quirked up at the corners. "You got it, D-Baby."

Okay. I had to stop smiling. I felt like a goof. I put my focus on the menu, just as a waiter appeared. Deke ordered a regular orange mimosa, and I decided to go with a mango version.

"But real talk, you look good, D," Deke said, when the waiter took off with our drink orders. "Thank you for joining me . . . and for shooting me your number."

I smiled again. "It felt right."

"How was your flight back from Miami?"

"Terrible." I waved a hand. "There was a lot of turbulence for such a short flight."

"Damn, that sucks."

"You don't have to worry about that, though, with your private jets and all. Doesn't your team have a private charter or something?"

"We do, yeah, but it's mostly used during the season. I can get you on a private jet if you want. Just say when."

"I'll hold you to that."

The waiter returned with our drinks, we placed our entrée orders, and Deke cleared his throat after taking a sip of his mimosa. With his back resting against the chair, he studied me with a smile.

"You're staring," I informed him.

"I can't help it when there's such a nice view in front of me."

I pursed my lips after taking a sip of my drink. This guy. May as well have called himself Prince Charming. "So . . . there's something I want to talk to you about."

At that, he sat forward and folded his long arms on the tabletop. "I'm listening."

"The . . . *thing* that happened on the rooftop . . ."

He fought a smile. "Go on."

"I didn't realize how badly I needed it."

One of his brows inclined. "When was the last time you had it?"

"I don't know. Months ago." *Over a year, actually.* I took another nervous sip of mimosa.

I dared a glance at him, and he seemed to be mulling my statement over. "I'll be more than happy to fuck you if that's what you need, D."

I nearly spit out my drink, and a laugh burst out of him. "How blunt of you," I said after swallowing the drink down.

"Just ask for what you want. I won't judge, and I *definitely* won't tell."

"I never said that was what I wanted," I claimed, but my voice was much too soft for even *myself* to believe those words.

"You said last night that you liked me, right?"

"Yeah, I do."

"And you enjoyed how I ate your pussy in that cabana?"

"Deke," I whispered, looking around like there were other people in the room who could hear us. There weren't any, but still.

"What? I'm just asking. I mean, I enjoyed feasting on you, and I like you, too, so let's be straight up about it. Whenever you need it again, we'll fuck. I satisfy you, you satisfy me, and we'll go on with our lives until the next time you need it. We'll keep it as simple as that."

That was tempting. "And you wouldn't want more?" I challenged.

He leaned in closer. "As long as I get the chance to bury my dick inside you, that's more than enough for me."

My face was on fire now. I'd *never* been talked to that way. I couldn't say I didn't love it. There was something illicit about his words. Every single one of them went straight to the warm area between my legs.

Lew was always so polite about sex. On rare occasions (likely when he'd been drinking) he'd be a little naughtier, and I loved when he took charge.

Nope. Stop comparing them.

"So we'll be fuck-buddies?"

He gave me a nod. "If that's what you want."

"It is what I want. Just sex."

He looked from my eyes to my lips. When he found my eyes again, he said, "All right then."

"Okay," I breathed, relaxing a bit. "Good."

"So let's start right now. They've got restrooms around the corner we can use," Deke said, cocking his head to the left. I fumbled over my words, which made him belt out a belly-deep laugh. "I'm just messing with you, D. Relax." He picked up his glass and took a swig, while I tossed out a nervous laugh. "We'll start when you're ready. Just say the word, D-Baby."

I ran a finger over the edge of my cloth napkin. "What is the word, by the way?"

He thought about it a second, then said, *"Brunch."*

"Brunch?" I repeated, laughing. "Why that word?"

"We're making this arrangement over brunch. Seems fitting."

"Okay." I sat back and crossed my legs beneath the table. "So if I randomly text you the word *brunch*, you're gonna drop whatever you're doing to come fuck me?"

"Ooohh, Davina Klein." Deke's expression was priceless. His mouth parted, and his eyes sparked beneath the chandeliers as he said, "Keep talking to me like that, and we'll *definitely* be making use of those restrooms." I giggled as he sat back again and spread his legs. I wanted to sit on his lap. Hell, I wanted to climb him like a tree. "If I can swing it, I'll be there," he stated.

"Wait. This isn't going to be a one-and-done thing, is it?" I asked. "Because if so, let's not even worry about it. I'm not looking for a one-night stand situation."

"Nah." He looked up at the ceiling before dropping his gaze and caging his bottom lip in his teeth. "I've been waiting too long to have you to make this a one-night stand. If we agree on this, I don't want there to be an end. I want to savor every second I get with you."

A smirk claimed my lips. "You're a patient man, Deke Bishop."

He winked. "Only for you, D."

THIRTY-EIGHT

DAVINA

After brunch, Deke walked with me to the valet booth to collect our keys. The valet could've gotten our cars for us, but Deke wanted to walk me to mine.

"Just want more time with you before I head back home," he said when I asked why he didn't let the valet do their job. I had to admit that was cute. I felt a flutter in my lower belly when he started walking beside me.

Now we were walking through the private parking deck the valet had directed us to. The concrete deck was reserved only for people like Deke: famous or rich as hell in some fashion.

I spotted my car at the end of the lot, and along the way, Deke pointed to his right and said, "That's me."

"A Ferrari," I noted, studying the gleaming black vehicle. "Can't say I'm surprised."

"Wanna know something?" he asked with a lopsided grin.

"What?"

"When I visit my sisters, I rent the cheapest economy car so no one notices me. One time, I had to drive a Prius."

I busted out laughing. "You did not!"

"No lie!" He laughed. "It was all they had. Now imagine this six-three dude stuffing himself into a Prius. Crazy, right?"

"I can't imagine that at all," I laughed.

"The shit we do for family."

"It's sweet that you're so close to your siblings, though." I gently bumped his side with my shoulder. "Sounds like you'd do anything for them."

"Oh yeah. I hit the jackpot with them. Whitney loved you when she met you, and I'm sure Camille will too." His smile slipped just a bit, and his face warped like something was bothering him. I started to ask what was wrong (though I had an idea that it might've been about Damon), but he looked at me again and flashed that million-dollar smile. "Shouldn't talk about meeting family with you so soon, huh?"

I shrugged. "If I happen to meet Camille in passing, I'm sure it'll be fine. Besides, you've met my sister."

"I have. Javier won't stop talking about how rude she is, by the way." He scratched the skin above his eyebrow. "I think he likes her."

"No!" I gasped. "Wait, are you serious?"

"I don't know!" He threw his hands into the air. "I'm just saying. I haven't heard him talk nonstop about a woman since his wife passed away. Even though he's talking about your sister with implied annoyance, it's still *talking*. I don't know. Guess your sister calling him a helicopter asshole really got to him."

"Oh, well, now I *have* to tell Octavia this."

"You better not!" Deke shouted, reeling me in with an arm around the shoulders. "I could be way off. I don't know what really goes on inside that dude's head."

"So I *shouldn't* say anything?" I asked, trying hard not to think about how warm his body was next to mine, the safe feeling I got with just his arm over my shoulders.

"Nah. That's my boy. I don't want his business getting out unless he wants it out."

"Okay." My head bobbed. "I respect that. I'll keep it quiet for now." But for how long? Because seriously, Octavia was my sister *and* my best friend. I told her pretty much everything.

The last thing I wanted was for Javier to feel some type of way because his best friend *assumed* he liked my sister, though. For all we knew, Javier really was annoyed by what Octavia said and was taking it to heart. That, or he was supersensitive.

"This is me," I said, gesturing to the white BMW a couple of steps away. I lowered the strap of my purse from my shoulder to dig my car key out and moved to the driver's door. "Thank you for brunch, Deke. This place was beautiful."

"Glad you liked it." He scanned my face, moving in closer. "When do I get to see you again?"

My back pressed against the cool metal of the vehicle. "That depends."

"On what?"

"Our schedules. But you're the big shot. You sure you'll have time to squeeze me in?" I teased.

"Oh, I'll make the time," he insisted with a crooked smile. "But I do have some commercial shoots here and there—oh, and a feature in this sitcom."

"A sitcom? Now that's interesting."

"Yeah, I'm the guy the main dude bumps into and he's all 'Holy shit, you're Deke Bishop!'" Deke waved a hand. "Super-small role. I'm technically not supposed to talk about it yet." He pretended to zip his lips.

I giggled. "You'll be pretty busy then."

"Other than that and some intense training coming up, it shouldn't be too bad. Season starts in a couple months. My coach and trainer are cracking down on me, but you're only a few hours away." He paused, studying my face. "You should come to one of my games."

I peered up at him from beneath my lashes. "Maybe one day."

He paused. "Don't look at me like that, D."

"Like what?"

"Like you want me to fuck you against this car."

My teeth sank into my bottom lip as he pressed a hand to the side of the car and caged me in from one side.

"Take a trip with me soon."

That caught me off guard, and I half laughed, half blurted the word "What?"

"A trip. Just you and me. Let's take one before my training camp starts."

I swallowed. "That sounds . . . intimate."

"I know." The corner of his lip quirked up. "That's the point."

"But we haven't even done the fuck-buddy part yet."

"By the time we take that trip, we'll have fucked plenty of times, D." He dropped his forehead, and the tip of his nose grazed mine. "The trip is just to sweeten the deal, proof that this isn't a one-and-done thing."

"Hmm." I lowered my eyes to the chains dangling from his neck, twinkling in the light. "Can I think about it?"

He gripped my chin in his fingers and raised it to place a slow, gentle kiss on my lips. I wasn't expecting it and shouldn't have been so surprised when that clench between my thighs transitioned to a hungry throb.

"Sure, you can." He kissed me again slowly, sweetly, and heat blossomed in my lower belly just as an unexpected moan filled my throat. "But don't think too long."

"Why not?"

"Because you'll miss out," he murmured, skimming the hand that wasn't on the car down my waist.

"On what?" I tempted him. I shouldn't have tempted him. I of all people knew better, especially after last time.

"All the things I wanna do to you," he answered.

He lowered his head so his mouth was near the bend of my neck. His palm skated down to my thigh, then traveled beneath the hem of my dress. In a delicate manner, his fingers tiptoed their way up to trace the fabric of my panties.

He leaned back just a bit to connect those heated brown eyes with mine, and his fingers traced my panties as I fought another moan.

"What exactly do you want to do to me?" I breathed, responding to his statement.

"Better if I show you." His mouth twitched, and he lifted his large hand higher, hiking my dress up and digging into my panties to cup my pussy. I moaned. "Mmm. Looks like somebody did a little upkeep," he said with a crooked grin.

A breath got stuck in my chest as he slowly spread the lips of my pussy apart and slipped a finger inside me. That same finger slid up to apply pressure to the most sensitive part of my body, and I released a sharp gasp, clutching his stiff arm. He worked those fingers up and down repeatedly before plunging two of them inside me.

"So wet, D," he rasped on my mouth.

He repeated the movements, making me wetter as his mouth hovered over mine, taunting me. I tried leaning in to kiss him, but he leaned back just enough so I couldn't reach.

"Deke," I breathed, mildly frustrated but more turned on, because he was still working magic with his hand.

"You wanna kiss me?" His voice made me tremble in the best way.

I nodded, and my knees went weak as he circled the pad of one of his fingers around that sweet, tender button of mine craving all the attention.

"Agree to take a trip with me then," he purred on my mouth.

I moaned louder as he kept massaging my clit. It was crazy, this moment. We were in a parking deck, and *anyone* could've driven by and seen us, but I didn't give a damn. All I cared about was coming around Deke's long, gifted fingers.

"Do you agree, Davina?"

I attempted another kiss, but again, he dipped his head back and chuckled deeply this time.

"Okay," I panted as he pumped his fingers faster, thrusting in and out of me, then sliding them back up to graze my clit. "Okay, I'll go on a trip with you."

"No bullshit?"

"No bullshit," I moaned.

"Okay, baby." He pressed his forehead to mine, and I felt the hardness of his dick press on my thigh as he moved in closer. "I'll make you come now." His nose skimmed my cheek, and his mouth ghosted my jawline.

When his face was front and center again and his lips came crashing down on mine, I fucking *melted*. That kiss was all I needed to finish.

"Oh, Deke!" I cried as he pressed harder, rubbed faster. A hiss slipped through his teeth, and a guttural groan lingered in his throat. The hardness of his dick rubbed against me as I came so hard I couldn't think straight. I moaned into his mouth as he finished me off with gentle loops of his finger.

He kissed me firmly as he dragged his hand out of my panties, then straightened the bottom of my dress.

He cleared his throat. "You look good when you come, D."

He said it like he was telling me he liked ice cream or something.

I huffed a laugh, standing up straight and looking around as he did. I was so glad this was a *private* parking area. After double-checking that my dress was straightened, I cleared my throat, too, and met his eyes.

"I'm going home to do my laundry now, Bishop," I told him, removing my purse from my shoulder to take my keys out. I had to really concentrate to do it. All my limbs felt like liquid. "And I promise you, this isn't me running away."

His smile was smug. "Good to know. And even if you are, I've got your number." He winked.

I unlocked my car and climbed inside, and he bent down to get eye level with me. "I'm gonna hold you to that trip."

I bit back a smile. "I know you are."

He stroked my chin with his thumb and forefinger, sending another wave of pleasure through me. I could smell myself on his fingers. I wanted to pounce on him like a jaguar, but the first time couldn't happen here. Not in a parking deck.

With one last kiss, he pulled away and said, "Text me when you want more brunch." Then he winked before standing tall again, closing my door, and walking away.

I took a second to snap out of my lustful haze, then started the car and put it in reverse. Deke was close to his lit-up Ferrari as I drove toward the exit, and when he heard my car coming, he peered over his shoulder with a smug smile.

All the blood crept up from my neck to my face as I drove past and threw a quick wave at him, but before I could fully get away, he yelled, "You're blushing, D!"

THIRTY-NINE

DEKE

"So what you're saying is y'all went on a date?" EJ threw the ball at the goal and made the net swish. He didn't watch the rock sink in, though. He was too busy staring at me and waiting for an answer.

I met with him and Javier the morning after having brunch with Davina. We were at Element and did a quick workout before a few guys from the team swung by for a practice scrimmage. They'd all left by now, but the three of us stuck around to go over a few drills.

EJ didn't usually tag along with us, but he claimed he wanted to take his career more seriously. Though he was a goof who loved partying, drinking, and sleeping with any woman who blinked at him, the kid could hoop.

"I guess you could call it that," I said, referring to his date question as I dribbled a ball between my legs.

"Hold on." EJ planted his hands on his waist. "Don't tell me you stopped fucking with Giselle for Davina?"

I frowned at him. "Me and Giselle were done a long time ago. And even if I did, so fucking what?"

"No wonder she's been talking shit about you." EJ shook his head and walked toward the towel rack.

"I think it is nice. You two seem to have a connection," Javier said from where he stood. "A *real* connection, not any of that forced bullshit you were involved with before."

"I guess it doesn't matter." EJ shrugged as he went for a water bottle. "Both of them are sexy as fuck." I lifted my ball and chucked it at EJ, making the water bottle fall out of his hands. "'Ey, man! What's wrong with you?"

I raised a brow, looking him over. He could talk about Giselle all he wanted, but Davina was out of the question.

EJ sucked his teeth, staring at me as I met him at the water station. "You really not gonna apologize for that?"

"Hell no." I sat on one of the chairs, lifting my bottle and taking a swig. EJ claimed a chair a few seats away from me as Javier picked up a ball, bouncing it from hand to hand.

"How did you get her to fold, anyway?" Javier asked. "She was glaring daggers at you at the Miami lunch—and I don't blame her. You might as well have been dragging her through the mud."

"I don't know." I laughed. "But I will say if she hadn't come to that man Chester's party, we probably wouldn't be talking right now."

"So you two did something at the party?" Javier's bushy brows inclined. "I was wondering why you had disappeared."

I hid a smirk as I took another drink of water. "I don't kiss and tell like EJ," I said after a wet gasp.

EJ poured some water into his hand and flung it at me.

"Can't believe you left me alone with her sister." Javier tossed the ball at the net but missed. He wasn't the best shooter. Best on the defensive end, though.

"Man, just admit you like her and stop beating around the bush." I hopped up and grabbed the ball he'd thrown, dribbling my way back to him.

"What the hell are you talking about?" His eyebrows bunched together as he tossed his hands in the air. "I don't like her."

"You keep talking about her." I stood at the three-point line and aimed for the goal. The ball sank in with hardly a shift in the net. "Must mean something, right?" I cut my eyes to his, and he still had his arms out with an incredulous look on his face.

"Deke, you are wrong. I do not like her."

"What are you getting so worked up for then?" I asked, chuckling.

"I am not worked up." He looked around the gym as if searching for the person who was worked up. "I mean, I am considering hiring her later to take care of Aleesa, but that is all it is. I need to make sure she is a good fit for my daughter. That is all. I *do not* like her."

I stifled a laugh. "If that's your truth, so be it."

"It is," Javier insisted, bringing his shirt up to wipe the sweat from his forehead.

"Oh shit! Deke, have you seen this?" EJ jogged toward me with his phone in hand. When he handed it to me, the first thing I saw was Davina on the screen. She was in the orangish dress she'd worn to brunch, and I was right beside her with my hand extremely low on her back.

"The fuck?" I scrolled down to find another picture. This one was of us in the parking deck. My forehead was pressed to hers. We looked like we were about to kiss. My heart almost dropped until I realized the image was only of our shoulders and up. "Who posted this?" I asked, frowning at EJ.

"BOBBLE dropped it."

"You've gotta be fucking kidding me." I handed EJ his phone back and ran across the court to get to my gym bag. When I dug it out, there were four missed calls from Arnold, a text from Giselle, and two missed calls from Whitney.

Arnold was most likely calling because of this news leak. I hadn't told him about me and Davina, so he was probably checking to see if it was true.

Whitney had most likely seen the article (she loved keeping up with celebrity gossip) and was calling to cuss me the hell out, seeing as she'd warned me to leave Davina alone.

And Giselle . . . well, I knew why she'd text me, but I didn't give a damn about her feelings at the moment.

The only person I was worried about was a state away. I grabbed my bag and hustled out of the building to call Davina.

FORTY

DAVINA

Tish was my best friend for many reasons, and one of them was her thoughtfulness.

This girl bought me a foot-massage machine to go beneath my desk. She said she'd been shopping and was thinking about me when she bought it. When I saw it on my desk with a pink ribbon, I hugged her so hard I was surprised she didn't pop.

I sat at my desk, deep in my cushioned leather chair, sipping my lavender-honey tea with one hand while scrolling through ad designs with the other.

The view outside was perfect, a clear blue sky and trees in the distance, gradually transitioning into warm fall colors. Just past them, the Charlotte skyline towered. It was a good day . . . or maybe I just felt that way after my brunch with Deke.

I felt *good*, and I couldn't quite explain this bubble of heat building in my chest, but it grew day by day. One day it would pop, and I'd be full of those hot, gushy feelings he'd created, and I wouldn't be able to stop them no matter how hard I tried.

As if I'd thought him up, my phone buzzed on the desk, and Deke's name appeared on the screen.

I set my tea mug on the coaster and swiped to answer. "Hi, Deke."

"Hey, D. You got a minute?" He sounded breathless and not his usual self.

I sat up taller in my chair as the knobs of the foot massager rolled toward my heels. "Uh, sure. What's going on? Everything okay?"

"I just left the gym. EJ was showing me some . . ." I lost Deke's voice as I heard commotion outside my office and then someone yelling, "Where the hell is she?!"

What the hell?

". . . and now there are pictures that have been leaked. I didn't think anyone would bother taking any, let alone share them. I—I mean, I tried to be discreet about it with you, but *fuck*, D . . ."

My office door swung open, and a woman I did *not* want to see appeared in the frame. Gloria stormed in, with a raging fire in her eyes, her lips pinched tight, and her nostrils flared. Her face was scarlet.

"How *could* you?" she shouted.

"Davina?" Deke called, but I lowered the phone from my ear and placed it on the desktop as I stared at my former mother-in-law.

Tish stood behind Gloria, her eyes wide with shock. "I tried to stop her, Vina! She went right through me."

"No, it's okay. Tish. Don't worry about it." I kept my eyes locked on Gloria as I took my feet off the massager and stood up. "Gloria, it's one thing to show up at my house, but to barge in to my office like this? Are you serious right now? What are you doing here?"

"Oh, you want to act like you don't know?" she spit, her face reddening even more.

"What the hell are you talking about?" I snapped.

"This!" She stormed across the room in her flats and shoved her phone in my face.

I snatched it away from her, and when I caught an image of me and Deke leaving Manhattan Rose, my heart plummeted.

"What?" I breathed. "What is . . ."

"You just couldn't wait to spread your legs for another man when Lew died, could you?"

I snapped my head up, pinning her with my eyes. "Tish," I said as calmly as I could. "Close the door."

Tish closed it without hesitation, and I tossed Gloria's phone onto a pile of papers on the desk before folding my arms. "First of all, what I do with my life is no business of yours," I retorted as she snatched up her phone. The calm was wearing off me now. My heart was pounding, fury simmering in my veins. "Secondly, how dare you come to *my* office shouting at me about *my* life!"

I mean, who the fuck did she think she was, coming in like this? She could show up at my house all she wanted, but coming to my job was crossing the line.

"Are you sleeping with the guy in these pictures?" she asked in a hiss. "You're so pathetic, Davina. You were a terrible match for Lew. God, I don't even know why he chose you!"

"Oh, *fuck you*, Gloria!" I shouted, and damn, did it feel good. Out of respect for Lew, I always kept my mouth shut. I always kept it respectful, and if I couldn't contain it, I'd walk away so I wouldn't go off on her.

Not this time, though. This time she'd pushed every single one of my buttons, and there was no patience left within me for her.

I marched around my desk, and she took a step back as I neared her. "Do you really have the nerve to show up here and reprimand me when you couldn't even be there for your own son? Lew called you every day, but did you answer? No. You only did when *you* felt like it."

"I was traveling!"

"Oh, right. *Gloria Travels*," I said in a jeer, referring to her stupid blog, where she traveled and wrote about it. And no, she wasn't paid to do this. She did this willingly with the life insurance payout she'd acquired from her husband's—Lewis's dad—death. "Traveling meant more to you than coming to see Lew? Those last few weeks, he *asked* for you, Gloria. He was waiting for you to walk through that door, but you never showed up. Typical Gloria, always making an excuse to not take care of her own child."

"I birthed and raised him!" she countered, getting in my face again. "He wouldn't have been the man he was without me!"

"Wrong. He wouldn't have been the man he was without his father, who also died when you weren't there. Don't act like you were the good parent to him."

Gloria sucked in a sharp breath, and her eyes glistened.

I'd had enough of backing down from her—from handling things so kindly. Why the hell was she even here? I hadn't heard from her since she showed up about the photo album. Now all of a sudden she was charging into my office and shouting at me? What was wrong with this woman? I get she was lonely and miserable, but I'd never seen someone try so hard to drag another person into their misery.

I took a moment to collect myself, realizing her barging in like this wasn't about me. All of this was from a problem she had brewing within herself, and she was looking for someone else to blame.

"Look, I get that everyone grieves in their own way, but this is not it, Gloria. Taking your anger out on me because you didn't do your part as a mother is wrong, so don't you *ever* come into my space pointing fingers at me when I did *everything* for Lewis. He was the love of my life, and I would've done anything for him, but he was dying. Do you think I asked for that? Do you think I walked into our marriage wishing he'd die when he was in his thirties? *I loved him*, Gloria! I never wanted him to leave me!"

She blinked as she backed away, but I couldn't see her clearly anymore, because my vision had blurred. I blinked and waited to hear what else she could spew at me as she shifted on her feet.

She looked awful, like she hadn't slept properly in months, and she reeked of stale cigarettes. She normally wore a lot of makeup but not that day. It was like she rolled out of bed, saw the news leak on BOBBLE, and drove straight to my office.

When she didn't speak, I pointed at the door. "If that's all, you can leave now. I have work to do."

"I can't believe you." Gloria pointed an angry finger at me. "I hope this new guy you're with forgets about you like you've forgotten about Lew."

She turned on her heel, snatched the door open, and stormed out. I stared after her until my vision grew blurry again, then rushed to slam the door.

My knees felt like they were going to give out on me as I walked back to my chair to sink into it. I glanced at my phone and was shocked when I realized Deke was still on the line.

I picked the phone up and brought it to my ear with a shaky hand. "Oh my goodness. *Deke?*"

"I'm here," he murmured.

I swallowed thickly and tried fighting my tears. To stop them, I closed my eyes. "Please don't tell me you heard all of that."

"I didn't want to hang up until I knew you were okay." He paused. "*Are* you okay?" His voice was soft and sincere, like he felt sorry for me. It was enough to make me break.

I placed the phone down and dropped my face into my hands. I couldn't fight the sobs, couldn't stop the tears. The emotion had accumulated into a large monster inside me, and this monster was wreaking havoc. There she was again, that bitch Grief. Always coming in swinging.

I heard my office door open, heard the faint voice from Deke as he called my name, felt a hand rub circles on my back.

"She'll call you back, Deke," Tish murmured. After ending the call, she guided me to the sofa and helped me sit.

"Look at me," I cried. "I'm the worst, Tish!"

"Davina, no."

"She's right. I—I'm moving too fast. This isn't normal!"

"Who said there were rules on the timeline of dating?" Tish asked, her brows dipping. "Davina, you told me yourself that the true intimacy between you and Lew was lost months before he died. You knew the day he passed away would come, and you did your best to prepare for it. You can't blame yourself for liking who you like, and you can't fight how you feel when you feel it. What good will that do for you?"

"I just feel so guilty," I said thickly. "Every time I'm with Deke, I feel like I'm betraying my husband. Sometimes I feel like he's still here—like he's just waiting for me at home so I can tell him about my day."

Tish slid closer to me and hugged me from the side. "I think you're being way too hard on yourself."

She was right, but how could I *not* be? It'd only been a little under a year, and I was already going out to brunches with another man and letting him finger-fuck me in parking decks.

When you love someone but have to part ways, it's normally a struggle to move on, because that person is familiar to you. That person, at one point, was who you centered your whole life on. I was ashamed to admit I was losing touch with that familiarity. The presence of my husband had been washed away long ago, and though our memories lingered in my heart, something had changed—and not just now, or even when he died, but well before that.

I lost my husband as soon as he was diagnosed. He wasn't the same man. He hated his life. He was miserable and didn't want me being miserable with him, so he pushed me away at first. He wouldn't talk to me, didn't want to watch movies, didn't want to cuddle, kiss, or any of it. It wasn't until he lost some of his ability to walk that he reeled me in again, and I embraced it because every second with him was even more valuable than it had been before.

It was so hard with him in the end. *So damn hard.* And maybe that was why I was running with this fling I had with Deke—because it was so freaking *easy*. This bond I'd created with Deke was effortless and simple. It was right there in my face, and no one was stopping me from having it but myself and my guilt. Just when I felt I was overcoming that guilt, situations like the one with Gloria happened and my choices felt like mistakes.

I reached for my chest, clutching the dragonfly pendant.

"Have you ever considered the possibility that you can grieve and embrace change at the same time?" Tish asked in a quiet voice. "Grieving is not linear, Vina. Some days will hit you harder than others, but that doesn't stop you from living. Sometimes you have to swallow it down and work through it. It's even better when you can work through it with a person who *gets* it."

I raised my chin to look at her. She was talking about Deke. "Yeah, well . . ." I sniffed, dragging the tips of my fingers over my cheek to wipe the tears away. "Regardless of what BOBBLE or anyone else thinks, me and Deke aren't a couple. We just like each other's company."

"And you're fuck-buddies," Tish added, grinning.

I hiccuped a laugh. "Yeah. That too."

"That's all it is now, but if it transitions to more, don't be afraid of it, babe, and don't feel guilty for something that makes you happy." She grabbed my hand and gave it a squeeze. "At the end of the day, we're all humans, and we're all just trying to make it through this thing called life. We only get one shot at it, too, so we might as well live it the way we want. It annoys me, because if you were a man, no one would bat an eye that you've moved on or found happiness with another person. Hell, they'd be praising you for it! I think Gloria is just mad because she'll never have what you have with Deke. The fact that you've found so much comfort with him at this moment is rare, so stop letting these judgmental people get to your head. When it comes to Lew, there's nothing you can do anymore. Okay? He's gone, and you're still here, and that's fine, Vina. For him, you'll live."

I nodded, then wrapped her in my arms with a comforted groan.

As simple as Tish made that sound, though, not caring about what anyone thought was so much easier said than done.

FORTY-ONE

DAVINA

"Assholes," I grumbled as I lay flat on the love seat in my office.

It was a little after nine o'clock, and now that all the drama and commotion had settled and Tish had gone home, I was looking at the pictures of me and Deke from Sunday's brunch. Who even took these? And why the hell did it matter who Deke was talking to?

The caption was so stupid: Deke Bishop Spotted with Unknown Woman during Giselle Grace Rumors.

At first, I thought the article wouldn't be so bad. It was only an image of us walking out of Manhattan Rose, and he was hardly touching me, only escorting me toward the valet. But then I scrolled down and saw the image of us almost kissing in the parking deck and his hand propped on my car.

I was so glad the photo had only caught our upper bodies. I couldn't imagine how humiliated I would feel if they'd captured him with his hand in my panties.

I sat up and crossed my legs, grabbing the Chinese-food carton on the table in front of me. Tish, for the first time in months, didn't care that I stayed in the office late. After the fiasco from earlier, I hadn't gotten much work done. I was too busy stewing over what Gloria had said and drowning in a pool of betrayal.

Our new products were going to be launching in a week, and I had some work to catch up on. I also didn't want to go home and see all those pictures of me and Lew.

Besides, my office was where I produced the clearest thoughts. It was my domain and mine only, and it gave me a boost of confidence knowing I'd worked so hard to have a place like this with a city view.

I slurped noodles into my mouth as my phone rang.

Deke was calling. *Again.*

I ignored the call.

After that stunt from Gloria, I was so embarrassed that I didn't want to speak to him. I had to think of the right words to say, first. He'd heard me throw everything on the table about Lew, things that were too personal to discuss with him so soon.

I was surprised to see he was still calling anyway. Any other guy who'd heard a conversation like that probably would've blocked my ass. But not Deke.

My phone buzzed loudly, and once again, it was Deke.

With a sigh, I picked it up and answered. "You don't have to keep calling me. I'm fine, Deke."

He ignored me to say, "I'm in Charlotte."

"What?" My eyes stretched as I set the greasy carton on the coffee table again. "What are you talking about? Why are you here?"

"Where are you?" he asked, once again ignoring me.

"Deke—what are you doing? You didn't have to come here. I'm fine, and I'm not mad at you. I just needed time to think—"

"Davina, *where are you?*" His voice held more bass. It sent a jolt down my spine and not in a bad way.

"I'm at my office, but Deke, you really don't have to—"

"I'm on the way." He hung up before I could get another word in, and I lowered the phone, shocked and confused.

I didn't know why the hell he was in Charlotte, but I closed the lid of my food carton, placed the chopsticks in the brown bag the food had been delivered in, then rushed to the mirror in the corner to check my appearance.

I'd reapplied makeup after all that crying and looked okay, minus that one pesky curl at my temple. I tried smoothing it down, until I heard my phone vibrate on the table. I popped a mint into my mouth before grabbing it.

Deke: Come unlock the door.

I darkened the screen of my phone and left the office, carrying myself through the hallways and past the lobby, until I was at the main entrance.

I could see Deke before I reached the glass doors, dressed in black basketball shorts and a white sleeveless athletic shirt. His shoes looked like the kind players wore during games, and I remembered him saying he had a practice scrimmage earlier with a few teammates.

When he caught sight of me, a faint smile appeared on his lips.

I couldn't help returning one.

I tapped the code into the security box and unlocked the door, pushing it open to let him inside. I took a step back as he entered, and his eyes never left mine as he twisted the lock back in place.

"You good?" His voice was low, husky.

I looked up at him as he moved closer, towering above me. "Yeah. I'm good."

"You weren't answering my calls, D."

I swallowed as I looked away. "I know. I'm sorry. Please don't take it personally." I was apologizing a lot lately. How was he not sick of me?

Like always, Deke's fingers came to my chin, and he tipped my head back up so I could look at him. "I dropped everything and drove here when you didn't answer the first two calls. I know it sounds desperate as fuck, but I needed to know you were okay. I needed to see it for myself."

"Well . . ." I threw my hands up quickly and let them fall so hard they slapped my outer thighs. "I'm okay, Deke. You didn't have to drive all this way just to check on me."

"I know I didn't. I *wanted* to."

My eyes softened, and my heart sped up. "Why?"

"I don't think you realize it yet, but I care about you, Davina. You have me doing things I don't usually do just so I can see a smile on your face."

I couldn't help smiling at that. "Well, it's very thoughtful, Deke. Thank you." I grabbed his hand that was still touching my chin and laced my fingers with his. "Come on. Let's go to my office."

I led the way and didn't let go of his hand until we walked into the office. But it was at that moment I realized I only had one lamp on, leaving the room dimly lit. The warm white light created a calming, romantic ambience.

My wax melt burner was lit up in one of the corners, allowing a warm pear scent to fill the room, and it didn't help that outside all those windows was one of the most beautiful city views to behold.

"Davina's domain," Deke said as he walked deeper into the office.

I laughed. "You could call it that."

He looked through the floor-to-ceiling windows, soaking in the skyline. He was like a god with those sculpted arms revealed and his head tipped just so.

When he stood a foot away from the window, I met up with him and absorbed the view too. His head turned, and he put on a cute grin as he reached for my temple. He tugged on my unruly curl.

"That piece of hair is the bane of my existence."

"I think it's cute," he said. His phone rang, and he dropped his eyes, sighing as he fished it out of his pocket. "It's Arnold."

"Oh?"

"I'm supposed to be meeting him tomorrow so we can fly to LA for some dunk contest. He's probably calling about that and all this BOBBLE shit."

"Tomorrow?" I asked, though my voice came out higher than usual. "Well, what the hell are you doing here, Deke? You should be home preparing for it."

215

"You're right. Plus, I signed a contract, so if I don't show, they'll probably sue the fuck out of me." He laughed dryly.

I blinked at him, stunned. "Deke, please tell me you're joking."

"I'm not." He laughed for real this time, slipping the phone into his pocket as I shook my head. "I'll make it back in time. Don't worry about that right now." He closed the gap between us and gripped my waist. "The woman I heard earlier. That was your husband's mom?"

"Yeah." I smashed my lips.

"I just wanted to make sure. We don't have to talk about it."

"You heard everything," I muttered with a shake of my head. "I'm sorry you had to hear that. I've never had a good relationship with her. She saw all that BOBBLE stuff and—"

"Davina," Deke said, voice soft. "We don't have to talk about it, if you don't want to."

I nodded. Good, because I didn't want to.

He turned me so my back was facing the window, and as he moved forward, I moved backward.

"What are you doing?" I laughed as he lowered his head.

"Just wanna kiss you," he murmured on my lips. "Make you forget all about it."

I felt a flutter in my belly as my back hit the cool glass. "So do it," I challenged.

"Is that all you want me to do?"

"No," I breathed.

"What else then?" His mouth was closer. He slid one of the hands on my waist down to the curve of my ass.

"I don't know," I said, and he gave my butt a squeeze, which caused a needy breath to catch in my throat.

"Well, I know what I wanna do."

"What's that?" I asked.

"Take this skirt off and fuck you against the window." His mouth grazed my jawline, and his voice carried up to the shell of my ear. "Can I do that to you, D?"

His voice nearly made me fold. My lips parted as he hovered his mouth above mine. "Yes."

"What's the magic word?"

I leaned in and kissed him softly, slowly, coaxing an illicit groan out of him before whispering the answer. *"Brunch."*

His mouth curved into a smile, and before I knew it, he was taking his shirt off and I was tearing at the buttons of my blouse. He reached for my skirt and unzipped it from the back, and when it and my panties were a puddle around my feet, he took off his basketball shorts and boxers and picked me up in his arms.

I gasped and wrapped my arms around the back of his neck, afraid I'd fall.

"I got you, D," he murmured. There was safeness in his voice. A sureness. I relaxed.

Deke adjusted me in his arms and pressed my upper back to the window. The glass was cool on my skin, but when I looked into his eyes, all I saw was heat that could melt a glacier.

"Should I get a condom?" he asked.

"If you want to," I whispered. Then I added, "I'm protected, though. I assume you're clean?"

"All clean."

With one arm holding me steady, his other went down to grip the base of his dick. I couldn't help but look. It was dark and thick, with a round, dark-pink head. He was already hard, stroking it up and down. The tip of it glistened with anticipation, and I drew in a steady breath as he inched closer.

"You're protected, huh?" he breathed out, like he was surprised to hear that I was.

"Yes."

I wasn't about to get into a whole spiel about how I hadn't stopped taking birth control after Lewis had passed, or the months before that, when he was diagnosed. We barely had sex after that crippling news was delivered, and though I had a feeling we never would again, I still held out hope.

And just because I hadn't wanted to find love again, it didn't mean I wouldn't want to have *sex* again.

"That's all I need to know," Deke said, bringing me back to the present. He pushed the head of his dick into me, and a breath escaped me as I dug my fingernails into his shoulder blades.

Shit.

I couldn't remember the last time I'd felt this sort of penetration, and with it came a familiar sting. He pushed in deeper, before lifting his head to find my eyes.

"This okay?" he breathed.

"Yeah. Keep going."

He cupped me in his hands while giving me what I wanted. Each thick inch of him stretched me more, and I caged the corner of my bottom lip between my teeth.

A groan rattled in his chest, and when he was all in, I couldn't resist the satisfied moan that slipped out. He was so big—bigger than I expected—and I loved it.

"Damn, Davina," he groaned. "I knew you'd feel good."

He held my gaze, searching my face until I finally dropped my mouth on his. He pressed me flush against the window, and our kiss was wild, sloppy, and eager. Our tongues twirled and entwined as he pumped his hips.

He thrust into me again and again, hissing through his teeth when he tore his mouth away.

"Oh, fuck," he groaned, gripping my waist and bouncing me on his dick. He took a step back so that only my upper back remained on the glass, and he clutched my waist tighter as he looked down at where we were connected.

"Damn," he rumbled. "You look so good with me inside you." His heated eyes flickered up to mine, and he pulled me off the window to carry me to the sofa, not once pulling out.

My back hit the cushions, and if I thought he felt big standing up, missionary was out of this world. I moaned as he thrust back in and spread my legs farther apart as he kissed me.

"Tell me how you want it, baby," he said on my lips.

"Faster," I breathed, and he moved his hips faster, delivering rapid thrusts. I collected his face in my hands, and with my mouth close to his, I said, "Harder."

He went harder, burying into me in repeated strokes, his groans thickening by the second. I felt all the blood in my body rushing to that sweet spot between my legs, and every time he drove into me, I was sinking into a delicious abyss.

My back arched, and Deke sat up, tilting my hips upward so that all that was left on the sofa were my shoulder blades and the back of my head.

"Look at you," he rasped again, his voice sending a tingle through me. His voice was strained, like he was trying his hardest not to come yet. "You're gripping me so tight, Davina."

"Oh my—" He had to stop talking or I swear I was gonna come.

As if he sensed it, he lifted my hips up and down effortlessly, pushing me closer to climax. I felt like a rag doll in his hands, like I was the weight of a feather. He was too good at this. I could feel him even more, and an intoxicated yelp bubbled out of me.

"Look at me."

I dropped my chin, and he lowered my hips to the sofa again. When he pulled out, I couldn't help the whining noise that pushed through my lips.

"What are you doing? Why are you stopping?" I asked.

He flipped me over to my stomach, and when he said, "Bend over," I understood exactly what he wanted. I bent over and arched my back, looking over my shoulder to watch him fist his dick. When he was ready, he placed a flat hand on my lower back and drove into me.

I cried out in bliss, clutching the couch cushion.

"I've wanted to see your ass bouncing around my dick for months now," he said after a carnal groan. "You know I had to hit it from the back, D."

He spanked my right cheek before gripping my ass with both hands and thrusting. Every time he went deep, my eyes rolled farther to the back of my head. I could feel his dick rubbing against my G-spot. I was going to come. I couldn't hold back anymore.

The noise that came out of me was a mixture of pain and pleasure. Sex had the tendency to feel so good that it hurt, but sex with *Deke* felt so good that it annihilated me.

"Oh, yeah. That's good, D," he said. "Come for me. It's all yours, right?"

I sucked in a breath, nodding as he pushed in deeper. It *was* mine right now. *All mine.* Nothing could take it away.

"You have the perfect ass, baby. Keep your back arched just like that." His voice was thick and sweet like honey. "I wanna keep looking at that beautiful ass while I fuck you."

This man.

His voice.

He was beyond anything my mind could comprehend. He was so primal, so blunt, so damn sexy.

I pressed my cheek to the cushion and moaned. I swear he felt harder, bigger, like he was swelling inside me with every pump. His breathing quickened, and he gripped my waist so tight I was sure it would leave a bruise, but I didn't care.

"You're about to make me come, baby," he panted.

After several rigid thrusts, Deke sunk his full length into me while unleashing a thunderous groan.

Then he yanked himself out just as quickly and came on my lower back. His come was hot as it spilled downward, and as he breathed raggedly, I collapsed, belly flat on the sofa.

We stayed that way a moment, catching our breath, letting the moment sink in.

Deke finally got up to find some napkins and wipe his release away. When it was gone, he lowered to his knees beside the sofa and met my eyes.

"You good?" he asked with a playful laugh.

I smiled at him, and his smile turned into a grin. He was so boyishly handsome, with his brown eyes sparkling and those adorable dimples popping out.

When I sat up, Deke claimed the spot next to me. He tugged on my hand and pulled me toward him. I bit a smile as I climbed onto his lap, then settled myself on top of his sated dick.

Wrapping my arms around the back of his neck, I leaned forward and kissed him. He groaned behind the kiss, palming me in his hands. I felt him spasm beneath me.

"You trying to get me hard again?" he mumbled on my mouth.

"Maybe," I returned with a coy smile, and he laughed, spanking me. After another deep kiss, I sighed. "Let me find my panties."

I climbed off his lap, but it was when I stood in front of him that Deke caught my hand and stopped me, before I could move away.

I looked down at him as he leaned forward, with his face so close to my sex I could feel his breath running between my thighs. With ease, he gripped one of my legs and propped my foot on the sofa cushion, leaving me spread wide open.

I suppose he hadn't completely gotten his fill, because he looked up at me, held my waist, and buried his tongue in my pussy.

I gasped, my knees buckling, but he kept me steady with one hand at my hip and the other clutching the outer thigh of my propped-up leg.

"Deke," I moaned. "You're just . . . you're too much."

A throaty laugh vibrated through him, and to show me just how much he was, he took my hand and placed the palm of it on the back of his head. That action alone sent a spiral of pleasure through me. He was telling me to own him, to *control* him, that he was mine to use and that I could do whatever I wanted to him.

I skimmed my fingers down the coarse hair at the nape of his neck and brought them back up again to rest my hand on the back of his head. I pushed his face in deeper, moaning as I looked down the soft, curvy hills of my body to lock eyes with him. Just like I had on the rooftop cabana, I held his head, but this time I wanted to ride his face, so I rocked my hips.

His tongue slid from my clit to just around my entrance, and when he picked up on what I was doing, he repeated that same motion over and over again until I threw my head back and cried out with pleasure. It felt so good, so bad, so fucking delicious.

When Deke pulled his mouth away, I staggered backward and attempted to catch my breath. He rested his back against the sofa again, spreading his legs apart as he swiped the pad of his thumb over his glistening bottom lip.

"I swear I love watching you come, D," he said, giving me a mildly arrogant grin.

I huffed a laugh, and because I couldn't help myself, I straddled his lap and kissed him. With thick, heavy breaths, he kissed the hollow of my throat and the crook of my neck and then gripped my face in one of his large hands to press his hot mouth to mine.

He coaxed my lips apart so our tongues collided, then gave my ass a squeeze. I sighed in ecstasy, feeling him grow hard again.

It was that night when I realized I'd hit the hookup jackpot.

Not only was Deke exceptional in his career; he was an incredibly gifted fuck-buddy too.

I could live with that.

FORTY-TWO

DEKE

The last thing I wanted to do was leave Davina's office.

I had the woman of my dreams lying next to me, her warm breath on my skin, and her scent still on my mouth. She was next to me on a futon floor mattress that'd been crammed into one of her closets.

As I'd helped her haul it out (after having my way with her several times), she'd informed me that she'd gotten the mattress when she and Tisha had to stay overnight in her previous office.

It was around the time her products went viral, and since it was such a big moment for her company, she didn't want to risk going home and missing out on something. It was a pivotal point in her career, so I completely understood that.

She'd told me the story about how she stuck around the building to make sure orders were fulfilled and packages were neatly curated. It was nice knowing she cared about her business. Most people's hearts aren't invested in what they do. They just do it for the sake of a check or attention, but not Davina. She loved GOC from the bottom of her heart, and that passion radiated from her.

It was six thirty in the morning. I'd woken up about twenty minutes earlier, when my phone alarm went off, but she didn't budge a bit. I remained at her side on the mattress, watching as she slept peacefully on her stomach, her arms folded and tucked beneath her head as a makeshift pillow.

Her thick mop of curls covered half her face, and her magenta lips were pouty, begging me to kiss them. She was still naked from the night before, with only a blanket covering her butt and thighs.

I sat up and stared out the window as the sun slowly made its debut. It was so quiet in this office. So serene. I didn't want to leave . . . but I'd already made an obligation, so I had to be there. Plus, Arnold would've flipped his shit if I didn't show. If I drove back to ATL now, I could pack a quick bag and still make my flight at twelve.

I put my focus on Davina again and brushed some of the hair away from her cheek so I could place a kiss there. I wanted to wake her up but remembered her telling me how she'd been restless the last couple of months. At this moment, she was sleeping like a baby.

As much as I wanted to kiss her mouth, then trail kisses down her naked body until my tongue woke her up, I didn't. I had no doubt I'd have another chance to do what I really wanted soon enough. Instead, I went to her desk, grabbed a loose sheet of paper and a pen, and left a quick note.

Before I walked out the door, I stopped and took one last look at her. As I watched her, something expanded in my chest like the swelling of a hot-air balloon. The heat was rising, the flames growing, filling the hollowness of my heart with warmth. Everything in me wanted to stay and hold her a few seconds longer.

This woman was doing strange things to me—things I couldn't explain or understand—but there was one thing I knew for certain.

Davina Klein had all of me. Every cell, every breath, every heartbeat—she had it all.

She just didn't know it yet.

FORTY-THREE

DAVINA

My phone chimed with the familiar 7:00 a.m. alarm, and I groaned, blinking to get rid of the bleariness.

When my surroundings were clear, I stopped the alarm, then stared up at the vaulted ceiling. Then I smiled when it all came rushing back to me.

I had sex with Deke.

I brought a hand to my mouth, trying to conceal the goofy smile as I looked where he'd been lying last night. I felt both relieved and disappointed to not see him there.

Half of me wished he were there to talk to—maybe even have a quickie before I got my day started—but the other half knew it was better that he'd left. After all, this *was* just sex. That was the agreement we'd made, so it was fine.

I sat up as the sunlight spilled over the spiked skyscrapers. There was a raw feeling between my legs, a sheer reminder that a well-known basketball player had been buried there.

With a blissful sigh, I stood up and collected my bra and panties. When I found my clothes from random corners of the office, I slipped into them, then walked to my desk. There was a folded sheet of paper lying on top of it that wasn't there last night.

I picked it up, and my heart pounded a little bit faster as I read it.

> Hey D,
>
> Didn't want to wake you up. You were sleeping peacefully and I figured you needed the rest after the way I put it down on you. Want to see you again soon. I'll call you when it's calmer on my end.
>
> Btw you're so pretty when you sleep. Hope I get to see you like that again.
>
> Deke

I couldn't help the laugh that bubbled out of me. *Put it down on me?* He was silly. I liked that about him, though, and it felt good knowing he'd enjoyed me the night before too.

Of course, if he didn't get around to texting or calling me, then maybe he'd left the note as a courtesy. I *was* a little rusty, I admit, and I was sure he'd had sex with women ten times better than me. I would've understood him not coming back for seconds, though it would've hurt the hell out of my feelings.

I shoved that thought aside and folded the floor mattress, cleaned up my greasy dinner from last night, then collected my sandals and purse. When I locked up the office, I walked barefoot through the building to reach the parking lot.

It wasn't until I was in the car and driving that I thought of Deke all over again.

His hot mouth on my skin.

The way he kissed me like he *owned* me, like my lips were the only lips he wanted to feel.

The way we talked until we fell asleep with such ease, like we'd known each other our whole lives.

I ordered a quick coffee from my favorite family-owned coffee shop and drove home. When I walked in and dumped my things on the table, I couldn't help looking at the pictures on the wall.

Lew was everywhere, and I expected to feel a sense of betrayal or a pang of guilt when I saw them, but for once, I didn't. It caught me by surprise.

Something had shifted since the last time I'd set foot in my house . . . or maybe I was still drowning in lust and delirium and couldn't be bothered with sadness.

I sipped my coffee and stared at a wedding portrait of us on one of the bookshelves. I smiled at the couple smiling back at me. *Yeah. Something is definitely changing.*

I glanced down at the wedding rings on my finger. The diamond glittered from the recessed lighting, and my eyes stung. I blinked, cooling the burn and setting my coffee down.

I headed to my bedroom and hovered by the bed a moment, taking note of the tiny changes that'd happened in the last couple of weeks.

The changed sheets, the dusted blinds, and Lew's clothes packed into containers, which were stacked neatly beneath the window.

The vintage hat rack, now with more space since I organized his baseball caps in the closet.

These were all small changes—baby steps I took with Octavia that I didn't realize were so monumental at the time.

I'd wanted to keep my house the same and let Lew's former presence linger so I could find him in every corner, in every accidental spill of juice on the carpet, and even the SNICKERS candy wrappers on his side of the bed.

A few days after he died, I'd found a SNICKERS wrapper beneath his side and couldn't bring myself to throw it away. I'd let it sit there for weeks just to look at it and remember the way the caramel drooped to his chin with every first bite of his favorite chocolate bar.

I turned toward my dresser in the corner and opened the jewelry box on top of it. The box was made of black velvet, with glass knobs. Lew had given it to me as a Christmas gift two years ago.

I released a ragged breath as I looked down at my wedding rings. My fingers were shaking, and my throat thickened with emotion. I swallowed to remove the blockage building in my throat, then inhaled as I twisted them off.

I'd never taken them off—not since Lew and I got married . . . but we weren't married anymore, *were we*? I was a widow who grieved my husband's loss every single day, but what Tish said the night before rang true.

There was no dedicated time to accept someone's loss, to be happy, or to embrace a new chapter. There was only today and the future. Lewis was *never* coming back to me, and for the first time in *months*, I was willing to accept that.

All this time, I'd had this stupid notion in my head that if I hung on long enough—if I thought about him hard enough—he would materialize in some way. I'd imagined he'd reappear, waltz through the front door of our house, and wrap me in his arms.

His death hadn't been real to me. I couldn't fathom it—my best friend being gone, the light of my life out of the picture. Denial, oddly enough, was the worst part of grieving. Holding on to all that hope, for nothing to happen.

No, he wasn't coming back, but he hadn't left me either. He was still there in that beating heart of mine. I was still his, and he was right. I needed to be happy. For once in my life, I needed to choose myself and to put *me* first.

After swiping the moisture from my eyes, I placed the rings inside the jewelry box and closed it.

FORTY-FOUR

DEKE

It'd been three weeks since I last saw Davina, and it was killing me. During my personal training and practices, she was all I could think about.

The good thing is we stayed in touch. I loved getting to hear her voice and see her on FaceTime. I loved hearing her bubbly laugh and watching her blush.

We probably could've seen each other sooner, had our schedules not been so hectic. Whenever I wasn't booked up for business-related stuff or attending an event, Davina was busy.

Her products had hit the shelves of some pretty popular retail stores. She sent me a picture of herself standing in front of the display shelves with an open-mouthed grin and a thumbs-up, like it was the best day of her life. And maybe it was. It was a proud moment for her. All that hard work and time she'd invested into GOC was paying off. Attached to the shelf was a life-size cutout of me modeling the products.

"I'm jealous of that paper model," I told her when she'd FaceTimed me that night. I was lying on my couch, holding the phone with one hand and stroking Zeke's head with the other.

"Why?" She smiled behind a mouthful of pasta.

"Because that should've been me there. Paper Deke could've taken my place here at home, waiting for a flight."

She giggled at that.

"When am I going to see you again?" I asked, tucking a throw pillow behind my head.

"Not sure. I'll be meeting with Kyla soon to discuss some stuff. Next couple of days will be busy."

"I miss you," I told her.

She stuffed her mouth with more pasta, then after chewing and swallowing, asked, "Have you ever tried Madonna's? Their carbonara is so good."

"I haven't."

"Maybe I can take you there one day."

I smiled, trying to ignore the stupid nagging in my brain. *She's not going to tell you she misses you. This is your second time saying it since you last saw her. Stop being so fucking desperate.*

I shook the thought away just as Davina said, "I'm getting another call. I'll text you after."

When the call ended, I lowered the phone with a defeated sigh. As annoying as that inner voice was, it was right. I had to chill. Davina had made it clear we were *only* sleeping together, and the conversations we were having in between were to stay in touch. I could respect that.

Besides, if I wanted to keep talking to her and keep this thing between us going, I couldn't push the boundaries.

To my luck, our schedules finally aligned toward the end of September. With training camp and the season starting soon, that meant less movement and traveling for me. I had to get my mind right and prepare mentally and physically for a successful season.

Normally, women were the *last* thing on my mind this close to the games, but there was no way in hell I was passing up a night with her.

It was cute the way she'd set everything up. She'd sent me a text, asking if I was free for *brunch* on a Saturday. I shot a text right back and told her I'd been dying to have brunch with her since the last time. Then she followed it up with an address and room number for a hotel in her city.

I packed a bag and drove to Charlotte, and when I knocked on the door of her hotel room and she swung it open, my jaw dropped.

Davina stood in front of me in a satin pink robe and black lingerie that hardly concealed her brown nipples. Her hair was piled up into a sleek bun, and there was a glint in her eyes as she hung on to the edge of the door.

There were no words I could form—nothing I could say at that particular moment. All I could do was act. It'd been weeks since I last saw her in person, and now I had her, this sexy gift before me, ready to be unwrapped.

I cupped the back of her head while dropping my lips to hers, guiding her body back until I had enough room to shut the door. She laughed behind the kiss and laced her arms around the back of my neck.

Dropping my duffle bag, I picked her up in my arms and stumbled toward the bed. She tasted like red wine and smelled like coconut and that signature warm vanilla. I missed her smell. I missed *her*.

When her back landed on the plush comforter, I stood tall between her legs, and while I peeled my T-shirt off, she tugged at the buckle of my belt and undid it before going for the button and zipper.

When my clothes were removed, I dove in for another taste of her lips. Our next kiss was heated and deep as I tugged her panties down. She slipped out of her robe, and I knelt on the bed, clutching her hips and centering myself between her thighs.

"Come here," I growled, bringing her closer. When I felt the head of my dick sink into her, a hiss slipped through my teeth.

The first time I'd felt her, I had to take a moment and breathe so I wouldn't come on the spot. I swear this was just like the first time all over again, pushing into her nice and slow, feeling her pussy wrap tight around me.

Her eyes slid up to mine, and when she cupped her tits and pushed her hips upward to guide me deeper, I couldn't hold off anymore. I buried myself inside her, and her moan pierced the air.

Fuck, she felt so tight. So wet. *So damn good.*

I leaned down, resting on one elbow as I wedged a hand between our bodies. Using the pads of my fingers, I rubbed her slick clit, and her back arched as she moaned again. I kept rubbing, circling, teasing, my dick hard as stone, ready to fucking explode while watching her unravel.

"Oh, Deke," she whimpered. "I'm gonna . . ."

"Gonna what, baby?" I asked, my mouth grazing hers.

"Come," she cried. "I'm gonna come."

She gripped my forearm that was next to her head, and when she threw her head back farther and moaned, the warmth of her orgasm coated my dick.

"Damn. You're coming all over me, D," I rasped, still rubbing. "You just couldn't wait, could you?"

She threw her arms over my shoulders to bring my chest to hers. I buried my face into the crook of her neck, groaning as I lost control.

I sucked hard on her neck while throbbing, pulsing, until a deep moan ripped out of me.

I pressed a hand to the bed and snatched myself out, stroking rapidly and watching my come spill in thick ropes on her pelvis.

"Fuck, you're too good," I breathed.

Her body settled, and a goofy smile spread across her face.

"What's funny?" I asked, caging her head between my arms.

"You."

"What about me?"

"You have a strong pull-out game." She smirked, sitting up on her elbows. "I don't even want to *think* about how you've mastered that."

"So don't," I murmured on her lips. Truth was I always used a condom with other women. With Davina, though? I had to have her raw.

I kissed her slowly this time, savoring the feel of her soft lips on mine and basking in her sweet perfume and those pheromones that drove my senses wild.

When the kiss broke, I rushed to grab a towel from the bathroom, helped her clean up, then sat on the edge of the bed. She sat right next to me, and I stole a glance at her. She was looking ahead, soaking in the city view.

"How long do you think this'll go on for?" she asked.

"How long do you want it to go on for?"

She replied with a shrug, then lowered her head to study her hands. I looked at her hands, too, and realized her wedding rings were missing. In place of them was a line several shades lighter than her regular skin tone.

Interesting.

The first time we had sex, she had those rings on. I couldn't say it wasn't a distraction, seeing that diamond glint beneath the dim lights while I had my way with her. Knowing another man had probably done the same things I was doing irritated me a bit, but I understood why she kept them on, so I ignored it as best I could. I had no right to feel that way either.

To see the rings gone . . . well, something must've changed since then. Maybe she was finally starting to trust me. I tried not to smile at the thought and instead took her hand, purposely rubbing the tan line.

She noticed and swooped her gaze up to mine. Her eyes grew glossy, but she tore them away, blinking rapidly.

"Sometimes I think God purposely made my life complicated," she murmured. "Everything in my life—every decision, every choice, every romantic relationship—has always been complicated." Her velvety-brown irises turned up to me again. "It's a shitty feeling, because when I finally get to do something for myself or decide to be selfish with my decisions, it feels like everything is going to fall through the cracks."

"Is that why you won't say you miss me when I tell you I miss you?" I asked, and she huffed a laugh, shaking her head.

"No. I *did* miss you. I just wasn't sure I was ready to say it." She locked on my eyes again, and my heart pumped a little faster. I took her hand in mine and lifted her knuckles to my lips to kiss each one.

"You don't have to worry about me falling through the cracks, D. I'm not going anywhere. Hell, I'll be the glue to piece it all together again, if that's what you need."

"You're really sweet, Deke." She sighed, studying her bare thighs.

I tipped her chin so she could look at me. "Next week. Take that trip with me."

"Where?"

"I share a rental property with Whitney near Santeetlah Lake. It's not too far from Charlotte. I told Whitney to leave next weekend open for me. I want you to come."

"Is it a lake house?" she asked.

"It is, and I think you'll love it. Whitney designed the whole place. It has really nice water views. A dock. We even have a boat. I'll have it all planned out. All you gotta do is show up."

She bit a grin. "How do you know I won't be busy next weekend?"

"Make room for it. I'm sure you'll figure it out."

She bumped my shoulder. "What exactly are you expecting from this trip to Santeetlah, Deke?"

I pressed my lips, giving the question some thought. I wasn't going to tell her that I wanted her at that house so I could fuck her in every position, or to spoil the hell out of her with food, wine, and attention.

Sure, I wanted that . . . but I also wanted to get to know Davina for who she truly was. I wanted to catch her while her guard was completely down and understand what was in her heart. And, if she was open to it, I'd tell her what was in mine.

But instead of saying all that, I said, "There are no expectations, D. I just like your company."

At that, she put on a broad smile, and because I couldn't help myself, I collected her chin in my fingers, leaned in, and kissed her.

She lay back, and I climbed on top of her, grazing the ridge of my semihard dick through the slit of her pussy. I kept skimming up and down while taking shallow dips inside to tease her.

Her breaths thickened, and her eyes pooled with heat and desire. She ran a gentle hand across my shoulder as I slipped into her with ease.

When I was all in, I claimed those pouty lips and kissed her like I meant it. Because I did. I meant it when I said I wasn't going anywhere.

FORTY-FIVE

DAVINA

By the time Monday rolled around, I felt like a new woman.

I walked into my office with a burst of energy and a pep in my step. It was as if the thick gray cloud that once hovered above my head and blocked my vision was slowly lifting. And as the cloud lifted higher and higher, it soon began to drift, so I could witness the world before me again.

I could see that things weren't all so bad and that I *could* live my life despite all I'd been through.

I wanted to attribute most of it to Deke, but it wasn't just him who checked on me, brought me out of a funk, and made sure I was okay. I had my sister, my best friend, and even some of my employees, who checked in whenever they caught me in the warehouse.

It was nice knowing there were people who cared and people who accepted me for who I was. No one tried rushing me into a happy place. They all just let me be what I needed to be in the moment and embraced it. I was shocked Deke did too.

I sat behind my desk, completely zoned out as I thought about my time with him. We'd eventually found the will to leave the hotel room and sit at the hotel bar, where we sipped on those waters I had rain checked him for. It was his turn not to drink that night. He had team training coming up and wanted to keep his mind and body clear.

It was amazing how disciplined he was, and I was curious who'd instilled that discipline in him, because a man like Deke Bishop wasn't just born. He was raised and molded to be the person he was. Though a part of him was clearly damaged (something he *never* talked about), he still seemed like a good man with good morals and hella patience.

It made me feel bad that what I had with him would only be temporary. I knew one day he'd grow tired of seeing me for brunches. He'd find another woman to catch his eye, and I'd hear less and less from him.

That was fine. In fact, I was preparing myself mentally to not be disappointed by it. The last thing I'd expected was for him to stick to only sleeping with me . . . but then I'd see the look in his eyes—the longing, as if he wanted more than just brunch and kisses.

It was as if he wanted me to wrap him in my arms so I could caress the flat waves in his hair while he listened to my heartbeat. Both of us would be in complete silence, enjoying one another's company. Holding on tight because it would feel safe . . .

I shook my head and sat up in my chair. It was a nice thought, but it wouldn't happen. It *couldn't* . . . could it? I was nowhere near prepared for something that deep. What we had now was good. It was safe—one foot in and one foot out, just in case.

There was a knock at my office door, and Tish popped her head in. "Don't forget about that meeting with Cassie Lee."

My brows dipped. "Who?"

Tish stepped deeper into the office, checking her phone. "Says here you have a meeting with Cassie Lee. She's a rep for a small storefront. You said it was fine to see her today at eleven."

"Oh. Right." I remembered now and also remembered thinking it was very strange that anyone wanted to schedule a meeting with me. The only in-person meetings I ever had were with Chester or, on the rare occasion, Deke. The rest were done via Zoom, or I had to travel for them.

"She'll likely be here in the next couple of minutes," Tish added before she left the office.

I glanced at the time on my computer screen. *Shit.* Time was flying. I straightened my desk and stuffed my feet back into my shoes, and right on cue, there was another knock at the door.

This time, Tish walked in without a trace of a smile. Her eyes were wide—panicked, almost—and my smile collapsed as a tall bronzed woman sauntered in behind her.

She wore high heels and a tan blazer over a skintight white dress, and her hair was so polished and silky it seemed unreal. But it wasn't. That hair was hers, and this was no Cassie Lee. This was Giselle Grace, Deke's past fling.

"Should I cancel this appointment?" Tish asked, looking between us with her arms folded. Her defensive side was coming out.

"No," I murmured, standing taller and raising my chin. "I'll take it."

Tish cleared her throat and walked past Giselle, who pressed her lips as my best friend went by. "Let me know if you need me," Tish called, and when she left, she didn't close the door like she often did. She left it cracked open.

I inhaled through my nose and released the air through my mouth as Giselle's almond-green eyes looked me up and down. She walked in the opposite direction of me, her heels clicking with each step, her gaze sweeping the area thoroughly. What was up with people bringing beef to my office?

"I assume you know who I am," Giselle said, facing me again. She had a mild accent. Caribbean.

I folded my arms, keeping my chin raised. "I do."

"Yeah, I bet Deke's told you all about me."

I held back a grimace when she said his name, and by the smirk on her lips and the fierceness in her eyes, I knew exactly what this was. She wasn't just here to see the woman who now had Deke's attention. She was here to strike discouragement, to intimidate.

I almost choked on a laugh at the thought. If only she knew I was hardly ever intimidated by anyone. She had no idea the shit I'd gone through in my life to be where I was.

"What do you want?" I asked, keeping my voice level.

"I keep seeing news on BOBBLE. Everyone has been trying to figure out what it is about this new woman Deke Bishop has been seen with on multiple occasions. First at a restaurant and then at a hotel bar." She trailed the pad of a manicured finger over one of my lamps. "I had to see this woman for myself. In person."

"So you booked an appointment under a fake name just to see me?"

She didn't answer that and instead peered out the windows. "All of this is very nice, what you have here. Why risk letting it drown for him?"

"You don't know what kind of relationship I have with him."

"Hmm . . . well, he broke it off with me without much of a reason and lost complete interest way before that. I could only assume another woman had stolen that from me."

I scoffed, my brows shooting to my forehead. "Stolen?"

"I can also assume he's fucking you now." She narrowed her eyes at me, and I sighed.

"Is this why you came here? For me to admit that we're sleeping together?"

"No," she said, and she steeled her jaw, glowering. "I came here to tell you that Deke is not who you think he is. He's a user and a manipulator. He makes you believe that he cares because he's so nice and charming and always has the right things to say, but it is all false. The truth is that he is a loner who will only hurt you because he knows he's a shitty human inside. Being with him is a *mistake*."

Her words made my heart stutter. Deke wasn't perfect, I knew this, but there was no way he was a manipulator, a user. Why would he use me when he had everything?

I swallowed thickly. "Is that all?" I asked.

"You don't belong in his world, Davina Klein. Or should I say Davina Klein-*Roberts*. Didn't your husband die last year? It's none of my business, but how are you even okay with this? Sneaking around with a basketball player, knowing people will find out more about you and start sniffing around your husband's grave. Because you know they will do that, right? These people, they don't care. I'm not sure what he's using you for, but I'll tell you now. When I was with him, there was no love inside him, no romance—*nothing*. He's empty inside. Everything is just a game to him, and right now you're no different than the ball he dribbles. Whatever it is you're looking for in him, you won't find it. He'll let you down before you even get the chance to ask why."

I blinked quickly, fighting the stupid urge to cry. I didn't have the urge because I was sad to hear this but because I was angry and trying to swallow it all down and hold my ground. Lew was a sensitive subject for me, and I was pissed she knew about it.

"If that's the case, why do you care?" I asked. "Why do you want him back? Because that's what you're implying, right? That you want me to leave him alone so you can have him to yourself again?"

She looked me all over. "I'm used to men like him. And though he's a shitty person and a lousy date, I made a great living by having him in my back pocket. My career blew up."

"So, remind me again who the user is?"

At that, her mouth pinched tight, and her nostrils flared. It was shocking, really, how the whole world thought she was this beautiful, ethnic, untouchable woman, yet up close she wasn't all they made her out to be. Hell, I thought she was stunning in the photos, but up close, behind the heavy makeup, designer clothes, polished hair, and filters, she was just a regular woman. A bitter, ladder-climbing woman.

I dropped my arms and walked to the door, pulling it open wider. "Thank you for the knowledge, Giselle, but I'm a grown woman who can make decisions for herself. You can leave now."

I remained by the door as she glared at me. Then she lifted her expensive leather purse and walked to me with a sheet of paper in hand. When she was closer, I realized it was a check made out to me for $60,000.

"I will give you this if you stop seeing him," she said in a lowered voice. I looked from the paper to her face, and her glossed bottom lip was slightly trembling.

Sixty grand? Was she serious? My company made twice that in two weeks. Many people would've been grateful for a check that size, but I didn't want or *need* her damn money, and this was clearly an insult— not only to me, because she thought I'd be shallow enough to take it, but to Deke as well.

I gently pushed her hand down. "Is that really all he's worth to you?" I asked in an even lower voice.

I know she heard me clearly, because her eyes expanded and she yanked her hand back. Stepping away, she whirled around and slammed the check on my desk.

"When you come to your senses, cash the check and walk away. Leave him where he belongs." She stormed out of my office, the click-clack of her heels growing faint the farther she was away from me.

When she was gone, my shoulders sagged, and I released the shaky breath trapped inside me.

FORTY-SIX

DEKE

Jacobi Bennet, one of the Ravens' power forwards, passed me the ball, and when the rock hit my hands, I positioned myself to shoot.

The ball sank into the net, and the nine other men on the court hollered at the tops of their lungs.

"Let's go!"

"Hell yeah, that's game, baby!"

"That's what I'm talking about, Bishop!"

A hand clapped my shoulder as I placed my hands on my hips to catch my breath. We were in the stadium where all the magic happened. Training camp wasn't starting for another week, but Coach Harrison gave us the green light to scrimmage with some of the rookies.

I preferred it this way—getting to know the new guys and building a connection with them before we got into the heavy hitting. In my opinion, a team couldn't be a team if we didn't trust each other.

Jacobi gave my shoulder a proud shake before he let it go and snatched off his headband. "I see you're ready to ball, Bishop."

"I am, man. Been training with Ken all summer."

Jacobi hissed through his teeth. "*Ken Massey?* Yo, I know he's been drilling your ass. That man is tough as hell, but that only means you'll be ready. Nobody'll be able to stop you, my boy." He tapped the heart of my chest with the back of his hand before walking backward. "I'll catch you in a couple weeks, though. Stay up, Bishop!"

I gave him a nod, then jogged toward Javier. We grabbed our stuff from the locker room, then headed to the private garage, where our cars were parked.

There were bound to be people lurking outside the building, trying to catch a glimpse of the team. Though we loved our fans, most of us were tired and ready to go home and chill.

"I am telling you, Deke. If I do not hire someone soon, I will lose my mind. Aleesa has been having these tantrums. I am not understanding why. It is like she is a whole new person." Javier stopped at his black Range Rover with a frustrated huff. I could see the tiredness in his eyes, the heaviness on his shoulders. "My mother has been helping out, but she has to leave for Argentina soon."

"Hire Octavia," I offered, swinging the door of my car open and dumping my gym bag on the passenger seat.

"You would like that, wouldn't you?" He inhaled deeply, his chest inflating, before letting the air out in a sharp exhale. "I will decide closer to the start of the season."

"Don't wait too long."

I focused on Javier, who was about to climb behind the steering wheel of his vehicle but ended up doing a double take over my shoulder. When his brows furrowed, I looked with him, and my smile collapsed.

Giselle was walking through the private parking deck. Some of the teammates drove by and whistled at her, which only made her grin and swing her hips harder.

I slammed the passenger door of my car and marched her way. "What the hell are you doing here?"

"Hey to you, too, Deke."

"Stop with the bullshit, Giselle. Why the hell are you here? How did you even get in this garage?"

"Security let me in. I told him it was urgent. He remembers my face. Besides, I could've been waiting for you at your condo, but my key doesn't work anymore, and Justin said you removed me from your visitors list."

"Yeah, I changed the locks and removed you from the list because you don't get the fucking point."

"I don't think we're really done," she said, stepping in closer. She tugged on the hem of my shirt, but I pushed her hand away. She frowned.

"Go home, Giselle," I said, turning away.

"I went to see her!"

I stopped in my tracks, glaring at her over my shoulder. "What?"

"That Davina woman you've been doing stuff with. I saw her yesterday. Are you really dropping *me* for *her*? Wasting so much opportunity for *that*?"

I twisted around until I was in front of her again, but Javier was right behind me, tugging on my shirt. "Deke," he said. "Let's just go."

"She's not going to talk to you again," Giselle went on smugly. "I told her about you and how you really are. Using women for your own satisfaction, then neglecting them. Lying to them. Disowning them. She doesn't strike me as the woman who likes to be used, Deke. Or the type who likes playing the games you play. And didn't her husband die? Don't you think it'll break her even more if you make her fall for you and then disappear? Because that's what you love to do. Hide. Disappear. Ignore the people who actually care about you. It's a sick game with you. It's like you get a kick out of making women love you just to discard them like trash."

I clenched my teeth together as Javier pulled harder on my shirt, a warning for me to move now before I did something I regretted. But I couldn't contain the anger simmering inside me, the rage coursing through my bloodstream.

"Deke," Javier said again, but I yanked my shirt out of his grasp and got closer to Giselle's face.

She smirked like she was winning—like she could control me with her words, *rule* me. Nobody controlled me anymore. I'd worked hard at being my own damn person and making my own damn rules.

I thought about Davina and how I'd called her last night only to get no answer. I assumed she was either sleeping or busy, so I thought nothing of it and figured I'd try again the next day, but now that Giselle was saying this, I realized she was ignoring me. She was afraid of the risk, and once again, the trust she had in me was severed.

My upper lip twitched as a hotness slid down my throat. I swallowed and took a deep breath to cool my temper.

"You know what, Giselle? I used to feel sorry for you. A woman without parents, adopted into a family that ended up despising you." At that, her cocky little smile sagged, and her mouth pushed downward. "But now I see why they hated you—why they didn't want you. You're a miserable, shallow person who only gives a damn about herself. Yeah, the world looks at you and sees your face, your body, but what they don't see is how fucking *ugly* you are inside. And that's why you're mad I moved on and why you went behind my back to find the woman who was *actually* making me happy. Because she's beautiful inside and out and you wanted to see it for yourself. You wanted to see what it was like to be her—what it was about her that makes *me* want her, makes *me* smile, makes *me* feel like an actual person and not just a damn prop. You wanted to witness a good woman and not the woman you are now—one who is rotten to her *fucking* core."

The parking deck was completely silent as we stared at each other.

Her bottom lip trembled, and her eyes became misty as she stared right back. When she finally blinked, she took a step away from me, but only to extend her arm and slap me across the face. The slap stung, but I barely flinched.

"*Fuck you*, Deke," she snarled before twisting on her heels and scampering away.

I watched until I could no longer see her, then dropped my head and stared at my shoes. A hand touched my shoulder, and I cut my eyes to Javier, who wore a mask of concern.

"Go get her back," he finally said after some time, and for a split second I thought he was talking about Giselle. When he realized I was about to protest, he held up his free hand and said, "Davina. Go get *Davina* back."

I felt a stinging in my eyes, which I kept trying to blink away. I hated this feeling, this disappointment. For once, I just wanted shit to go right in my life and to remain on a steady path. It felt like no matter what I did or how hard I tried, it was never easy.

I had to agree with Davina. Sometimes it felt like God made my life complicated too. I don't think it was to punish me, though, but to help me learn lessons—lessons that often left me feeling raw and gutted afterward.

"Do not let this defeat you, Deke," Javier said. "Get Davina back, and prove to her and everyone else how wrong they are about you."

FORTY-SEVEN

DAVINA

My phone buzzed on the kitchen counter as I dunked a tea bag into a porcelain mug. I gave it a glance, not surprised to see Deke's name on the screen.

"Is that him again?" Tish asked from the living room. Her eyes were glued to the TV, her hand deep in a bowl of popcorn as a reality show streamed.

"Yep," I muttered, picking up my mug and phone and carrying it with me to the living room.

"You're gonna have to answer one day, Vina," she said, still staring at the TV. "Oh! I knew that girl was lying! She was all over Darrell in the last season!" She pointed at the TV, and I huffed a laugh as a woman with red hair commentated.

As I settled onto the couch and sipped my tea, my phone rang once again. I sighed. It wasn't that I *didn't* want to talk to Deke, I just wasn't sure what to say to him or what the hell to even ask.

What'll happen when you're tired of me too? Will you toss me to the side like trash? Pretend I never existed?

I knew one day our fling would end, but that didn't mean it'd be on good terms . . . and that's probably what was scaring me about this whole agreement. Deke seemed like a great man, but the way he handled his relationships with women, sex buddies or not, seemed completely unhealthy. My heart couldn't handle being scarred again, especially not while it was still in the process of healing.

Frankly, I was afraid that if I asked anything about it, he'd give the wrong answer and I'd have no choice but to look at him differently. I'd be disappointed in a person I thought was making my life better.

"Girl, just answer the phone," Tish insisted, finally putting her attention on me.

"I don't know what to say to him, Tish."

"Don't say anything. Just answer and let him do all the talking." Her shoulders hiked up, nearly touching her earlobes. "That's what I do to Lorenzo when he's pissed me off."

"That sounds *very* immature," I laughed.

"Who cares? It works." She winked at me before climbing off the recliner, with the popcorn. "I'll get the face masks." Right. Because we'd rescheduled our self-care Sunday to a self-care Thursday . . . all because I was still in a hotel with Deke and tangled between his legs.

Ugh.

I swiped the Answer button and put it on speakerphone. "What is it, Deke?"

"Davina," he said with way more enthusiasm than I expected. "Finally. I, um . . . I've been calling you for days."

"I know." I sipped my tea and cut my eyes to Tish, who was ripping a pink face mask packet open while fighting a smile.

"Listen, I'm sorry about Giselle. If I'd known she would come to you, I would've warned you, D." Hearing him call me that one letter made my heart stutter. I couldn't stand that he had this effect on me, this strong hold that made me feel like I was important. He continued when I didn't say anything. "What all did she say to you?"

I let my head tilt back a bit so I could look at the flat ceiling. "Not much. Just that you're a manipulator who'll most likely hurt me when you're ready to dispose of me." Okay, so maybe those weren't her words exactly, but that's how I digested them. "I don't take any of it personally,

Deke. You're a famous person who is surrounded by temptations and opportunities. I know what we have going on is just fun to you. That's all we agreed to, right? So whenever this thing between us loses its appeal, just promise me you'll handle it gently."

"No—Davina, listen." He released an exasperated sigh. I could hear basketballs dribbling in the background. Was he practicing but took a break to call me? To check on me? I tried not to melt at the thought. "Just give me the chance to explain everything, all right? Let me prove to you that I do care and that I'm not using you. Let me show you that I'm not just wasting your time. Come to the lake house tomorrow. I'll email you the details, and I'll wait for you there."

"Deke, I can't go to that lake house with you."

"Why not, Davina?"

I swung my head to Tish, searching for a cop-out, but she simply sipped her tea and raised her free hand, refusing to intervene.

When I didn't say anything, Deke spoke again.

"See? You have no reason not to. You know me, D. You know deep in your heart that I would never hurt you. We've got a good thing going. Don't let Giselle fuck it up."

I swallowed and lowered my gaze to my lap.

"I'm tired of pretending we're these surface-level friends who don't know each other. Let me prove to you that I'm not a flake, that I'm not someone who'll abandon you. Just give me that chance, Davina, and I promise I'll make it worth it."

Still, I didn't say much. I closed my eyes for a moment, feeling an unexpected tug in my belly. A tug of hope.

"Look, we don't have to get all deep at the lake house," he said in a huskier voice. "I know you're not ready for that—I can sense it—but you can't deny that you like being around me, D. And I know you can't because I like being around you." The tugging was stronger. I adjusted on the sofa, trying to get rid of the feeling. "But I also get why you wouldn't trust my word after hearing that firsthand from Giselle and with my reputation, so we'll keep it simple. A few days ago, you asked me how long I thought this would go on for. Well, we can figure it out this weekend. If you decide by the time the weekend is over that you want to walk away from it, I'll respect it. You won't have to worry about me hurting you, lying to you, or any of that other shit. We'll walk away and be done with it in a cordial way. I'll stop calling, stop texting, stop emailing. It'll remain strictly professional, but that's *only* if you give me a chance this weekend."

"Deke . . ."

"Think about it before you answer."

I placed my tea on the coffee table to run my palm over my sweat-pants. "Okay. I'll think about it."

"Cool. Just let me know."

I hung up before any more seconds ticked by. If I'd stayed on the phone with him, I probably would've cried. I felt so bad for ignoring him, knowing he was stressing himself out and worried sick.

But how could I answer after hearing that from Giselle? Because I'll be honest, other than knowing Deke was a professional NBA player, that he had two sisters and a dog, and that he'd lost a brother at a young age, I didn't know much else about him.

I didn't know what was beneath the exterior, if he had a temper, if he lied to and used women he wanted—like me and Giselle—just to satisfy some black hole within himself that could never be filled. Not that I believed everything Giselle said, but still. There had to be *some* truth to it, no? You never really know a person, and with Deke, there was only one way to find out who he really was.

"You know you have to go, right?" Tish asked, carrying the face masks into the living room.

I dragged a hand down my cheek. "Why should I?"

Tish sat in the recliner again. "Because you like him, I can tell. And it's been clear from the beginning that he likes your ass too. Y'all aren't just fuck-buddies anymore. I sense something deeper."

"*Deeper* how?" I asked to entertain her.

"Davina, be real. If you were only in it for the sex, you wouldn't have been so upset about the Giselle thing. It wouldn't have mattered what she said if you were only in it for the D."

"I don't believe that. There may be no strings attached, but I still expect a little respect. This is probably just a phase for him, Tish. Like he said, we can have this weekend to get it out of our systems and then we can move on." I waved a dismissive hand. "No point in prolonging the inevitable."

"And what, pray tell, is the inevitable?"

"What we have, Tish. This thing between me and Deke has only ever been physical. It'll never reach a level deeper than that for us, and frankly, I'm fine with that because I don't want more. Yes, I want to live my life, but settling down and falling for someone again is not in the plans. I just . . . I don't think I can do that to myself again."

Suddenly, all I could think about was Lewis. He had my all. I invested so much into our relationship and gave him every ounce of love I had.

I wasn't sure I had it in me to give it to another . . . or maybe I was just too much of a chicken to find out if it was possible.

FORTY-EIGHT

DAVINA

I adjusted my visor mirror, catching the reflection of my eyes. They were rimmed with dark mascara and only a light swoop of black eyeliner.

My hair was in tight coils that shaped my face, my brows freshly plucked. The sky was thick with clouds, an attempt to block the sun's radiant shine. Birds flew past, dipping and bobbing.

I glanced at the packed bag on my passenger seat, the bag I'd taken my time to pack that morning, ruminating between the idea of abandoning it or packing extra clothes just in case. The teal straps of one of my tank tops stuck out, and I tucked it into place before starting my car and pulling out of the driveway.

When Tish and I had discussed more about my weekend with Deke, I kept telling her how I needed to be working anyway and couldn't go to the lake house. She wasn't having it, though. She knew they were all excuses for me to not be with Deke.

"I'll have all of that covered," Tish had said as she replaced my tea with a glass of chardonnay. "If you don't go, you might not get the chance again later."

For some reason, her words struck fear in my heart, as if not getting to be solo with Deke again was a loss my body couldn't handle. Those words stuck to me like glue as I lay in bed, restless, reading the email he'd sent with the address of the lake house.

I filled my gas tank, then took the freeway, chewing on the inside of my cheek until it was raw. I spotted the sign for Graham County, and my heart thundered in my chest as I made a turn onto an unmarked road and drove until I spotted a cottage in the distance.

The cottage was enveloped in sweet gum trees with saffron-and-gold leaves. A few pine trees and red maples blended in, the reds of the maples standing out boldly beneath the remaining sunlight.

It would be dark soon, and I was glad I left when I did, because the view was spectacular already. It *screamed* autumn, and I could feel a persuading breeze sneaking through my cracked window.

I turned into the driveway and killed the engine, staring at the over-size lake house ahead of me. The exterior was made of wood beams and panels, had a wraparound porch with cable railing, and was furnished with a combination of cushioned seats and rocking chairs.

I spotted the familiar black Ferrari parked close to the cottage and gleaming in the light. I closed my eyes for a second, taking a quick breath before opening them again and climbing out of my car, with my purse and overnight bag.

As I clutched my keys in hand, I smelled the salt of the lake, the sweet stickiness of the maple trees, and the muskiness of the damp, earthy soil.

It was in this moment that I felt I was no longer controlling my body. My mind took the back seat as I put one foot in front of the other, and the gravel crunched beneath my Air Maxes.

I walked along the wooden porch until I found the front door. It was painted black, which was a nice contrast to all the wood. I pressed the doorbell with my thumb as my pulse rattled in my ears, and my hands grew slick with sweat. I had the entry code, but I didn't have the courage to just walk right in. Deke and I weren't there yet . . . *were we?*

Footsteps sounded on the other side of the door, then a curtain near the window shifted so someone could peek out. Just as quickly, the locks of the door clinked, and it swung open.

My breathing slowed—as well as my heart—when I looked into Deke's deep-brown eyes. He was shirtless, wearing only a pair of gray basketball shorts that did nothing to hide his bulging print.

His chest was a delicious, satiny brown, and I studied every single detail of him in what was left of the daylight. The sharp collarbones followed by the pecs below them. His dark-brown nipples and how they were positioned perfectly on his chest. The six-pack of muscles on his abdomen leading to a carved V hidden beneath the thin material of his shorts.

He smelled like men's bodywash—a sensual, warm, earthy scent—along with a subtle hint of cocoa butter.

When I found his eyes again, he smiled a little, as if he had to take caution—like if he smiled too hard, he might risk me walking away. But I wasn't walking away. I was here, and as it digested, I realized there was no going back.

And perhaps that's why my heart was beating so chaotically and why I was so afraid to come here in the first place. Because deep down, I knew this weekend was going to either push us closer together or tear us apart, and I didn't want it to come to either of those outcomes. I just wanted us to exist in the same world and breathe the same air.

I wanted us to just *be*.

Regardless of what I wanted, I had to cherish this time with him and be grateful for it. There were thousands of women in the world he could've picked to be at the lake house, but he chose *me*. That had to mean something.

I took a step closer, and his face softened. He brought a hand up and slid the pad of his thumb over my mouth, then carried that hand over until it was cupping the side of my face.

A sigh rippled out of me, and I buried my face into his palm, grabbing his inked forearm, silently begging him not to take this comfort away. His hand slipped through mine, and I swallowed hard as I stared up at him, studying the cognac flecks in his eyes.

With a crooked white smile, he said, "Come here," then his hand cupped my waist, and he reeled me in. I was left with no choice but to drop my bags at the door and sink into his arms.

I was hungry for his lips, feeling complete satisfaction when they landed on mine, and he kissed me fiercely, *hungrily*, like he'd been craving the taste of my mouth.

He stumbled backward into the house and picked me up in his arms. When he kicked the door shut, I didn't know where he was taking me, nor did I care. My butt landed on something hard and cold, and he snatched his lips away to kiss my throat.

As my head fell back, I saw we were in a spacious kitchen. He had me on the countertop and was deep between my legs, leaving no gaps between us.

We were both in a frenzy then, hurrying to take my leggings off, to remove my jacket. He helped me discard the panties, then pulled my shirt over my head, revealing my white lace bra. When he caught sight of it, he marveled at it for a moment before diving back in and kissing me.

He shoved his shorts down, then angled the lower half of my body just right so that my legs hung over his forearms. And when he pressed the head of his dick to my entrance and sank into me at a torturous pace, I lost it. He sank all the way until he was balls deep and kept his hips completely still. A throaty groan was stuck in his throat as he eyed me.

Damn. I loved it when he did that. The first stroke in, keeping it there so we could both feel it, to prove this was real—that this was happening. I clasped his face in my hands as he drew his hips back to slam into me, and he kept going this way, our skin clapping, our tongues overlapping, our moans and groans floating up to the vaulted ceilings.

I held on to him tightly, resting the back of my head against the cabinet as he pawed at my bra and forced the cups down. His mouth wrapped around my nipple, sucking, nipping, and he slowed his strokes, focusing on driving into me while simultaneously using his mouth to go from nipple to nipple.

There weren't many words that could be spoken.

We were here, tangled in each other's arms, and the thought of that sent a shot of euphoria through me.

Deke gripped my ass in his hands and pulled me closer to the edge of the counter, burrowing deeper until a loud groan rocked through him. I felt him pulsing inside me, like his dick had taken a life of its own.

Our eyes connected, and his pupils dilated, and when I sank my teeth into my bottom lip, he grunted and pulled out with a deep moan, coming on the kitchen floor.

"Oh, fuck," he gasped, stroking his dick as more come dribbled downward. "*Fuck*, Davina."

I moaned, looking at him as he studied his glistening dick. His eyes shifted up to mine again, and he picked me up, carrying me to the living room.

"Are you going to clean that up?" I laughed.

"Later," he said, laying my back on the edge of the nearest sofa. He dropped to his knees and lifted my legs so they hung over his shoulders.

Oh, goodness. Is he about to . . .

His hot tongue slid right through my pussy.

Yeah. He's doing it.

A ragged breath burst out of me as he licked and sucked, focusing directly on my clit. There was no teasing this time, no delay. He went straight for it, pressing his tongue in and looping it round and round like he had something to prove.

"Deke," I breathed. I gripped the top of his head, and he took that as an invitation to bury his face deeper. He made hungry noises, *kissing* noises, eating me like I was a meal he'd never had. It was enough to make me explode.

I clutched the upholstered couch with one hand and arched my back as I cried to the ceiling. The orgasm swept through me, and he swallowed it all down with deep little grunts, vibrating between my legs to finish me off.

I had to push his head away for him to pull back because it felt so incredible—*too incredible*. I was stuck in the kind of pleasure that overwhelmed me—the kind that pushed me into another universe and caused my eyes to roll to the back of my skull. It was the rare kind of orgasm that could make a woman cry.

When I came down, Deke placed my feet on the floor.

I gulped down a few breaths as he hovered above me and planted his large hands on top of the couch.

With a boyish smile, he asked, "You good, D-Baby?"

I couldn't help laughing as I gave his chest a playful smack.

FORTY-NINE

DEKE

I don't know what came over me when I saw Davina at that door. For a second there, I thought she wouldn't come.

I came to the lake house that morning to mentally prepare myself for her arrival. I missed her, and I didn't want to waste a single second, but as the clock ticked and the sun made its descent, I figured she wouldn't show.

I tried swallowing my pride and accepting the loss before the night could end . . . but then I heard that doorbell ring, and I'd never jumped up so quickly. My heart was hammering, and I was as giddy as a kid on Christmas morning.

When I saw her, I wanted to cry, I shit you not. I'd never felt such relief, such joy.

After I finally cleaned my mess on the kitchen floor and helped her find her clothes, Davina went for a shower while I ordered dinner. When she came back down, the pizza boxes were set up in a row on the countertop, with a wine bottle freshly removed from the fridge and two cool bottles of water right next to it. She wore white shorts that I wouldn't have exactly called shorts and a teal cropped tank top with no bra.

I fought a smile and cleared my throat as I grabbed two plates from the cabinet.

"What?" she asked, meeting me in the kitchen.

"Nothing." I laughed anyway, like a dumbass.

"Deke, seriously? What's funny?" she asked, her smile melting a bit.

"Nothing," I tried again, placing the plates on the counter. "It just hit me how it was a waste of time for you to take a shower when those clothes are gonna come off again."

She sunk her teeth into her bottom lip and leaned over the counter. "We'll see about that."

I jerked a thumb over my shoulder, pointing to the deck. "I've got a fire going if you wanna eat outside."

"*Ooohhh.* Yes, please."

I filled two wineglasses while she grabbed one of the boxes of pizza and a roll of paper towels. I eyed the fancy plates from the cabinet, realizing they were kinda pointless. I was trying so hard to impress her.

When we were on the deck, she shivered as she placed the pizza box on the four-top table.

"Yeah, it got cool out here. Let me grab a blanket." I collected one from the basket full of blankets Whitney had handpicked herself and brought it outside, wrapping it around Davina's shoulders as she sat.

"Thanks." She looked up at me with a coy smile, a hand on one shoulder to keep the blanket in place.

I grabbed a slice of pizza after she did and listened to the fire crackle, sinking into my chair and basking in the moment. It was too dark to see much of anything beyond the water flowing beneath a swollen crescent moon and the silhouette of mountains.

When she took a bite of her pizza and some of the cheese drooped onto her chin, I ripped off a paper towel and handed it to her.

"What made you come?" I asked as she wiped grease from her chin.

Her eyes connected to mine, and the bright embers of the fire reflected in them. "It felt like something I needed to do."

I nodded, biting into my pizza. "I think it was the right choice."

She laughed. "Of course you'd think so."

"I'm sorry about Giselle," I said, studying her face. Her features softened as she placed her pizza on a loose paper towel.

"What did you do for her to talk that way about you?"

"I didn't do anything," I returned. "I just saw her for who she really was."

"And that is?"

"A selfish person."

"Hmm." She dropped her gaze. "So you're telling me that you'd rather be in this lake house with me, an ordinary woman, than with a supermodel most of the world knows and adores?"

"Damn right."

"Why?" she asked, and there was genuine curiosity in her eyes.

"Because you're not just ordinary to me, Davina. You're beautiful, nice, and you give back. You empathize."

"I'm not perfect, Deke."

"Neither am I."

She accepted that, picking up her pizza again and finishing it off.

As she sipped some wine, she sat back and said, "You know this won't last forever, right?"

I smirked, grabbing my wine too. "We'll see about that."

~

After eating, we went inside, and Davina did a little squeal when she noticed the stack of board games beneath the TV stand.

"We *have* to play Scrabble." She pulled the red box out and waved it in the air, causing the wooden letters to rattle.

She was really good at Scrabble. I, on the other hand, was trash at it. This game had never been my strong suit.

"What happened?" she asked when the game concluded. She was studying the final score on the loose sheet of paper on the coffee table.

"I have a confession to make," I said, stifling a laugh.

"What?"

"I'm the *worst* at Scrabble. My sisters used to whip my ass in this game. I'm more of a Trouble or card game type of guy. Play me in Uno and I'll win every time."

"Well, that's okay." She came my way and straddled my lap. We were sitting on the floor next to the coffee table, my back resting against the bottom of one of the couches. It was the perfect position. "Not everyone can be smart like me and your sisters," she murmured on my lips.

She kissed me slowly, gently, and my dick twitched as she settled into my lap and laced her arms around the back of my neck. She stroked the hair at the nape of my neck and rocked her hips. The sweet wine was still fresh on her tongue, and she gave me a taste as she slid it between my lips.

I groaned as she kept rocking her hips, making me hard as fuck again. We kept going this way, breaths ragged and my hands sliding beneath her shirt to palm her breasts, until she broke the kiss and laughed.

She climbed off my lap, picked up her wineglass, and grinned over her shoulder.

"Getting a refill," she announced.

"Wow. So you're teasing me now?" I watched her walk away, her ass bouncing with each step in those white shorts.

I looked at my own shorts, and it seemed like someone had pitched a tent in them.

This woman was going to be the death of me.

FIFTY

DAVINA

I wasn't sure when we went upstairs. Between the bottles of wine and making out on the sofa, time was lost on me.

All I could remember was us playing a game of twenty questions (well, it was more like six questions before we got carried away with the heavy petting and lip locking again).

I found out a few important facts about him in those six questions, like that his birthday was December 8 and that his favorite cereal was Cocoa Puffs. I told him my favorite color was purple and my birthday was February 22.

"Your emotional personality makes sense now," he'd said after finding out I was a Pisces. I couldn't help laughing at that.

I shifted in the bed of the master bedroom and looked up at the vaulted ceiling, which seemed endless in the night. Wooden beams were built into it, and a chandelier dangled from the center, bathed in moonlight. I could hear water trickling, frogs croaking, cicadas chirping.

I checked my phone on the nightstand to see it was four in the morning, then sighed, glancing at Deke, who was lying right next to me. His feathery lashes kissed his cheekbones, and he only wore a pair of briefs. His long arm was draped over my middle, and his groin was pressed into my hip.

I was tired, but my body still had the habit of waking me up between the hours of three and four in the morning. I turned onto my side so my back was to Deke, and he instinctively shifted, too, pressing in closer. He spooned me from behind, and it didn't take long for something hard to press into my backside.

Smiling, I pushed my hips back and shifted my butt up and down just enough to cause friction. Deke groaned, and I felt his lips on my shoulder blade, slowly moving up as he rocked his hips in sync with mine. One of his hands slid down the length of my hip to reach my thigh before riding up again.

With ease, he tucked a finger beneath the top of my shorts and pulled them down on one side. I tilted over and pushed the other side down, and when the shorts were tangled around my ankles, his hot body was flush against mine.

His lips trailed kisses up my shoulder, and I pushed my hair out of the way so he could keep dropping them on the crook of my neck, my spine, my jawline. That hardness of his ground against my ass, and his breathing became thicker.

One of his hands capped my knee, and he guided it upward, still kissing. I felt his long fingers run through the slick slit between my thighs, and another groan caught in his throat.

As if he couldn't stand it any longer, he removed his fingers to angle himself just right and slowly eased into me. I released a trapped breath as he clutched my hip and thrust into me from behind, his mouth still hot on my neck and switching between kisses and nips.

I lifted a hand so it could rest on the back of his head, my moans coming out hot and labored. I turned my head just enough so he could kiss my lips instead, and his tongue dipped into my mouth, teasing, tasting, as he kept pumping deeper.

"Damn, baby," he rasped on my mouth. "I swear I could fuck you all night long."

His gruff voice made me clench. When he felt it, he pulled out to flip me onto my back, but before he could slip inside me again, I stopped him with a hand to his chest.

"No," I breathed as I sat up. "You lay down."

His brows shifted up a notch, a mixture of delight and confusion swirling in his eyes. He lay down, and I climbed on top of him, but I didn't face him this time. I sat in reverse so he could see my ass and *everything* behind me. As I slowly sank down on him, he clutched my hips tighter and cursed under his breath.

"Shit, Davina."

I rode him slowly at first, moaning as he spanked me. "Look at this ass," he sighed. "You look so sexy riding me."

His words were my ammunition. I rode him faster, my breaths quickening as I clutched my breasts and tossed my head back. I didn't know what it was about having sex this early in the morning. There was a slight exhilaration to it, like I was chasing a high or slipping between a state of consciousness and unconsciousness, where every sense was heightened.

It seemed Deke felt the same, because his grunts came out louder and he felt harder inside me. I glanced over my shoulder, and his eyes were hooded, his mouth slightly ajar, as if me riding him was too much to handle right now.

"I'm gonna bust, Davina," he rumbled. "I can't hold it anymore. Get up before I come inside you."

I climbed off and turned to face him. When I wrapped my lips around his dick, he damn near melted.

"Oh shit." He looked at me, the weight of his hand pressing on the back of my head so I could take him deeper. Veins bulged on his neck as he moaned so loudly it reverberated off the walls.

When I unlatched, Deke lay there a moment to catch his breath, with his eyes shut. I lay next to him and rested my head on his chest, while he brought a hand up to run it over my cheek.

When he focused on me, I bit back a smile, and he chuckled as he said, "Nah, don't act all shy now. I don't even wanna *think* about how you mastered that."

I couldn't help giggling at that because, once again, he'd used my words against me.

"So don't," I murmured.

He studied my eyes in the moonlight before leaning forward to consume my mouth.

I fell asleep in his arms that night, satisfied.

FIFTY-ONE

DAVINA

I woke up for the second time that morning, to the sun beaming through the sheer curtains, birds singing in the distance, and the cottage much louder now than it had been the night before.

I checked the time on my phone, and it was nearing ten in the morning. I rolled over to find Deke, but he wasn't there. I ran a hand over his side of the bed, and it was cool to the touch. I sat up and yawned, then I heard dishes clattering in the distance.

I climbed out of bed, feeling raw between the legs, and dug into my bag until I came across a pair of sweatpants. I tugged them on and grabbed Lew's UNCC hoodie, and that's when something on one of the mirrors in the room caught my eye.

A yellow sticky note was stuck to it, and I moved forward to get a closer look. An arrow was drawn on it and was pointing to the left. I looked that way, and there was another sticky note pressed to the wall, also with an arrow, but this one was pointing to the bedroom door.

Another was on the door, pointing out of the room. I followed the sticky notes, only to see there was a whole trail of them leading down the stairs, and they didn't stop until a new path appeared, made of red rose petals.

I stopped at the kitchen, searching for Deke, because I could've sworn I heard him moving dishes around. My phone buzzed in my hoodie pocket, and I plucked it out and read a text from the man I was just thinking about: Keep going 😏

I looked around again, my heart beating a tad bit faster as I followed the petals. I walked barefoot along the wooden deck and stairs until the trail stopped. When I raised my chin, an overwater bridge leading to a dock was just ahead.

Deke stood there in a black T-shirt and shorts and tossed a wave at me when our eyes connected. I couldn't help my grin as I walked ahead, taking in everything that was set up behind him.

A plush white blanket was spread out on the square dock, two large floor pillows placed opposite of each other, and in the center was a spread of chocolate croissants, mini waffles, finger sandwiches, a glass cup of syrup, and a bowl of fresh fruit.

A kettle was there as well, steam rising through the spout, along with two ceramic mugs. Also there, a slender cup filled with plastic utensils, and pink tulips lying flat on one of the pillows.

"Deke." I pressed my fingers to my face, stunned. "What in the world? What is this?"

He smiled like a child who'd been complimented on something he was proud of and gestured to it. "Brunch."

"Are you serious?" I stepped closer to him in complete awe. "You didn't have to do all of this, Deke!"

He lifted a shoulder like it was no big deal. "I wanted to."

I studied the spread again before looking into his eyes. "I—I don't know what to say."

"You don't have to say anything. Just sit and eat with me." He pressed a hand to the small of my back, and I stood by the pillow with the tulips.

"These aren't even in season anymore," I said.

"Yeah, I lucked out and found some from a local florist. He said they'd probably be the last of them until spring." Deke swallowed, looking me over in my hoodie and sweats.

I sat with the tulips on my lap as he lowered down and stretched his long legs, focusing on the lake. The water rippled softly, and beyond it were groves of autumn trees and lush green mountains that seemed to touch the blue sky. The sun felt good on my skin, and with the gentle breeze going, it was the perfect combination.

"This is nice," I said.

"I had the food catered." Deke fixed his eyes on me. "They dropped it off this morning. I, uh, I remember my mom and Camille telling me women like to be surprised, so I thought of this."

"Well, they were right. This is a really nice surprise. You even have tea. That's a nice touch."

"At the hotel you said you're sensitive to too much caffeine, so you don't drink much coffee. Tea is your go-to."

I couldn't help smiling at that. "How do you even remember me saying that? *I* can't even remember it."

"I don't know. I just remember us ordering my coffee and finding it interesting that you went with a tea, and before I could ask about it, you explained why you always picked tea." He shrugged. "It's the little things."

His eyes sparkled in the sunlight as they locked with mine. He was looking at me again with that glint in them, one full of longing and desire. For some odd reason my chest tightened and I felt a drop in my stomach.

"Well," I said, gesturing to all the food. "Let's eat!"

Deke finally blinked and lowered his head, grabbing a mini sandwich. As I dunked a waffle into the syrup and ate, I tried ignoring what I saw in his eyes, because it couldn't have been that.

Mixed in with the longing, the excitement, and the satisfaction was something I was all too familiar with.

Love.

FIFTY-TWO

DEKE

"I wanna show you something." I took Davina's hand, after she'd showered and put on a pair of leggings and an oversize Tupac T-shirt that didn't do anything to hide her curves. "You might want to put on those Air Maxes you brought."

When she had her shoes on, I led her out the front door and gripped her hand as we rounded the house and reached a flagstone path. We made our way between oversize pine trees while skipping broken stones, until I spotted the fence veiled in black netting.

"No way." Davina gaped.

"Yep." I released her hand to open the gate, and when we stepped onto the smooth basketball court, she laughed and said, "Of course you would have this here!"

It was blacktop, with white lines and goals on both ends. It was surrounded by trees, so we couldn't even see the house from here. A basketball rack protected by a weatherproof cover was near one of the goals.

"It might've been my idea," I said to Davina as I uncovered the rack of basketballs. "Can't go in on a property without a court, man. It's just not right."

She laughed as I grabbed one of the balls and dribbled. I bounced it from hand to hand, sidestepping, then circling around her before rising on my toes and aiming for the goal.

"That defense is weak, baby!"

"Oh, really?" Davina cocked a brow, then she nodded slowly, like she felt challenged and wanted to prove me wrong. She jogged away to scoop up the ball, and I was surprised to see how well she handled it.

"Hold on now. Don't tell me you've been keeping this side of you a secret," I said, grinning.

She kept dribbling, moving the ball between her legs before stepping back to the three-point line and taking a shot. When the rock slipped through the net, I exaggeratedly cupped my mouth and stared at her.

"Who taught you that?" I asked, dropping my hands.

She busted out laughing as I met up with her. "Remember me telling you about my little brother, Abe? Well, he needed someone to practice with when he was younger. I used to take him to basketball practices and camps during the summer. And while I worked on GOC ideas, I'd sit and watch him. I helped his team as a coach once." She paused, fighting a smile. "And I might've played varsity in high school, too, so . . ."

"How did I not know this?" This woman had to be after my heart.

"I wasn't all that good at it. Honestly, it was so long ago. Feels like a blip."

"What position did you play?"

"Point guard."

"The one." I couldn't help my smile. I ran around her to grab the ball. "Well, how about we play a match. The one against the two. We can make a bet on whoever gets to five first."

"Oh yeah? And what will I get when I win?"

I tucked the ball beneath my arm, meeting up with her again. Her eyes radiated sunlight, a smile teasing her lips. "Depends on what you want."

She thought about that while nibbling at her bottom lip. "I want ice cream," she replied, which made me laugh.

"Okay. That's doable. But if I win, you gotta come to one of my games." I knew I was testing her. This weekend was an all-or-nothing thing—we both knew it deep down—and a part of her was still reserved, but if I could get her to agree to show up for me later, then it wouldn't be over. What we had wouldn't be limited to one weekend.

She dropped her chin, running her tongue over her plump bottom lip. Then she nodded and said, "Okay. It's a bet."

"Cool." I stepped back and dribbled the ball. "You gotta get that defense up, though. I'm not taking it easy on you."

"I don't expect you to." She tugged on her leggings, hiking them up at the knees as she lowered into a defensive position.

"Now *that's* cute," I said, dribbling around her, then taking my first shot. The ball sunk in, and I tossed my hands in the air as she narrowed her eyes at me and pointed a finger.

"Okay, I see how it is." She collected the ball, bouncing her way around me. When she leaned forward, I did the same, looking into her eyes and anticipating her next move.

She started to go right, so I did, too, but then she pump-faked it and stepped left, aiming for the goal. The ball hit the backboard and slid right in.

She grinned, and I nodded, huffing a laugh as I grabbed the ball this time. She tried squaring up with me, swatting at the ball, and I took that opportunity to run around her, leap in the air, and dunk it.

"Oh, *really*? It's like that, Bishop?" she called, with a hand on her hips.

"Yeah, baby," I said, planting a kiss on her cheek as I passed her. "It's like that."

The game went on for at least fifteen more minutes. She missed her next shot, while I landed my next two. Sweat beaded on my forehead as she swiped at hers with the back of her hand.

"Four–one," I called out, and clearly that fueled her, because she took control of the ball and landed her next shot.

"Two–four," she announced, skipping off.

"I'm about to win, so it doesn't even matter," I taunted, loving that fire in her eyes. She was competitive just like me, and there was something about seeing that heat in her eyes that turned me on.

"Go on, then. Take your shot," she said, back in her defensive stance. Then her face warped as she narrowed her eyes and leaned inward. "Oh wait, I think you have something right there."

"Huh?" I swiped at my cheek.

"No, there," she said, pointing to the right side of my face. I swiped that side as she moved in so close her lips grazed mine. I froze, waiting for her to wipe whatever it was away *and* give me a kiss, but then she moved back and swiped the ball out of my hand. She hustled toward the goal with a smooth layup.

"Three–four. Gotta get that defense up, honey," she sang.

"Oh wow! A distraction, I see!" I couldn't help feeling both stupid and proud. "That never would've happened on a real court! Let me see that ball."

She passed the rock to me, and this time I didn't wait for her to come up. I lifted on my toes and aimed for the goal. It hit the rim but tipped over and dropped through the net.

"Deke!" she shouted with a breathy laugh.

"What?" I smirked. "It was only right. Five–three. That's game, D."

"I hope you don't cheat like that on the court."

"Never," I said, draping an arm over her shoulder.

"I *guess* you won." She looked up at me as we walked toward the gate. "Looks like I'll be seeing you at one of your games, then."

"For real?"

"Yeah. Why not?"

My heart pumped faster, not only from the match we played but also from knowing I'd see her again after the weekend was over. Maybe

I was wrong, and this wasn't a one-and-done thing. Maybe she was realizing that, just like me, she wanted more.

Before we left the court, I faced her and clasped her face in my hands. She kissed me back and moaned as I bumped her back until her backside hit the gate.

As if we both had the same thing on our minds, she reached for my shorts and pushed them down. I went for her leggings, helping her step out of one of the legs before tucking my forearm beneath one of her thighs. The gate creaked as our weight pressed against it, and I wasted no time sliding into her.

I'd had sex in *many* places and in *many* ways, but never on a court— never like this. This woman made me feel invincible. She made me whole every time I was inside her, and every time I held her—like all the worries, all the problems, all the guilt, and all the shame were washed away by her presence alone.

If only she knew how I felt.

If only she knew I'd give her the world if she let me.

FIFTY-THREE

DAVINA

When the sun was nearing the horizon, Deke took me on a boat ride. His boat was named *The Saint*.

"Because Bishops are far from saints," he told me when I asked why he and Whitney chose that name for it. "When we go for a ride, it feels like our sins are being washed away."

We cruised the lake, the mist sprinkling my face and the wind blowing through my blown-out curls. Lake Santeetlah was absolutely breathtaking. The clouds hung low, blending with the emerald mountains. The air smelled sweet, like remnants of honeysuckle and tree sap.

When Deke stopped the boat, he walked around the steering wheel and sat next to me on the padded bench. "Did you know the name *Santeetlah* derives from Native Americans?"

"No," I said, meeting his eyes. "I didn't know that."

"Yep. Whitney told me. It means 'blue waters.'"

I looked past Deke to the water, which looked more like a dark turquoise. "It's really beautiful here." *And romantic,* I thought, but I wasn't about to say that out loud.

Deke leaned forward to grab the handle of the cooler and popped it open. He plucked out two Drumstick ice cream cones and offered one to me.

"Does this mean I won the bet?" I asked, grinning as I unwrapped it.

"You came close, but no one can beat the king of the court." He cracked a smile and turned on the portable speaker he brought with him.

When his phone's Bluetooth was connected, a song by Khalid and Normani played. I bit into my ice cream cone, and Deke opened his, too, spreading his legs and looking ahead.

"So what's with the dragonfly necklace?" he asked. "You wear it a lot. Does it mean something?"

"Oh." I grappled nervously at the pendant. "Yeah, Lewis gave it to me. My, uh . . . my late husband. It was an anniversary gift."

"Oh." He nodded. "Nice."

I avoided his eyes, feeling the need to explain further. "It's supposed to represent love and changes that are promising. I don't take it off much."

"I see." Deke was quiet for a moment. "Can I ask you something?"

"Sure."

"Why don't you ever talk about him?"

"Oh . . . um . . ." My chest tightened, and I blinked rapidly as I looked away. "I guess I thought you didn't want to hear about him."

Deke gave me his full attention. "I don't mind hearing about him. I don't want you feeling like you have to hide that part of your life or anything."

"It's not that I'm hiding it—it's just hard to talk about him. Even with my sister and Tisha. Talking about him with you would be twice as hard."

"Well, I want you to know I won't feel any kind of way if you ever decide to bring him up. This is a safe place. I'll never judge."

"Okay." Some of the vanilla dripped over my fingers, and I licked it away. Silence settled between us.

"He was nice," I offered after a while. "Got along with everyone."

Deke nodded with a soft, sincere smile.

"Everyone loved him. He was just one of those people who could find anything to talk about and had a way of making others feel special." I felt my mouth twitch as I thought about my first date with Lewis.

We had gone to eat expensive burgers and milkshakes at Five Guys, and our conversations were so simple, so seamless. I didn't have to force anything with him. It had been almost second nature, like he and I had met in another lifetime and were picking up where we left off. Funnily enough, it had been like that with Deke too. *Effortless.*

"Anyway, you probably would've really liked him. And I know he would've loved you. Football had his heart, but he was also a *huge* basketball fan. His favorite college team was Clemson."

"That's a shame," he said, head shaking. "Clemson was good, but he should've been riding with the Blue Devils." He was referring to Duke University. I remembered seeing in his file that he played for Duke. "Who was his favorite NBA team?"

"The Wasps, of course! Home team!"

"Boo!" Deke threw a thumbs-down at that. "We've whooped their asses so many times. He should've been flying with the birds, not the bees."

I tossed my head back to laugh. "I think that was the corniest thing I ever heard you say, Deke!"

"Oh, for real? You think I'm corny?" He set his ice cream down on the wrapper next to him to haul me across his lap. I couldn't help laughing as he nuzzled his nose into the bend of my neck while holding me in his arms.

When he'd had enough, he sat me upright again. My cone had fallen to the floor, but I couldn't bother myself to pick it up, because Deke leaned forward to cup the back of my head. His forehead pressed to mine, and his eyes traveled to my lips. And when he kissed me, I melted into it and sighed as his hand curled around my waist to reel me closer.

We stayed like that for a while, kissing hotly, gasping for breath, sticky from ice cream, tasting like vanilla, chocolate, and a hint of peanuts. He was such a good kisser, his lips the perfect mixture of firm and soft. His hands roamed my body, squeezing, claiming.

"I want more nights like this with you, D," he breathed when our swollen lips parted. "Tell me you want the same."

My breaths came out ragged as I clasped his face in my hands. "I think I do."

"But?"

"But . . . it makes me nervous. Feels too soon."

He thought about that as he studied my face, drinking in every feature, every detail, with mellow eyes. When he leaned back, he reached for my head to smooth down the unruly curl at my temple.

"I'm willing to wait for as long as you need me to," he murmured.

Then he kissed me again.

FIFTY-FOUR

DAVINA

"Now I want to ask *you* something." I pushed my plate of pasta away and folded my fingers beneath my chin.

While steering *The Saint* back to the cottage, Deke had suggested we go to a restaurant to eat, but after what'd happened with Manhattan Rose and the pictures of us at the hotel floating around, the last thing I wanted was more private photos of us taken just to be sold to some tabloid.

Instead, we had ordered the food for pickup so we could eat in the cottage. For the first time, I'd ridden in his leather-scented Ferrari, watching as he drove past thick-trunked trees and coasted along black pavement peppered with leaves.

Deke sat up in his chair and picked up a napkin from the glass table to wipe his mouth. "What's up?"

"Well, it's a personal question, so you don't have to answer if you don't want to."

His throat bobbed, and his features hardened just a little as he said, "Okay . . ."

"So, when we first started emailing, you said something about how grief never goes away."

He stared at me blankly before lowering his head, like he knew where this was headed.

"I only say that because I, um . . . I saw a picture your mom posted about your brother from several years ago. I guess I'm wondering why you never talk about him like how you talk about your sisters."

Deke's nostrils flared as he stood up and grabbed my plate. "You done with this?" he asked, already carrying it to the kitchen.

"Deke, you know what? It's fine. I don't mean to pry. I'm sorry."

His back was to me as he set the plates on the island counter. He planted his fists on the quartz countertop, his shoulders tense. Then his shoulders relaxed, and he threw his head back, pointing his face to the ceiling.

"Is this why you sent her to me?" he mumbled. He said the words lowly, a quiet whisper to God, but I heard every single one.

Deke turned and rested his lower back against the counter edge, his biceps bulging beneath his shirt. "I don't talk about him for the same reasons you don't talk much about your husband."

It was my turn to look away. I focused on the leftover garlic knots on the table.

"You asked about him earlier, and I told you," I reminded him. A silence fell down on us, thick and tense. I heard him release a belly-deep sigh.

"I'm sorry," Deke whispered. He maneuvered his way back to me and lowered to a squat next to my chair. He took my hand and held it tight, but I couldn't bring myself to look at him. "Davina, *I'm sorry*," he repeated. "That wasn't fair. That's just a sensitive topic for me. I don't like thinking about it." I turned my head a fraction to find his eyes, only to realize my vision was blurry.

Damn it. No. I was *not* about to cry in front of him. I pulled my hand out of his and left the table to sit on one of the couches. As I sank into the plush material, I closed my eyes and let out a trembling breath.

Deke circled the couch and sat next to me.

"You're right," I muttered. "If you hadn't brought him up, I wouldn't have told you about him, so I get it. Forget I even asked anything."

"No," Deke murmured. "I feel like I should tell you something about him so you can understand why he's a sore subject for me."

His eyes were glossy. He was trying desperately hard not to cry. *Way to ruin a great weekend, Davina.*

"His name was Damon," Deke said. "He died when I was fourteen, so he was seventeen. And I, uh . . ." He scratched the top of his head, eyes bouncing around the room. "I don't like bringing it up because he committed suicide."

At that, my eyes stretched, and my heart dropped. No longer was my guard rising. It had slammed back down again, and I instinctively took Deke's hand in mine.

"Deke. Oh my God, I'm so sorry. I—I didn't know."

"Yeah, well . . . now you know." He offered a pathetic smile, one that didn't reach his eyes.

"But . . . why did he do it? If you don't mind me asking."

Deke shrugged. "I have my assumptions for why he did it, but we'll never really know."

I started to ask something else, but his phone buzzed on the coffee table, and he grabbed it, almost like he was in the center of the ocean and it was a raft he could hang on to. Something to save him, spare him from remembering the overwhelming details.

I could see the relief in his eyes, how quick he was to stand. All the other times when his phone rang, he ignored the calls, but not now.

"It's Camille. Gotta take this." He was up and out of the room before I could respond.

I sat for a moment, tucking my hands between my thighs. His brother committed *suicide*? And at such a young age too. I couldn't imagine that pain. It's one thing for a person to be sick, or to die in an accident, but it's another to know that a person inflicted pain upon themselves to end their own life.

I couldn't wrap my head around it. It made sense that Deke didn't want to talk about it. Suicide never made sense to the people closest to the victim. All they were left with were questions and anger.

How do you discuss something like that without feeling that pang of sadness, or guilt, even? Because I was sure there was some part of Deke that blamed himself for what his brother did.

We all blame ourselves after a death, wishing we'd talked to that person more, or hugged them one last time. Wishing we hadn't yelled at them, cursed them out, or ignored their phone calls.

Guilt.

Shame.

Hurt.

It's all tangled in the same web.

While Deke talked to his sister on the deck, I cleaned the kitchen. My mind was racing so fast I couldn't keep my thoughts straight. I kept cleaning, clinging to the distraction, even going so far as to wipe the inside of the microwave.

It wasn't until I'd cleared the counters that he walked inside again. He met up with me, holding my eyes while taking one of my damp hands in his.

"Come to the room with me."

I let him lead the way, but with each step we took up the stairs, my heart was hammering. I wasn't sure what had me going or what was making me so nervous. It was like all the emotion I was trying to swallow was bubbling up and the lid on the pot was wobbling and ready to fly off.

When we entered the master bedroom, Deke released my hand to sit on the edge of the bed. "I feel like I should tell you more about my brother so you can better understand."

"No, Deke. Don't." I waved my hands and took a minor step back. My breath was coming out heavier. "You don't have to. Seriously."

He noticed me backing away, and a slight dip formed between his eyebrows. I thought about what Deke said on the boat, about how I

281

could talk to him about Lewis. How could I just talk about my dead husband knowing his pain was probably much worse?

All these thoughts of death, of suicide, of sickness . . . it hit me so hard. Suddenly that giant room, with the endless ceiling, felt too small, and I couldn't breathe. My head was spinning, my throat drying . . .

Oh, God. I'm having a panic attack.

I hadn't had one in so long. The first time was after Daddy died. I was ten, sitting in my classroom and gasping for breath. I had several of them throughout that year, to the point where my doctor suggested to my mother that I see a therapist.

The last time was a week after Lew died, when the funeral and wake were over, the people had left, and I was alone in my room, with no noise.

I thought that after Lew, I was officially done having them, but there was something about this moment. The weight of it was crippling, like a giant thumb was pressing down on me and smashing me down until I was flat.

It wasn't until Deke was in front of me, his hands on my shoulders and his eyes full of concern, that I realized I was hyperventilating.

"Davina, breathe. Look at me. I've got you. *Breathe.*"

I tried collecting breaths, but that only made my chest tighter.

I pulled away from him, rushing around him to get to my bag in the corner. I scrambled through it, searching for my phone. I wanted to call my sister or Tish. They were the only two people who could take me off the ledge. I stopped a moment, flinging my hands as if they were on fire.

"Where's my phone? I—I need my phone."

"Davina," Deke called again, but I didn't want to hear him. I remembered I left my phone downstairs. *All the way downstairs.* My body couldn't handle it. I would've fallen if I tried going down there.

I glanced at Deke, watching as pity consumed him, and because I didn't know what else to do, I ran past him to get to the bathroom. I slammed the door behind me and locked it. I should've left, but I couldn't drive in that state, panting wildly, my heart racing, fear sinking into my heart.

It was all coming at me at the wrong fucking time.

All the memories.

All the panic attacks I'd had when I was younger as I feared the unknown.

The depression I was in, wondering how life was worth living when it was *so, so* hard.

Always putting on a brave face, when deep down I was weak. I was soft. I was far from brave.

I thought back to a time way before I'd met Lew, back when my daddy would play hopscotch with me, or fail at braiding my hair into two thick braids. Back when I realized my dad was the first man I ever loved. And then he was gone—snatched away in the blink of an eye. And then there was Lewis. *My sweet, sweet Lewis.* Gone too. Forever.

A wail broke through my lips, and I dropped my face into my hands as I slid down the door. I could hear Deke calling my name, tapping on the other side of the door, begging to be let in.

Why is this happening now? Why now? Deke was the last person I wanted to see me like this. What the hell was wrong with me, anyway? Why was I in that damn lake house in the first place?

It hadn't even been a full year since my husband died, and there I was in a house with another man, acting like my husband never existed. Acting like I hadn't just clung to his cold, dead body while sobbing all over his chest.

Then there was Deke. I'd been so focused on my own grief that I hadn't taken the time to explore his. All this time he'd been dealing with that heartbreak, and I didn't know because I was so selfish, so stupid, so *worthless*.

No wonder everything was constantly ripped away from me. I didn't deserve any of it.

I broke down in tears, letting myself feel it, take it in, just like Octavia had told me to do. She was my mini therapist. My safety net. I wanted to call her. I breathed in and out, and when I felt stable enough, I stood as Deke knocked on the door again.

"Davina, please. Let me in," he pleaded.

I faced the door with wobbly knees and swiped at my tight eyes. Then I opened it. When Deke caught sight of me, relief washed over him, and the edge melted from his shoulders.

I walked past him, going for my bag again and stuffing my clothes into it.

"I need to go home." I swiped hard at my face with the back of my arm.

"What? No. Why?" he asked, and I don't think I'd ever heard such desperation in his voice. That cool-guy facade was cracking, the charming Deke being replaced by a helpless, confused one. "D, come on. Why are you packing?"

"Don't call me that right now. Please," I said, moving past him to collect my toiletries from the bathroom.

"Okay, okay. I'm sorry."

I grabbed my bodywash and deodorant.

"You don't have to go, though, Davina," he said as I slipped past him again, stuffing the toiletries into one of the side pockets.

"Yes, I do."

"Why?"

Ugh. Why couldn't he let this go? Why couldn't he let *me* go? How could he not see that I wasn't worth it? That he deserved more? That just like the other men in my life, he would probably be taken from me, too, if I gave in to him?

I couldn't risk that. The thought of it *petrified* me. If another person I cared about got snatched away somehow, my mind wouldn't be able to handle it. I stared at him for a moment and shook my head. There was only one way I could think of to make him let go.

"I can't be here, Deke. I can't sit here and pretend that all this shit I'm doing with you is okay, because it's not! I lost my *husband*. He was . . . he was supposed to be the love of my life, but now you're here and you're *so perfect*, and I just . . ." I cupped my mouth as the tears thickened. My throat felt raw, like my vocal cords were on fire. "I just have to go, okay? This whole thing with us has just been too much, too fast, and—"

"You're scared," he stated, and there was a hint of agitation in his voice. He may as well have called me a coward to my face.

"You're right!" I shot back. "I *am* scared! I told you that from the beginning!"

"But what are you so scared of, Davina? I'm right here! I haven't gone anywhere!" His voice had risen in volume to match mine.

I zipped my bag and slung it over my shoulder. I started for the door, but he stepped in front of me and blocked the way.

"No. Don't fucking run this time! Tell me the truth. What are you so afraid of when it comes to me?"

"*Everything*, Deke!" I yelled, glaring up at him. He blinked down at me like I'd sprouted another head, but he didn't startle, didn't flinch. "I could hardly love Lewis the right way, but I knew when I met him, he was the one for me, okay? He was the one I was supposed to take care of, to nurture, to fuck, and whatever else a wife is supposed to do! I'm not supposed to be with a fucking *basketball player*! I'm not supposed to be with a guy who treats women like objects—who makes a game out of catching a grieving widow and having his way with her because he can!"

Deke flinched this time and staggered backward like I'd slapped him. I felt horrible, but this was good. Now he'd know I wasn't perfect, that I wasn't the woman for him. He could let go. Move on . . . even if it hurt.

"Wow," he said, so low it was more like he'd expelled a breath. "How long have you been keeping that bottled in?"

I swallowed salty snot and tears as I tore my eyes away. I couldn't look at him. I'd only cry again. I was hurting him, I knew this, but I had to. He *had* to find someone else.

"You know what, Davina? One thing you said about me is true. I *did* have a point in my life where I treated women like objects. I made it into the league and became a man who gave zero fucks, because I didn't have to! For once, it was *my* life and I was in control, so yes, I did whatever the hell I wanted, with whoever the hell I wanted, because I felt like it! But do you think that shit made me happy? Do you think I wanted to be with women whose names I couldn't even remember the next morning? With women like Giselle, who don't give a single fuck about me? Do you think I would be standing here right now explaining all of this to you if I was just some man who wanted to make a game out of catching a *widow*? Do you really think I'm that selfish—that *petty*?"

He took a step closer, and my pulse swam to my ears.

"Davina, I know you don't want to hear me say this, but *I love you*, all right? And there's nothing you can say that'll change my mind, because you're speaking out of anger and hurt, and I know those feelings. I *embodied* those feelings for years. Angry all the time, pissed off at the world, wondering why it had to be my brother, wondering what the hell I did to deserve *any* of what I went through."

"No," I whimpered, backing away. "You don't. You *can't* love me."

"Yes, I can," he declared. "I fucking *love you*. Since the day I set foot in your office, way before I even noticed those rings on your finger, I took one look into your eyes, and you had me. I wanted something with you, and I didn't care what it was. All I knew was that I could *not* let you get away from me. You could not leave my life."

"Deke, please," I cried, bowing my head. "Just stop talking, please."

"No, because I want you to know it, Davina. I'm tired of hiding it." He caught my hand and clasped it in his, trying to catch my eyes, too, but I wouldn't look. I *couldn't* look, or I'd break. "When you're away from me, my heart *bleeds*, Davina. My chest hurts and I drown in my own misery every time I have to watch you walk away from me. I can't think straight. I can't sleep. I can barely eat. All those times before, I just let you go because I knew I couldn't have you, or that you weren't ready for it yet, but I can't keep letting you slip away from me. I want you in ways I never thought possible, and I have *never* felt this way about a woman in my life. You might think I'm lying to you, but I would never lie about something like this." He held on to my hand tighter, pressing my palm to his chest and sealing the gap between us. I could feel his heart beating hard, fast.

"I hear all these stories about how being in love makes you feel a different way. Being without that person makes you physically sick—makes you feel like you can't do life without them—and I'm telling you, Davina. If you leave this house, if you walk out that door . . . I will be *sick* without you. You're my cure, D. Regardless of what you've gone through or what *I've* been through, I have no doubt we're in this house together and talking about this for a reason. You can't stand here and tell me what we have isn't real. Even the first letters of our names are a damn match. You're my other half, and I feel that deep in my soul. And look, I know you made a lifelong promise to Lewis when you married him. I *know*, okay?"

I tried snatching my hands away when he said Lew's name, but he held on tighter. I'd never heard Deke say it, and it struck a chord in me. God, it hurt so bad, and he kept holding on, kept talking, kept pleading with me.

"I get why you're torn with your feelings and with what you want, but he's gone now, baby. He's gone, and I know that shit hurts. I know it cuts you up inside, like annoying little fucking paper cuts, but I'm *here*, Davina. I'm here right now, willing to wait, willing to be patient with you, to let you process it all and talk about it whenever you want to. I'm *here*. I'm giving my heart to you, and that can't be for nothing. It just can't, baby. So *please*, just this once, don't walk away from me. Don't leave, because if you go, you and I both know what that means."

All of his words hit me like a ton of bricks, and because I couldn't contain my emotions anymore, a sob bubbled out of me.

When he brought me into his arms and hugged me against his broad chest, I cried like I never had before. I cried so hard and for so long my stomach became sore and my eyes felt stretched thin.

We lay on the bed, the hours passing, my body still racked with pain and guilt. We didn't utter a word. We just lay there, breathing in sync, thinking.

I hadn't cried so much in months, but it was like my soul needed the cleanse. I'd bottled the emotions in for a while, thinking one day they'd go away or even become dull and muted, but all they'd done was accumulate.

At some point, Deke fell asleep while holding me in his arms. I shifted a bit, and his arms tensed. Even in his sleep he didn't want to let go. I managed to free myself, then sat up to look at him—*really* look at him.

This beautiful man with the world as his oyster. This kind soul who loved *me*, who wanted *me* . . . and it made no sense at all. Giselle was right. A woman like me didn't belong in his world, because his world was meant to be easy and satisfying after all that hardship with his brother, and I was a complicated, mourning mess. I was a literal trigger to him. One pull on that traumatic gun, and it'd pierce him right in the heart.

My bottom lip trembled as I leaned forward and placed a kiss on his forehead. I left my lips on his skin a few seconds too long, and a hot tear slid down my cheek. I wiped the tear away before it could land on him, then climbed off the bed and grabbed my bag.

I looked at him one last time, and before my eyes could fill with tears, I closed the door and walked away.

FIFTY-FIVE

DEKE

When I was thirteen, I remembered, Camille had once burst into our house, run up to her room, and thrown herself onto her bed. She buried her face into purple pillows and sobbed while our mama stroked her back and told her she would be okay.

I stood at the door watching, confused as to why she was crying so hard over a boy she'd only been dating for a couple of weeks.

"My heart is broken, Mommy," Camille had whined, and I remembered thinking how stupid that sounded and how dramatic she was being.

Hearts can't break. How does that even feel? I wondered. I was fortunate enough to grow up not knowing that feeling with a significant other. But when I woke up in that bed and saw Davina was gone, I felt exactly how my sister had that day when she'd stormed to her room.

It starts off small, a wave of disappointment followed by mild frustration. But as you sit with it, it snowballs into something bigger, something monstrous, and suddenly your eyes sting and the center of your chest aches, and it literally feels like someone has stuck their hand down your throat and ripped your beating heart out.

I sat in a chair on the deck, hunched over, with my face in my palms. The cool air nipped at the bare skin on my back, and though goose bumps were on my arms, I didn't shiver.

My heart was pounding alone, yearning for a woman who wanted to be as far away from me as possible. All it wanted was her, but she was gone, despite me stripping myself bare and laying it all out for her. Despite me trying desperately hard to prove that I loved her.

She'd made her point. Her decision was to walk away. So be it. That was it.

Truth is, grieving people hurt in a different way. Sometimes we punish or blame ourselves. We act like we don't deserve good things when we lose someone, because good things mean happiness, and happiness means moving on, and no one wants to move on from what's familiar to them.

No one wants to face a new chapter after such devastation or fill themselves with fresh ideas and perspectives. Some people cling to whatever is left of their old lives, even if that means pushing everything else away.

I should know. I was one of those people.

When I looked up, focusing on the lake and the gray clouds in the sky, hearing the thunder roll in the distance and the leaves rustle from the wind, I came to the most heartbreaking realization of all.

No matter how badly I wanted Davina Klein, I was never going to have her the way I wanted.

Her heart belonged to a man I could *never* compete with, and I was simply an obstacle she had to conquer so she could cling to whatever was left of him.

FIFTY-SIX

DAVINA

When a week passed since the lake and I hadn't heard from Deke, I wasn't surprised.

But when *another* week crept by and there wasn't a single peep, I drowned in guilt and immediately wanted to call him.

After the way I'd bolted, I couldn't blame him for not reaching out. I did that a lot—bolted when things got complicated. I was tempted to text him sometimes while at work to check in with him and see if he was okay, but I knew he wasn't. Texting him would've been torturing him, and I'd done that enough.

During that last night with him, I developed a feeling I couldn't quite put my finger on. It was a feeling that made me question the love I'd shared with Lewis and the years spent with him.

It contradicted what I'd told myself the day of Lew's funeral about melting in another man's hands. Deke had lowered my guard completely in such a short span of time, and for a split second, I felt safe because it was only us.

No one else was around.

No one could interrupt.

I could be me, and he could be himself.

It was perfect . . . but maybe a little *too* perfect, if there was such a thing.

Regardless, that safety with him scared the *shit* out of me.

I lowered the wand of my mascara, studying my reflection. So put together on the outside but a mess inside. With a huff, I stuffed the mascara into my makeup bag and left the bathroom to find my shoes.

I couldn't stay in my house a minute longer, with everything I had on my mind. Octavia insisted I come home and take a breather, and she was right. I was going to Maple Cove to see her, Mama, and my little brother, Abe.

Maple Cove was a small town that was only a fifteen-minute drive from Asheville. It was so small, in fact, that many people liked to lump Maple Cove in with Asheville, but the true natives never did. Maple was much more secluded.

I drove on a four-block road lined with cars, passing Mrs. Rina's coffee shop, which I'd spent many days studying in; the bed-and-breakfast Mrs. Buttle owned, where tourists loved sleeping in; and then the barbershop where Daddy used to get his haircuts.

Octavia and I would sit on the curb waiting for Daddy to get his shape-up. His barber, Bradley, would hand us Dum Dum lollipops and wink for behaving afterward.

There was the familiar hair salon, but the name had changed to Clara's, and two stores away was a brand-new candy shop, with taffy rolling in the window.

Then there was Mama's candle shop, Aromantic, with its gold sign and black drapes in the window.

When I drove through town, it only took about a minute more before I was making a right turn and taking a familiar dirt path that led to a two-bedroom house.

Sunlight filtered through the leaves of the hovering trees and beamed on the newly built roof. The tan exterior had been refreshed with another coat of paint.

Bold emerald box hedges hugged the lower half of the house, and the porch (which you had to get to with a four-step stoop) had plants hanging from the ceiling in baskets that swayed with the breeze. Two wicker chairs with waterproof cushions were nestled in the corners, and as I walked up the stoop, I noticed more plants and flowers had been added.

It was like a mini jungle on the porch, and I loved it. Sure, I had my place in Charlotte, but this was my real home.

I dug into my purse until I found my key, then gave the lock a twist and turned the doorknob to get inside. Dishes clanked from a distance, and I could smell something savory cooking.

I took a quick sweep of the front room. Dark hardwood floors and shelves built into the walls, topped with books and plants. A love seat and a recliner, neither of which matched, were set near the walls, and a TV was mounted to face them both.

A bohemian red rug was placed beneath a round wooden coffee table, and on one of the side tables was an essential oil diffuser steadily blowing out mist and whatever scent Mama had picked for the day. Today it smelled citrusy, like lemon and a hint of clove. This house I grew up in wasn't much, but it was cozy.

"Mama?" I called from the door. The clanking of dishes stopped, and as I set my purse down, I saw her head pop around a corner.

"Davina Bobina!" she sang, rushing out of the kitchen, wearing an apron with cartoonish avocados on it. She threw her arms around my neck and hugged me tight, and I huffed a laugh as I held her back.

My mom may have worked my nerves a lot, but if there was one thing about her, she could deliver an amazing hug.

"I'm so happy to see you, baby," she said over my shoulder. She leaned back and held on to my shoulders as she looked me all over. "You look good."

"Compared to what?" I asked, half-teasing.

"Oh, stop it. You always look good."

"You do, too, Mama." For a woman who'd be turning sixty in two months, she was flawless, really.

Her face had hardly a wrinkle in sight, other than the laugh lines around her mouth and the faint crow's-feet around her light-brown eyes. Her hair had flourished, and what were once simple natural curls a decade ago had been transformed into unruly locs. She reminded me of Lisa Bonet, and I recalled a lot of men in town loving that about her.

"Thank you, honey. Come on, you're just in time to have lunch with me."

"Where's Abe?" I asked, following her into the kitchen.

"He's at therapy right now but should be done within forty-five minutes or so." Mama sauntered barefoot through the kitchen to open one of the opaque glass cabinets. "Made us some chicken and chickpea soup."

"That sounds good." I went to the drawer where the utensils were while she ladled soup into porcelain bowls. After she grabbed a pitcher of lemonade, we sat at the four-top table and dug in.

"Octavia told me y'all went to Miami," she said after chewing. "What was that like?"

I met her eager eyes and shrugged. "It was for business, so I didn't really get to see much."

"Oh. Well, your sister said y'all went to some fancy party in a penthouse too."

"It wasn't *that* fancy." I laughed.

I looked up, and Mama was studying my face.

I didn't know what she was looking for but I wasn't in the mood to have her read me right now, so I said, "I can ride with you to pick Abe up if you want."

"He'll love that, Vina." She took a sip of lemonade. "So how are you lately? I mean after the last few months . . ."

"You know you can just say it," I told her.

"I know, but I don't want to be insensitive."

"I'm okay, if that's what you're asking."

"That's good."

I took a look around the kitchen, before my eyes ventured to the living room. This house had changed so much in the last decade. When Octavia and I were younger, this place was sparse and lacked many of the decorations it had now. But back then all Mama cared about was going out with her friends or staying the night with one of her flings.

It was a surprise knowing all it took for her to get her act together was birthing a son.

When Daddy died, I was the one taking care of Octavia and making her peanut-butter-and-jelly sandwiches and pouring her milk after school. And during the first year of Abe's life, I had to secure a part-time job just so Mama could have enough money for formula and diapers.

Whenever I wasn't working, I'd be watching after him and Octavia while our mother slept or worked part time at a retail store. I was forced to mature, and to this day I don't feel like I had much of a childhood.

Maybe that's part of the reason why I'm so fucked up inside.

I shifted my gaze to Mama's, but she was already looking at me. "You look troubled, Vina," she said. "What's going on in that brain of yours?"

I debated whether to speak on the issue that'd been bothering me for years now. I didn't want to come across as bitter for how I felt.

And don't get me wrong, Abe deserved the world. I loved that kid from the moment I laid eyes on him, but I became angry sometimes when I thought about how simple it was for him and how hard it was for me and Octavia.

I moved my spoon around in my soup, pushing one of the chickpeas toward the edge of the bowl. "Do you think I'd be different if I was raised like Abe was?"

Mama sat up straight, her rosy lips parting. She stared at me a moment before lowering her gaze with a defeated sigh. "Davina . . . I know what this is about."

"What do you mean?"

"When you were young, I wasn't there like I should've been."

I swallowed thickly and placed my spoon on a napkin, bumping my bowl away.

"I wasn't a good parent to you. You relied on me, and I wasn't there half the time. You . . . you lost your daddy at such a young age, and I could tell it really affected you. And you were always so sweet and kind and understanding about everything I did. Always looking after your sister, making sure she was fed and bathed and—" Mama gasped and pressed her hands to her chest. "I've thought long and hard about this moment, you know? How I would bring it up to you—how I would apologize for everything. I've been waiting for you to confront me because bringing it up myself never felt right. I was a terrible mother, and I know it. And this is no excuse, but I simply wasn't ready for the role back then."

I nodded, combating tears.

"But let me be clear when I tell you that your resilience and your shine cannot be replaced," she said. "No matter how you grew up, or if the tables had been turned, you would still be the Davina you are now, and I *love* that about you." Her voice broke during the last sentence, and I tucked my hands between my thighs. "I'm so sorry it took me so long to pull myself together. I'm so sorry if my actions have damaged you in any way or made you feel like you don't deserve to be cared about or loved. I love you from the depths of my heart, and you should know that I'm here now. I'm not going anywhere, and if it's not too late for you, I want to keep being here for you, baby. You, your sister, and your brother are my world. Nothing will ever come before my babies again."

At this point, Mama had become a blur. A part of me figured maybe I was being too emotional about this, but the rational part of me knew I had a lot to be emotional about.

I wasn't sure what'd come over me. I thought I'd done all my crying at the damn lake house, but it turns out I had a lot more pent up inside me. So at my Mama's dining table I cried, and didn't realize I was crying until she curled her arms around me and held me close.

As she did, all I could think was that the last few months I'd spent with Lew were just like it had been when I was a child.

Inconsistent.

Lonely.

That feeling of abandonment, even though he had no control over his situation.

I'd been in complete survival mode, trying to take care of everything and make all the ends meet just so the people around me would be okay.

But what about me? What if I'm not okay?

That question tormented me in so many ways. I was *not* okay. Like I told Deke, I was in shambles, and I meant that in every sense of the word. My heart, my mind, my body—all of me was so bleak and broken.

And maybe that was why I ran from him. Maybe that was why I was so scared of what was budding between us. Because I didn't want someone so *perfect* to see how fucked up I truly was.

It'd taken a while for me to fully commit to Lewis, when we first met. I didn't feel like it was real or like my relationship with him was something I could keep. Even after we married, I kept waiting for the other shoe to drop, just like it had with my dad, and it came stomping down when he was diagnosed with cancer.

To me, that was all the proof I needed to know I was better off alone. Why suffer if I didn't have to? Hell, I'd suffered enough. I didn't think I could share that side of me with another man again. I kept saying this, but it was true. Deke deserved better than me. *Lewis* deserved better than me.

Like a light bulb flashing above my head, a clear realization hit me, and my mind circled back to one of the last things my husband had said: *"I love you, Vina Boo. But I know you, and I don't want you shutting the world out when I'm gone."*

Lewis had seen how lonely I was after his diagnosis, how isolated I felt, how tired I was. He saw me move at lightning speed just to make sure he'd survive. He saw *everything* I couldn't see. Now it made sense why he said those things the night he died. He was trying to save me from *myself.*

A door closed from a distance, and after hearing footsteps drift through the house, I picked my head up and spotted my sister through bleary eyes.

"Mama! Why did you make her cry?" Octavia exclaimed, frowning at Mama. "She just got here!"

Mama laughed, rubbing my back in soothing circles. "She's just processing a few things. Right, Vina?"

I smiled up at my mom, and she returned a warm smile.

"Yeah." I sniffed. "That's right."

FIFTY-SEVEN

DEKE

The Ravens lost the first official game of the season, and it was because of me.

Afterward, I had to sit behind a table with reporters in my face, telling them I'd messed up—that I had a lack of sleep or something—just to cover my own ass. My coaches were pissed, and my teammates hardly recognized me on the court. So many faces in that stadium looked up to me, all for me to fail them.

After fulfilling my part with the media after the game, I went straight home. I wasn't in the mood to sign autographs or make conversation. Coach could shout at me the next day. I just wanted to go home.

Justin tossed a wave at me as I approached my condo building, and I waved back. "Heads up," he said with a smile. The smile meant someone that I actually liked was visiting.

"Thanks, Justin."

"Hey," Justin called, and I stopped next to him. "You okay?" He studied my face, his peppery eyebrows stitching together.

I studied his black vest and the gold name tag at the heart of it, and for a split second I wished I could be like Justin. Living an ordinary life with a happy wife and family he'd built. Smiling through each day as if he had everything he needed in the world. Maybe he did.

I'd thought when I got into the NBA, it would solve all my problems. If anything, all the money and the fame had made things worse.

I forced a smile and capped his shoulder. "All good, J."

I walked away, before he could look at me a second longer, and took the elevator up, the key to my condo already in my hand. I unlocked the door, and as soon as I stepped inside, Zeke dashed across the penthouse and threw his front paws on me.

I closed the door, rubbing his head and giving him a good scratch behind the ears. I noticed all the lights were on and the curtains were drawn, despite it being dark outside, and sitting on the sofa was none other than my sister Whitney.

She'd gotten the key to my condo a few weeks ago so she could feed Zeke while I was traveling. She also needed a place to crash in ATL for a couple of days while searching for properties to renovate, so I offered her mine. That was weeks ago, though, so I didn't understand why she was still lingering around.

"What are you doing here, Whit?" I dropped my keys onto the counter and let my gym bag hit the floor. The black-and-red T-shirt peeked through the open zipper, and I tried not to frown at it.

The general manager had gotten the players shirts with our numbers on them that we could take home. The number seventeen stared up at me. I lowered down to zip the bag and hide it.

"How about a *Hello? How are you? I miss you, sis?*" Whitney stood up, walking around the couch and folding her arms. "Me and Camille have been trying to call you for weeks."

"I know. Got busy," I told her, heading to the kitchen to pluck a Gatorade from the fridge.

"Too busy to talk to your sisters?"

I closed the fridge and cracked the bottle open, keeping my back to her. When I didn't answer, Whitney met me in the kitchen and grabbed my arm, twisting me around gently to face her. She studied my face for so long I had to back up.

She was reading me. She and Camille were good at that. My mom too.

"You messed things up with her, didn't you?" she asked in a low voice. There was no judgment in her tone. In fact, she asked the question as more of a statement, like she already knew the answer.

"Not now, Whitney." I stepped around her to sit on the couch and turn the TV on. I tapped the Netflix button, but Whitney stepped right in front of the TV and blocked my view. "Whitney!"

"Deke, I told you not to do it!"

"It's whatever," I muttered.

"Look at you, bro. You're hurting. I can see it all over your face! I told you not to get involved with her, but you never listen! I'm not trying to make this an *I told you so* moment, but, Deke, even I could've seen this coming from a mile away. Is that why you asked me to take the lake house off the books? 'Cause Camille said the day after that is when you stopped answering the phone."

I looked away.

Zeke trotted my way, whining as he rested his head on top of my thigh. With a heavy sigh, Whitney moved from in front of the TV to sit on the couch too.

We sat this way for a few seconds, quiet and still, until Whitney spoke again.

"I never thought I'd see you fall in love," she murmured, and my eyes flickered to hers quickly before dropping to Zeke's head. "I saw it the night of her rebranding party. I saw the way you looked at her, the way you spoke to her. I saw you searching for her when she disappeared after your speech. I've never seen you care about *any* woman like that other than your family."

My throat thickened when I met her eyes again. I expected her to be staring at me with pity but there was only sympathy.

I closed my eyes, letting them cool before I opened them again and clicked on my Netflix profile.

"Yeah, you're right. You warned me, but I pushed for it anyway. It is what it is."

"What even happened?" she asked.

I gave that question some thought. I'd wondered the same thing for a while. I thought I did everything right, treated her well, took care of her, showed her new things . . . but she still left.

The truth hit me on my drive home from the lake, and I realized her departure had *nothing* to do with me. This was a war Davina had going on within herself, and it was clear she wasn't winning it. Knowing that still didn't make it hurt any less.

"She was too afraid to let me in," I finally answered, meeting my sister's eyes. "She wasn't ready."

FIFTY-EIGHT

DAVINA

"What's the matter, Vina?" My brother, Abe, pulled out of my arms and focused on my ear.

I smiled as I capped his shoulders in the parking lot. I'd decided to pick my sixteen-year-old brother up myself while Mama ran to the store to get a few groceries and Octavia showered.

"Why would something be wrong, Abraham?"

He squinted like the sun was directly in his eyes, then cut a glance at me before looking elsewhere. "Your face is puffy, and your eyes are red like you've been crying."

"I might've been," I told him, releasing his shoulders and walking to my car. He followed along, tucking a thumb beneath the strap of his backpack.

"You cry a lot," he said when we were seated on the leather. "But Lewis died and you loved him, so I get it."

"Yep." I started the car with a reluctant nod. "That's right. He died." No one could be as blunt as my baby brother, and I mean that literally. If he had a thought, he said it. He'd been diagnosed with Asperger's when he was six.

We always knew he was different from the other kids. He didn't learn to speak in clear sentences until he was seven, he hated going out in public because it was often too loud for him, and he didn't like being touched a certain way.

He would cry a lot when he was a toddler. He'd outgrown the crying but was still sensitive to a lot of noise. Mama had him going to classes with a woman in town named Patricia, who homeschooled him in her house. It worked for him, plus he got along great with Patricia's teenage son. He was also in therapy, which helped a lot.

"You still hate donuts?" I asked, reaching between his feet for the pink bakery box.

"Yes," he said, peering out the window.

I huffed a laugh. "More for me."

Abe was quiet. He was always quiet, but I hadn't seen him in so long and wanted to make conversation. The one thing I could think of was something I didn't want to bring up, but I went with it just to hear Abe's voice again.

"You know I worked with an NBA player for my company?"

At that, my brother whipped his head to look in my direction. Like a fish on a hook. "What team does he play for?"

"The Atlanta Ravens."

"Is it Javier Valdez? He's a really good center. He has long arms. And I also hear that he's a nice guy even though people think he's mean because his wife died."

"Well, I *have* met Javier Valdez, and he's pretty cool, but it's not him I'm talking about."

Abe's eyes stretched, and for a split second he looked me in the eye. He pulled away just as quickly to stare at his lap, hold his hands out, and say, "Is it Deke Bishop?"

"Ding ding ding!"

Abe's mouth twitched like he wanted to smile as he kept staring at his lap. "He's really cool. I check his stats all the time. I want to play like him, but he has much better control of the ball than me. Did you know Mama put me in basketball camp again? Yeah, it's for teens like me. It starts around the time school starts, and I think it's for three hours a day. But I watch so many of Deke Bishop's videos and highlights. He's such a beast. I wish I could play like him. Did you know he's had the most assists on the team since . . ."

My brother was on a tangent now, and I loved it. He only talked nonstop about the things he loved, and what he loved most was basketball and math. He'd been a lover of basketball since he was a kid. As far as math goes, you'd never catch me talking about it during casual conversations.

We made it back home, and Abe was still talking about Deke and the Atlanta Ravens, even when Mama greeted him with a peck on the cheek.

"Sorry." I laughed. "I got him going."

She gave him a kiss on the forehead, when he sat at the table, and placed an already-prepared grilled cheese down for him. "Go ahead and eat, Abe. Then I want you to shower and put on your comfortable clothes."

"'Kay, Mama."

He dug into his grilled cheese, and while he did, Mama went to the fridge, pulled out a bottle of merlot, and said, "Vina, let's have a drink on the porch."

FIFTY-NINE

DAVINA

The sun was setting, and I had a cool glass of much-needed wine in hand. There was a cool, soothing breeze going, causing the wind chimes to collide.

Mama was sitting in one of the chairs, I occupied the other, and Octavia had joined us. She was sitting on the ottoman for my chair.

She and Octavia talked about Aromantic while I scrolled through my phone. As I was reading a few of the comments on the GOC page, a text notification popped up from Tish, and I tapped it. I refrained from rolling my eyes as I clicked the link.

The headline was:

DEKE BISHOP'S FIRST GAME A BIG LETDOWN

Oh boy. *Really?* It was obvious she wanted me to feel worse, as if I didn't feel bad enough. She wasn't in support of me leaving while he was sleeping, but when I explained how I felt and that I'd had a panic attack, she understood.

I darkened the screen of my phone, took a sip of wine, then climbed out of the chair to use the bathroom. Abe was sitting on the couch in fresh clothes, the scent of his citrusy bodywash filling half the room.

His phone was in his hand, and though the volume was low, I could hear people speaking. When they said a familiar name, I stopped in the hallway to listen.

"I'm sorry, Doug. I know you like the guy, but he's starting a brand-new season with *weak* attempts. Bishop claimed he had intense training over the summer, but I gotta tell ya. I'm not seeing it! He lost control of the ball four times in the span of thirty minutes, and he was eight for twenty, which is the lowest I've ever seen for this guy, even when he was in college."

"Yeah, Deke Bishop normally brings the heat, but all I saw were ice-cold bricks," another said.

The commentators laughed together, and that's when I hurried into the bathroom.

Of course, when I emerged, I could still hear them.

"It's not looking good for him. The Ravens signed him for one of their biggest contracts yet, and I bet they're regretting it."

"Yikes," one of them said. "All I know is if Bishop doesn't get his head in the game, the Ravens aren't going to send him packing. They're going to send him *flying*." To make matters worse, a bird cawed at the end of their chat.

Good Lord. Deke was right. They *did* talk a lot of shit.

I went back to my seat on the porch, pulling my phone out again and searching for highlights from Deke's game. Seeing him pop up on my screen caused a wrenching in my chest.

I watched one clip, where he let the ball slip out of his hands, followed by another, where he took a shot and missed. Right after missing, he turned away, with his head shaking in defeat and his hands low on his hips.

There was another of him dropping the ball, which resulted in a turnover.

There was a close-up of him bent over, hands on his knees, eyes ahead, sweat dripping from his forehead to the tip of his nose. He was looking around the stadium like he was searching for something. Or *someone*.

Nothing could beat the last clip I saw, where Deke missed the buzzer shot, walked toward the chairs, and kicked one so hard it flew back and slammed into the rails. Right after, he walked to the locker rooms with his head down. Apparently, he was fined for that.

I turned my phone on its face and swallowed. This was my fault.

"You know I lost your grandma right around the time I met your daddy, right?" Mama asked with a lazy smile. She was talking to Octavia, but the question caught my ear.

"Wait, what? I didn't know that," I said.

"Oh yeah!" She sat higher in her chair. "We met when I had a job at the blood bank. He was smitten." She chuckled. "The day he came in was about three or so days after my mom passed, and I was so upset. I didn't want to work, but I had to, because I needed money. All he wanted was to make me smile, and he accomplished it. He made me feel better in a lot of ways, even though I didn't really want to be with him—or anyone for that matter." She tapped her chin. "Yeah, after meeting him, I sort of spiraled. And I could never figure out why he stuck around when all I cared about was drinking and partying and hanging with my girls. There was a point where I was flat-out telling him to leave, because he could do better than me. I mean, really? He was such a nice, handsome man. He didn't need to waste his time on me."

Wow. That sounds awfully familiar.

"Sounds like somebody was a bitch." Octavia snickered into her glass.

Mama picked up something next to her and threw it at my sister, and I busted out laughing when I realized it was a gardening glove.

"*Anyway* . . . I was not so wise then. I should've loved him properly while I had the chance."

My heart ached a little hearing that. I remembered all the times my dad put in effort for Mama, only for her to brush it off or pretend it was no big deal. There were women who *craved* the kind of love and attention he poured on her. She never seemed to care, though . . . but she did take advantage of it. I didn't want to be like that.

"I'm going to make a sandwich," Octavia said, already standing and heading for the door.

"Bring me a water!" Mama called.

When the door clicked shut, I put my attention on Mama again. "I feel guilty about a situation similar to what you went through with Daddy."

Her brows dipped. "How do you mean?"

"There's this guy I've been working with who's been giving me a lot of his attention. He's so sweet and funny, but . . . I'm rejecting him." I paused, rubbing the rim of my wineglass. "I guess I feel the same as you did. Like he deserves better. Plus, it feels too soon after Lew to even *think* about going that deep with anyone else. It just progressed so fast, and it completely blindsided me when I thought about it."

Mama scanned me with her eyes, before setting her wineglass down and scooching to the end of the cushioned chair. "Who is this guy you're talking about?"

I glanced at her. "His name is Deke."

"Well, what does he look like?"

"Why does that matter?" I asked, cracking a smile.

"Girl, it matters a whole lot! What does he look like? I need to see who has you all torn up! I knew something else was wrong when you first walked into the house."

I choked on a laugh as I unlocked my phone and went to Deke's Instagram. I clicked on one of his recent pictures, where he was at a charity function at the recreational center he owned, and handed the phone to her.

She looked down at the screen the way older people tend to do, with their chins tipped and their eyes pointed downward. "That is one fine-looking man."

I threw my head back to laugh. "Mama!"

"What? He is!" she said with a guilty smile. She handed the phone back to me and crossed her legs in the chair. "Do you wanna know one of the things I regret most in my life so far?" she asked after a stretch of silence.

"What?"

"Not having the courage to love your daddy back. I held back from him because I knew he deserved better and figured one day he'd see that and he'd walk away. But when he passed, I was heartbroken all over again, and I started looking for that love anywhere I could find it. But what I really wanted was to pour that love back into your daddy. I took such a beautiful soul for granted. If I had the chance to do it all over again, I would love him so much he couldn't stand me." She wore a soft smile, and I couldn't help smiling with her, though my heart ached.

"I guess what I'm trying to say is you shouldn't hold back based on how you feel about yourself, Davina, because at the end of the day we are our own worst critics. We're hardest on ourselves and only see the flaws when all another person sees is the beauty."

"Yeah," I murmured, dropping my head.

"And don't take this the wrong way, honey, but Lew was sick for a *long* time, and deep down, *you knew* the day when you lost him would come. You knew he'd have to go." She swept me up in her gaze while I bit back tears. "The only difference between my situation and yours is that you had time to prepare for the worst. To accept it. But if this Deke fellow likes you the way you say he does and if you like him, why *not* go there? Why not try a deeper level before denying it? You have to ask yourself, what's stopping you?"

I sniffled and wiped at my nose. "I'm scared," I whispered as a tear crept down my cheek.

"Of what, sweetie?"

"Of him seeing the *real* me. Of him taking the short end of the stick because of my loss. Of having him pick up all those broken pieces and trying to mend them just to make me happy. He doesn't need someone so damaged. He needs someone good. Someone *healed*. He's such an amazing person, and I'll only drag him down."

"Oh, honey. Love always comes with the good and bad." She walked across the porch and sat on the ottoman near me. Clasping my hands in hers, she said, "I don't think that's fear you're feeling. That's just a test of your faith. You know what you need to do. All you have to do is gain the courage to take that step again, and you're there, baby. And whatever happens, happens. I know it was easy to think ahead when you were with Lew. You were looking for solutions and only wanted the best for your future, but in a situation like you have now, you can't look ahead and you *definitely* shouldn't look back. You can only focus on what or *who* is in front of you at this present moment. Does this unexpected man make you laugh? Does he make you feel like yourself? Does he comfort you relentlessly, unconditionally? Do you ever feel judged by him? Does he understand you, even at your lowest? Is he patient even when you feel like he's sick and tired of you?"

With each question she asked, all I could think about were the last few months I'd spent with Deke.

Yes, he made me laugh.

Yes, he made me feel like myself.

Yes, he comforted me relentlessly. Unconditionally.

No, he never, *ever* judged me for the way I cried at the fountain around goose shit or even when I ran away from him on the rooftop. He understood me during my low points, held me at the lake house and refused to let go . . . but I did. Like an idiot, I let him go.

And most of all, through every single strife, every tear, every disappointment, every dumb or rude remark from me, he remained patient. Not once did he waver.

"Oh, God." *What have I done?* I cupped my mouth as hot tears gathered on my cheeks. Everything Mama said was true. I peered up at her, this woman full of wisdom and reason. "Wow. Who knew a woman who used to get lit for a living could have such great advice?" I said, and she reeled me in for a hug so I could hiccup a laugh into her chest.

"That's what happens when you get to be my age. You live and you learn, and most of that knowledge was gained the hard way." She pulled back to swipe a stray tear from my cheek. "If that man loves you, *let him love you*, Vina. Don't deny yourself something good just because you think you don't deserve it."

"I won't," I whispered, and I never would again.

The screen door creaked open, and I looked back as Octavia and Abe walked out the door.

"Again, Mama?" Octavia garbled out around a mouthful of sandwich.

"Hey, Davina, I want Deke Bishop's signature," Abe said, completely disregarding my sister and pushing past her. "You said you work with him, so you can get it. He had a bad game last night, but we all have bad games and bad days. I still think he's a good player. Can you get it?"

I smiled at my little brother, taking his hand and giving it a squeeze. I knew what I had to do, and it was time to lower my guard once and for all and get my man back.

"When I make things up to him, I'll be sure to get his signature and more just for you, Abe."

SIXTY

DEKE

EDGE was my favorite barbershop in Atlanta. I greeted my barber Scottie with a dap and bumped fists with the other barbers.

It wasn't until I sat down in the barber's seat that my phone buzzed in my hoodie pocket. There was a tightening in my chest when I saw the single letter *D*. I'd seen it twice the day before and once the day before that. Davina had called multiple times for three days in a row, and I ignored every single one. I had nothing else to say to her.

"I need you to make sure the next game is a good one, man," Scottie said, bringing the razor closer to my hairline. "I had a hundred dollars riding on the Ravens. I just knew my team was gonna win."

Scottie was my barber, a heavyset dude with tawny skin and a thick black beard. The barbershop was light today, which I expected for a Tuesday, but those who were inside waiting or getting haircuts agreed with him.

"Yeah, man. Wasn't my best game," I said. "But the next will be." At least I hoped it would.

My first game of the season was shitty because my mind wasn't in it and neither was my heart. Coach Harrison chewed me out like a dog the day after, screaming at me across the office, spittle flying onto the papers on his desk.

"You're supposed to be the star player! Act like one!"

If I didn't pull out of this funk soon, I wasn't going to have a career for much longer. I watched my phone until the vibrating stopped and the home screen appeared, then slid it into my pocket again. If I wanted to get my head back in the game, step one was to forget about Davina.

When Scottie was done and I dropped some cash with a hefty tip in his palm, my phone vibrated again. I took a selfie with a man who caught me at the door before I could escape, then whipped my phone out, seeing that same letter. *D.*

Why the hell does she keep calling me? Now she wanted to reach out, after damn near two weeks of not saying a fucking thing?

I worked my jaw and stuffed the phone into my pocket again. I hit up my personal chef when I was in the car so I could have a healthy lunch delivered to the condo, and on my way home, my phone rang again.

I expected it to be Davina—and this time I was prepared to shoot her a text and tell her to stop calling—but it wasn't her. It was Javier.

"What's going on, Valdez?"

"Hey, Deke." His voice streamed through the speakers of my car. "I completely forgot that I have a meeting with Coach Harrison, and the sitter will not be here until seven. Do you think you can swing by with Aleesa for an hour or two? Only if you are not busy."

"Oh, yeah. I got you," I told him. "I'm on the way."

"Thanks, man. You're a lifesaver." He hung up, and I made a U-turn to get to his house. As I did, I couldn't help glancing at my phone. I had the urge to call Davina back, to lower my damn pride and see what she wanted.

As badly as I wanted to, though, I couldn't bring myself to do it. She'd made her point. At this rate, she was just playing games, and that was the last thing I had time for.

I drove through the iron gates of Javier's house, the wheels of my car coasting along the cobblestone drive. His home was a two-story structure with a stucco roof. The exterior was ivory, and palm trees were planted around it. It felt very coastal for a home in Georgia. I supposed he wanted to stick with his roots.

I climbed out, headed for the front door, and gave the doorbell a ring. Javier answered in a matter of seconds, with Aleesa on his hip.

"Deke," he said, breathless. "You are here. Good."

"Uh, why aren't you dressed?" I asked when he let me in.

"Oh, right. I was feeding Aleesa. All I have to do is toss some jeans on. It will be quick."

Aleesa smiled at me. "Deke. Canny?" she asked in that adorable voice.

"Ah, I'm sorry, Aleesa. I didn't bring any. I was trying to hurry over here so I could hang with you."

She pouted, and I reached for her. She came to me, her smile returning.

"Don't worry," I whispered loudly. "As soon as your daddy leaves, I'll order us some candy on Instacart."

"Deke," Javier warned, raising a brow.

"I'm just playing, man."

Aleesa reached for her dad again, and Javier made his way toward the living room. I rounded the corner, ready to slip out of my shoes and hoodie and get comfortable, until I saw someone else standing in the middle of the room.

I stopped dead in my tracks, and my heart sank to my stomach as Davina tossed a wave at me.

"Hi, Deke," she murmured.

"Javier, *what the fuck?*" I snapped, turning my eyes on him.

"Deke, calm down," Javier said, raising a patient hand. "She said she has been calling you for days. You were not answering, so she had her sister call me yesterday so she could get in touch with me. She was worried and arrived in Atlanta last night because she needs to talk to you."

"Yeah, I wasn't answering because I didn't wanna talk to her," I snapped and noticed her tense up a bit.

"Look," Javier said, his voice lowering. "You know the last thing I wanted to do was blindside you, but she begged me to do this, Deke. I know how much you care about her, and that is the *only* reason I did not turn her away. Something tells me this needs to happen or you'll regret it, so just hear her out."

"Nah. It's too late for all that." I turned around, ready to storm out of the house, but Javier made his way around me and stopped me with a firm hand to the chest.

"Listen to me, Deke. You are reacting emotionally, and I completely understand why, but I refuse to let you do something that I know will only cause you suffering later. I *know you*, Deke. I know going out that door isn't what your heart wants."

"Javier," I grumbled. "Get out of my way."

"If you do not like what she has to say *after* you hear her out, you can walk away and I won't stop you again," he went on, holding steady. "It is that simple. If you decide to walk, I will promise to *never* interfere with your relationships again. But right now, because I am your friend and because I care about what is best for *you*, I really think you should stick around and listen."

I looked down, and there was a mixture of shock and fear in Aleesa's eyes as she stared at me.

"Dee, wha' happen? Dee okay?" she asked in a soft whimper. Guilt ate me alive. She was so young. So innocent. She didn't understand what was going on—this animosity taking over her own home.

"I'm okay, Aleesa." I gripped her little chin and forced a smile. I had to calm down. I was scaring her.

I focused on Javier again. "I just do not want you to have any regrets," he said.

I wanted to ask Davina if she regretted when she walked out the fucking door, but instead I exhaled and took a step back.

"Fine."

Javier slipped his feet into athletic slides and hiked Aleesa higher up his hip. "I will take Aleesa for a walk, give you two a moment."

"Thank you, Javier," Davina said, and I hated that my heart betrayed me by beating faster at the sound of her voice.

When Javier left, it was just us in his oversize living room. I turned to face the woman who'd broken my heart, and she took a step toward me. She looked good, even in something as simple as jeans and a halter-top shirt. Curls dangled around her ears, the rest pulled up into a puffy bun, diamond studs in her ears.

Light poured through the blocky windows above, beaming down on her and making her look like a damn angel. It was becoming really hard to stay mad at her when she looked like that.

"Look, I know I'm the last person you want to see right now," Davina said, and I loosely folded my arms, clinging to my guard. "I know that I hurt you, and I never should've walked away like I did at the lake. I was just scared, and I kept telling myself that you deserved better than me—which I still believe—but I wasn't looking at the bigger picture. I was only focusing on *my* pain and what'd happened to *me*. I wasn't thinking about a future, because I didn't care about the future. I—I was stuck in the moment and only thinking about myself, and that wasn't fair to you. I was so selfish, Deke. So damn selfish." She took a few steps closer, making the space between us smaller. I could smell her now, vanilla and shea butter. Warm and familiar. "I just wanted to come to you, like you came to me all those times before, to tell you that *I'm sorry* and that I'm here."

I dropped my arms. "Oh, you're *here*? Now, after stomping on my heart and leaving it there to rot?"

"I know, I know, and I'm so sorry," she pleaded, another inch closer. "You're such a good guy, Deke. You're so kind and respectful and hilarious, and I *love* that about you. And with all the time that has passed since the lake, I realize just how much I miss you being in my life! I had time to think about everything the last few weeks, and it hit me—like *really* hit me—that I would not have made it through the end of that sad, selfish season of my life without you. I never would've pushed through. I would've willingly remained stuck. Yes, I had my family and my best friend, but you checked on me every day. You made me smile *every single day*. You put me first, even when you had other places to be and other things to do. You were there for me so many times, and I didn't appreciate it in the moment . . . and I guess I didn't trust it or you because I didn't know what you were after, but I see the truth now. I can see it just like I saw it in your eyes on that dock."

She was right in front of me now, taking my hands in hers and holding them tight. Her eyes shimmered like she wanted to cry, and I wanted to pull her into my arms and kiss those tears away as soon as they fell.

Still, I remained stubborn.

"You said you were in love with me, so I came here to let you know my truth. *I love you*, Deke Bishop," she said with a breath of elation. "I'm in love with you, too, and I know it, because I can never get you out of my head. I crave your presence more every day, and believe me, my chest hurts, too, when I'm away from you. I've tried fighting that ache, but it's impossible. I resisted for so long because I didn't understand how it could be, you know? How I could love two men with one heart, even when the other is gone. I didn't think it was possible or that I could feel so much with another man so quickly, but I felt it all and possibly even more with you."

Those tears dripped down her cheeks, and I stared into her eyes for so long my vision grew blurry.

"So why did you run away?" I asked in a whisper. "Why did you leave me like that?"

"Because I was stupid," she croaked. "I was so stupid and so wrong, and I promise you I will *never* run away again."

I pulled my hand away, and a wave of defeat washed over her until I cupped my ear and leaned down so her lips were next to it. "I'm sorry. Can you repeat that?"

She bubbled out a sad laugh, and I couldn't help cracking a smile.

"I said I was stupid and I was wrong!" she yelled in my ear, giggling. "I'll never run from what we have again."

I chuckled, cupping her face in my hands and planting a drawn-out kiss on her forehead.

"I know you're mad at me. And even though I'm here, I'll understand if you don't want to be with me anymore," she said softly, studying my face when I pulled away.

I pressed a finger beneath her chin and lifted it so our eyes could connect. "I'm not walking away, Davina. I'm not afraid to love you or to shout it so the whole world can hear it."

Her eyes grew misty again, her mouth trembling, like she had so much more to say but wasn't sure how to express it. I leaned down, kissing her with all the love and passion I had in me.

Damn, I missed her soft lips and smooth skin. I didn't care about the salty taste of her tears or her mini sobs. If it came from her—if it involved her in *any* way—it was all mine now.

Her fingers curled into my hoodie, and I sighed behind our kiss. I loved the hell out of this woman. She had no damn idea.

How was it possible that this woman, who was once a stranger, was now the epitome of my life? She was the center of my thoughts, the reason I finally believed in those two things many people talk about: *love and soulmates.*

She was mine, despite the circumstances, the losses, and the pain. She belonged to me and I to her. There was no doubt in my mind that we'd met in other lifetimes, destined to be, and now we were meeting again.

"I'm yours, D," I whispered on her lips. "No matter what, I'm always going to be yours."

SIXTY-ONE

DAVINA

After thanking Javier for helping me and giving cuddly hugs to Aleesa, I followed after Deke in his Ferrari to get to his condo.

He led me to the private parking deck and gave me a pass to stick on top of my dashboard as a guest. As we rode up the elevator, he took my hand in his, and I squeezed it, smiling up at him.

"So, does this make you my girlfriend?" he asked.

I laughed. "I don't know, does it? Because I'm pretty sure you have to ask for someone to be your girlfriend." I smirked, looking ahead.

"Oh, word? Okay, I see."

The elevator doors split apart, and he led the way to his door. He let me in first, and I drank in the interior of his home, but not for long, because a large black dog came pouncing toward me.

"Zeke! You better not!" Deke called, but Zeke was already on his hind legs with his paws on my stomach.

"Oh my goodness, hi!" I rubbed his head as his tongue hung out and his stubby tail wagged. He panted, licking my hand every time I tried to stroke his head. "So you're the roommate this guy talks all about?" I laughed as I looked up at Deke. "Don't tell me you gave him the name Zeke to match yours?"

Deke smirked. "Damn right I did."

I laughed as Zeke licked my cheek.

"All right, man. All right," Deke said, tapping his butt. "Down, Zeke."

Zeke obeyed, rushing to his owner, who chuckled and made his way to a glass container on the counter full of dog treats. He took three out and dropped them onto Zeke's doggy pillow in the corner. I watched as Zeke sat on the pillow to devour his snacks.

"He likes you," Deke said behind me. He wrapped me in his arms, reeling me back so that my butt was pressed to his groin. I held on to his arms as he buried his face into the crook of my neck. "You always smell so good."

"Thanks." I smiled. "I like your bachelor pad."

"Appreciate it." His lips pressed to my jawline. "Wanna see the bachelor's room?"

I turned my head to look up at him, grinning. He released me but only to take my hand and guide me to the bedroom. I heard Zeke's paws on the floor, but Deke commanded him to stay, then said, "I need a few minutes alone with my girl." He winked at me, and I swear I melted.

When the door was shut, I studied his room. It was simple, masculine. The regular walls were painted a smoky gray, but the wall behind the bed had built-in panels. His bed was dressed in all black, with a black leather headboard.

Two nightstands were on either side, and floating lamps were above them. The other side of the room had floor-to-ceiling windows revealing the Atlanta skyscrapers.

"Wow," I breathed. "This is not what I expected. I love it."

"Yeah? Whitney designed it for me."

I turned around to face him, about to apologize again about the lake house, but he swooped in and cupped the back of my head to kiss me. I moaned as I stumbled backward while he held on to my hip, guiding me to the side of the bed. When I sat, he pulled his hoodie and shirt over his head, and I removed my shirt too.

"Deke," I sighed as he climbed on top of me, kissing my throat. "I'm still so sorry."

"I know you are," he rasped.

"So let me make it up to you."

"How?" he asked, planting a kiss on my collarbone.

I pressed a hand to his chest so I could sit up, then pushed his body to the right. He flopped onto his back, and I climbed off the bed to take my jeans off. He watched as I slipped out of my panties and bra, too, his eyes growing wider as he scanned me.

"Oohh, Davina Klein. Don't tell me you're about to do what I think you're about to do."

I laughed and lowered my knees to the floor, wedging my upper body between his thighs. When I tugged at his briefs, he lifted his hips so I could pull them down. When I removed them, I leaned upward, and his breath hitched as I kissed the tip of his hardening dick.

"Is it okay to make it up to you this way?" I asked, my mouth hovering over him.

"Yeah," he breathed, staring down at me with hooded eyes.

"'Kay." I smiled, then parted my lips and wrapped my mouth around him.

He tensed beneath me, one hand clutching the gray duvet. I took more of him into my mouth, and he stifled a groan, but when I gripped the base while simultaneously massaging his balls, he palmed the back of my head.

"I'm gonna end up coming in your mouth, D," he rumbled, and his voice made me clench. I kept sucking him, making his dick wetter, dragging my tongue down his shaft and circling his balls with it.

I could hear him breathing faster, and when I looked up at him, he shook his head with his fingers tangled in my hair. "Don't look at me like that, D."

"Like what?" I asked, suckling on the tip, then running my tongue over the slit.

"Like *that*," he rasped. "Gonna make me come if you keep looking at me with my dick in your mouth."

I smiled around him and eased him down my throat again. He released a heavy groan, and I used my hand to stroke while I sucked.

There was something empowering about doing this to him. Watching this man who seemingly had it all together come apart as I sucked, stroked, slurped, and gagged around him.

I pumped faster, moaning as he grew harder in my palm. His breaths were rapid, his body twice as tense.

When I lapped my tongue around his balls again, he sat up fully and said, "I need you up here. Get up here." He was already hauling me off my knees so I could climb on top of him.

As I held his shoulders, he gripped the base of his dick and placed his other hand on my hip. I slowly slid down the length of him, and his lips spread farther apart until they'd formed a wide O.

I rode him slowly on the edge of the bed, looking into his eyes and gasping when he tilted his hips to be deeper. He cupped my ass and thrust upward as he moaned.

He felt so hard inside me, so big. I could tell he was already close, so I clasped his face in my hands and kissed him. I rolled my hips and moaned into his mouth as he propelled upward.

We moved in sync, lips locked, tongues colliding, and Deke snatched his mouth away to look at me. His lips were swollen, and mine felt raw. His eyes were like two brown pools. He gazed at me with so much adoration, so much desire, so much tenderness.

"I love you," I whispered on his mouth.

"Yeah?" he breathed.

"I do," I sighed. "I love you, Deke."

Before I knew it, he stopped pumping to go completely still beneath me. While he looked up at me, I kissed him slowly, claiming his mouth as mine, and he moaned, clutching my ass tighter.

"I'm about to come," he rasped, urging me to climb off.

I climbed off and moved between his legs again to let him finish in my mouth. He let out a carnal groan like I'd never heard before as he came. His come was hot and salty, and I swallowed it down as he lay on his back again with a moan and several twitches.

He clung to my head as I pulled back up for air, and while he lay like that, subdued and spasming, I licked him once more, which really made him lose it.

I climbed on the bed to lie next to him. One of his arms was resting on his forehead, and his chest rose and fell as he caught his breath. I peeled his arm away, and he cracked a lazy smile.

When he sat up on his elbows, he gripped my chin in his fingers and brought his mouth to mine.

"I fucking love you," he whispered. "Will you be my girlfriend?"

I giggled, kissed him again, and said, "Only if you'll be my boyfriend."

SIXTY-TWO

DAVINA

Deke's away game after we made up proved all the naysayers wrong.

It was one of his best games yet, and suddenly the commentators were trying to figure out how he'd made such a strong comeback.

Truth is, he'd never lost his touch; it was just his gloomy heart that'd weighed him down. I promised him I would never do that to him again—walk away, leave him alone. This time, I was here to stay, and unless he gave me a reason to leave, I wasn't going anywhere.

Three weeks had passed since I'd gone to Deke's condo, but we made a way to see each other every weekend. It was that third week when I realized it would be a full year since Lewis died.

One full year.

I couldn't believe it.

I expected to feel completely broken and torn up when I saw the reminder in my calendar, but I wasn't. For once I was okay. I cried (of course I did), but after pulling myself together, I called my mom and Octavia and asked them to come to Charlotte for the weekend to honor him.

On November 2, my house was full of familiar faces. Tish had come with Lorenzo; my sister, brother, and mother were there, as well as a few of Lew's old friends and football teammates from college. And though I didn't want to, I invited Gloria. She still wasn't happy with me, but she lowered her pride just a notch to make an appearance.

We took turns going around the room and sharing our favorite memories of Lewis, then we ate a cake with his face on it. It was a nice night.

I was sure Deke would've come, too, but he had a game in Houston. He called me as soon as he got home, but by that time, it was nearing midnight and everyone was gone except Mama, Octavia, and Abe.

"I'm sorry I missed it," Deke said as I threw plastic cups in the trash.

"Deke, it's fine," I assured him.

"I bet it was nice."

I studied his face on the screen and how his eyes turned away. "I think you should do something like that for your brother."

"Yeah. I should. I'll tell my sisters about it." He set his phone down to pour himself a bowl of Cocoa Puffs. That was his treat after every game, and hearing the cereal clink in the bowl always made me smile.

"My mom wants me to come to her place for Thanksgiving," he said, pouring the milk.

"That's a good thing, right?"

He propped the phone up on something so I could see him straight on. "No. She invited my dad."

My brows drew together, confused. "What's wrong with that?"

"I despise that motherfucker," he said, then shoveled a big scoop into his mouth.

"Why?"

After he chewed, he asked, "Do you wanna know the whole story over the phone or in person?"

"I think in person would be better, but now I'll be wondering why you hate him until the next time I see you," I said, laughing, and he gave me a closed-lip smile.

"It won't be long until I see you again."

"Vina?" I looked to find the voice, and it was Abe standing in his pajamas and rubbing his eyes.

"Hey, Abe. What's wrong?"

"I can hear you talking," he informed me, then moseyed around me to take a cup out of one of the cupboards. He filled it with water and gulped some down. He glanced at my phone and did a double take before leaning in and narrowing his eyes.

"Is that Deke Bishop?" he asked, and I could see his face light up, even though he avoided mine.

"It is." I laughed. "Would you like to speak to him?"

"No, no." Abe backed away, excited but nervous.

"Is that King Abe?" Deke asked, and for the first time that day, Abe connected his eyes with mine. It was brief, but still something.

"He knows my name? H-how does he know my name?"

I moved closer, wrapping an arm around him. "I told him all about you. He signed a basketball for you, by the way. All I have to do is pick it up."

"No way." Abe grinned a little, and I dropped a kiss on his cheek. He peeled out of my arm to finish his water, set the cup down, and said, "I'm going back to bed." On his way, he mumbled under his breath, "That's Deke Bishop. He knows my name. Deke Bishop knows my name."

"Cute kid," Deke chuckled.

"Yeah. He's the best. And so freaking smart."

"You should bring him to one of the games."

"I'm sure he wants to go to one, but he's sensitive to a lot of noise. He gets overstimulated very fast, so being surrounded by loud crowds and buzzers wouldn't work."

"I can get you box seats," he offered.

"Aw, Deke. You don't have to do that. Plus, knowing Abe, if he ever did build up the courage to go, he'd want to be front and center."

"Hmm. Well, maybe I can figure something out."

"We watched some of your game earlier."

"Yeah?" He quirked a brow. "Like what you saw?"

"You just love going for threes, don't you?"

"Where do you think most of my points come from?" he asked, grinning. Then he yawned right after.

"Get some sleep, Bishop."

"But I wanna sleep with you," he returned.

"Maybe this weekend?"

"Yeah. This weekend for sure."

And sure enough, he was in Charlotte for the weekend, and for the first time I let him visit my house. It was weird having this giant man in my home. There were still pictures of Lew on the walls, and it wasn't as impressive as his condo.

I'd held off on inviting him to my place for a while, but the hotels were getting stale, and our relationship was past that now.

"So, this is Davina the Divine's *real* domain."

"I swear you have a name for everything!" I said as he walked to the living room.

"What?" He smiled over his shoulder. "I can't help it."

He walked toward one of the shelves, studying the images in their frames. I stood by the island counter, watching as he picked one of them up. It was a picture of me and Lew at Niagara Falls. I loved that picture, because it was captured randomly by a photographer on the boat. Lew was looking at me like I was the only girl in this world, his face soft, eyes low. I was cheesing hard, not even realizing he was looking at me.

"He loved you. I can tell," Deke said, glancing at me. I walked toward him as he set the picture on the shelf again.

"If this is weird for you or anything, we can go somewhere else," I said.

"It's not weird to me, D. I've always wanted to see your place. Is it weird to you?"

I hesitated. "A little . . . but I'll get used to it."

"I don't think you should hide him," Deke said. "He was a part of your life for years. No one can take that away. Not even me."

I pressed my lips as he took my hands. "I'm glad you understand. I mean, one day I will put most of the pictures somewhere else, along with the boxes full of his clothes and hats and stuff. Just not right now. I don't think I'm ready."

Deke smiled down at me. "Take all the time you need."

SIXTY-THREE

DEKE

When Davina invited me to her place, I wasn't entirely sure I was ready for it yet. I was hit with a wave of discouragement knowing it was once a house she shared with another man.

I could never compete with her husband, and frankly, I never wanted to. But sometimes I wondered if she looked at those pictures and longed for the traits in him that she couldn't find in me.

It was tricky thinking of the comparisons, but I had to remind myself just as Camille reminded me over and over again: love is different with every individual.

While Davina finished tossing a salad, I set up the table for her. When the food was ready and she'd prepared the plates, she set one in front of me, and it was piping-hot homemade lasagna.

"Oh shit. Let me find out my girl can cook!"

"I'm okay at it," she said, sitting in the chair next to mine. "Octavia is the one who can throw down. I make a mean batch of pancakes, though."

"I'll have to try some of those soon, see what they're all about."

She smiled at me, and we dug in. It was really good, by the way. She had to stop discrediting herself.

"So, I don't want to push too hard, but I am curious, Deke."

I glanced at her as she cut into her lasagna. I already knew what topic she was about to bring up.

"My dad," I sighed.

"Yes. I'm sorry, I just keep wondering what happened, then I think about your brother, and I'm just trying to connect the dots."

"Yeah. I did promise to tell you." I took a sip of sweet tea. "To put it simply, he's an alcoholic. Well—according to my sisters and my mama, he *was* one. He's sober now." I scoffed at the thought, taking another bite of lasagna. "Anyway, uh, he used to drink a lot in the afternoons. Every day he'd have a six- or twelve-pack of beer. Sometimes he'd go to the liquor cabinet. Didn't matter what kind of alcohol it was, so long as he was drunk."

Davina nodded, with sympathetic eyes.

"Whenever he drank, he became hostile and violent. He didn't get heavily into drinking until I was around eleven, but before that, he was all right. He's the one who got me and my brother into basketball. He showed us the fundamentals, taught us how to be respectful. He even taught us how to ride our bikes. To see him go from a stand-up dad to a raging alcoholic was shocking to me. My mom says it was because he was injured on the job and they let him go. He worked in construction, broke his arm somehow, and when they said it was his fault for not following protocol, they fired him.

"She said he was broke, injured, and angry, and that's why he resorted to drinking. He was struggling to find another job that could pay him enough to provide for four kids, so my mom would do double shifts at the hospital. She was a triage nurse—still is to this day. I can only assume he wasn't pleased that she was bringing in all the money and that he couldn't find a job, so he started drinking." I paused, swallowing thickly.

"It started slow, you know? Like a snowball effect. It started with him shouting at us, telling us to pick up our stuff or to clean something, and he only ever directed it to me and Damon. But we listened, because, you know, he was our dad, and back then, he was still a good man to us. But eventually the yelling shifted to grabbing and shaking. Then he'd slap us or push us, tell us to buck up and stop acting like girls. And then it progressed to punches and beatings.

"He never did it to our sisters, though. Camille was already on her way to college, and Whitney was hardly ever home. Damon got the worst of it, though. If Damon lost a game, there my dad was throwing shit at him and punching him. Shouting at him about how sorry he was. If I lost, he did the same to me. Sometimes he took out a belt and hit us. Sometimes he grabbed us by the backs of our necks and would drag us all the way outside, force us to grab a basketball, and run drills until we were bone tired. And during all this, my mom would try and stop him, but whenever she did, he'd hit her too."

I sucked in a breath, realizing Davina's hand was on top of mine. I met her eyes, and they were glossy, her mouth trembling. "Deke," she whispered. "I'm so sorry."

"Yeah, but that's not the worst of it. The thing is, back then, Damon was the weakest of us mentally. He constantly doubted himself, constantly worried, but if there was one thing he was confident in, it was protecting us. There was one night when our dad was beating on him *so bad* for something *I* did. I can't even remember what it was about, that's how stupid and minuscule it was. Damon took the fall for me, and our dad beat him until his eye was swollen and his bottom lip was busted." I clenched my other fist.

"Deke, you don't have to keep going," Davina whispered. "You can stop if this is triggering you."

"No." I swallowed again and stared down at my plate. "Because this shit *haunts* me, Davina. I feel like it's my fault Damon killed himself. After my dad beat him like that, my mom was hysterical. She said she was calling the police, and there was a big argument between them. She kicked our dad out that night, and I used to share a room with Damon, so I saw all the mess in there, the broken chair, blood on the floor. When he got back from the hospital, he was crying harder than I'd ever seen him cry before. He was *moaning*—I can still remember the sound of it." I squeezed my eyes shut. "It's been embedded in my brain—it wakes me out of my sleep sometimes, D. Damon kept saying he hated his life that night, that he was tired, that everything hurt. Me and Whitney tried comforting him, and he did eventually fall asleep.

"The next day, me and Whitney went to school, and Damon stayed in bed. My mom had to work a double, so no one was home with him, but he knew how to take care of himself, so we figured he'd be fine. When I got back, I saw he was still in bed, but he wasn't moving. I tried waking him up, but I—I found a letter in his hand. All it said was 'I'm sorry. It's all too much.' I saw deep gashes on his wrist, and there was so much blood beneath him. I saw a knife. I . . . *fuck*. I didn't know what to do, so I just started screaming for Whitney to come to the room.

"Whitney saw and called our mom, but it was too late. Damon had just started his senior year. He had so much ahead of him. He . . . he sliced his own wrists with a kitchen knife. He bled out on that bed by himself. I really don't know why he'd taken such a drastic approach. I mean, I knew he was sad, I knew he was hurting, but I just . . . I never thought he would *kill* himself. And that note in his hand, I kept reading it, knowing exactly what he meant.

"Our dad was an abusive asshole who was too hard on us. He coached me and Damon for years and taught us everything we knew, but he was too much. He was too strict, too harsh, just . . . over the fucking top. Even before he started drinking so much, if we lost a game, he'd punch us dead in the chest for however many points we lost by, but we considered it tough love then. Damon was talented, but I remember him getting to a point where he didn't want to practice or play anymore because he hated the consequences of losing.

"But of course, our dad kept making him. He wouldn't let him quit, and Damon was good—hell, he was better than I was on the court, and my dad made sure to let me know that. I guess it all came crashing down on him, though. It had to for him to take his own life. My dad got arrested for what he did to Damon, but my mom dropped the fucking charges just so he could attend the funeral. I was so fucking mad, D. My anger has always gotten the best of me, and I was so heartsick and pissed off because he was just back in our house like nothing happened, groveling to our mom, manipulating her while she was sad and weak, but I saw right through that shit, so while my mom was sleeping, I told him he needed to leave. And if he didn't leave, I'd tell the police that he'd been hitting me too.

"He left for a couple hours but came back later that night. He was so fucking drunk, stumbling through the house like an idiot. I was in my room and all I could hear was him screaming my name, 'Declan! Declan! Declan! Who the hell do you think you are? Get the fuck out here, *Declan*!' Then I heard a bunch of commotion. I heard my mama screaming at him, so I opened the door, and my mama was trying to push him back down the hallway, but he was so drunk and furious that he pushed her to the side, and she hit her head on one of the picture frames. She hit it so hard the glass cut her head. I saw her bleeding, but I had no time to go and help her because my dad charged toward me and wrapped his hands around my throat.

"He shoved me back on my bed, and he kept choking me and yelling in my face. He kept telling me I would never be as good as Damon, that I'd never amount to anything, that I should've been happy to be trained by him and that I wouldn't have any of the talent I had if it weren't for him. He kept saying I should've been the one to go, not Damon. And in that moment, I was so scared. But not because he was choking me out or anything. It was because his words were sinking into me like seeds, planting themselves there and taking root.

"I knew I'd never be as good as Damon—and I didn't want to be. I didn't care. But I also knew that since Damon was gone, I was going to have to carry on his legacy in some way. That's why I wear the number seventeen. That was his number and the age he died. I was scared people would see me as this fraud, or the person who wasn't worth a damn, you know? I was scared that he was *right* . . . that I'd never amount to a damn thing. But here I am, best of my team and one of the biggest faces of the NBA franchise, and there's still this hollowness inside me," I said, tapping the center of my chest with the tips of my fingers.

"There's this part of me who knows all of this wasn't for *me*, Davina. I have this life and this fame because I wanted to prove that mother-fucker wrong. A lot of what fueled me was heart and passion for the game, yes, but what *really* got me going was the *rage*. I'd see my opponents on the court, and all of them had one face: my dad's. I'd run circles around them. I'd prove my point, I'd win, and I'd walk away." I felt my eyes getting hot, burning from the unshed tears.

"My mom managed to get him off of me and call the police, and this time he was locked up for a while. It was only eight years, but it was enough for us to uproot. When he was out, she divorced him, and I thought that would be the end of it. I thought we'd never have to see his face again, but here we are. About to have Thanksgiving with this motherfucker."

"My goodness. I can't imagine how scared you were or how much pain you were in over your brother, Deke. I'm so sorry that happened to you. I get why you don't like talking about it now," Davina said.

I shrugged. "The pain never left, honestly. Just got easier to manage."

Her throat bobbed, and her eyes were lined with tears. One blink and they'd fall.

I huffed a humorless laugh. "The worst part is that, to this day, I don't know if I'm angry at my brother for leaving me back then or envious that he escaped that hell."

The tears dripped down Davina's cheeks. She pulled her hand away to swipe at them, and I stood up, taking her hand and leading her to the couch.

I held her in my arms, and the emotion in my throat thickened. I was so close to crying, myself. I hadn't cried about my brother in years, and didn't want to start now. I wanted to be strong for Davina. I told my story, and now she knew. It was up in the air and off my chest, and frankly, I was relieved.

"Don't cry for me, D," I whispered in her hair. "I'm past all that."

"No," she muttered. "You're not, Deke." She sat up to look at me. "Listen to me. You're an *amazing* person, okay? Your life is *yours*. You built this for yourself. You are talented and handsome and smart. Everyone loves you, Deke. Everyone wants to be you."

"Yeah, but what they see isn't the real me. That's just a front I put on to prove I'm okay and to tell myself that my past will never define me."

"It doesn't have to define you, but you can't run from it either. I see the real you, and I know your heart. You're worthy, baby. You're *so* worthy. Don't let your dad or anyone else in this world tell you otherwise."

I felt a hot streak fall down my cheek, and I closed my eyes as she used her thumb to swipe it away.

When I opened them again, I said, "This is why I could understand you and why I wanted to be patient with you. Because I know that pain. I live it every single day, and I know how hard it is to let people in when you're hurting. It took me a while to step out of my shell when Damon died."

"Thank you for that. Seriously." She laid her head on my chest and was quiet for a few seconds. "Is that why you don't like to be called by your real name? Why you corrected me every time when we first met?"

I had a feeling she already knew the answer to that, but I responded anyway. "Yeah. That's why. When anyone calls me that, all I can hear is my dad shouting my name down the hallway. All I can remember is his hands around my throat, my brother's blood on the mattress. You wanna talk about triggers? *That* fucking triggers me."

She tilted her head back, peering up at me. "You can't let him have your name. He took enough away from you. You were born with that. Don't let him keep it."

I couldn't help smiling. "My mom says the same thing."

"See? And if she raised you, I'm sure she's a wise woman."

I gave her a peck on the cheek before consuming her lips. When our mouths parted, I hugged her tight, because there was nowhere else I wanted to be than with her. Outside of my family and a few people who knew Damon, no one else was aware of his suicide, not even Javier. I'd purposely kept it buried when high school was over and never wanted to revisit it again, because when my dad was in jail, I worked on becoming a new man.

Telling Davina took a weight off my shoulders, though. One that'd been dragging me down for nineteen long years. And for the first time that night, as our lasagna went cold and we curled up on the couch, I felt nothing but sweet relief.

For the first time, I lit a match to my past and warmed up to the flames.

"Will you join me for Thanksgiving?" I asked.

Davina rubbed my arm. "Of course I will."

SIXTY-FOUR

DAVINA

Deke took off the following morning to return to Atlanta.

He had conditioning and therapy, then film sessions, and prior to even visiting me, he said his time would be very slim and apologized for his upcoming absence.

I don't even know why he bothered apologizing. I knew he'd be busy and was okay with that. I most likely wasn't going to see him again until Thanksgiving, but that was fine. After what he'd told me, I was looking forward to going with him.

I couldn't imagine how he felt knowing he had to face a man who abused him—a man who was supposed to protect and love him but had done the complete opposite.

Regardless, Deke stayed himself. There was one day when I got home and saw a package at the door. It was made out to me but had no return address. I carried it into the house, opened it, and found a voucher for four tickets to an Atlanta Ravens game in December as well as a brand-new pair of noise-canceling headphones.

There was also a handwritten note inside:

Davina,

Tell Abe I'm looking forward to meeting him.

Make sure you bring the whole family.

See you courtside, D-Baby.

Deke

I knew he had an away game that night, so I eagerly waited for him to call me when he was home. It wasn't until the next morning that he called me via FaceTime before heading to an event, and by then I couldn't contain myself.

"Deke, I got the headphones! You didn't have to do this! Abe is going to lose his mind!"

Deke chuckled on the other end. "I told you I'd figure something out."

"That was so thoughtful. But are you sure you want to meet my mom? She literally has no filter."

"Hell yeah, I want to meet the woman who birthed the love of my life. Besides, I've dealt with enough people to handle someone without a filter. Trust me."

"Okay." I laughed. "Only if you're sure."

Deke studied the screen. "You look sexy right now."

I busted out laughing. "Please. I haven't even changed into my work clothes yet." I had on a baggy *Purple Rain* T-shirt, and my hair was still tucked into a bonnet.

"Yeah. You're natural. That's what makes you sexy. Let me get a full view."

"Deke," I laughed.

"Come on, D. Show me what I'm missing."

I sank my teeth into my bottom lip. I couldn't believe I was even considering it, but I missed him, and honestly it'd been a while since I had a thrill like this. I propped the phone up on an oatmeal box and stepped back.

"Damn, girl!" He whistled. "Turn around and let me see the back."

I laughed, spinning around.

"Yeah," he said. "You're lucky I'm not there. I'd be bending you over that counter right now."

At that, I busted out laughing.

He cracked a smile. "I'm walking up to the building now, but I'll call you when I get a free moment, 'kay?"

"Okay."

"I love you, D."

"I love you, too, Bishop."

SIXTY-FIVE

DAVINA

The morning of Thanksgiving, I woke up in a hotel bed with my boy-friend. It was nearing seven in the morning, and he was still asleep.

We'd taken a private jet Deke had booked, and I swear it was the most luxurious experience of my life. The leather seats were plush and comfortable, the champagne was aplenty, and we talked about the game he'd just had the day before. He was bone tired but still smiling.

I sat up on my elbow and stared at him. He looked childlike lying there, with his features soft and one hand on his heart. The other was tucked beneath his pillow.

I didn't want to wake him, so I climbed out of bed and went to the bathroom to brush my teeth. When I walked back out, Deke's back was perched against the headboard as he looked at me.

"Did I wake you?" I asked, climbing back into bed.

"No. Phone was vibrating. Camille called, asked me to bring drinks."

He flipped onto his side to face me, then wrapped his arms around me, pulling me in close so the fronts of our bodies were pressed together. I could feel his semihard erection, and as if he knew I'd feel it, he grinned.

I cupped his face and kissed him. He groaned, kissing me back, and before I knew it, he was between my legs and grinding himself on me. I let out a ragged breath as he kissed my throat and carried his lips down to my pelvis.

"Is it wrong to have an appetizer before a Thanksgiving dinner?" he asked between my legs.

I laughed. "I don't know. Is it?"

He smiled up at me, pushing my T-shirt up and revealing my panties. I lifted my hips so he could take them off, and he buried his face between my thighs, groaning as he pushed one of them up to my chest.

I ran my fingers over the coarse waves of his hair, arching my back as I closed my eyes.

"I love how you taste, Davina," he breathed. He slid his tongue into me, teasing before gliding it back up to the tenderest spot.

I was getting worked up, breathing harder, faster, and just when I felt like I was about to reach my peak, Deke took his mouth away and sat up to center himself between my thighs.

He shoved his boxers down and freed himself. The man was massive. I still had moments where I wondered how he could fit the whole thing inside me.

"Wanna make love to you," he mumbled, placing his elbow outside my head. He pushed into me at a deliberate pace, watching my lips part and my eyes glaze over. His mouth came to mine, and he swallowed my moan, stroking while kissing me. With a groan, he tore his mouth away to look into my eyes.

"You love me?" he asked, voice raspy.

I nodded, clinging to him as he rocked into me. "Yes, I love you."

"Good. 'Cause I love the hell out of you."

He stole my lips again, thrusting faster. When he slammed into me and stilled, his dick felt twice as hard. It was the stillness of it, the feeling of him pulsing so hard and deep, that sent me over the edge. I threw my head back and clutched the sheets, crying out his name.

Seconds later, he hauled himself out and came too. When he met my eyes again, he huffed a laugh.

"Damn," he sighed.

"What?" I asked.

"I'll never get tired of making love to you. That's all." He hovered above me, kissing me once more and sighing behind the kiss before climbing off the bed. After he cleaned me up, he took my hand, helped me off the bed, and said, "Now let's go make love in the shower too."

~

When Deke pulled up to his mom's house, he released a breath. The driveway was full of cars, which made me wonder if we were the last to show. If we were, I had no doubt it was intentional.

The house was gorgeous, a simple ranch home with a farmhouse flair. The exterior was white, the gabled roof black, and the porch large enough to fit four rocking chairs. A handful of trees were spread throughout the massive yard, the grass a neat, pedicured green.

Deke killed the engine of the rental car and sat a moment, staring ahead. I placed my hand on top of his, and he shifted his gaze to mine.

"You ready?" I asked.

He nodded and unclipped his seat belt. "Might as well get it over with."

When he took my hand, we walked along the driveway and onto the porch so Deke could give the doorbell a ring. He shifted a bit, cleared his throat, then jostled the grocery bags with the sodas and juices in his other hand.

"It'll be okay," I assured him. "Whenever you're ready to go, I'll be ready too."

He gave me a quick nod, then we heard rapid clip-clopping on the other side. When the door swung open, a woman with dark-brown hair and streaks of gray appeared. Her skin was a beautiful, deep brown with warm red undertones, her lips coated in ruby lipstick and her natural hair in big bouncy curls. Her eyes were a familiar brown, with hints of cognac in the sunlight, and they lit up when she spotted Deke.

It was Olivia Blake, Deke's mother. Even if I hadn't seen that picture of her on Facebook with Damon, I could've guessed she was his mom, because Deke was the spitting image of her.

"Declan, honey! Oh!" She wrangled him into her arms and hugged him tight around the neck. I released his hand so he could hug his mom back and smiled at their interaction.

That's when I noticed the scar on her temple. It was slightly raised and about the length of a newborn's pinkie. I instantly thought of Deke's story and him mentioning how his dad had pushed her out of the way and caused her to hit her head on a portrait.

"Hey, Ma," Deke murmured over her shoulder. I blinked, snapping myself out of it.

She leaned back a bit to look up at him, holding one side of his face. "My sweet boy. Look at you."

He smiled down at her, then gestured my way. "Ma, this is my girlfriend, Davina. Davina, this is my mom, Olivia Blake."

"I know exactly who she is," Mrs. Blake said, a wide smile claiming her lips. She moved closer to me and took my hands in hers. "You're even more beautiful in person, sweetheart."

"Thank you, Mrs. Blake. It's so nice to finally meet you."

"Girl, stop it! Call me Olivia."

"Okay, *Mrs. Blake*." I winked at her, and she chuckled. I'd call her Olivia one day, but not on my first day of meeting her. She deserved all my respect.

"Oh, I can tell I'm gonna have a lot of fun with her," Mrs. Blake said. "Come inside, both of you! I'm finishing up with the turkey, then we can dig in."

SIXTY-SIX

DEKE

As soon as I entered my mom's house and walked around the corner, I spotted my sisters, Jack, and Elias in the living room. My sisters were sitting on one of the sofas with glasses of wine in hand, Jack had a beer, and Eli was on the floor doing a puzzle.

It was tradition not to have the TV on the day of Thanksgiving. My mom insisted that for one day of the year, we all focus on each other and not lose ourselves in the screens. Talking on the phone was limited too.

There was a time when she used to take our phones and store them in a basket, up until she realized we actually needed our phones for our jobs. Camille had missed a call from a client, and it'd cost her a massive delay. A hearing had to be rescheduled and everything. Since then, Mama gave a little leeway.

"Deke!" Whitney squealed as she hopped off the couch. She hugged me tight, and I hugged her back, laughing.

"What's good, sis?" I asked, but she completely ignored me to hug Davina twice as hard.

"Davina, as pretty as ever." Whitney grinned.

"I could say the same about you!" Davina returned. "I love your dress."

Whitney did a little curtsy. "Why, thank you."

Camille approached me as they chatted, wrapping one arm around me while her other hand kept the wineglass steady. "Hey, little brother," she sighed over my shoulder.

"Hey, Mill."

"Bringing girlfriends to Thanksgiving? That's new." She sipped her wine and looked from me to Davina, who was snickering at something Whitney was saying.

"Yeah," I said, smiling. "Guess so."

"How does it feel?" she asked.

"Good as hell."

She shot me a wink.

"Hey, D, this is my sister, Camille. Camille, this is Davina."

"Davina, hi! It's so nice to meet the woman my brother never shuts up about," Camille said, taking her hand.

"Come on, Mill! Don't be like that!"

Davina wore a bashful smile. "Well, that's good to know. It's really nice to meet you, too, Camille. Deke talks about you all the time."

My sister was instantly flattered, and that was all it took for Davina to reel her in. While they got acquainted, I greeted Jack (who gave me a hug that was too tight and too long), and Eli ran my way, hugging me around the waist.

"Uncle Deke, we shootin' some hoops today?"

"I don't know, nephew. After last night's game, I'm kinda tired. You might get all the points today."

Eli donned a proud grin. "Yeah, you're right. It's better if you chill today. Don't wanna whip you too bad."

I chuckled, watching him walk to the kitchen to find his grandma, but as I looked that way, I noticed someone standing near the dining area. My hand curled into a fist as I stared at him.

He looked different from the last time I'd seen him—then again, nineteen years did that to a person. He was pudgier, with a bit of a gut beneath his plaid button-down shirt. His hair was peppered with gray, and wrinkles were around his eyes and on his forehead, like he'd frowned so much they became permanent. His hands were buried in the front pockets of his jeans, but he took one out to wave at me.

It was Joshua Bishop. My father.

I swallowed, ignoring his wave and facing my sisters again.

"Behave, Deke," Camille said, tapping my fist.

"Trying," I muttered, loosening my hand.

I looked at Davina as she studied my dad briefly before fixing her eyes on mine. *You okay?* she mouthed.

I'm good.

"Let's eat!" my mom shouted, placing the turkey on the center of the table.

I helped Davina settle in and took the seat beside her. My mom sat at the head of the table in the chair next to mine, Camille across from me and Eli between her and Jack. Whitney took the seat next to Davina, and at the other end of the table was my dad.

"How about a prayer?" Mama said, extending both her arms. I placed my hand in hers and started to reach for Davina's until she pressed a hand to the top of my thigh to stop it from bouncing. Our eyes connected, and she gave me a warm smile before weaving her fingers through mine. Mama led us in prayer, and afterward we all dug in.

"All of this looks really good, Liv," a deep voice said from the end of the table. I cut my eyes to my dad's, and he was smiling proudly at my mom as he placed a few cuts of turkey on his plate.

"Thank you, Josh."

I clenched my jaw, dumping a spoonful of macaroni and cheese onto my plate.

"How about we go around the table and share a reason why we're thankful this year. Yeah?" Mama insisted, looking at everyone.

I shook my head as Whitney groaned and Eli said "Yay!"

"I'll go first." Mama took a sip of sweet tea, then rubbed her lips together. "I'm thankful that I have my children here with me and my sweet little Eli," she cooed, pointing her fork at him. "I'm also thankful for this food that took me all morning to finish up, so y'all better eat up and make sure you take some home with you."

Everyone laughed as she gestured to Camille.

"I'm thankful for wine," Camille said, raising her glass, and Mama swatted at her. I smiled as Camille grinned. "Okay, okay. I'm thankful for being alive today and being surrounded by family."

"I'm thankful for my family and the sweet potato pie we get to eat after this!" Eli shouted, making us all chuckle.

"I'm thankful for football," Jack said with sorrow. He was upset that he was missing some of the NFL game due to Mama's limited-screen-time rule.

"Aw, Jack. It'll be okay. You can watch it when you get back home," Mama said. She pointed her gaze to her former husband. "And you, Josh?"

He sat up taller in his chair and cleared his throat as he glanced at all the food on the table. He then shifted his gaze to each of us. It didn't surprise me that he couldn't look into our eyes for long.

"I'm thankful to be here, to see my kids again, and for your delicious cooking, Liv. I, uh . . . I know you all probably wish I wasn't here, but I appreciate you for embracing me and letting me share a meal with you. I've, uh . . . well, I know I've missed out on so many years, and I'm sorry for that. But I've missed you all, and I hope to rebuild a relationship with you, if you let me."

The table fell silent, minus the scraping and clinking of silverware. I couldn't stand it.

"Are you not going to mention Damon?" I asked, looking from my plate to him.

His eyes rounded, then he blinked rapidly, turning his attention to my mother, who said my name in a calm warning. "You know Damon is with us in spirit," Mama said.

"He could be here right now in the physical sense if it weren't for *him*. I really don't understand why he's here."

"Declan," Mama hissed at me.

"Deke, come on," Camille chided.

Davina's hand was on my lap, rubbing, and I swear that was the only thing calming me down. "You're right. You're right." I raised both my hands in a guiltless resolve. "Let's get back to this good food."

A stretch of awkward silence filled the room, then Mama cleared her throat and said, "Whitney? Anything you're thankful for?"

"Yeah, Mama. I'm just thankful to be here . . . and for wine, like Camille said."

That got them to laugh and to erase the awkward spell.

"Davina, how about you, love?" Mama asked, popping a piece of moist turkey into her mouth.

"Oh. Um . . . well, I'm thankful to be with you all this year. I'm glad I met Deke and that he felt comfortable enough to introduce me to all of you. It's so nice to be surrounded by the people he loves, and I see why he can never stop talking about any of you." Davina gave my arm a squeeze, and I leaned over, kissing her cheek.

"Well, we are *so happy* to have you, Davina, and we hope to have many more holidays with you. Trust me, I never thought I'd see the day this boy brought a girl home." Mama tapped my nose, and I fought a smile. "What are you thankful for, son?"

I lowered my fork and took a look at everyone around the table. Then I said, "Survival. I'm thankful we all survived and came out on the other side."

I glanced at my dad, and he stared right back at me with glossy eyes. He lowered his head to focus on his food, and I wasn't sure what it was about the way he did it, but for the first time since I was a teenager, I actually felt sorry for him.

SIXTY-SEVEN

DEKE

As much as I would have loved staying with my family a bit longer, I had to leave if I wanted to make it back to Atlanta for my next game.

When it was time to go, I hugged my mom and sisters, bid farewell to Eli and Jack, then eyed my dad, who stood in a corner, drinking sweet tea.

I was surprised I made it through the damn dinner, let alone another two hours after it with him still in the house. That should've counted for something.

I turned away, taking Davina's hand, ready to get the hell away from him. But as soon as we neared the car, I heard a deep voice call my name.

I stopped at the bumper but didn't look back. Instead, I closed my eyes and inhaled before exhaling. Should've known walking away wouldn't be so simple. Turning around, I spotted my dad as he lumbered down the stoop and came in my direction.

"I'll meet you in the car," Davina whispered, patting my arm. "Will you be okay?"

My eyes dropped to hers, and I gave her chin a light squeeze. "Yeah. Meet you there."

When she was settled in the passenger seat with the door closed, I refrained from balling my fists as I looked into my dad's eyes.

I tried not to focus on the bridge of his nose and how he had a slight hook to it like mine, or the way his ears stuck out just a bit . . . like mine. I didn't want *any* part of myself to be like him.

"What do you want?"

He stepped closer with a pleading hand in the air. "Son . . ."

"Don't call me that."

"Okay. Declan, look—"

"Try again."

He inhaled and exhaled deeply, dropping his hand. "Deke, I was hoping I could get the chance to talk to you."

"There isn't much to talk about."

"I know you're angry with me, okay? I know you are, and trust me, I will *never* forgive myself for what I did to you . . . or to your brother."

My eyes burned, and I tried not to blink. I wanted to turn my back on him and bail, but my feet wouldn't fucking move.

He took another step closer, but not too close that he could touch me. I looked past him at the door, where Mama and my sisters were now standing.

"Look, even though I know you'll never forgive me and that you'll likely hate me for as long as I live, I just want to tell you how proud I am of you, son. I—I watch your games every time they're on. I see how hard you ball and how much heart you have, and you've worked hard for it. There's no one else who deserves it more than you."

I felt my guard lowering, but all I wanted was for it to go back up. What the hell was wrong with me? All these years spent hating this man and fantasizing about how I'd punch him square in the face if I ever saw him again, and now I was softening.

"It's a little too late to say all this, man," I muttered.

"Yeah, I know it is, but whether I get to speak to you again or not, I just want you to know I love you, Deke. You may not think so, but I do. I know I did some messed-up things, but I pray to God every day and ask him to let you, your mom, and your sisters forgive me. I made mistakes—actually, let me rephrase that. *I fucked up.* All right? Lord, forgive me for my language, but I really fucked up, and I know you think people don't change, but I have been working really hard on becoming a better man and a better person overall so that those mistakes I made never happen again. I work on myself so lives like Damon's aren't lost. I . . . I think about him *every single day*, and it tears me up," he said, voice cracking. "You gotta know that. It eats me alive, robs me of my sleep. I'll never come back from that."

I smashed my lips together, looking away when his eyes grew misty. I couldn't believe I wanted to cry over this motherfucker. Even though he'd ruined me and I knew I'd never forgive him for what he did, I couldn't help thinking about all those moments *before* he started drinking.

I thought back to when I was just a kid and he taught me how to handle a ball, how to shoot, and how to correct my form. He taught me how to cook spaghetti, how to swim, how to tie my shoes, how to flip a pancake. He took me to practice and showed up to every single one of my games.

Though the last memories of him were shitty and twisted, he was still my damn father. That's what was messing me up—because I of all people know humans have their weak moments, and what he did to us was him at his weakest. He needed help, that's a fact, and he never got it.

But no matter how sorry I felt for him or how much I missed that version of him who taught me everything, I couldn't look at him and *not* think of my brother or that blood on the bed, the knife lying next to him, that letter crumpled in his hand saying it was all *too much*.

I looked over my shoulder at Davina, whose eyes were wide and worried. Then I looked at Mama and my sisters, who were clearly on edge and waiting for my reaction with bated breath.

All of them had chosen to live, despite their murky pasts. They no longer let those circumstances weigh them down. Instead, they carried them with them and found the joy day by day.

It was my turn to choose the same thing. Joy.

I closed the gap between me and my dad and instead of punching him, I hugged him. This wasn't a hug of reminiscing, forgiveness, or even sorrow. It was a hug to let him know that I loved him—that I'd *always* love him—but that I'd *never* see him as the same man who taught me all my firsts.

There may have been a lot more meaning to it, but the best way to sum it up is to call it closure. This chapter of my life, where I carried all that sadness, rage, and guilt, was coming to an end. It was time to turn the page and start a new one.

My dad froze a moment before hugging me back and holding on tight. I heard him wheeze a bit, like the hug had given him so much comfort it hurt. He and I were about the same height, so it was an even hug, our heads over each other's shoulders.

When he sniffled, I pulled away. "Just promise to keep working on yourself," I said.

He nodded, swiping the tears off his cheeks. "I will. I promise."

I scanned him one last time, then went to the car to get inside it. When I was on the main road and driving away from Mama's house, Davina reached over the middle console and took my hand in hers.

"I'm proud of you, Deke."

I glanced at her and smiled a little.

"Yeah," I said. "I'm proud of me too."

SIXTY-EIGHT

DAVINA

When March rolled around, I drove to Atlanta with Mama, Abe, and a swirl of excitement. We had our Atlanta Ravens gear on, all of us wearing number seventeen as we walked toward the stadium.

This was the third time we attended one of Deke's home games, and it was one of the last games before playoffs. The temperature was perfectly warm, and the spring air caressed my skin.

As soon as we checked in and took our courtside seats, I was bursting with energy. There was just something about coming to a basketball stadium—inhaling the scent of buttery popcorn and greasy pizza, the lively chatter as everyone took their seats and sat with drinks, sipping and laughing. The sight of the fans who appeared, decked out in team colors, with colorful wigs and face paint.

It was glorious.

Octavia met us at the gates so we could all go in together. Abe sat between Mama and Octavia, while I sat next to Octavia, who had Aleesa on her lap. Aleesa was squirming, ready to get down and make a show cheering for her dad.

"She's a handful, but an angel compared to Roger," Octavia said, and I laughed, remembering the bratty three-year-old she last nannied.

Shortly after Javier let me into his house to talk to Deke (something I would be *forever* grateful for) he called Octavia back and asked if she could look after his daughter. I couldn't say I was surprised. Even before she was officially hired, Deke insisted that Javier talked nonstop about whether or not to hire her. Deke and I knew what that meant: she was still on his mind, even months later.

According to Octavia, Javier was a pure grump who mostly ignored her when she was around. He did, however, enjoy her cooking, and she was positive that was her only saving grace.

I leaned forward as Aleesa looked up at me with round green eyes. "You ready to cheer for your daddy?" I asked.

"Yeah! Daddy!" she shrilled, and I gave her cheek a little squeeze.

As the stadium filled, I noticed some familiar faces and gasped when I realized it was Whitney and Camille making their way toward us. Whitney squealed, and I hopped up to hug her.

"Whitney! Hi!"

"Hey, Vina!" she sang over my shoulder. She stepped past me to hug Octavia and to introduce herself to Mama and Abe. I could tell Abe wanted to ignore her and sit still with his soundproof headphones and Ravens hoodie on, but Mama insisted he say something.

"Camille, as beautiful as always." I gave her a big hug and then fist-bumped Eli, who was next to her.

"He bought tickets for everyone, huh?" I asked, sitting.

"He did! He even got Mama and her new boo seats in the box." Whitney bumped my shoulder, and I laughed. I'd heard all about Mrs. Blake's new boyfriend through Deke, who constantly griped about it but was willing to do anything to make her happy (like get them tickets for a date in box seats).

It didn't take long for the lights to dim and the players to be announced. When they said Deke's name (and they saved it for last, of course), the entire stadium went into an uproar as he jogged out.

I swear I was never going to get tired of this image. My man running out, a wide smile and dimples, both of his hands up as he basked in the attention and love he most definitely deserved.

I screamed his name as Whitney whistled and Aleesa tried reaching for him, which was adorable.

When the players lined up to prepare for the national anthem, Deke's eyes found mine. I grinned while waving at him.

Deke waved back, then mouthed, "You're blushing, D."

I laughed, and he winked, raising two fingers to his lips, kissing the pads of them, and then pointing them toward me. I kissed mine, too, and pointed them his way. It was the silent message we sent to each other before every game. Even if the game was televised and I couldn't make it, whenever he dropped that first bucket, he'd kiss his fingers and point them at one of the cameras. It was damn sweet, and I would never get enough of it.

Deke balled his heart out that day. I hadn't seen him shine so brightly in so long, but it must've been an amazing feeling, knowing all the people he cared about—his *1 percent*—were in the stadium cheering him on. All he had to do was look over his shoulder, and we were there, rooting for him.

When halftime rolled around, there were a few shooting contests and T-shirt launches into the crowd from the Ravens mascot, a big black raven in a red uniform.

But just as quickly as the halftime show started, the people dispersed, and I noticed Deke emerging from the locker rooms to accept a mic from the announcer.

"What's up, Ravens!" Deke yelled into the mic as he made his way to the middle of the court. The stadium went wild, people screaming at the tops of their lungs and crying out his name. Deke chuckled into the mic, and when the crowd settled a bit, he spoke again. "Listen, I don't usually do this. If you know me, you know I can't stand giving public speeches unless I absolutely have to, but I need to do it right

now, because there is someone in this crowd I have to send my love to."
Deke turned my way, eyes latching with mine, and I stifled a breath.

"What is he doing?!" I whisper-hissed to Whitney.

She pressed her lips and shrugged, making an *I don't know* noise.

"This person has been there for me like never before. I have this thing I like to call my *one percent*, and there are only a handful of people who make it there. These are the people I love with my whole heart, the people I care about, the people I respect, and right now not only do I give thanks to my family and friends for showing up for me today, but also to the beautiful woman sitting right there. Davina Klein."

My eyes rounded as a gentle applause filled the building.

"This woman is the other half of me that I never knew I was missing. When I had that rocky game at the start of the season, it was because I couldn't get her off of my mind, y'all. Y'all remember that, right? Yeah, I bet you do, 'cause the whole crowd was mad at me." He chuckled, and so did many others. "Hold on—I just want to show her off to y'all really quick so we can squash all the gossip going around. D, can you come here?" He curled his fingers, gesturing for me to come.

I swallowed as Whitney and Octavia pressed their hands to my back to push me out of my seat.

"Go, girl!" Octavia insisted.

"Get it, Vina!" Whitney hooted.

My heart raced as I walked across the court, fighting a goofy smile. *What are you doing?!* I mouthed at Deke, but he kept his hand held out and waited for me to take it. He then requested one of the people on the sidelines to toss him a ball. When he handed the basketball to me, I looked from it to his eyes.

"What am I supposed to do with this?" My question came out breathy and quick. All these people were watching us. I didn't mind crowds, but this was new territory for me, standing in the middle of a jam-packed stadium with a megastar basketball player.

"Y'all should see how she shoots. I play her one on one all the time, and she's got a nice form. Go ahead, baby. Show 'em," Deke insisted, one hand gripping the mic.

"Deke, I can't. This is—"

He tapped the ball, shot me a wink, and stepped back. I sighed as I looked around the stadium. If I got this over with, I could sit back down and pretend this wasn't happening. I couldn't say I was surprised Deke was doing this. He *did* tell me repeatedly that he was going to show me off to the whole world.

I drew in a breath and faced the goal. I rose to my toes to shoot the ball and thanked my sweet Heavenly Father for allowing it to sink into the net. I expected cheers and applause afterward, but the crowd gasped instead, and a wave of murmurs erupted.

The speed of my heart picked up again. I twisted around to find Deke, but when I saw him, I gasped too.

He was on one knee, a velvety black box in his hand with an oval-shaped diamond ring nestled inside it. The diamond gleamed in the light, and I didn't even want to think about how much he'd shoveled out for it.

"Deke." My eyes stretched as I stood there like a gaping idiot.

He smiled up at me with a glint in his eyes. He'd gotten rid of the mic, so the only person who could hear him speaking was me. Reaching for my hand with his other, he gave it a squeeze.

"Davina, there aren't many things I've been sure of in my life, but when I met you, I was positive you were the one for me. Whether I could have you or not, you were the one my heart yearned for. I want to spend the rest of my life with you. I want to kiss you every single morning and night, to hold you when you're down and lift you up when you feel weakest. I want to see your smile every single day and hear you laugh about my corny jokes and nicknames. You've always been the woman for me, and I love you so much, D. I've never felt a love like this, and I can't let it go, which is why I have to ask you right now . . . *Will you marry me?*"

I squeezed his hand back and bobbed my head, a hot tear sliding down my cheek. "Yes," I said in a half sob. "Yes, I'll marry you, Declan Bishop."

He cracked a smile, taking the ring out of the box and sliding it onto the finger I swore would never belong to anyone else again.

But like a hurricane, Deke barreled right in and swept me up. There was no way of missing him, no way to avoid him. He was right there, leaving me no choice but to fall for him more and more each day.

When he rose to a stand, he reeled me in by the waist and held me tight as I laced my arms around the back of his neck. And when we kissed, the crowd cheered.

I couldn't believe this was happening—this raw, romantic moment that was certainly in Deke fashion. All this time we'd been hiding from the press and keeping our relationship out of the public eye because *I* was afraid they wouldn't accept me. But there was something about hearing those cheers fill up the stadium. They were rooting for our happiness, rooting for *us*.

My heart filled like air in a balloon, swelling to the point I swore it would burst from how much love I felt, not only from him, but from his fans too.

When you first learn how to play basketball, you stumble a few times and miss a lot of the shots you take. You grow frustrated, but you keep dribbling that ball, keep shooting, keep moving your feet. Your chin stays up, and even when you feel like you'll never be great—that you'll never accomplish your goals—that's when it all falls into place.

Our love was a lot like that. Bumpy at the start as we learned, stumbling through feelings and grief, but coming out the other side with our heads up and our dreams in our grasps.

We had a love like no other—a beautiful, broken love that healed us when we needed it most.

EPILOGUE

DAVINA

I carried a small bouquet of sunflowers as I walked through a field of soft grass. It was fairly hot for a June morning, but there was a nice breeze going, causing my pink sundress to blow in the wind.

I passed through rows and rows of flat marker headstones until I found the one I was looking for. It was next to a cluster of bushes, the stone a glossy black with white lettering.

I read the headstone, which was flush with grass, the flower container empty, proof that no one had been here in a while. That hurt my heart a little. The headstone shimmered in the sunlight like it was smiling at me.

LEWIS C. ROBERTS

1988–2021

LOVING SON, HUSBAND, AND FRIEND

I bent over, tucking the sunflowers into the container and adjusting them. A breeze sailed by as I cleared my throat.

"Hey, Lew. It's been a while." I huffed a laugh, studying his name. "I'm sorry I haven't visited as much, but like I told Octavia, I don't think you're really here. Your soul isn't, anyway. But just in case you are, I want you to know that I'm engaged now—wanted to tell you that. The wedding will be next summer." I bit into my bottom lip, running the sole of my sandal over a patch of grass. My eyes prickled, but I blinked and drew in a breath.

"You told me it was okay to move on and be happy, and I didn't believe you. I couldn't see how I could move on when you weren't there. It just didn't feel possible. But you should know that I appreciate you so much for leaving me with that—for letting me know it was okay. It's still taking me a while to block out most of the guilt, but I'm getting there. And even when the time comes when I'm numb to it, it won't stop me from missing you."

I lowered to a squat and ran my hand over his headstone to swipe some of the dirt away. When I stood up again, a dragonfly swooped down and landed on top of it. I sucked in a sharp breath, and there was no stopping the tears this time, because I knew what the dragonfly signified and who it was from.

I grabbed at the collar of my dress, pulling out my dragonfly pendant.

"I see you," I whispered, voice cracking. "Thank you." The dragonfly took off, and I watched it fly away until I could no longer see it.

I returned to the parking lot, where Deke was leaning against the side of my car. His eyes lit up when he saw me, and a smile graced his lips as he offered me a hand. I smiled back and felt my heart skip a beat. Sometimes it still surprised me that I would be marrying this gorgeous man.

"You ready?" he asked, stroking the top of my hand with his thumb.

That seemed like such a loaded question at the time.

Was I ready to let go?

Ready to move on?

Ready to create new adventures and a new life?

Ready to leave the past in the past to make space for an undefined future with him?

I looked into my fiancé's eyes, rose to my toes, and kissed him.

"Yeah," I said when our lips parted. "I'm ready."

Thank you so much for reading *Beautiful Broken Love*!

I hope you enjoyed Deke and Vina's story!

For a steamy bonus epilogue in Deke's POV, visit https://bit.ly/dekeandvinabonus, sign up, and enjoy!

ACKNOWLEDGMENTS

There are so many places I could start and many people I could thank with these acknowledgments, but I first have to give my glory to God. If it weren't for Him, I never would've found the strength or the courage to write this book.

Here's a little backstory on what inspired me to write *Beautiful Broken Love*. (Bear with me.) Some people may already know this, but for those who don't, my brother Demontez Stitt passed away in July 2016. He was my first impression of a big brother and protector.

As a kid, you think you'll grow old with your siblings and continue the laughs and the jokes till you're old and gray. Unfortunately, that wasn't in the plans for us.

A few months after he passed away, this story began to sprout, and I wrote my notes and plot ideas, as usual, but I didn't dare open a document to try my hand at writing a manuscript for it. To put it simply, I wasn't ready, and I was also afraid because the grief was still weighing heavily on me. I hadn't healed from his loss and had even lost myself in the process.

But here we are now, eight years later, and I have never been prouder. This book is a tribute to my brother, who played basketball the whole twenty-seven years of his life. He was a Clemson alumnus (you can catch murals of him on some of the walls in the basketball stadium), and he played professional basketball overseas in countries like Israel and Turkey.

Deke Bishop is a character who embodies many of the traits I miss in my brother. His laid-back attitude, his silliness, his tender heart, his patience, and the way he cared about every single person who was important to him off the court. Deke held his family close and put them first, and my brother did the same. He was so passionate about basketball (and a damn good point guard), so to write this was an incredible, freeing journey.

All those memories of Demontez were poured into these pages. My tears nearly ruined my keyboard, because I was bawling my eyes out, but trust me, they were tears of bittersweet joy.

And that epilogue . . . well, that's a chapter I wrote to express my own personal healing. I realize I'm telling you a lot of personal things, but I wanted to share this side of me with you so you could understand the reason why I wrote a story such as this.

Okay. Now that I've shared that tidbit, I want to express my gratitude! Thank you to my husband, Juan, for sitting around the corner while I wrote this book and for holding down the fort with our wild boys. Your unconditional love and support mean the world to me, and I know for a fact I wouldn't be able to continue this career without you.

To my whole family—this one's for you! I know you all miss Montez as much as I do, but his memory lives on, and hopefully this book will continue that legacy with each printed copy.

To my amazing agent, Georgana Grinstead, thank you for championing this book and being in full support of Deke and Davina! I can't wait for us to bring more magic to the book world.

To my awesome editor at Montlake, Anh Schluep, and developmental editor, Lindsey Faber, thank you both for loving this book as much as I did. You kept me inspired and motivated to make this the best version possible of *Beautiful Broken Love*. And I will never, ever forget that first call shared with Alison Dasho! You saw the potential in my angsty little submission, and I'm eternally grateful you gave me a chance.

To my readers who are always so eager for my next book to drop—thank you so much for taking a chance on this novel. Without you, I wouldn't have anyone to share my words with. You make my dreams come true every single day, and I will never, ever take it for granted.

And finally, to the person reading this very sentence. Yes, you, lovely reader. Whether this book was your cup of tea or not, if you made it this far, I'm *so* glad you gave it a chance. Thank you, thank you, thank you.

LET'S STAY CONNECTED

Sign up for my newsletter to stay updated and to receive exclusive information, graphics, teasers, and so much more!

For updates, teasers, and more fun exclusives:

Follow me on Instagram: @reallyshanora

Follow me on TikTok: @theshanorawilliams

Follow me on X: @shanorawilliams

Visit www.shanorawilliams.com for merch, info, and details.

Psssttt . . . I'm most active on Instagram, by the way!

ABOUT THE AUTHOR

Photo © 2023 Ericka Leigh Photography

Shanora Williams is a *New York Times* and *USA Today* bestselling author of over thirty romance novels and diverse thrillers. She lives near Charlotte, North Carolina, with her husband and three boys and is a sister to eleven siblings. When she isn't writing, Shanora's spending time with her family, binge reading, or running marathons on TV streaming services.